The
Entanglement
of Rival
Wizards

Other Books by Sara Raasch

The Nightmare Before Kissmas

Go Luck Yourself

The
Entanglement
of Rival
Wizards

Sara Raasch

BRAMBLE

Tor Publishing Group
New York

THE ENTANGLEMENT OF RIVAL WIZARDS

A Bramble Book
Published by Tom Doherty Associates / Tor Publishing Group
120 Broadway
New York, NY 10271

www.torpublishinggroup.com

Bramble™ is a trademark of Macmillan Publishing Group, LLC.

EU Representative: Macmillan Publishers Ireland Ltd, 1st Floor, The Liffey Trust Centre, 117–126 Sheriff Street Upper, Dublin 1, D01 YC43

The Library of Congress Cataloging-in-Publication Data is available upon request.

ISBN 978-1-250-33323-0 (trade paperback)
ISBN 978-1-250-33324-7 (ebook)

Our books may be purchased in bulk for specialty retail/wholesale, literacy, corporate/premium, educational, and subscription box use. Please contact MacmillanSpecialMarkets@macmillan.com.

First Edition: 2025

Printed in the United States of America

10 9 8 7 6 5 4 3 2 1

To everyone who found themselves at a DND table

The
Entanglement
of Rival
Wizards

Chapter One

We've come all this way to get stopped by a *door*.

I recheck the runes I scrawled in chalk around the frame. I accounted for any fail-safe we might trigger, and even padded in unnecessarily complex runes for any *fail-safe* fail-safe; I would not put it past these assholes to have traps on traps just to fuck with me.

But Seb, Orok had said, *isn't it egotistical to think the Conjuration Department beefed up their security to spite you and not to, say, protect the thousands of dollars' worth of spell components in their lab?*

To which I'd responded with a deadpan stare. The protection ward currently keeping me out of the second-floor Conjuration Lab might as well have *To Sebastian Walsh, With Love* woven into the fabric of the barrier that glimmers an ethereal blue every time I try to break it.

I roll my shoulders, shake out my hands, and start the incantation. Again.

"You get one more shot," Orok interrupts from where he leans against the wall behind me, "then I'm climbing the side of the building."

"They'll have wards on the windows, too."

"Not ones this intense. They *expect* thieves to come through this way—"

"Thieves." I snort derisively.

I can feel Orok's eye roll as strongly as I can feel his next words coming, and I mouth along with him—

"And puny evocation wizards."

Only I don't add that descriptor, and I flip a glare back at him. "Puny?"

Orok eyes me head to toe, then holds his arms out in an unspoken comparison.

He's got the height and bulk from his half-giant lineage, which has made him broader and taller than I am at every stage of our lives. My family had been thrilled when we glommed on to each other in grade school, exclaiming what a *good influence* he'd be on me—right up until he opted into academia, and it turned out Orok Monroe wasn't a good influence on me; I was a bad influence on him.

Lock up your kids, Sebastian Walsh might come along and tempt them to fall upon the sacrificial altar of student debt.

Orok lets his arms drop. "I meant that they probably only have simple locking wards on the windows. I can break those mid-jump."

"All the more reason to get through this," I say. "Prove to these dickheads that I cannot be stopped. I cannot be contained. I am inescapable, damn it, and I will not—"

"Your villain victory speech would be more impressive if you hadn't already been at this for twenty minutes."

I check my phone—ignoring texts from my mom—and sigh. Security only walks the upper levels a few times a night, but they could be due for their sweep soon.

I grab the little vial hanging at my side.

Orok groans. "No."

"I need the boost. It'll be quick."

"If you're that desperate *over a locked door,* I'm climbing the building."

I elbow him back into place as he tries to pass me. "You gave me one more chance. Stand down, Monroe."

"You know I hate your fox familiar, Walsh."

"Because you're heartless. Nick's adorable."

"He's *invisible.*"

"And when he wasn't invisible, he was adorable, ergo, he's still adorable. Now—" I bat Orok back to the wall and he goes with a resigned sigh.

I spill the spell components into my hand. With a whispered incantation they disperse, and the air at my feet grows hazy before clearing.

To anyone else, it'd look like I had tanked the Call Familiar spell. But I know better, and Orok knows better.

He presses closer to the wall like he's trying to climb it and grumbles, "Where is he."

Then chirps loudly and grabs his ankle. "*Motherfucker—*"

He kicks blindly and I smack his chest. "Don't kill him! I'll have to call him again, and I don't have another vial prepared, and it'll be a delay we can't afford."

"He *bit me.*"

"Because Nick knows you don't like him."

"Because he *bites me* every time you call him."

I scramble into one of the pouches on my component belt—the leather contraption around my waist that holds an array of pockets, loops, and buckles to store whatever spell supplies I might need—and pull out a tiny top hat on a string, brandishing it at Orok with a smile. I click my tongue until I feel a soft brush against my calves, and I bend down to tie the hat onto Nick's head so we can more easily tell where he is.

"Happy?" I say to Orok, who continues to rub his ankle. "Geez, you big baby."

"Gods know what kinds of diseases familiars carry." Orok holds firm that his physical strength and size compensate for any shortcomings he might run into by choosing not to call a familiar. How he expects punching to have the same effect as the occasional magic boost, I have no idea.

"Gods know what kinds of diseases *you* carry," I mutter at Orok and scratch Nick's chin now that I know where it is. He rumbles against my fingers. "Ready to power me up, buddy?"

Nick answers with a screeching bark that sounds like a dog with laryngitis.

I shush him, and he nuzzles his cold nose against my palm.

Orok's phone pings and he checks it with a passive-aggressive exhale. "Oh, look. Another picture of another end-of-semester party currently happening. And, oh, wait—yep, yep, we're *not in that picture.* Because we're here."

I face the door again, trying to refocus on the incantation. "Toddle on off to whatever party you're missing. I can handle getting revenge on the Conjuration Department all by myself."

Nick chirrups.

"I mean, Nick and I can handle it."

He purrs happily.

The first few words of the incantation roll off my tongue, boosted now by Nick's connection, the magic he pours into me from the Familiar Plane. It won't last forever and is generally considered to be a last resort during spell work, but the cheerful squeaks Nick's making confirm that he's glad to be here, so why should I feel guilty for wasting a high-level spell on a prank?

What's the point of magic if you don't get to use it for silly shit anyway.

"The Conjuration Department only retaliated for what we did to them," Orok says quickly.

I stop the incantation again and look at him.

His pale skin is washed out in the safety lights that cast the hallway in a faint milky white, but is that exasperation on his face?

"What's with the tone?"

He shoves his phone into the pocket of his purple Lesiara University hoodie. The bright gold Manticore logo has a scorpion tail curving around a snarling lion face. "They'll retaliate for this, too, and on and on, and we fucking *graduate* in the spring. Shouldn't we, I don't know, focus on *that* instead of this dumbass rivalry?"

I sparred with him once. And only once. His words hit now like his fists did then, in rapid succession, chest then stomach.

Yeah. We graduate in the spring.

Yeah. This rivalry is dumb. Evocation and conjuration are under the umbrella of the Mageus Studies Department, but unlike other focuses, we have *similar needs* and *aligned goals* according to university funding, so we've been in the same building for decades—which put us at odds long before I enrolled at Lesiara U. I just took what was a simple *we're clearly better than them* attitude and cranked it up a few notches: spelling their dried insect wings to fly around the storage room or all the books in their library to scream upon opening.

And for a while, the Conjuration Department responded in kind. Fake plastic spills on our expensive equipment, dozens of pictures of famous conjuration wizards taped all over our walls.

Until I put a spell on their lab's door to make it look like it'd vanished—it was just an illusion; it didn't go anywhere—and the Conjuration Department *did not like that.*

Namely, the Conjuration Department's golden boy, *Elethior Tourael,* did not like that. His ranting could be heard all the way down to our floor.

And the next day, the Evocation Department's ash tree dew we painstakingly gathered during the super blood moon had been replaced with ocean water, but we didn't notice until after a number of experiments had already been fucked up.

Line. Crossed.

Nothing I've done ever damaged any of the Conjuration Department's shit. I'm a *professional,* unlike elitist, trust-fund nepo babies who rest easy on beds of blood money.

The Evocation Department will get our revenge, and the piece of me that's always a little on fire, always a little shaky, always a little *livid* will be satiated.

We graduate *in the spring.*

Tomorrow, I learn whether I even *do* graduate in the spring.

Nick pushes against my leg again, a solid, warm weight.

I flex my shaking hands, all too aware of the way that shake reverberates up my arms, down into my chest, my anxiety plucking each rib like harp strings.

Tomorrow, I have to stand in front of the Mageus Research Grant Committee and listen to their verdict, and that imagined scenario has all my internal shivering ramping up to earthquake levels.

They get to decide my future.

And I have to let them.

I almost tell Orok to fuck off if he's over this prank war. *He* doesn't have to worry about funding his final project, with the Church of Urzoth Shieldsworn sponsoring everything he's doing, since his focus is on drawing magical energy out of holy items. *He* doesn't have to worry about a job after he graduates, since he's similarly guaranteed a position in any Urzoth church across the country.

Meanwhile, I managed to snag a job post-graduation with Clawstar Foundation, a nonprofit that specializes in protective spell research, but I know the cutthroat drive is alive and well. If I slip up, Clawstar will be well within their rights to rescind their offer and shift it over to a wizard who was able to fund their final research project.

But what comes out is the worst thing I could say. A simple, brittle "Please, O."

His annoyance vanishes in understanding. I can't be a mystery to him. I can't *hide*.

Orok sighs—inward, at himself—and waves his hand at me. "Proceed."

I grin. "We'll go to the party of your choosing right after this."

"Yeah, yeah."

"Now stop distracting me. I need to— Oh! Wait—"

"Good gods, what now?"

"The pièce de résistance, my friend." I grab the bag I'd stashed off to the side before crouching and tipping it upside down.

When magic wielders discovered other planes, it was cool and all, but the real mark of brilliance was from whoever decided to take all that interdimensional magic and put it in storage containers.

I jump to my feet, whipping the bag away with a flourish, revealing a dazed corpse who blinks cataract-white eyes at me.

My showmanship is immediately overshadowed by—

"*Holy shit, he reeks.*" Orok slaps his hands over his nose and mouth.

I also fight the urge to gag, but I don't win, and end up hacking aggressively at the floor.

The corpse doesn't seem offended. He doesn't seem like he can feel much of anything, which is good. If he were alive, he'd be freaking out. And he would've suffocated in the interdimensional bag, but whatever.

Most of his bones are visible beneath sagging clumps of what I assume were once muscles. Or skin? Organs, even. A scraggly beard clings optimistically to what's left of his chin, and he has very little else in the way of fleshy human bits.

I grab another vial and dump out the components as I mutter a quick preservation spell. The corpse shimmers head to toe before the smell dies down and a few of the more precarious skin flaps settle into place.

"There." I dust off my hands. "All better."

Orok chokes again. "You said you were going to leave an animated corpse in the Conjuration Lab."

I waggle my hands in a rather pathetic display of razzle-dazzle. "*Corpse.*"

"No, *skeleton.* He's gonna shatter the moment we're not there to lay preservation spells on him."

The corpse turns sharply on his heels and the bones of his feet *click-clack* a few steps across the tiled floor before I stop him by grabbing his decaying arm.

It's squishy. A bit chalky.

I compartmentalize that and say, "Woah now, Sten," in the soothing voice of someone talking to a child. "We took a field trip, remember? Stay."

"*Bqllr*," the corpse mumbles, and a tooth falls out of his mouth.

I don't bother with a translation spell; the Necromancy Lab two buildings over said he mostly mutters Nordic cuss words when he's not under the effect of a full-blown repossession.

Orok rubs his thumb against the skin between his eyes. "What'd you call him? Stan?"

"Sten. The Nec Lab said he was a Viking. He was one of the corpses that freshmen practice talking to, but he was due to be disintegrated since he's, well . . ." I wave at his condition. "Plus, apparently the only stories he tells are brutal recountings of raids on Danish villages that get a little racist. No one wants to work with him."

Orok eyes Sten. Then me.

He pushes off the wall. "I'm climbing the building."

"Wait!" I grab for spell components with one hand, the other still holding Sten in place. "I can—"

But Orok flips me off over his shoulder, then he's gone, jogging toward the stairs.

I look down at Nick's floating top hat. "I get no respect around here."

Nick twitters.

And Sten seems determined to meander up the hall, his bones tapping as he basically walks in place against my grip.

Probably should've waited to dump him out until we were *in* the lab, now that I think of it.

Impulsive? Me? How dare you.

The stillness lets the absurdity of this situation sink in. I feel Orok's words creep back on me. How maybe I should give all this up.

My eyes snag on the plaque next to the Conjuration Lab's door.

REFURBISHED THANKS TO A GENEROUS DONATION FROM THE TOURAEL FAMILY

A molten burn gathers in my stomach.

Yeah, fuck taking the high road. I'm going to put an animated corpse in the Conjuration Lab like any perfectly sane twenty-four-year-old almost-grad-school alumnus.

A minute or two later, the magic over the door shimmers, vanishes, and the door pops open to reveal Orok.

He gives a smile that's brought more than a handful of Lesiara U's single population to their knees and shows me the timer he has running on his phone. "Forty-two seconds."

"You didn't let me—"

"*Thank you, Orok.*" He pitches his voice up several octaves. I don't sound like that. "*You're the most amazing wizard in our graduating class, Orok. I bow to your prowess, Orok.*"

I sigh. "Thank you, Orok."

"You're welcome."

"My GPA's still higher than yours."

I duck his attempt to smack the back of my head and shuffle Sten past him into the dim lab space. I'm sure Orok already checked as part of his forty-two seconds of speed magic, but I wrestle one-handed to pull out mirror dust and cast a spell to find any scrying enchantments or stuff that might be recording our presence here. I get nothing, not even extra levels of traps or security precautions.

Wow. They really didn't think I'd get past the ward on the door.

I mean. Technically, I didn't.

That's not important.

This lab takes up most of the second floor, with one section farther down for lowerclassmen, and the rest segregated by half walls into individual lab spaces for students who get dedicated areas. Each one is neatly tucked away, most experiments and research locked up since the semester's winding down. Huge windows throw hazy moonlight into the room, giving enough illumination to see by.

For comparison, the Evocation Lab, a floor down, is a quarter this size. And has one window.

"What now, O Captain, my Captain?" Orok sidles up next to me.

"Give me a sec. Here—hold him."

I shove Sten toward Orok, but Orok lurches back with a shudder.

"I'm not touching it."

"This one won't bite you. I promise."

"That wasn't a fear until just now, thank you. No—I meant I'm not touching *dead flesh*."

I grunt. "Fine, gods; just don't let him wander into the hall. Pretend he's one of the people you have to tackle on the field, but corral him."

That seems to register with Orok. He stands straighter, refocusing on Sten with the intensity that makes him one of the university's top athletes.

Mildly confident, I release the corpse, who wobbles, only toward the wall, not the door.

I fold to my knees and scramble for other components, laying them out in a quick seeking spell. There's still a magical trace left from whoever cast the ward on the door—and I know very well who cast the ward on the door—so I link to it, let it spread out to find more of the same signature.

A trailing vapor of glowing blue sizzles through the air, leading from the door to the third lab space on the left.

That blue glow vanishes when I scoop up the spell bits and climb to my feet.

The Nec Lab gave me a few spells to control Sten, basic first-year necromancy stuff, and I rattle one off now.

Could I have used one to keep him in place instead of making

Orok hover around him, doing some weird herding dance? Yes. Would it have been as fun? No.

Sten jolts into action, marching like a soldier for the lab space. He stops inside and his arms snap straight, at attention.

A huge chunk of skin—muscle?—falls off his body and plops onto the floor.

I grin. "*Perfect.*"

Orok gags. "You need help, Seb."

In this space, the tops of the desk and worktable are mostly clear, a few stacks of papers, a jar of pencils. The whiteboard has some equations on it, spells that are just conjuration bullshit. But there's nothing of importance lying around. I do have my limits, unlike *some* people.

I recite the command spell for Sten, adding a few instructions— *stay* and *messy*, followed by *jump out and scare the first person who comes over here*.

Sten shudders as the magic sinks in.

Then he bends and licks the desk, leaving a good amount of his tongue behind.

Orok gags again.

I grin again.

"Good boy, Sten," I say in a cutesy voice.

Something sharp digs into my calf and I yelp, only to look down and see a top hat bobbing away.

Orok cackles. "Someone's jealous of your new pet."

I rub my leg—damn, that does hurt.

"The Nec Lab doesn't expect the corpse back, do they?" Orok asks, head cocked as he watches Sten wobble to the window, bump into it, back up, walk forward, bump into it, back up, and stare impassively at it.

"Technically they're supposed to dispose of Sten through proper channels, but I worked out a trade of services with the guy there."

Orok catches me with an accusatory stare. "A trade of *what* services?"

"I volunteered in the Nec Lab." They infamously can't get students to volunteer in their experiments no matter how well they pay. Shockingly, few people are cool with being test dummies for protection spells against decomp attacks, let alone more advanced shit. There was a rumor that a student's leg fully decayed once.

My own experience was hardly a danger to my person; a couple of sophomores resurrected a guy, and I had to talk to four people and give my guess who the resurrected corpse was. Something about believability, how well they healed the decomp, and so on.

But Orok's implication clicks and I tip my chin down, vaulting my eyebrows seductively. "Did you think I was trading *sexual favors* for a *dead body*?"

"Like you haven't done shit more reckless than that." His accusation holds. Intensifies. "You've been more . . . unhinged lately."

I sober, feeling an immediate kick to match up with his energy. "I have not."

Orok looks pointedly over my shoulder.

Sten is scratching his bony finger down the dry-erase board, pulling lines through the writing. Meanwhile, pieces of . . . something . . . are falling off his pelvis and down around his feet.

This is harmless.

Tomorrow will be fine.

Despite that, my stomach turns to lead.

All I see is the grant committee. How desperately I need that money to finish my degree and keep the job offer with Clawstar.

Doing spells in an experimentation capacity adds up, especially once you factor in the need for component purity and consistency. And here Elethior Tourael's family paid for a whole lab refurbishment while he was still in undergrad.

Which sector of the Tourael fortune paid for it—their magical weapons manufacturing? The patents they hoard for spell developments? The Arcane Forces training camp they run?

I breathe out so deep my sides ache.

"I'm not going too far," I tell Orok. Which sounds, like, so convincing. "Elethior deserves this. Don't do the war crime if you can't do the time."

"I don't think Elethior has committed any actual war crimes."

"How would you know? And if he hasn't, his family has."

Orok's chuckle is humorless. "And we should be held responsible for what our families do?"

Even in this hazy moonlight, I know the red flush heating my pale face is visible. Not embarrassment, not quite; just the shame of being called out.

"Don't bring logic into my feud," I mutter and throw another preservation spell at Sten so the poor guy has a hope of lasting the night.

Orok wrestles me into a headlock, nearly dislodging my glasses, and plants a kiss on the blond mess I call a hairstyle.

Unfortunately, Nick takes that as an attack, because by the way Orok yells and flails his leg to the side, I'm guessing Nick bit him again.

Orok hauls me to multiple parties. By the time two of his teammates text him about a fourth that we stumble over to—or, well, *he* stumbles; I'm maintaining a delicate buzz due to my grant ceremony in the morning—he decides to enter the house by bellowing, "Feel the sting, Feel the sting!"

Orok's normal state has him collecting friends and acquaintances like a golden retriever. Add on him being a lethal defensive tank on the university's rawball team, and everyone picks up the chant until the first level of what might be a frat house is caught up in the swell of school spirit, high-fiving Orok and calling out greetings as we wind our way inside.

Two of Orok's teammates are in a dining room off the main hall. As grad students, none of them should still be playing, what with college rawball participation capped at four years; but every player during the past year and a half got special permission to extend their time thanks to a particularly gnarly accident that caused the entire field to get sucked into a portal dimension. Luckily, all the players and fans who happened to be in the stadium were recovered, but it took a while to get back the various bits of the field itself.

You'd think complications like that would make rawball ban interdimensional spells, but *noooo*, where's the fun in a safe sport?

Ivo's a tank like Orok, though short and stocky, dwarven, with a buzzed head and a dark beard. Crescentia's a rogue on the team, human, with neon-pink hair and a quirky art-student vibe, currently sporting her purple-and-gold jersey.

Orok hooks his arm around my waist and bends down to prop his chin on my shoulder, ever the touchy-feely drunk.

I nod at Crescentia's jersey. Orok rocks with the motion. "That helping you pull tonight?"

Crescentia leers and puffs out her chest. "I dunno. Is it?"

Ivo elbows her. "His boyfriend's *right there.*"

Orok rockets away from me at the same moment I glower back at him.

"You have *got* to stop cuddling me in public," I say.

Ivo shrugs. "Crescentia was out of line to—"

"We're not *together,*" I cut him off. "Crescentia, feel free to hit on me."

Orok groans. "Please don't hook up with one of my teammates."

Crescentia sizes me up and sips her beer. "Actually, pass. You're always giving off high-maintenance vibes."

My squeak of offense is swallowed in music blaring from the kitchen. "Fuck you very much, I am not *high maintenance.*"

"Eh." Orok rocks his hand back and forth.

I punch him in the stomach. He doesn't flinch.

Ivo points between Orok and me. "Back up. You two are constantly hanging off each other, and you mean to tell me you're *not* fucking? Are you *serious?*" He looks at Orok. "Do you have any idea how many of my friends have asked for your number, and I always brush them off with a *sorry, he's basically married?*"

"Two masculine people can't be physically affectionate without being in a relationship," I say, "but if two feminine people were, they'd be cuddly friends, right? Neanderthals."

I allow myself one more drink and snatch a red cup from the dining room table. The contents smell like cheap vodka and grenadine, but I down it, wincing at the slight cough-syrup flavor.

Orok plants his palm on the side of my head and shoves until I'm standing between Crescentia and Ivo, no longer next to him. "This is the last time our codependency cockblocks me. You are whatever's the opposite of a wingman."

"A thigh-woman," I say without missing a beat.

Orok glares at me, or tries to, but he's half laughing and can't stand up straight without bobbling. "Keep away from me for the rest of the night. I'm not going home alone."

"You're right, you're not. We live together."

He notes my empty cup and gasps like a hole opened up in the floor. "*Bad.* I'll fix this."

He snatches it and he's off, the crowd easily parting for his substantial size, and I'm honestly not sure where he's wandering to, given that the table where I got the drink is right here, spread with dozens of various alcoholic options. And more than a few potion bottles with labels like PROPER FUCKED-UP—NO HANGOVER, GUARANTEED! and LIQUEFIED MAGIC SHROOMS: PINEAPPLE PIZZA FLAVOR.

My nose curls.

Gods, I hope whatever I drank was cheap vodka.

Crescentia takes another sip of her beer. My eyes get caught on her lips around the bottle's rim, and my reaction conflicts with Orok's plea not to hook up with his teammates. Was that a serious plea? Is it worth having to prove to Crescentia that I'm not *high maintenance*?

Though if I do try to get with her, even for a one-night thing, would Orok be all accusatory again about me slipping back into reckless behavior? I have had hookups without his judgment, so maybe it was the bit where he thought I'd connected it to a favor.

This is a lot of mental hoops for an orgasm I'm not sure I—

I'm flung into Crescentia, who flattens against the wall with a shout of surprise.

I whirl on Orok and steady him. "Dude, what the—"

"We gotta *go*," he says, putting his face right up in mine. "Seb. We need to *leave*."

"You were gone two seconds. There's no way you fucked something up that—"

"Elethior is here."

My grip on Orok's shirt tightens. I pop my eyes past his shoulder, scanning the party.

People press around us, everyone well past inebriated, limbs strewn in the air and heads lolling to the music or thrown back in laughter.

A figure leans against the wall that divides the dining room from the kitchen. Elethior Tourael is all length and height—long black hair buzzed on one side; long, slender, half-elven ears; long limbs under a black T-shirt and black pants; thick boots like he rode here on a motorcycle, though I think the fuck not. It's okay for a Tourael to play pretend at being some kind of badass, with the black tattoos up the side of his neck and along his arms contrasting against his pale skin, but for him to actually be a badass would require a level of slumming it that he's not capable of.

He's listening to whatever someone in his group is saying, but he reaches for his drink on a table behind him and his eyes lock with mine.

Recognition transforms Elethior's expression. Seizes him in a cringe of revulsion.

My already rapid-fire pulse goes ultrasonic. I can't even hear the hum of it in my ears anymore.

"*Seb*," Orok pleads. "We gotta go. What if he knows we were in his lab? *Oh my gods.*"

"Hey." I break my gaze from Elethior like I'm emerging from underwater—sound throbs again, movement speeds back up—and I cup Orok's face so his bloodshot eyes focus on me. "You always get super paranoid when you drink. We're good."

Ivo pats Orok's shoulder. "Maybe lay off the hard stuff. And stop doing whatever this moron tells you to do."

Crescentia tips her beer at Ivo. "I'll drink to that. What is this rivalry about, anyway? Evocation and conjuration are basically the same thing."

My hands are still cupped around Orok's face, so when we both turn to look at her, it's more than a little ridiculous.

There are a good number of spells all wizards are capable of. Once you get into higher-level stuff, things break into rigid class structures—and evocation uses magical energy to create nonliving things, like magically generated fire. But conjuration uses magical energy to pull inanimate shit to the caster, regardless of where it came from; no creation, nothing new, just something fully formed that belonged to someone else, then *poof.*

"Evocation creates from magical energy. *Creates.* Like a—like a— We're *artists.*" I release Orok to point at Crescentia, who looks like she's regretting ever having said anything, or maybe being this side of sober when she did. "Conjuration wizards are *thieves*—"

"Funny. I was going to say the same about you."

The words are only spoken loud enough to be heard over the music, but the voice itself is a thunderhead, and it crashes into my nerve endings like each one was caught unaware in a storm.

Our group turns.

To Elethior.

Orok curses, Crescentia chugs the rest of her beer, and Ivo rolls his eyes and ducks around Elethior to slip off into the house.

I'm only vaguely aware of these things, tuned in to Elethior in a tunnel of narrowed awareness, the primitive part of my monkey brain screaming *threat, threat, threat.*

Elethior gives me a flat, cold stare.

I return it with a confident grin. "Can I help you?"

He tips his head, his dark hair catching the yellow light with a sheen. A cloud of cologne, smelling of floral vetiver, billows over me, so thick it takes a beat for it to emanate from him.

"Though *thief* is the incorrect word," he carries on like I didn't speak. "What's the name for a person who breaks in and leaves something?"

My grin widens, more a baring of teeth than a smile. "Santa Claus."

Elethior's jaw twitches. "I got a call earlier tonight from campus security," he tells me. His voice stays even, despite the rise and fall of the music, and I have to watch his mouth to catch what he's saying.

He has snake-bite piercings through his bottom lip. "Apparently, someone left bones, skin, and a chattering skull in my lab space. Are you saying I have Santa Claus to thank for that?"

He wasn't the one to find Sten? Damn.

I resist the urge to check the time, but by my calculation, Sten barely lasted four hours before the preservation spells failed him. Double damn.

"Wow," I say. "You must've been *really* naughty if that's what Santa left you."

Elethior sucks his teeth. "You're lucky nothing important was damaged."

"Wait." I fake a gasp. "Are you accusing me of something? I've been out all night, partying it up. These guys can vouch for me."

Orok sways on his feet and shrugs. Way to back me up, dude.

It's Crescentia who leaps to the rescue.

She tosses her empty beer bottle onto the table while glaring daggers at Elethior. "Awfully hypocritical of you to come over here and lob baseless accusations when your family has been proven guilty of more than a few heinous crimes."

Oh. Maybe we *should* hook up after this.

Crescentia missed a party one time when she was off in DC lobbying for a ceasefire after another portal to the Demonic Plane popped open somewhere in the Midwest. The Arcane Forces always respond to those with an aggressive counterstrike before any demons or fire elementals can sneak through, but destroying the portal so violently causes untold damage to the surrounding area.

And who provides the bulk of shit used for these counterstrikes? Who has the market cornered on magical weapons, deadly spells, even the specialized training those soldiers receive?

The Tourael family.

But Elethior is ignoring Crescentia's social justice energy, his focus on me.

The fact that he looks smug sends a shiver of ice down my spine.

"I didn't accuse anyone of anything," he says to me. "I know for a fact it couldn't have been you to break into my lab. Do you want to know why I'm so certain? Why I didn't throw your name to the security guard who called me?"

"Because I'm the picture of motherfucking innocence?" I give him my best syrupy smile.

His nostrils flare and he leans in. I hold my ground and let him get an inch from me, the heft of his cologne clotting the air, choking me with earthiness and roses.

"Hardly," he growls. "It's because I know you're not good enough to have broken my ward, like you're not good enough to win that grant tomorrow. Are you, sweetheart?"

The fucker pats my cheek.

Maybe that last cup of vodka cherry whatever did have a mystery potion in it because I blink, then Orok's holding me back by the collar of my gray T-shirt, his other arm belted around my waist.

Elethior's torso is bent slightly backward like he was dodging me, and I don't remember lunging. But I definitely did; I feel the burn of movement sizzling in my muscles, feel the flash-bang of fury aching along the sides of my body.

"Don't you *fucking* touch me," I snarl, and Elethior plunges right back, getting so close that the world is consumed in the harsh angles of his half-elven features, the abyss of his eyes.

"Don't fuck with my lab," he snaps, and I wrench against Orok's hold.

"*Seb*," Orok hisses.

We've drawn attention. A dozen or so people watch us, and the music still plays, but one idiot chants, "Fight, fight, fight." It doesn't catch, especially when Elethior pivots his glare in the guy's direction, and the attitude plummets from the crackle of entertainment to the lightning strike of *This is not a joke.*

Elethior faces me again and straightens his tight black shirt like it somehow got mussed in his few sharp movements. He licks at the silver ring on the left side of his mouth and sizes me up before shooting a bored look at Orok.

"When he loses the grant to me tomorrow," Elethior tells him, "don't let him come near me. I'm done with his bullshit."

I laugh. It rattles out of me, half-hysterical, pushing me right up to the threshold of unhinged, like Orok had been worried about.

I'm done with his bullshit.

His words set off other voices in my head, a swelling, overlapping symphony.

Is that all you've got?

Pathetic.

This was wasted on you.

I shove Orok off, and he lets me go. I'm not sure why. Maybe he can sense the dip in my rigidity.

"I'll happily leave you alone after tomorrow," I tell Elethior. "They're going to award that grant to me, then I'm never going to think about you or your family again."

"Oh, baby boy," he coos. "We both know every bit of that's a lie."

I spin away from him, seeing red, seeing flashes of things that slither along my arms and creep across my body and—*fuck.*

My skin is too tight and my chest hurts and I try to unbutton my collar, only to remember I'm wearing a T-shirt and can only ineffectively tug at the cotton that's trying to suffocate me.

I trip on the rug in the entryway, wrench open the front door, and plunge into the night.

The autumn-chilled air stabs into my lungs. It smells like damp leaves. Dying, mildewy rot, but in the comforting way that promises the season's changing so you can change with it.

Orok follows me. Crescentia, too. But it's Orok who grabs my arm and tugs me to a stop, and I spin on him.

He gets it. He gets it instantly, and he lets me go.

"Unclench your hands, Seb," he tells me.

I obey, flexing my fingers, but it's *bullshit.* It does *nothing.* Several therapists got me on exercises like this—in the throes of anger, focus on relaxing tense muscles; breathe deep; get yourself back in your body—but these techniques only make me more pissed that I need help calming down at all.

I don't want to calm down.

I don't want to let it go.

No one else had to calm down, so why do I?

"Fucking Tourael," Crescentia says. "Right? Blood-money rich rat bastard."

That, in spite of everything, makes me laugh. A real laugh, not the bitter, harsh thing Elethior got out of me.

I rip my glasses off, scrub them clean, and shove them back on.

Crescentia turns to Orok. "Think Seb can handle a few rounds of Blast Off?"

He doesn't get a chance to answer. I groan, head thrown back, it's damn near pornographic. "*Gods yes.*"

Blast Off is a rawball training game Orok complains about doing every few weeks. It involves a fire-blasting machine, and the only way to shut it down is to get it to burn to a certain temperature which, for wizards, means one gloriously destructive and explosive spell: fireball.

With my head still thrown back, I turn my groan into a mewl of unease. "Wait. Are you asking me to *go raw,* then *blast a load* with you?"

I tip a cheesy grin at Orok and Crescentia.

They share a long-suffering look.

Orok holds up a nonexistent watch on his wrist. "You went almost half an hour hanging around my teammates without making a rawball joke. I'm pretty proud."

"Aw, babe, your approval means everything."

Orok drops his wrist and frowns at me. "You sure you're good to play, though?"

There's a lot unsaid in his question.

I nod. "End tonight by burning the shit out of something? This is exactly what I need."

There's a lot unsaid in my response, too.

Small things. Focus on small things. Pretend and pretend and maybe I won't have to pretend eventually.

Orok exhales. But he manages a smile. "All right. Let's burn some shit."

Crescentia cheers.

We all turn, weaving through parked cars to cross the road and head to campus.

Even with the briefly heightened emotions, I'm the only one who seems to have burned through what little alcohol I'd pumped into my body, or maybe Orok and Crescentia drank way more than I did. But Orok slants to the right until I tuck myself under his arm to steer him toward the rawball field, while Crescentia dances ahead of us with hiccupping giggles.

Enacting pranks: a good way to burn off stress.

Going to parties: a bad way to burn off stress.

But actually burning things? The *best* way to burn off stress.

Chapter Two

TRAFFIC ALERT: Troll warning at the South Street Bridge. Travelers advised to seek alternative routes even if they believe they can answer the troll's riddle. Adventure party dispatched. Expected time to all clear: two and a half hours.

Normally, a notification about an adventure party so close would have me wrestling Orok out of his hangover so the two of us could play gawkers with a few dozen other people. On the spectrum of defensive magic users, adventure parties sit on one end while the Arcane Forces cap off the other; it's the difference between using an explosion spell to close old subway tunnels so they can flush out a horde of undead pixies versus using it to level half a town along with alleged stores of dragon eggs. A friendly neighborhood adventure party is typically an entertaining start to the day—

—except the South Street Bridge is the path I take to campus.

I was *ready* for this morning. Before I went to the Conjuration Lab with Orok last night, all my nice clothes were tucked in a garment bag and my messenger satchel was packed next to my laptop, along with printed copies of my grant proposal and my travel case of spell components since my leather belt isn't exactly fancy. I ordered breakfast to be dropped off at the ass crack of dawn despite Ghostmates' exorbitant fees and the tendency of their delivery spirits to slam kitchen cupboards and rattle plumbing. All I had to do was wake up this morning, hop in the shower, grab my shit, and get to campus not just on time, but *early*, so I could change in my TA office instead of wearing my nice clothes on the bus.

But what's that saying? When mortals laugh, gods make plans? Or maybe it's the other way around, but I must've laughed way too much last night playing drunken Blast Off with Orok and Crescentia, because holy *shit*, am I getting fucked by a god's plans now.

My dress shirt never made it into my garment bag. Hell, it didn't even make it from the washer to the dryer, so it was a stiff, mildewy mess that's currently rattling around with hopes, prayers, and extra static sheets on the quick-dry cycle.

And my coffee order, which was supposed to have an extra shot of charisma—yeah, okay, those potions are generally sugar syrup, but I'll take whatever placebo effect I can get—had an extra shot of *something*, but it was *nothing* close to charisma. I am vibrating out of my skin as I pull up the Philadelphia transpo app and check what other routes are available, and, wait, are my nails a little jagged? Does that matter? This brunch is for the announcement of the grant recipient, but this is still a chance to network with university uppity-ups and alumni who felt like coming and—shit. I should bring business cards, too. Do I have time to get some? Is there a spell to make business cards? Can I—

What was in that coffee.

I pace my bedroom, window to door, and growl at my phone as the transpo app loads.

New estimated route: forty minutes to campus.

I factored in *fifteen minutes*, which is what it usually takes.

I shove my phone in my messenger satchel, grab my garment bag, and sprint into the hall. The bathroom is still open, steam from my shower making the upper floor of our two-level apartment muggy. I clatter down the stairs, the ratty carpet slick from decades of tenants, and nearly twist my ankle as I trip-tumble into the living room.

"Mom, I'm not hungover, I swear."

Orok's huge frame is sprawled on our couch, one leg across the back, a bottle of water balanced on his forehead. He's still in last night's clothes that make everything smell vaguely of smoke, his phone pressed to his ear. His eyes are pinched shut even though the curtain's drawn tight and the only light comes from our dinky-ass kitchen, where the dryer chugs, the buttons on my nice dress shirt dinging around inside the drum.

"Yes, I can handle my alcohol," he says into the phone. "I'm not—Mom. *Mom.* No, I didn't challenge anyone to a fight." He rubs the skin between his eyes. "Yeah, Seb was there. He had nothing to do with me not wanting to punch people."

I rush past, tripping on a pair of Converse—mine, oh, I need those; I tug them on, keep walking—but Orok's eyes stay closed, and he's now rolling the water bottle back and forth across his forehead.

The Church of Urzoth Shieldsworn is all about strength and physical prowess. Most of what I've heard is rhetoric from his mom about how real devotees of Urzoth don't show weaknesses like getting sick from alcohol—which is just, *what*—or how they don't *stumble down paths of nonsensical frailness* like academia rather than doing something that requires brute strength. Orok's wrested some saving graces by focusing his studies on Urzoth's relics and playing on the rawball team. Despite being proud of these accomplishments, and generally loving her son, his mom refuses to see me as anything other than a black mark against him.

I should send Mrs. Monroe a photo of her baby in all his *I can handle my alcohol* glory, then explain that I'm the one who is *not* hungover despite the rampant anti-Sebastian propaganda she pushes. He did drink more than I did, but whatever.

Though being *not hungover* is all I've got going for me this morning.

The dryer lurches worryingly, jostling everything in the kitchen, but the cycle continues, and my frantic rushing throws me to a stop in front of it.

Do I need a shirt? Is it that important?

If I leave right now, I'll make it to campus on time. Ish.

I look down at my threadbare AC/DC shirt and briefly think it'd be pretty badass to do the T-shirt-under-a-suit-jacket look, but am I capable of pulling that off?

Doubt hits me, or rather, catches up to me, and I stagger from the force of it body-slamming my brain.

You know who could pull off that look? Who probably isn't running late. Who's likely already at campus, polished and chatting up the grant committee, not at all worried about his post-graduation plans being dependent on this grant because if (*when*) he doesn't get it, he'll still have a cushy job lined up in any number of his family's businesses.

I grab my half-drunk coffee from the counter—but no, okay, I rethink *that* at the last second and check the label.

No charisma potion, like I suspected, but it does have a quad shot of espresso added to my regular drip coffee. I've only been poisoned by caffeine and my own neuroses.

Great, great morning. It's fine. Everything's fine.

I'll get to campus, change at warp speed, and sneak in while everyone's getting their brunch food bits. No harm done. The decision about who gets the grant has already been made, anyway; I doubt the committee will change their mind based on a few minutes of tardiness. Right?

I glare at the dryer and seriously consider blasting it with a fireball.

"Yeah, I'm still going to church," Orok says behind me.

I laugh. Loudly.

He lets go of the water bottle to flip me off.

"I know," he keeps saying to his mom. "I'm still working with Reverend Dregu. Yeah, we get together every week. Mom. *Mom.* I'm not sending you my research reports. There's nothing in them you'd care about! They're all spells and equations, not—yeah, I talk to Reverend Dregu about *my soul,* too. No, I didn't take a tone with you. I'm sorry. *I said*—"

Ironic how Orok's mom is all about pushing him to exert his strength, but him standing up to her isn't something she tolerates.

There is no sweeter sound in the world than our crappy dryer beeping.

I chirp triumphantly and open it. My shirt is dry, wrinkle-free, and doesn't have that weird mildew smell.

Things are looking up, see? *Everything is fine.*

The knot in my stomach that has nothing to do with strong coffee pulls tighter.

I delicately tuck my shirt into the garment bag and double-check

I have everything. Why do I feel like I'm forgetting something? I probably am. I'll probably get to the brunch and realize I forgot pants and have to go in wearing my gray sweats.

But no, I packed pants. And a normal belt, too. Look at me, adulting.

My unsteady hands fumble the garment bag's zipper and I spin around to down the rest of my coffee—I really, *really* don't need it— only to slam right into Orok's chest.

Still on the phone, he clamps his free arm around me and draws me into a brutal hug. He *reeks* of smoke, and the side of his shirt is crunchy where it got singed during Blast Off.

But I let him hug me. Just for a second.

"While I appreciate the sentiment," I whisper, "you're making me stink."

He squeezes me tighter before releasing me with a pat on the head. "Good luck," he says softly. "You're gonna kick his ass." He flinches. "No, Mom, *I'm* not kicking someone's ass; it was metaphorical. I'm not—" He sighs, and the sound of his mom guilt-tripping him for not embracing his family's religion by randomly crushing skulls is a muffled drone between us.

I grin, and Orok winks at me, and that gnawing worry abates enough that I manage a clear breath.

I'll make it to the brunch. I'll get that grant. I'll do my final project, complete my degree, and start at Clawstar next summer.

It's going to be fine.

I grab the rest of my stuff as Orok plants his hip against the kitchen counter.

"No, Seb's not been going to church with me," he tells her and smirks at me like he's tattling. "He's still a heathen."

Asshole, I mouth.

"You're right, he *is* puny!" he says brightly. "That's what I said yesterday."

"I'm leaving," I shout too loud as I open the door. "Have you told your mom you got kicked off the rawball team yet?"

Orok's eyes peel wide a beat before I hear his mom shriek "*WHAT?!*" through the phone.

He hasn't been kicked off the team. Shit-stirring is my love language.

I smile sweetly as I close the door.

Transportation spells are banned within city limits. It's an under-handed political move by the transportation authority to stay nec-essary; but never in my life have I come this close to breaking the law, and that includes last night's B&E and a few other questionable moments in my past.

The rerouted path to campus throws me on a trolley and two dif-ferent buses, and since the closed bridge has mucked up more than my plans, everything's overcrowded and traffic's moving at a snail's pace. By the time the bus clatters to my stop, every conceivable *what could go wrong* scenario has played through my head at least twice, and it isn't until a dwarven woman with her two kids frowns at me that I realize I've been muttering to myself.

The brunch started ten minutes ago.

I all-out *sprint* across campus. It's humming with Friday activ-ity as I zigzag between buildings and across the Quad, the massive grassy area that sits between a few of the biggest buildings. Bellanor Hall, the place I've seen more of than my own apartment the past few years, towers on the south side of it, playing host to the Evoca-tion and Conjuration Departments.

The banquet room where the brunch is being held sits at the back of the building, on the opposite end from my TA office. I'd burn precious extra minutes rushing there to change when I know there's a perfectly good restroom not far from the banquet room. Are the odds going to work in my favor and leave that restroom empty and not, say, packed with grant committee members doing up their flies at the urinals?

I roll the dice on the banquet restroom, the rubber soles of my Converse squeaking on the tile floor as I slide into the hall. At the far end, people in suits and nice dresses mill in and out of the banquet room. The only noise is chatter from conversation and the ting of cutlery, no official announcements yet—okay, I have time.

But I'm gasping and my overcaffeinated heart is doing its level best to sucker punch its way out of my rib cage, and part of me wonders why I never took Orok up on his offers to, quote-unquote, *whip my ass into shape.* I wheeze a pathetically shrill breath and heave into the bathroom off the hall—

—only for the gods to hatch their final plan at my expense.

Elethior's at the sink, washing his hands.

He glances up when I none too gracefully plunge inside, garment bag and messenger satchel clutched to my chest.

He's not wearing sweatpants and a T-shirt.

He's looking like a walking advertisement for why suits should always be tailored. His long hair is slicked over the side of his head and he's in a double-breasted black suit with a black shirt and tie, his shoes gleaming—

Fuck me up a wall.

I forgot my shoes.

My focus pings to my ratty blue Converse before I force myself to meet Elethior's eyes, feeling every bit of the sweat drying on my skin, of my frizzed-out hair, of my pulse jackhammering in my wrists and throat.

I look around, desperately hoping someone else is in here to serve as a barrier, but nope. We're alone.

Elethior scans me in a quick head-to-toe analysis and arrives at the same conclusion I would've come to had our situations been reversed: I'm screwed.

A satisfied smile unfurls across his face.

He calmly dries his hands, throws away the paper towel, and leans against the sink. "And here I thought you'd made the first smart decision of your academic career and decided to skip the brunch. I must say, showing up, having just rolled out of bed? *Much* better. For me. For you?" He clicks his tongue.

"I didn't just roll out of bed. Not all of us have chauffeurs who can cart us around the city."

"True. But all of us have at least alarm clocks, don't we?" His grin is caustic. "Some might see your tardiness as proof that you don't take this program seriously, Sebastian. Others, like the grant committee, know you've already proven that tenfold."

My jaw sets. Our interaction last night is still raw, and everything I've toppled through this morning has fallen on it like slow drips of vinegar—so I have no resolve to shrug off the attacks he fires with an archer's precision. Especially when he's looking like he leaped off a fragrance billboard, making every word he spews feel so much weightier, casting judgment and finding me wanting in every possible way.

He's polished and pristine, composed and orderly.

Why wouldn't he get the grant instead of me?

The knot in my stomach is rock-hard. Takes up every free space inside me.

He doesn't matter. None of this matters, remember? It's all noise. Get to the brunch. Get the grant. Rub his smug face in it.

I shift my garment bag and eye the bathroom stalls, but I'm hit with an image of dunking my shirtsleeve into a toilet, which leaves changing out here.

Elethior must follow my train of thought. His smile grows slyer, and he doesn't move from where he's reclined against the sink, ankles crossed so the leg of his pants rides up and a flash of skin shows above his low-cut sock.

"They're due to begin the presentation in"—he checks a watch that likely cost more than my rent for a year—"seven minutes."

His eyes pop up to me, amused and daring.

I think one of my molars cracks. "You gonna leave?"

With overemphasized deliberateness, he turns back to the mirror and swipes a finger along his eyebrow. "I don't think so. It *is* a public restroom, isn't it?"

It's a game of chicken.

Fuck him. Fuck this morning. *Fuck all of this.*

I toss my garment bag over one of the stall doors and plop my satchel on the sink next to him.

His eyes flash to mine in the mirror. For a too-long second, we stare at each other, challenge as thick as humidity in July.

Wrong day to mess with me, buddy.

The part of me that Orok's always worried will take over bursts up out of my soul like a rabid dog, feral and snarling, and before I can think anything else through, I shrug off my coat, remove my glasses, grab the hem of my T-shirt, and yank it off.

Our eyes disconnect. The moment the T-shirt brushes across my face, I slide my glasses back on and I can see him again.

The silence arching between us stretches. The difference between *come at me, bruh,* and something that takes the knot in my stomach and douses it with kerosene and scrapes a match against my nerve endings to light it.

That light flares, illuminating a singular fact:

I'm half naked in front of him.

Elethior blinks twice, in rapid succession.

Prickles of chill race across my skin, goose bumps that make me shiver even though the bathroom's pretty warm, heated for late November.

Elethior switches his gaze back to his own reflection. "Classy," he says, but it comes out rough.

"Never claimed to be," I bite back.

I move to untie my sweatpants, and he coughs, some jagged, garbled sound.

"For gods' sakes," Elethior rasps and hurries past me for the door.

I should feel vindicated for winning this game. But something's off-balance, thrown into tumult by *him* again, and I'm so tired of him rocking me, and I'm tired of this rivalry, and I'm *done.*

"Why are you here?" I bark as he reaches for the door handle. "Why do you give a shit about this grant? What are you going to do with it that your family can't fund anyway?"

"It's not just about funding," he says to the door. "This grant carries weight."

The flames take me. The rage, the months of strain, all of it scorches through me and my mouth moves independently of my brain. "This is only about *prestige* to you? Gods, that's worse. Even if you win this grant, those of us out here in the real world will always know you didn't deserve it; you got it because of your last name. You're not capable of earning anything yourself, you pompous prick."

His shoulders go rigid under that suit jacket that fits him like it's made of liquid. Color stains the part of his neck not covered by his hair, a bright crimson that spreads up the side of his face.

Slowly, he pivots to me again. My hackles rise, that hindbrain awareness of a predator nearby.

His glower flits down my body, and when I shiver this time, it's from feeling exposed.

"At least people will know me," he says, eyes returning to mine. There's no challenge in them anymore. Just excruciating hatred. "Meanwhile, you will remain an immature fuckup who will die in obscurity because you have nothing substantial to contribute to this world."

He says it with such certainty that it knocks the wind out of me.

The restroom echoes with the door banging shut in his wake.

"Mr. Walsh, where have you been hiding?"

Professor Thompson claps my shoulder as I take my seat beside him. I discreetly shove my garment bag and satchel under the table, along with my Converse-clad feet. Luckily, everyone else seated at our table is engaged in conversation, chatting easily and snacking on bits of quiche and mini pastries.

The wide banquet room is lined with windows on one side, casting bright midmorning light on half a dozen circular tables set with linens and flowers, while buffet tables piled with brunch bites at the edge of the room billow out scents of syrup and bacon. Most of the guests are alumni and faculty of the Mageus Studies departments, but I clock the other applicants.

There are only four of us. Elethior and I are the front-runners, according to my faculty advisor.

Due to the oftentimes intensely competitive natures that tend to crop up in our field, the selection committee has only announced minimal details about each project. I have no real idea what the other applicants are hoping to use the money for, merely that Elethior's topic caused *quite a stir* among the selection board, as did mine.

My gaze snags on him, where he sits at one of the tables closest to the front podium, smiling amicably at a man seated with him.

I pivot back to Thompson. "Sorry, sir. I—"

Dr. Davyeras steps up to the podium at the front of the room. He's on the university board and heads up the selection committee—and he's in the Conjuration Department, but I try not to read too much into that.

He adjusts the microphone. "Thank you all for coming," he says, and the crowd's conversation dies down.

Thompson lifts one eyebrow at me. "Don't stress about it," he whispers. "We did all we could."

He's not only the professor I'm a TA for, but the one who recommended me for this grant and helped me fine-tune my proposal.

I shift on the chair and wish I'd had time to grab something to drink. My throat is sandpaper while I feel like I might sweat right through my blue button-down and gray suit. I did what I could in the bathroom, but I still probably look like I got swept up in a windstorm on my way to campus.

"We are pleased to present another Mageus Research Grant," Davyeras says. "Every year, we are amazed by the quality of the proposals we receive. This year was no exception. The caliber of students gracing Lesiara University continues to be set by those who study in the Mageus programs."

My knee bounces. I grip my hands into fists, my tongue caught between my teeth.

It's happening. It's too soon and not going fast enough and I can still feel the troubling amount of caffeine wreaking havoc with my blood vessels.

"There were two proposals in particular the committee wanted to call attention to."

Can't breathe. Won't ever again. *Here lies Sebastian Walsh; he suffocated at a brunch.*

"The first came from Elethior Tourael—"

Ugh.

"—a graduate student in the Conjuration Department who plans to use his degree to continue the vital work his family does for our country, and across the globe, in magical defense."

Magical defense. Sure. It's that harmless.

"Mr. Tourael's proposed research project involves studying the limitations of the energy connection between a conjurer and their conjured item."

I do not look at Elethior. Briefly, I feel his eyes on me, but I stay focused on the announcer.

Thompson nudges my shoe to get me to stop bouncing my leg.

"Our second applicant of note," Davyeras says. He shuffles some papers on his podium. "Is Sebastian Walsh, a graduate student in the Evocation Department—"

I can taste blood. I pry my teeth out of my tongue.

"—who plans to use his degree to contribute to spell work in the nonprofit sector. Mr. Walsh's proposed research project involves the limitation of energy drawn from components during spells."

Davyeras stops to look up at the crowd. "The committee was met with an interesting challenge this year," he says. "Both of our front-runners' projects deal with the connection and control of energy during spell work."

I barely stop myself from scoffing. Has this guy been talking to Crescentia?

"As you well know," Davyeras carries on, "there has always been a bit of friendly competition between the Conjuration and Evocation Departments. And at first, the committee's decision lay along those lines. Which should we support: Evocation or conjuration? But the issue is larger than a divide of department. The benefits of uncovering ways to cap and control energy in spell work appealed to those on not just the selection committee, but on the university board itself. Our decision came down to what would best serve the magical community as a whole."

My heart sinks like the rest of my chest cavity turned to quicksand.

Best serve the magical community.

The Tourael family is one of the heads of the elite *magical community.* They're going with Elethior, aren't they?

It hits me in a crashing wave, the reality of having to get funding from somewhere else. If I want to graduate. If I want to keep Clawstar impressed. If I want to be able to get spell work to people who *need* it. Sure, I can scramble to find other sources, maybe get one more loan, why not? But that would take time. Time I doubt I have, to get started next semester.

But. I could call my father.

I force myself to sit up straight. Like hell will I fold. Like hell will I show weakness. It ain't over 'til it's over, gods damn it.

"Given the potential benefits of exploring spell work energy limitations," Davyeras says, "and the importance of cross-disciplinary teamwork, the committee has decided to provide a dedicated lab space as well as increase the grant's funding—"

I jerk to the edge of my chair. What? A dedicated lab? And—*more* money?

"—in a collaborative state to both Elethior Tourael and Sebastian Walsh."

Everything in my body solidifies. Quick-set cement.

The crowd is dead silent for a beat. Then whispers ripple through, nothing negative, mostly curiosity and interest.

Thompson jostles my arm, his face stretched wide with happiness.

"Mr. Tourael and Mr. Walsh will be expected to make full use of these resources as they not only research their projects, but uncover the ways in which conjuration and evocation overlap in spell energy limitation," Davyeras tells us. "They will cooperatively present their findings next spring. A unified project between these departments is a mark of this community's growth, and we, the selection committee, are excited to see what Mr. Tourael and Mr. Walsh are able to do together."

Together.

Cooperatively.

Collaborative.

Oh. My. Gods.

The room breaks into applause and Thompson elbows me.

Again.

A third time.

"Go up there," he hisses, and I'm moving on autopilot.

I stand. People clap.

Across the room, Elethior stands, too. Everyone else remains sitting so it's impossible to look anywhere but at him as the two of us converge on the podium.

His face is impassive—until our gazes connect.

That wrath he'd shown in the restroom surges to life, wildfires running rampant.

I'm lodged too firmly in shock to do anything more than gape at him.

There was always going to be *one grant winner*. It was me or Elethior and it would've shut at least one of us up for good.

We reach the podium, and Davyeras pulls us on either side of him. The audience claps still, and a photographer takes pictures of the three of us.

I tell myself to smile.

Nope, not happening.

"Uh, sir—" I start, throat still sandpaper so it comes out scratchy.

Davyeras squeezes my shoulder. Hard. "I know it's unorthodox," he says out of the side of his mouth.

Elethior hears him, too, briefly glancing across to give me another cutting glare.

Davyeras catches it and sighs. "This community has no room for juvenile conflicts, boys." He smiles at me, then at Elethior, and more photos are taken. "You will work together. As part of the grant, you will have monthly check-ins with myself and your advisors to ensure progress is being achieved. I am excited to hear how you tackle this challenge. This is a great honor, and a testament to how much faith we have in each of you."

I expected to feel one of two things after the announcement: ecstasy or fury. I have no idea what to do with feeling . . . *numb*.

I got the grant. I got funding—*more* funding. *And* a dedicated lab space. I'll be able to do my project and graduate. My future's being handed to me.

Only I'll have to work with *Elethior Tourael* to get any of it.

Chapter Three

Sebastian—

I understand your concerns regarding your required partner. I myself partook in many a good-natured ribbing with the Conjuration Department during my time as a student. The fact that the selection committee not only saw value in your project, but in YOU, speaks volumes of your character and skill. Do not risk your future over this.

I look forward to hearing of your progress at the first monthly check-in,
Professor Thompson

Basically, *Suck it up, Sebastian, you're being a child.*

I would, however, like to point out that my issues working with Elethior have almost nothing to do with him being in the Conjuration Department—I'm not *that* much of a dumbass. As I told Thompson, my *very valid and professional concerns* stem from working with someone who represents magical corruption and elitism, the polar opposite of everything I stand for.

But Thompson seems unable to comprehend anyone *not* being over the moon to rub elbows with a Tourael, which means he's determined to view my concerns only as the result of a petty interdepartmental rivalry.

I swing back and forth in my desk chair, staring at my laptop, trying to decide how professional it would be to send back an email saying, *But I don't WANNAAAAAA.*

The floor outside my bedroom creaks and I swivel on Orok, nearly upending myself from the rickety chair.

"I'm not being childish. He's a Tourael," I tell him, like he doesn't know, like I haven't been having this argument with him and myself since I got home on Friday, and it's now Monday, and the semester is over and he's officially stuck with me for the next few weeks. "*That's* my problem. He's going to take what will now be *our project* and dump it into the Tourael magical defense conglomerate, and it'll be used to hurt people. Clawstar will see I'm working with a Tourael and think I've crossed over to the enemy. My research, my work will be tangled up in *Tourael shit,* and I get no say in it. *That's* my problem, and it's not a childish concern. Right?"

Orok's checking something on his phone, but he flicks his eyes up to me. "No. It's not a childish concern."

"Thank you."

"But—"

"Fuck you."

"—first of all, I doubt Clawstar is so petty that they'd boot you for working with a Tourael."

He's right. I did, actually, message my future boss the evening of the grant announcement to assure her I got it, remind her that my prearranged forthcoming job is still a good investment on her part, and try to get ahead of any issues. She'd congratulated me, and made no mention of my auspicious lab partner.

It's possible I might be overexaggerating the negative impact of this, but damn it if I'm not going to wallow.

"Second of all," Orok continues, "Elethior won't be able to *take* your joint project. You both own it equally. If you don't want it to end up in his family's hands, it won't. He's probably just as concerned that you'll try to get your joint project to go up online for free."

My smile is sinister. "*Oh.* Oh, that's a *lovely* idea." I was already planning on pushing this project out for free, so Elethior stewing is icing.

Orok winces at his phone and pockets it. But he refocuses on me before I can pry into that. "What is childish," he circles back, "is not accepting the situation *like an adult* and finding common ground so you do, in fact, *have* a final project to present."

I scowl at him and scramble for my phone on my desk. "I'm calling Crescentia. She'll take my side."

"You know I'm right, dipshit. But I didn't come up here for you to ignore me."

Orok's posture is . . . weird. He's leaning against the door like he's *trying* to be relaxed but tension's strung across his shoulders, one thumb tapping an anxious rhythm on his thigh.

Concern flares. "What's wrong?"

Our doorbell rings.

Orok holds up his hands. "Okay, so, I didn't *tell her* to come. Remember that."

That clears up nothing. "Who?"

He scrubs a hand across the back of his neck. "My mom wants me home for winter break. Our church is doing their usual ode to Urzoth Shieldsworn's birthday—even though I've told her that isn't his birthday, that church higher-ups just jumped on the trend centuries ago to throw big holidays in the winter season like a dozen other gods, so it doesn't—"

The doorbell rings again. A fist knocks.

He coughs. "Right. Anyway, my mom came to get me. And since she was coming, they decided to make it a road trip."

They.

Everything in my body shifts gears, only the clutch goes out so there's a lot of internal grinding and a little bit of smoke.

I snatch my phone, but swipe to the most recent—unread—texts from my mom.

MOM

Sebastian, sweetheart, we're on our way!

Ghorza's GPS says we should be there after lunch.

We'll visit then hit the road back home! And I do mean WE. It's been too long since you spent the holidays with us!

I stare at my phone in a stupor.

Until the screen lights up with an incoming call. From my mother. Who, I assume, is part of the knocking and doorbell-ringing racket downstairs.

Eyes pinched shut, I let my phone *thunk* onto my desk and take a beat to scrape through what the past few days have left of my sanity. There's nothing to do but face this like an adult. That's what I do now, apparently. It'll be good practice—if I can get through a few hours with my mom, I can handle Elethior. Probably.

"We should let them in before she chops down the door," I say, defeated.

"My mom hasn't used her strength like that in years."

"I wasn't talking about your mom."

He snorts as we clatter down the stairs—

—and I come to an abrupt halt.

Orok slams into me from behind, sending me stumbling forward.

I whirl on him with my mouth agape. "Did you clean our apartment?"

He rolls his lips between his teeth and gives a sheepish shrug. "Moms. Ya know?"

Yeah. I do know. I know that they'll deep-clean the whole place within an hour of being here no matter what state it's in, but Orok's attempt is good.

Every table is usually covered in old plates or takeout boxes, and books from classes or the library tend to stack up along with spell or research components. But there's nary a book or bit of trash in sight. Our ratty couch has a decorative quilt Orok's grandmother made folded on the back with two frilly pillows I've never seen in my life sitting on either end. The coffee table holds our unsorted mail in a neat stack. The dining table and kitchen are just as spotless—who knew our counters were blue?

I slug Orok in the shoulder. "A-plus, man. Is this why you've been clattering around down here all morning? You could've press-ganged me into service; I was just spiraling in my bullshit."

"Orok!" a voice calls through the door. His mom.

"Let us in, please," another voice. My mom. She must lean closer to the door, because the next part comes lower and more muffled. "This neighborhood isn't safe for us to be standing in the open."

Yeah, that's definitely my mom.

Orok moves for the door. "You don't have to come home," he whispers at me. "Don't let her pressure you. Remember, *no* is a complete sentence."

I flick him a deadpan look. The very idea of saying *no* to either of our mothers is, quite possibly, the most absurd thing he's ever said to me.

He grabs the doorknob but doesn't open it yet. "Just—them being here isn't my fault, okay? Don't be mad at me."

"Why would I be mad at you? For, like, anything. You're the one person who could dump a bowl of spaghetti on my head, and I'd assume you had a good reason and thank you."

Orok gives me a weak smile before he says, in one breath, "Well, it isn't spaghetti, but I've known your mom was coming since before the grant brunch, and I didn't tell you because I knew you weren't checking your messages from her so you wouldn't know, and this way, you didn't have to stress about it."

Okay, *now* I get pissed. "You son of a—"

He rips open the door. "Mom!"

Ghorza Monroe barges inside in a whirlwind of flailing arms. She squishes Orok's face in her hands with gushy proclamations of adoration like he's still the seven-year-old who'd cling to her arm on the walk to the bus stop. She's bigger than he is, and even her hair is huge, a giant arch of dark curls, so she has to crouch in the doorframe while she oohs and aahs over her son.

Then she steps aside, and my mom slides past her.

Abigail Walsh is the sixty-year-old female version of me. Or I guess I'm the twenty-four-year-old male version of her? Either way, pale skin, blond curls, short stature, poor eyesight. She's wearing a coat and a crisp Lesiara U collared shirt, death-gripping her purse over her shoulder because *I don't know why you chose to go to school in the city, Sebastian. There are pickpockets everywhere!*

The polo at least makes me smile. She's trying. I can, too.

"Hey, Mom," I say.

She shuts the door and leans in for a hug, but stops at the last second and zips her eyes over my outfit. Sweatpants and a T-shirt.

Her lips twist in distaste. "I told you we were coming. Would it have been so hard to clean up for us?"

Ah. Well. I guess we're not trying *that* hard.

"Yeah. Sorry. Been a busy weekend, what with the semester ending, and—"

"The semester *ended*," she repeats. "You had nothing to study for this weekend, and I know that job of yours doesn't start for months. There's no reason you couldn't have made an effort for our arrival."

I chew my tongue. "So. Good trip?"

"The drive was fine." She puts her purse on the counter. Or, rather, she *starts* to put her purse on the counter, but pulls a few components from said purse and does a spell she's done so many times I'm pretty sure she doesn't realize she's doing it: Detect Germs.

I've seen a lot of badass magic casting in my day, but watching my mother do a spell that makes germs glow green in an apartment owned by two university students, one of whom does sports, is a whole new level of courageous. Then again, she's a nurse who raised four kids, so what *hasn't* she endured.

The radius on the spell only covers the kitchen and a little in the dining room, but the counter lets out a faint green glow in a few places, as do the stove and floor. For the most part, though, everything looks pretty clean.

Mom sighs, pulls a sanitizing wipe from her coat pocket, rubs the counter, and finally sets her purse down.

"Ghorza," Mom says. "We can't leave the place like this. They'll get mice."

Ghorza takes in the area in one swoop and clucks her tongue. "Nothing we can't tidy up."

I give an apologetic cringe to Orok, but he's unbothered.

Mom takes off her coat and hands it to me as she rolls up her sleeves. "We'll have this place set to rights in no time. With you coming home for the holiday, it isn't sanitary to leave your home in such a state."

What state? Did they not see the *throw pillows*?

"I'm not coming home." I hang her coat by the door.

She digs under our sink for a sponge and soap, still not making eye contact. "Run upstairs and pack while we take care of this. Ghorza, can you handle the living room?"

But Ghorza's already there, refluffing the pillows Orok set out.

Orok takes an uncertain step toward her. "Mom, you don't have to do this. I'll grab my bag and we can head out, okay?"

"We're in no hurry to get back in the car," Ghorza tells him. She picks up the stack of unopened mail and flicks through it without hesitation at the privacy invasion. "Oh! Orok, you haven't opened your mail?"

Any bills or important things get picked through upon arrival; the rest—letters, mailers, and university notices—gets dumped for sorting at a later date that to this day has not arrived.

Ghorza plucks out an envelope. "This is the Simpsons' holiday card! Orok, you haven't even opened it." She throws a not at all thinly veiled glare—at me. "Let me guess. Sebastian is in charge of organizing your mail? You didn't know you'd gotten a card from them, did you?"

Orok sighs. "Seb didn't hide it from me."

"I wasn't implying he did."

Yeah, sure you weren't, Ghorza.

She holds the envelope out and Orok crosses the room to take it from her, obediently opening it while she watches on with a placated smile. It is, indeed, a holiday card; from where I'm still in the kitchen, I can see a picture of a smiling family all wearing matching red sweaters.

My mom is now fiddling with our wonky plumbing to get the hot water running. It chugs once, burbles, then spits out something I know will only be passably lukewarm.

She exhales in that passive aggressive way that says more than words ever could. *Oh, why would my youngest child choose to live in poverty? What did I do to make him hate me so much?*

But she gets to work scrubbing our countertops.

I give up, find another sponge, and join her. The faster they're done, the faster they'll leave.

"And here's one from the Horknuths!" Ghorza presents another envelope. We seem to have forgone cleaning in favor of shaming Orok into opening holiday cards from people who go to his parents' church. "Have you sent out your holiday cards yet, Orok?"

He fumbles opening the one from the Horknuths. "Uh—"

"You don't want to let it get too late. People will think you've forgotten them. You wouldn't want to upset the congregation, would you?"

"Our matching sweaters haven't arrived yet, Mrs. Monroe," I say as I throw half my body weight into scrubbing out a green glow by the fridge. "I got him one with Urzoth's symbol on it, and I got myself one with a symbol for Galaxrien Vossen. He was important to Urzoth, right?"

Galaxrien is a demon lord who's the sworn enemy of Urzoth. Urzoth famously locked him in a pit in the Demonic Plane, but Urzoth's devotees still get touchy when Galaxrien is mentioned.

Ghorza's face pales.

Next to her, Orok gives me a quick *don't antagonize her* look, but Ghorza finds fault in me no matter what. It's fun to poke her.

She must be at least sort of used to me, which is nice after knowing her for almost twenty years, because she recovers and says only, "That isn't funny."

I grin. "It's a little funny."

Mom scrubs the counter like cleaning will purge her of her snarky child. She's got two other sponges going under animation spells, but she tsks and holds up her own sponge. "This is falling apart, sweetheart. What happened to the birthday gift card I gave you to Bards, Blessings, and Beyond? Cleaning supplies are in the *beyond* part of that. Your sister promised they don't just sell spell components."

No one reacts; she doesn't expect anyone to.

Ghorza straightens, her chin jutting out. "I've been praying for you, Sebastian."

I count it as a mark of growth that I don't laugh.

"Thank you, Mrs. Monroe." I rewet my sponge in the sink. "I appreciate that."

"And how has your schedule been?" Ghorza continues, now idly flipping through the mail. "Do you often go out with Orok on the weekends?"

I pause, sponge soggy in my fingers.

This feels like a trap.

Ghorza pins her eyes on me with all the intensity of a government interrogator. "You do, don't you? If Orok was going out on his own, to parties of *his* choosing, I know he'd be spending far more time around people who encourage his natural strength. He hasn't challenged anyone to a fight in *more than a year*."

Orok, who'd taken to propping the holiday cards on the dining room table, startles and knocks them over. "I don't *have* to fight people. That's not one of Urzoth's commandments."

Ghorza smiles sweetly at him. "I know it isn't, honey, but where is your aggression? Your *passion*? You've been more and more timid each time I speak with you."

Orok snaps his mouth shut. "I'm fine. There's nothing wrong with *not* hitting people."

"You don't challenge anyone. You aren't sending holiday cards honoring Urzoth. What are you doing to uphold the teachings we instilled in you?"

"We graduate soon. I've been focusing on that."

"In strength lies power. I'm worried, Orok." Ghorza faces me again, scowling instantly. "And we all know who's to blame for encouraging you to not uphold our values."

I'm used to Orok's family—and, all right, my family—using me as a punching bag for bad behavior. And I'm ordinarily fine with it; I'm an easy target, and it lets Orok keep his relationship with his parents more or less copacetic.

But I flinch now. And I'm not immediately sure why.

"Sweetheart," Mom says. "Your sponge is dripping on the floor."

Dumbly, I plop it into the sink.

She and Ghorza probably talked about this all the way up here. *Poor Orok, Sebastian's got his claws in him.*

"I haven't been encouraging him one way or another, Mrs. Monroe." I step out of the kitchen. "There's nothing—"

"Exactly." Ghorza stabs her finger at me. "In *not* encouraging him to follow Urzoth's path, you have led him astray, and I am *sick* of your negative influence on him."

"Woah!" Orok lurches between me and his mom.

Again, I'm used to this. After the shit I dragged Orok into when we were younger, it's a wonder Ghorza didn't cut off contact between us. I take her scorn and her ridicule, and I take my mom's, too, because it's valid; plus, they'll go back home soon, and it's easier to endure it than try to convince them I've changed.

Because . . . maybe I haven't.

Maybe there's still a part of me that'll have Orok bailing me out of jail again. Or worse.

I have a number of dismissive smiles on hand. I have scripts prepared to brush off judgment.

But right now, every single one of them evaporates out of my mind, and it isn't Ghorza glowering at me.

It's Elethior.

Judging me. Finding me lacking.

I should say something to Ghorza but all I can feel is a rising need to get away. Or to scream at her, and Mom, once and for all, *Do you know why I started doing any of that stuff? Did you ever realize where it came from?*

"Stop blaming Seb," Orok barks at his mother.

My chin jerks back. I haven't heard him use that tone with her *ever*. That's his *back the fuck up* voice that he only has to break out when things get rowdy at parties.

"*I* choose not to fight people," Orok says. "I'm *twenty-four years old,* and I make my own choices. If anything, Seb's a great influence. He upholds more of Urzoth's traits than I do."

"Orok," Ghorza says. "You don't have to lie for—"

"I'm not lying. Seb's doing *amazing*. He got a grant. He got a *highly competitive* research grant that he fought hard for because he's brilliant and responsible. I know I've not done nearly enough to get you to stop blaming stuff on him, and I'm honestly not sure why he puts up with me as his friend, but I'm tired of letting him get pounded on. So *stop,* Mom."

Someone cast a silence spell on the room. That has to be it.

Ghorza gapes at her son. Orok's gone red, and he pants a little, staring at his mother like repercussions will swiftly rain down upon him.

And my mom's looking at me now, all her animated sponges halted in their scrubbing.

"You got a research grant?" she asks.

Her question is hung with such pride that it overturns me. A left hook to Ghorza's right uppercut.

She didn't act this proud when I told her about the job I have lined up. Then again, I told her over text, and her response was a GIF of a duck clapping, so.

"Y-yeah," I stammer. "It's not . . . it isn't a big deal."

"Liar," Orok counters.

I look up at him. He smiles.

"It's a big deal," he tells me. His focus shoots to my mom. "He's been preparing for months. Had to get references from his professors, pull his project into a cohesive proposal, provide documented plans and real-world applications. There was an award brunch. He crushed it." He includes his mom with a look. "It took *strength* to do all that."

Half my mouth tips up.

I haven't really *felt* all the work I've done, the accomplishment of it all. But yeah. It *is* a big deal; I *did* crush it. The same with getting that job—I've worked hard for all this shit, and I earned every bit of it.

Mom dries her hands and digs her phone out of her purse. "Did the university post photos of the brunch?"

My brief island of good feelings crumbles out from beneath me.

"Oh, ah—" I slip back into the kitchen and try to reach for her phone, but she holds it away.

"Sebastian," she says. "If it's such an accomplishment, then there are photos, aren't there? I want to see. We deserve to be a part of your life."

There's a lot to unpack in what she said, but under no circumstances can I let her see a picture of Elethior and me. Together. And the announcement that I'll be working with him.

The ramifications ripple out like a collapsing run of dominos.

"It's not a big deal," I repeat. And fling a helpless look at Orok. "Right? Orok's exaggerating."

He has the same realization and I see the *Oh shit* in his eyes. "There probably aren't pictures," he tries. "It was a small brunch—"

"The Mageus Research Grant?" Mom asks, reading on her phone, and my pulse hums a disjointed rhythm.

I've been unhappy about the grant decision, of course, but I haven't let it *in*. I've refused to think about what it means to work with Elethior—*for me,* beneath the implications of it on my degree, on my future career. It's easier to keep it distant. To be upset about it from a dozen other angles rather than think about how being in close proximity to Elethior will affect me on a personal level.

But I watch over my mom's shoulder as she clicks around the university site, and reality knocks the wind straight out of me.

I try to think of something to say. Something so the three of them can head out on the two-and-a-half-hour drive to our hometown. Then I can curl up in my room and spend the next few weeks cleansing myself of the brunch, and Mom, and Ghorza, and the Touraels. I can find a way to pack all this down into that space in my stomach where I've learned to store things until they become an unavoidable, painful knot that only releases when I do something stupid.

Mom scrolls through a few pages until she gets to a photo of Elethior, Dr. Davyeras, and me. The caption gives the details of the grant along with the vague descriptions of each of our projects.

Her face transforms into a gleaming smile, her initial swell of pride now a full-blown hurricane.

"*Sweetheart*. You were awarded a grant with a Tourael? You'll be *working* with him? Oh, Sebastian, this is—"

"Nothing. It's nothing." My fists beat on my thighs.

"Tourael?" Ghorza questions. Understanding dawns. "They ran the camp you boys went to? The one where—"

Just as quickly, her understanding folds back into blame directed at me.

But she doesn't continue her sentence. Doesn't say, *The one where Sebastian convinced Orok to drop out, thereby ruining his chances of being an arcane soldier like Urzoth intended.*

I feel the memory of it anyway. Feel it scrape along my spine and fizzle at the base of my neck. It's been six years but there's no protection from it, no dullness of time, no armor from any of the ineffective ways I try to shield myself. It's always right there. Waiting.

"Camp Merethyl," Mom says to Ghorza, beaming still, unaware of the way my breathing escalates. "Yes. The director of the camp is retiring, and we heard rumors that Mason's under consideration to replace him—Ghorza, I told you about that?"

I recoil at my dad's name.

Ghorza makes an affirmative noise.

"Well," Mom continues, "it's quite a big deal. Most of the Camp Merethyl directors have been Touraels. It's an honor he'd be considered. And now, it seems Sebastian's working with a member of their family." Mom studies the pictures—does she notice my lack of a smile in any of them? "Oh, Sebastian, this is wonderful!"

Orok watches me, and it agitates me even more. I don't want to need him. But I did back then, and I do now, and he was wrong. I don't embody any of Urzoth Shieldsworn's teachings about strength.

I scratch at my forearms, the sting of pain enough to ground me briefly.

"Mom," I say, but she won't hear me. She never does. "Elethior isn't—"

Her eyes mist. "Your father is going to be so proud."

And there it is.

Orok wasn't the only one whose legacy I destroyed. And you don't have to follow the teachings of Urzoth Shieldsworn to believe in a black-and-white duality between what makes someone strong and what makes them weak.

Colonel Mason Walsh has three children who went to Camp Merethyl every summer of high school, graduated from it, then were promptly recruited to join the Arcane Forces.

Then there's me. Who dropped out right before graduation. That plus my mild criminal record are the black marks on my father's résumé as he tiptoes toward the goal of heading up the foremost magical paramilitary training camp in the country.

Is that all you've got?

Pathetic.

My stomach caves.

I move around Mom to attack the kitchen, but it's spotless now, so I grab a towel and robotically dry the countertops.

She pats my arm. "This is what you two need: common ground, and you can—"

"Don't tell him." I pin my gaze on her. I want to glare. Maybe I am, maybe I only look pleading. "You are not to tell him about this grant. About Elethior. None of it."

Those blue eyes are full of hurt she has no right to feel. "Things have been strained between you for too long. This is a chance to start again. It's redemption, Sebastian."

Redemption.

It was my fault, dropping out.

It was my fault, and I need to prove myself to my father again, earn back his trust.

"Do. Not. Tell. Him." I say each word with its own beat, so there's no misunderstanding.

"Don't be disrespectful," Mom snaps, her cheeks pinking. "You know what scandal your withdrawal from the camp caused, and yes, it would help your father's chances of becoming director if you could smooth over your reputation among the Touraels—but you can also use this to heal your relationship with your father. This opportunity is more than a grant, Sebastian! You're being unreasonable."

"I'm really not."

Her face tightens in exasperation. "Fine. I won't tell him."

I go back to drying. "Thank you."

"As long as you tell him yourself when you come home."

I bend over the counter, teeth clenching. "I'm not going home, Mom."

She sucks in a shaky breath. "You haven't been home in months. *Months.* And you haven't spent the holidays with us in *years.* Your nieces and nephew miss you."

"I mailed them some presents."

"Your siblings miss you."

"Doubtful." An age gap of almost a decade between me and my next oldest sibling would've been enough of a divide without the addition of me being so . . . not them.

Mom's upper lip stiffens. "Your father misses you."

I have nothing left to give this conversation, hitting the bottom of my tolerance for speaking and not being heard.

So I turn and hug her.

She goes rigid before her thin arms come around my waist, her chin resting on my shoulder with a contented hum.

"Have a happy holiday season," I whisper.

"Sebastian—"

But I push around her.

Ghorza's got her arms folded, a look of smug confirmation on her face. Everything she believes about me is right. What son would treat his family this way?

"Happy Urzoth's birthday, Mrs. Monroe," I say politely, and it shocks her out of her victory, her smile shrinking.

I jog up the stairs, not at all surprised when Orok's feet pound after mine.

I reach the landing and scratch my arms harder, red lines growing in the wake of my nails.

This is enough. This is *enough.*

I stole shit from the convenience store in our neighborhood after the first summer at Camp Merethyl. Orok hated that, but he was always there to cover for me.

After the second summer, I stole my oldest brother's car. Crashed it into a telephone pole going about ten miles an hour because I'd never driven before, but it knocked the pole down and shattered the windshield. I still have a scar by my hairline where the glass cut me. Orok had been in the car, too, and he'd been unhurt, but the realization that *he* could've been the one getting stitches had me rethinking things.

After the third summer, I started cheating on all my work at school and selling answers to other students. That didn't last long—it never gave me the same rush—so I opted to use spells for the dumbest shit I could think of. Wizards have been experimenting with component amounts and quality for centuries, but I decided to do my *own* experiments. If I used a handful of sparrow feathers instead of one big eagle feather, how long could a levitation spell hold me up? Long enough to walk the length of the bridge that used to stretch over the gully behind the grocery store? What if I mumbled the verbal part of the spell while drunk? Would it still work, or would I fall?

I claimed it was all for science, but the kids from school who'd gather to watch saw through my excuses. I was an adrenaline junkie, nothing more.

And that's not touching on the shit I did once we got to college. Drinking. Questionable hookups. Needing to be bailed out for trying to spell all the flowers in the Quad to smell like sulfur; but I was with a huge group of bumbling idiots, so the charges were minor. Orok talked sense into me before I did anything too irreparable, and I backed off once my grades started to suffer. That was another effective wake-up call, that I was letting my chaos affect the one goal I had: to be able to create spells that would help people.

"Seb," Orok says now. He takes a step toward me like he's closing in on a startled animal. "Hands."

I relax my fingers where they're arched into my arms and sniff through the haze of moisture that stings my eyes.

"I'm fine," I whisper. "It wasn't anything unexpected. I—"

"Don't." Orok looks down the stairs before shifting closer to me. His voice lowers. "I'm sorry. I shouldn't have brought up your grant."

"Don't apologize. Their reaction wasn't your fault."

"Yeah, it was." He stuffs his fists in the pocket of the Lesiara U hoodie he's wearing again, his jaw firming. "I should've stood up for you years ago. I should've told you they were coming and I shouldn't have let my mom blame you for so long. Gods, Seb. I just wanted them to know how far you've come. How well you're doing."

His words dig into me. Burrs that stick fast.

I haven't come far. Only a few days ago, I left a zombie in the Conjuration Lab. How is that *doing well*?

What if I show up next semester and I can't get over working with Elethior? What if all I am, all I'll ever be, is an irresponsible, immature fuckup who can't cope with anything in a normal way? I won't be able to handle working with Elethior and I'll end up doing something reckless that gets me kicked out of school, and that'll be that.

Tension wends around my lungs again. Thick, inescapable chains of it.

"You think I can do it?" I was whispering before so our moms wouldn't overhear, but I whisper now because I'm incapable of asking that question at a reasonable decibel.

Orok cracks a smile.

"You'll do it," he tells me. "Fuck Elethior. You'll solve your research project. You'll graduate and Clawstar will realize how lucky they are to have you, and you'll churn out so many new protective spells that no one will ever have to hurt again."

I want to return his smile, but I can't.

Maybe over-the-top support isn't what I need right now.

Spells use certain amounts of components, like the *experiments* I used to do. But sometimes, a wizard only has a solid block of quartz when they need a sliver and they can't chip off the right amount for whatever reason, so they have to focus on not draining more of the component than they need. Using too much of a component can make spells go haywire, or it can bleed a component dry entirely.

That's my research project: developing a way to cap the energy drawn from components *in the spell,* rather than having wizards cap the amount through their own focus. A safety net thrown over every spell so parameters are set and, yeah, what Orok said.

I nod downstairs. "Was your mom right though? About you, I mean. Is there something different? Are you unhappy?"

He frowns with a curious look. "Have I seemed unhappy to you?"

"I don't think so. But I dunno—mom radar. I want to make sure she's not picking up on something I missed."

He's quiet. Considering. And that's enough to ping my concern, but he shakes his head.

"Starting to feel the pressures, ya know? Everything's changing. Or it will. And I *knew* it would, but knowing and living it are two very different things. I don't know what next year will look like and it's freaking me out."

"I thought you were going to be a priest of Urzoth?"

It's part of why his mom's come around. Her son's getting his Mageus of Theological Evocation with plans to join Urzoth's church, all while being a rawball star. If he isn't going to be a rampaging soldier in the Arcane Forces, what more could an Urzoth-worshipping mother want?

"I am. I—" He rocks on his heels. "You know that's all bullshit, right? That stuff about physical strength equating internal strength. It's antiquated and she's wrong. You're not a bad influence on me."

Yeah, I am. "Stop apologizing for her, you dingus."

Orok sputters such an abrupt laugh he spits all over me.

I flinch away. "Dude!"

"*Dingus?*"

"It's what you are. Especially now." I overexaggerate wiping my cheek. "Gross."

He keeps laughing.

I wait until he meets my eyes. "You don't have to be a priest. You don't have to do anything that doesn't work for *you.* If that makes me a bad influence on you, then hell yeah, I'll keep leading you to the dark side. I want you to be happy."

He sobers. "I *am* happy. I'm fine. And I won't let her talk bad about you anymore. I promise."

I hope my smile is appropriately unbothered. "The way I see it, your penance is dealing with both of them by yourself on the drive home."

He blanches. "Uh, I can stay home for break. Help distract you from next semester."

"I don't need a babysitter. Go home. Some alone time might be good. Get me all centered or whatever."

His eyes brighten. "You'll try meditating again?"

Every time I do, it's like non-sexy masochism, but I usually endure an hour of it every few months for his sake.

"Sure. I'll meditate."

It's more likely I'll lock myself away and drown in freak-outs, but even that might be cleansing. Purge me of all my anxiety so I can face the spring semester like the competent, mature wizard no one believes I can be.

Orok's look is full of such disbelief we could bottle and sell it.

But he relents, mostly because I don't give him a choice; I slip into my room.

"Happy Urzoth's birthday," I tell him.

"Love you," he calls as he heads downstairs.

"Fuck off," I singsong back to be a dick.

But Ghorza hears me. "*Sebastian!* How *dare* you—" Orok must cut her off, because she huffs. "I don't understand why you let him speak to you like that!"

I shut my bedroom door and pound my forehead against it.

Chapter Four

A competent, mature wizard.

There are, most assuredly, *parts* of those things in me, so I spend my Winter Break of Solitude desperately digging them out. I get up every day at a reasonable time and go to bed at an even more reasonable time and keep up with personal hygiene, all of which are at least nuggets of pyrite in mining for emotional intelligence, right?

On the first day of spring semester, as I head through campus toward my—sorry, *our*—new dedicated lab space in Bellanor Hall, I'm rather pleased with myself. I've got a whole new outlook on life. Live and let live, c'est la vie, and other such phrases I absorbed during 2 A.M. internet searches for *how to work with someone you hate without dreaming about murdering them.*

I said I went to bed and woke up at reasonable times, not that I *slept* at reasonable times.

But those aforementioned internet searches, while immediately telling me not to commit murder, led to an approach I have not yet tried: killing Elethior with kindness.

We've been at each other's throats. We've insulted each other and played dumb pranks. But neither of us has tried to be, gasp, *cordial,* so by gods, that's what I'll do.

And the fact that I'll be the first of us to attempt this feat of adult sensibility means I win the moral high ground forever and ever, so he can suck it.

I daresay I've got a pep in my step as I jog down the hall toward the lab, ready to test out this new resolve to extend an olive branch. Turn over a new leaf. Nurture a fresh seedling.

Why did the internet give me so many plant-based mantras? Are all psychologists druids?

I find the door to the lab on the first floor of Bellanor Hall, a keypad glowing arcane blue next to it. I half expect the code I was given not to work, for Elethior to have used his winter break to oust me—but I enter the four-digit number and there's a low beep before the keypad shifts to green and the door unlocks.

A sense of rightness settles over me. This is all really, actually happening.

The lab shows the Quad through huge windows. There are four workstations, as this is ordinarily a space for doctoral students, but two of them have been closed off. In the other two, I find everything Elethior and I might need: a desk, storage locker, electronic hookups, office supplies, and a rolling whiteboard each. A shared space at the back has a cabinet, fridge, and rows of shelves, all furnished with spell components, and a round dais made of smooth white marble in the middle of the room sits under a few protection glyphs embedded in the ceiling, perfect for testing out spell circles.

Elethior isn't here yet, so I claim the best workstation, the one with the most light near the window. I unpack the stuff I brought, mostly binders of research and texts from the library, and once I flip on my laptop, I lean back in the desk chair and . . . wait.

I don't know what Elethior's schedule is. We probably were expected to coordinate, but I don't have a way to contact him and didn't care to ask for one, and neither did he.

I roll idly in my desk chair and check how long until I have to go to work—one of my scholarships is dependent on work study, and since I'm not a TA this semester, I took a job stocking books in the library. It's sure to be mind-numbing, but I didn't want anything too taxing to compete with this research project. I've got several hours until my first shift.

Another ten minutes pass, 9 A.M. rolls around, and I think, why the hell am I waiting on Elethior? I've been wanting resources like these at my fingertips for *years*.

First things first: I summon Nick. I don't plan on doing any spell work, but I need someone to talk at, and he's a good listener.

He comes, curling his invisible body around my shin with deep, crackly fox purrs.

"Hey, buddy." I scratch what turns out to be his back, his spine arching under my fingertips. "Gotcha something over break."

I dig into my component belt and pull out a jaunty fedora.

I secure it to his head with an elastic band.

"You're dapper as hell, Nicholas," I tell him, and he chirps in what I interpret as delighted approval. "Now." I stand, clicking my tongue as I open one of my binders and flip through notes. "Ready to be the world's best sounding board?"

The fedora leaps up and lands about a foot above my desk.

I poked at my project over break but purposefully kept distance from it so I could come back fresh. But something's stalling out in my head.

My eyes flick to the lab's door.

A beat, and the lock pad on the other side disengages.

Elethior saunters in, peeling off aviator sunglasses, backpack hanging on his shoulder, black leather jacket tight over an eggshell-blue shirt. His hair is pulled up at the back of his head, showing the buzzed side and his slightly pointed ears, and he's in jeans with those dumbass motorcycle boots again. Black leather component harnesses squeeze each thigh.

He stops as the door closes behind him. He looks at the room from left to right with deliberate precision, surveying the workstations, the shelves, the marble dais, until he gets to me.

He sucks his teeth. "Sebastian."

I point at the clock over the door to make a crack about how he wasted the morning, but I catch myself. I'm supposed to be cruising down the high road, wind in my hair, one of those kitschy driving scarves fluttering behind me. We're *killing with kindness* now.

Only my hand's lifted.

I wave stupidly.

"Elethior," I return.

His eyes narrow in suspicion. Which, earned.

He crosses to the other workstation, his back to me as he slides off his coat and pulls stuff out of his bag.

He's got a few of the same textbooks I do.

I look at my books and frown.

Evocation and conjuration are nothing alike. Creation versus theft. So him having those books is an attempt at fucking with me, right?

My gaze lingers on my desk. Something's missing.

No fedora.

Elethior lets out a shriek that'd have me *rolling* if I wasn't clinging to a one-sided olive branch by my fingertips. I lurch toward him as he whirls around, whipping out spell components and dropping his weight into an expert attack stance.

I stop a few paces from him when I realize he's got stuff for a fireball. "Really?"

"What the *fuck* is in here?" he snaps, eyes darting around.

Nick's fedora bobs behind Elethior. I swear it bobs *smugly.*

Oblivious, Elethior hits me with a glare, and I open my mouth to explain Nick.

"What did you *do?*" Elethior cuts me off. He rises out of his attack stance, pockets his spell components, and redirects his defensiveness at me. "I refuse to spend the next several months fending off your idiotic pranks, so allow me to bring you in on a secret: I am not threatened by you. Yet you, obviously, feel threatened by me, and I am telling you right now that I won't tolerate petty insecurities from an obsolete man. I have a job to do here, and you will not interfere with that. I will *crush* you if you keep on with this time-wasting bullshit."

Three weeks of fortifying myself to face Elethior as a calm, level-headed adult.

Thirty seconds of him reminding me that that's not possible.

My chest seizes, stealing a breath that I cover by clamping my jaw tight.

"What you felt," I start through my teeth, "was my familiar."

I point to the fedora.

I see my words process. I see him realize he overreacted—is that regret in the smoothing of his forehead?

But he follows where I'm pointing and, of course, sees nothing. Nick's now tucked under Elethior's desk and the fedora is only half-visible behind one of the legs.

"I don't—" Elethior clears his throat. His voice is thinner. "What is it?"

"A fox."

He bends, still seeing nothing. "A—fox?"

"Yeah." I put my lip between my teeth and whistle. "Nick, c'mere."

The fedora bobs out.

Elethior jerks upright at the disembodied hat. "What are you playing at?"

My face stays neutral. I'm locked down now. He threw that lock, he melted the key. I'm a vault, baby, and he's getting *nothing* from me but what I choose to give.

"Huh? Oh, the hat?" I shrug. "He likes to dress up. Familiars, ya know? What can you do?"

"No, I—" Elethior studies the fedora. "He's . . . invisible?"

I scoff. "Good one."

Elethior points at the fedora. "He's *invisible*."

I put on my best *what the fuck* look. "Um. No. I think I'd know if I couldn't see my own familiar."

"But he's—"

I scoop Nick into my arms and hold him up for Elethior. "Wait, wait—are you telling me you can't see this *full-grown American red fox*? Elethior. I'm not sure I can, in good conscience, work with a lab partner who's such a moron."

I'm grinning when he looks at me.

"He's invisible," he says, this time flat and declarative.

I set Nick down. "Mad observation skills you have."

"Go fuck yourself, Walsh."

"I will, and I'll think of you while I do it."

His face flares red. *Bright* red, two near perfect lines along his cheekbones.

He doesn't give me any time to revel in embarrassing him before he juts his chin at Nick's fedora, still obediently next to me. "There are spells to undo that."

I roll my eyes and head back to my desk. Nick plods along beside me, rubbing against my calf and purring gently, which I'm almost certain is his way of asking if I want him to bite Elethior again. I'm undecided, so I sit in my chair and scratch under Nick's chin.

"He likes it," I say.

Elethior grunts. "I . . . might have overreacted. I can undo the spell. As an"—Gods, I can *hear* his shudder—"apology."

"No." That's all I give him.

Elethior pauses before he returns to his own desk. "Wow."

I snottily mouth *wow* to his back and bend over my notes.

But my concentration is shot to hell.

I'm painfully aware of him moving around, opening drawers, sorting his shit. Then of him exploring the room, looking in the fridge and storage areas, cataloguing the spell components.

Nick curls up in my lap, purring like a vibrating space heater.

I flip to a new page of notes that swims in front of my eyes, but when Elethior stops next to my desk, I am *deeply focused on reading*.

"So," Elethior says. "How do you want to do this?"

"Are you asking for my opinion?" I swing around in my chair so I can face him, feeling like an action movie villain with Nick in my lap and my fingers scratching his neck. The effect would probably land more if he weren't invisible. "Me, the *obsolete man*?"

It knocks the wind out of me when his chin lowers in—deference? What the fuck?

"I said I overreacted." He rubs a hand down his face and tugs on one of his lip piercings. "Had a rough morning. Had a rough whole—no, fuck that. We have to do this. I'm not going to waste time dancing around each other. Our first check-in with Davyeras and our advisors is in a month. We need to get to work, so step up. I'm giving you a chance to prove yourself."

I rocket out of my chair so fast Nick tumbles from my lap with an annoyed shriek. In a burst of magic that sizzles on the air, he vanishes back to the Familiar Plane, his fedora dropping limp to the floor.

"*Prove* myself?" I thrust right up into Elethior's face, so livid I can feel heat wavering out of me.

He rolls his eyes. "This is what I mean. You can't—"

"I have to *prove* myself? To *you*?"

"You spent the better part of the past few months fucking with not just my shit, but the whole Conjuration Department. You can't honestly tell me you don't understand where my distrust of you is coming from."

"And what about my distrust of *you*? I'll have you note, not *one* of the things I did ever damaged anything. *You* can't say the same. Your prank screwed with projects in the Evocation Department, so if either of us is deserving of *distrust*, it's you. *I* know when to—"

"Wait." Elethior sways back. "You think *I* had a hand in the pranks against you?"

I snort, unamused. "Don't try to tell me it wasn't you."

"*It wasn't me.*"

"I *heard you* complaining about the missing-door prank. Heard you *shouting* about the inconvenience of it. Then the next day, the Evocation Department's dew water gets screwed with? You're the chosen one of the Conjuration Department. Your name is on the fucking lab."

He's back again, leaning so close we're steaming each other's air. "I was *shouting* about the *inconvenience* of the lab being inaccessible because it made me late for a meeting with my cousin, and she doesn't—"

"Oh, gods forbid I upset the Touraels. My deepest condolences."

Elethior's shoulders rise, his face darkening. When he speaks again, he says each word with disturbing calmness. "I have never once partaken in the ridiculous and unfounded rivalry between our departments because I have better things to do with my time. Meanwhile, how much of your life have you wasted on useless tricks?"

My mind races over all the pranks the Conjuration Department enacted. So often, Elethior would be the first one I'd see in the aftermath, usually with a group of fellow conjuration wizards. He was there, watching whatever dumbassery unfold with that smug, self-righteous sneer.

Of course it was him.

Wasn't it?

I had never caught him doing anything. No one had ever caught *me* either, though.

"Oh, right." I knot my arms over my chest, upper lip curling. "You're *so* innocent. You admitted to laying the spell work on the Conjuration Lab door."

"Yes, I did, because I knew you'd try something else."

"Fuck off with this pious act, Tourael. It's beneath you."

"No—what's *beneath me* is *you!*"

He's damn near screaming, his face fully red, and I'm no better. It's a wonder no one's barged in to check what all the yelling's about, but given the nature of this lab, I wonder if it's soundproof? Great, Elethior and I can kill each other without being disturbed.

That sinks past my fury. The barest brush of shadow against the light.

No one can hear us in here. We're alone.

My breath snags.

Pathetic.

Is that all you've got?

I'm not trapped in here. I'm not locked in.

I can *leave.*

So I do.

I snatch my phone off the desk and knock all my stuff into my bag in a frantic, ungraceful shove. As I walk around Elethior, I pop him with my shoulder.

"Where the hell are you going?" he demands. "Giving up already?"

I slam back up close to him, unmasking all the anger in my eyes, but I think I show a little of my fear, too. "I'm going to cool down because if I stand here much longer, I'll fireball your ass. When I get back, you stay on your end of the lab. I'll stay on mine. Don't talk to me, don't so much as *breathe* in my direction."

Elethior's nostrils flare. "We have to work together."

"No. We have to report how conjuration and evocation overlap as we explore restricting spell energy," I quote the instructions the grant committee sent a few weeks back. "We'll conclude that our research topics were more different than initially thought, and we'll present two *separate* papers."

He looks like he'll fight me more. And I realize, in him trying to get us to work together, that *he's* being the bigger person and has therefore claimed the moral high ground.

Gods damn it.

But he scoffs in disgust. "Fine. You're nowhere near my level anyway. You can't even put aside this stupid rivalry when it matters."

"First of all, I'm so far above your level you'd choke from the lack of oxygen up here. Second—" I talk over him, and his lips shut with a snarl. "*Second,* I don't want to work with you, not because of any rivalry, but because you're an entitled asshole spawned from a family of entitled assholes, and I'm not playing into whatever Tourael jack-off fantasies you being here fulfills."

"I earned my place here," he says, speaking through his teeth. "And—"

"And, what, it looks good on your résumé? Like Mommy and Daddy don't have a cushy job waiting for you after you graduate."

The ferocity of our argument makes me physically aware of our silence. It grates against my skin like sand particles, and I realize it's Elethior who's stopped yelling, stopped talking, who is now watching me, his frown wilted.

"Stay away from me," I hiss, wrench open the door, and leave.

As I'm hunched over a mocha in the student center—a regular mocha, no extra shots or potions; I triple-checked with the barista—an email pings on my phone.

It's from Dr. Davyeras.

My heart sinks, reliving my interaction with Elethior and, again, wondering if he pulled strings to oust me. I'm pretty sure that'll be a concern of mine until I have my degree firmly in hand, because what's stopping him? He has the family heft to make my life very, very shitty.

I gulp the rest of my mocha, crack my neck, and open the email.

The first line is asking how I like the lab space, so I let myself breathe again.

But as I read, tension creeps back over me.

As part of your commitment to excellence through the Mageus Research Grant, you will be expected to participate in two university events.

The first is this Saturday, a welcome-back cocktail party on campus. An invitation will shortly be sent to you with the details.

The second will be part of the Lesiara Founder's Day festivities prior to spring break.

Attendance at both is mandatory.

I don't let myself do more than absorb this at surface level. I toss my coffee cup, grab my bag, and head back to the lab.

Elethior's still there, bent over open books, scribbling notes on a crowded piece of paper. He doesn't look up, so I don't say anything, just cross to my desk and pull all my stuff back out.

When I have nothing else to busy my hands, I flop into my chair and stare at the wall above my workstation. "You get the email from Davyeras?"

Out of the corner of my eye, I see Elethior's head lift.

He must not have. He shuffles through his books and papers until he unearths his phone.

A beat of silence passes as he reads.

"Shit," he hisses, so low I wonder if I wasn't meant to hear.

"What's wrong? Worried they won't have the right vintage of wine at the cocktail party?"

Elethior tosses his phone onto his desk. The position of our workstations is in an L shape, with his back to me while I face the wall, which honestly makes talking to him easier. Maybe this is how we'll survive the next semester: having full conversations with the ether instead of each other.

"Yeah," he says dryly. "Last time, they ran out of Domaine de la Romanée-Conti."

He's quiet when I scowl at his hair.

Was that a joke? I sort through it, trying to figure out how it was at my expense. Or maybe it was him showing off a flawless pronunciation to be pretentious.

Then he adds, "Just hate being on parade."

And that, more than offering to fix Nick's invisibility, feels like an apology. It's his tone, his words raw in a way that's—that's—*wrong*.

Don't try to *bond* with me, jerk.

"Then drop out of the grant," I tell him and open a textbook. "It looks like this is the beginning of our *commitment to excellence,* and I'll be at this cocktail party all set to charm the pants off the donors and board members if you can't handle it."

Elethior bends back over his own desk. "I have work to do. Stop bothering me."

My mouth opens, ready to rip into him again, but I clench my jaw. I have work to do, too, if I'm going to go to this party with any update on my plans for the semester and how I'll be using this grant money. It won't be as the committee intended, with Elethior, so I'll have to make my project sound strong enough on its own.

Elethior and I spend the next few hours ignoring each other in a tense, living silence. But nobody's dead by the time I leave for my shift at the library, so I'd call that a successful first day.

Only several more months to go.

Elethior and I fall into a rhythm.

We don't talk to each other. If one of us has to get up to leave the room or check something in a supply area, we don't look at each other. I don't summon Nick again; like hell am I going to talk through my theories and risk Elethior eavesdropping. The lab is so quiet I can hear the squish of my internal organs every time I move.

Elethior is as focused as I am. Neither of us will leave until the other does, which adds another self-sabotaging layer to the already toxic work ethic we both seem to share.

He eyes me a few times, flinches like the sheer act of moving is offensive. And I realize—he's waiting for me to play a prank. So I don't, because the *threat* of playing one is clearly enough to fuck with him. Plus, I don't have the time; I am, despite what he thinks, capable of hard work.

By Friday, we've spent more than fifty hours together without bloodshed, and I almost bring a bottle of champagne to mark the occasion. But the days have passed in a fugue state of research and work, that near-unhealthy level of single-mindedness that descends when I get into a project. Making it through this first week is celebration enough.

I get ready to leave the lab a few hours earlier than I have all week. I have to pass by his desk to get to the door, and he does that flinch thing again before his eyes meet mine with a challenging glint.

"Tapping out already?" he mocks. "Probably for the best. Not like a few extra hours will make all that much of a difference for you."

I stop midstride next to the disaster zone that is his workstation. He's a mess, I've learned. Coats and winter hats, an extra pair of shoes, a gym bag, a grocery sack of chips, a dumb amount of *stuff* is slowly encroaching on my area, while his desk has open books and uncapped highlighters and loose pieces of paper in a rising tide of disorganization. It's honestly impressive he's created this much disarray in one week. I should sic mine and Orok's mothers on him.

"Make a difference with what?" I let my eyes linger on the state of his workstation and overemphasize my nose curl.

"With impressing the donors and board members." He ignores my disgust. "That's what you're hoping to do for tomorrow's party, isn't it? Take advantage of this first chance to wow them with plans for your *solo* research project."

I glare at him. "Like that isn't your plan, too."

"Oh, it is. But I'll actually be successful at it."

"Why? Because you're staying and I'm leaving? If you haven't figured out your shit by now, I hate to break it to ya, but a few extra hours isn't going to save you. Excuse me for having a *smoking hot date* waiting for me so I can blow off steam before tomorrow. You can go in sleepless and stressed; I'll go in relaxed and freshly laid."

I have no date; I'm meeting Orok and a few of his teammates for dinner.

Though, maybe getting laid isn't such a bad idea. It's been . . . a few months? Gods damn my busy schedule. And general lack of what the poets call *game*.

Elethior's cheeks flood red again. He blushes so easily; it shouldn't feel like a victory every time I get one out of him, but it does.

"As tactful as always," he mutters.

I head for the door again but pause with it cracked open. "Oh, and Elethior?"

He looks up from his notebook.

"If your shit crosses the demarcation line"—I point to the space between our workstations, about half a foot from where his gym bag is vomiting a towel and sneakers onto the floor—"that will be taken as an act of aggression, and I'll have no choice but to declare an end to our ceasefire."

I let the door slam as he flips me off.

Orok's waiting at a place off campus that serves funky hot dogs, with toppings ranging from onions and chili to elote and pimento cheese. Students and weird, greasy hot dogs? Gold mine.

Orok blinks at me from the booth he's claimed near the back.

"Is that—" He rubs his eyes, squints, and I pause with my arms out, thinking I must have a stain somewhere. Fucking public buses.

But he gasps melodramatically. "Is that—it is! Sebastian Walsh! As I live and breathe. I barely recognized you."

I shrug off my puffer jacket. "Hilarious. You saw me this morning."

I up-nod two of his teammates—Ivo and Crescentia, unsurprisingly. The only grad students on the team tend to stick together.

"I saw a *blur* this morning," Orok says. "Like I've seen a sleep-deprived wraith stumble back home every night. You're taking this *last semester before we graduate* thing too seriously."

"Yeah." Ivo picks up a menu. "We're basically done. What could the university do to us at this point? *Not* give us our degrees? Coast, man. Coast."

I slide in next to Crescentia. "Sorry, not all of us can hang our hopes on being a professional at going bare."

The three of them stare at me.

"Getting drafted to a pro rawball team," I clarify.

Cue three simultaneous eye rolls.

Ivo points a threatening finger at me. "Don't jinx us. Joking about that shit isn't funny."

Orok waves off Ivo's concern. "It's the first week, Seb. You've been pulling crazy hours. You can't keep this up for the rest of the semester."

All the teasing melts away, Orok's eyes latching on to mine, and it's like I've been spinning in circles only to come to a crashing halt.

Between building a research plan, ignoring Elethior in the lab, and avoiding the fact that I'm failing this grant in the first week, I'm tantalizingly close to running on fumes.

The voice at the back of my head, the one I've been ignoring by working, working, *working*, whispers, *You're messing it up. The committee is going to see your refusal to get along with Elethior as a breach of the grant, and they'll pull you from it.*

I force a smile at Orok. "I won't keep this up forever. This is me getting the foundation solidified so everything else is smooth sailing. Promise."

"And Elethior?" Crescentia asks, elbowing me. "Need me to help stage a protest? Bet we can get him kicked out of the lab."

I cock a startled look at her. "What? Really?"

"Hell yeah. You know how many people on campus are anti-war? Him being a student here has always been a source of contention, but for the most part, the board and all the people with money shut down any concerns. We can get people riled up, though. Have them worry that his access to a lab that high-level could be *dangerous* for the rest of us."

My face droops. Why am I not jumping on this?

It feels . . . slimy.

I mean, he *is* a danger by the mere fact of him being a Tourael, but he isn't working on anything that could jeopardize the immediate vicinity or the school. Not like he's in there manufacturing arcane bombs.

He's just . . . studying the limitations of the connection between a conjurer and their conjured item. Whatever the hell that means.

I smile at Crescentia. "Thanks, but I can handle him."

Orok croaks. "You—you said no." He blinks at me. "Who are you, and where's Seb?"

I pick up a menu with unnecessary flare and make a great show of reading it. "I'm taking the high road. I'm a reformed wizard now, gods damn it."

Luckily, our waiter approaches, and we all order.

The shift in focus lets the conversation trajectory shift, too, and I ask how rawball practice is going and whether Ivo really does have a shot at getting drafted. Turns out, he does, and scouts will be at a few of their preseason games, which is another reason he, Crescentia, and Orok are all suiting up for the spring training season even though they won't be playing next year.

They're talking game strategy when our food comes, and I pretend I understand what they're saying. All these years of supporting Orok, and for the life of me, I still can't explain the *rules as written*—what the *raw* in *rawball* stands for. There's a ball that has to make it to one side of the field for a team to score, and each team is comprised of tanks like Orok and Ivo, rogues like Crescentia, and wizards and healers and other classes that adhere to the *rules as written,* but I swear to the *gods* they change those rules randomly to screw with me.

"—for Lesiara Founder's Day," Crescentia is saying, "we're doing the game against the kids' shelter again, but Coach said they want us in full uniform. Better photo ops."

Chewing the last of my banh mi hot dog, I groan and wrestle my phone out of my pocket. "I have to do something for Founder's Day, too. What day is it this year?"

"Same day it always is. Why don't you remember—*ohhhh*." Orok hisses between his teeth. "Because *someone* always gets a little too familiar with the Founder's Day punch."

Ivo cackles. "That's right! Last year, didn't you challenge our team to a funnel cake eating contest? Like, the *whole* team. Against *you*. Then—something with the powdered sugar—"

"He inhaled it." Orok's grinning. "Coughed white clouds all over himself like an asthmatic smoke dragon."

"Nah." I open my calendar app. "That doesn't sound like me. When is this carnival that I have definitely never experienced in my entire collegiate career?"

"Friday before spring break," says Orok, polishing off his third taco hot dog.

I add it in. "And even if I might have been a handful at previous carnivals—"

Someone tosses a wadded-up straw wrapper at me.

"—this year, I'll be there in a *professional capacity*, so not a drop of Founder's Day punch shall pass my—"

My phone rings.

It's my dad?

For a second, I stare.

Holy shit. My dad's calling.

He *never* calls me.

Dread chills everything in my body, a head-to-toe rush that has me answering in a scramble.

"What's wrong?" I demand before the phone's even against my ear.

Orok, Crescentia, and Ivo all look at me with furrowed brows.

"Sebastian," comes Dad's voice in my ear. There's a too-long pause, and that creeping sense of horror wraps around my throat.

Is it Mom? My brothers or sister, their kids? Shit, what the hell happened?

"You have a minute to chat with your father, don't you?" Dad continues.

I scramble up from the booth. Orok gives me a look that's a whole unspoken conversation, but I shake my head; I don't know, my heart's stopped.

"What's wrong?" I ask again and duck through the restaurant, toward the hall with the restrooms. "Is everyone okay? What did—"

"Everyone's fine, just fine. I was calling to see how your first week of classes went."

The back hall is dark, one side piled with boxes that advertise chili sauce and hot dog buns next to the bathroom. The door to the kitchen is on the other side, blocked by a frayed sheet, and the heater ripples it, the air rich with the smell of fried pork and garlic and sharp cheddar.

I'm grabbing at those small, mundane things that make sense. Because my dad calling like this? Does *not* make sense.

"I—" My heart beats again, heavy, painful thuds. "I assumed you were calling to tell me someone had been in a terrible accident."

He sighs. "Put aside your theatrics, Sebastian. I want to have an honest conversation. Are you capable of that?"

The adrenaline that spiked at his call comes hurtling down, a landslide barreling through my body in tiny, agonizing quakes.

"Yessir," I say mechanically.

Movement next to me is Orok, who stops fast.

The colonel? he mouths.

I nod.

His eyes widen.

"Good," Dad says. "Now tell me how your first week of classes went."

In my whole collegiate career, he's *never,* not once, called to *see how classes went.*

There'd been a time, though. Before high school. I always aced my arcane classes and I was well on my way to not only following in the Walsh family's footsteps, but to surpassing many of them.

And gods, my dad was so *proud* of me, asking about my classes then, and we'd talk spell work incessantly until Mom had to ban any magic topics at dinner. I knew I probably wouldn't go the military route, but for that small window before Camp Merethyl, I at least felt a *part* of this family, because that spark in my dad's eyes when we talked about spells? It burned in me, too. We had that connection.

I'm so blindsided by this phone call, by the overlapping vignette of sitting across from his pleased smile at the dinner table more than a decade ago, that I can't grab ahold of my senses.

"Classes?" I echo, scrambling. "I'm in the last semester of my graduate program. I'm not taking classes anymore. It's a research block."

With Elethior Tourael.

My shoulders wilt.

Of course.

"Then tell me how your research block is going," Dad says, like that isn't the actual point of his call. "Your mother said you have a lab partner. That you're working with a Tourael. It's important you make a good impression, you hear? It's important you apply yourself."

I don't interrupt him. Can't. My throat is swollen shut and I kick the floor, over and over, shoe scuffing the cheap peeling laminate.

Orok steps closer to me. "Seb?"

"This could be the kind of connection that makes your career," Dad tells me. "You—"

"Your career."

"What?"

"This could make *your* career," I hear myself say. "Not mine. Right? That's why you're calling."

Dad sighs again. "That is not, actually, why I—"

"Are you still in the running for that job?"

A pause. "The position doesn't officially open for several weeks."

I have no extra bandwidth to think about my father running that place.

"But yeah," I scoff, "you're calling about me."

"I called because I know how you are," Dad says. "And I won't see you wasting this opportunity *for yourself.*"

My arms itch, my vision goes starry, and I'm pacing now, in the tight hallway, nearly bumping into Orok with every pass, getting dizzy with the sharp turns.

Distantly, I think how dumb a place this is for a freak-out. I mean, there's a cartoon hot dog on the wall behind Orok, for fuck's sake.

"Tell me what you've been doing," Dad repeats, his voice harder. "I'll help you figure out how to best navigate the situation so you don't squander this connection. Not everyone gets a second chance. You had so much promise when you were younger."

You had such promise.

This was wasted on you.

Get out, get out, *get out—*

Sweat breaks out down my spine and I get in a jagged, shaky breath.

"I gotta go."

I hang up on him. I hang up on Colonel Mason Walsh so forcefully I nearly break the phone in half.

My ears ring. Ring and ring, a hollow clanging; and rage gathers, swelling up and out, and I want to call him back to scream at him.

"Seb?" Orok touches my shoulder. "Don't answer his calls anymore."

I bark a laugh and pocket my phone. "Lesson learned. Lesson *mastered.*"

Orok stretches his arms out for a hug. He's blocking the hall, and he knows it.

"I'm being held hostage."

"Yes. Hug me, dumbass."

I fall into the center of his wide chest. His thick arms pull me in and my breath leaves my lungs in an unsteady *whoosh.*

When I was sitting at the grant banquet, *knowing* they'd announce that Elethior got it, I remember thinking that I'd have to go to my dad to ask for the money instead. I *wouldn't,* but somewhere in the back of my mind, that's been the ghost of a safety net. Still is, I think. Or it *was,* until this moment, when I feel the impossibility of me ever asking him for support. Even if he'd give it, with his own messed-up stipulations, I wouldn't ask.

If I go to the party tomorrow, and tell the grant committee I haven't taken any steps toward doing the *one thing* they asked me to do, and they pull their funding . . .

I've got nothing.

The anger worsens, rising, anger at myself, at my dad, at this situation.

"Shit." I back away and try to wiggle around Orok, but he's still playing immovable object in the hallway. "Dude. Let me go."

"You're not going back to the lab. I'm serious, Seb; your work ethic isn't sustainable."

"I'm not going back to work."

He stares at me.

"I'm not going back to work *much*." Okay, that's a lie, too. Maybe Elethior's still at my lab—*our* lab, our our *our*—and I can, *ugh,* revert to my original intention and extend an olive branch, and the two of us can half-ass a plan in the fifteen or so hours until the cocktail party.

I can hear Dad's disappointment if I get pulled from the grant. How I failed again. How *expected* my collapse was because I'm all dramatics and overreacting.

I wince and see I've pushed my sleeve up to gouge my nails into the back of my arm, crescent moon arches purpling into bruises.

Orok bats my hand away. "Seb—"

"Please let me leave." I look up at him, not afraid to let him see that I'm not, actually, okay. "I promise, I'll take a break after this." Maybe.

He holds for a beat.

But he steps aside, and after grabbing my shit from the table and tossing a few bucks to cover my cut—and dodging *are you okay* questions from Ivo and Crescentia—I race to the lab.

When I burst through the door, Elethior's not there.

I slam into the chair at my desk, dig out my phone, and start to type up an email to one of the committee members, Davyeras maybe, to ask for Elethior's contact info, but—

Anyone I ask is going to want to know why I don't already have it. Why Elethior and I have been working together for a *week*, but I don't know his number.

"*Fuck,*" I bark at my desk.

Maybe Elethior'll stop by the lab tomorrow before the party. That'll be good, honestly. It'll give me time to cool down enough to extend a truce.

My fingers rub absently over the swollen marks on my arm and I manage a deep breath, like Orok taught me. In, hold it; out, slow.

All the breaths I'm taking make my lungs burn.

I'm breathing too much, too deeply. That's the reason my body feels like it's stuffed with embers, packed full of debris, waiting, waiting, waiting for something explosive to set it all off.

I'm fine. I have a plan.

It's all *fine*.

I grab a piece of paper from my desk and jot my number on it with a *very polite* request for Elethior to text me. Then I stand in front of his workstation—I think there's still a desk under there—and consider about half a dozen places to put it. It's going to get lost in his chaos no matter where it ends up. Unlikely he'll see it, so I toss the thing onto the mound.

The moment it crosses a hand's width above his desk, it incinerates.

I blink at the remnants of ash that drift down onto his textbooks, paper, and garbage.

Elethior put a protection ward around his desk.

For some reason, this blatant symbol of our divide is the last straw.

Explosion detonated.

A spell component is in my hand. I don't remember pulling it out. But I'm holding what I need and I chant the spell between my teeth, chant it and chant it, intensity building, anger surging to the tips of my hair. I feel them lift as the arcane power swells, magic that I draw from the component.

The spell needs a chip of iron from a lock, and I've got a whole gods-damned padlock in my palm. Chalk to draw sigils, but I can't dredge up the fortitude to scribble out anything right now.

I don't understand Orok's adherence to religion for many reasons, but especially in moments like this. How does he cast spells, then think he needs a god to give him strength?

The spell sucks like a vacuum, magic funneling through the component, into me, and *out*.

I fling one hand toward Elethior's workstation as the spell releases.

His protection ward shatters.

It doesn't just fall; it's *decimated,* the air alive with electrical currents so charged they could power the building.

I stand there, gasping, head pounding in the aftershocks. Prickles race up and down my arms and braid with my spine, making me shiver in the letdown.

But I look at my palm. The one that'd held the lock.

There's a gray stain on my skin where the lock had been.

The spell to break a ward only needs a sliver of iron. But I let my rage get away from me, let my focus slip and liquefy, and the magic ate up the entire lock. Nearly a pound of iron. And I didn't use any sigils, no way to focus the magic, to make sure it didn't flare or rebound.

My hands go up into my hair, probably streaking it with the iron stain, but I don't care.

I can't lose control like this. I *can't* fuck up, not anymore.

But this is why I'm here, isn't it? This is my research project. To develop a safeguard so stuff like this doesn't happen. So stuff *worse* than this doesn't happen.

A plan. I had a plan. What was it?

I'll find Elethior tomorrow. We'll get to work. The committee won't have any reason to take this opportunity away from me.

See? That's solid. That's *safe*.

I lower my trembling hands, sweat sheeting my face, eyes tearing, burning.

At least Elethior'll know I'm capable of breaking his wards now.

Semester's off to a bangin' start, lemme tell ya.

Chapter Five

The cocktail party's on campus, in an old building where a wall of windows faces a brick walkway, the protruding bays showing iron crossbars and engraved marble borders. People mill within, warped by the aged glass.

Elethior didn't come to the lab this morning. Or afternoon. And by the time I had to leave to get here, he still hadn't shown, and it didn't matter anyway; we wouldn't have had enough time to pull anything together.

I've got to go into this party, paste a smile on my face, own my mistakes, and hope the committee gives me a second chance.

It only takes remembering the way I rage-broke Elethior's protection ward last night to know that I fully deserve the repercussions for being such a stubborn, antagonistic pain in the ass. Why did I think I could show up with any game plan that'd appease the committee if that plan basically told their intentions to fuck off? Yeah, he's a Tourael. Yeah, I hate him. But *gods*, I'll hate not doing this project more.

I sink deeper into my puffer coat and jog up the steps.

Inside, the foyer is dim and cozy and warm, paneled in dark wood, with a mostly full rack of coats off to the side. I hang mine and duck through another set of doors.

This reception room is definitely nicer than the banquet hall where the grant award ceremony happened. Two chandeliers give off soft light against more of that dark wood paneling while dozens of dancing globes glitter across the ceiling; an easy enough enchantment that most kids figure out, but it creates a nice effect of glitz and glamour. There's a bar against the far wall and a fireplace to the left heating the already warm air. Guests push in around high-top tables, drinking and chatting and nibbling on finger food.

Davyeras is by the fireplace with a few committee members.

Thompson is here, along with the conjuration professor who sponsored Elethior, as well as faculty of both departments. But the majority are people I don't recognize, dressed the nicest by a long way in evening gowns and pricey suits, clearly not clinging to a university salary. Donors and board members, then.

I suddenly feel even more the status symbol of my Target white button-up and clearance black pants, and I let Orok talk me into a dark blue tie with snowflakes on it. At least I have my travel pack of spell components in my pocket and didn't wear my full belt; no one else here has any noticeable harnesses.

My eyes ping to each face, looking for—

Elethior's at the bar.

"Mr. Walsh!"

Before I can muster up the courage to cross the room, Davyeras crowds in on me and extends his hand.

I smile mechanically and shake it. "Doctor."

"Glad you got here." He slaps my shoulder as a way to steer me toward the fireplace.

I look back at the bar, where Elethior's talking with a tall blonde elven woman who reeks of money so strongly my nose tingles from here. "I should get a drink before—"

"In a moment, in a moment." Davyeras stops us in a group, half of which are committee members, half who must be donors. "I want to introduce you to a few people first."

My lips fight a hard battle to stay smiling, not grimacing.

Davyeras names off those in the group before gesturing to me. "And Sebastian Walsh here is one of the recipients of the Mageus Research Grant."

A woman with gray hair pulled back in a severe chignon puckers her lips in interest. "How has your first week gone?"

The group pins their eyes on me.

Right into the fire we go, then.

I resist looking over my shoulder for Elethior. "Ah. Well . . . have you spoken to—Mr. Tourael this evening? I wouldn't want to repeat him." *Or incriminate myself.*

"We've not had the pleasure yet," the woman says. "I admit, restructuring the grant was viewed as unnecessary by some, but I do hope to see stimulating results."

"Mr. Tourael and I are definitely"—I think of shattering the protection ward around his desk—"breaking down barriers."

"And what plans have you developed to explore the overlap of your two fields in spell energy limitations?" Davyeras asks. "Evocation and conjuration are famously at odds."

The group chuckles cordially.

"Yeah. At odds. Um . . . we're solidifying our projects individually before we begin seeing how they overlap." There. That's not a lie, but it sounds okay, right?

The group quiets. A few eye one another.

Davyeras clears his throat. "You mean, you are working separately?"

Unease wends in my stomach. "We've been firming up our own projects, so when we come together, we have a better understanding of all the pieces."

The woman who asked the initial question sips her drink. "Hm" is all she says.

Davyeras laughs. It's forced. "Well, we can hardly expect breakthroughs after only a few days, can we? Mr. Walsh, let's get you a drink. We'll discuss more later."

He nods our farewell to the group and steers me in another of those back-clapping maneuvers until we're a few yards away.

"Mr. Walsh." Davyeras smiles politely at someone who passes us. "We have put a great deal of faith in you and Mr. Tourael. Should we be worried?"

His mask of civility barely restrains the intent behind his smile.

"No," I say immediately. "No, sir. Like I said, we're getting foundations set in our projects before we come together. We know what an opportunity this is, and we don't want to waste it."

Davyeras stays quiet for a beat.

"That had better be the case, Mr. Walsh," he tells me. "And we will be seeing you both, with a *joint* report, at the first check-in a few weeks from now?" It's a question but it's definitely not a question.

"Of course, sir."

He studies me a beat longer before gesturing toward the bar. "Good. Now get that drink you're after."

"Thanks," I say and all but catapult my body to the bar.

Elethior's still at one end, still talking with that blonde woman, only there are a few other people with them now, too. He looks as comfortable as I did in the group with Davyeras, gritting his teeth with a strained smile and death-gripping a glass of red wine.

The bartender approaches me. "What'll you have?"

I collapse on my elbows. "Literally anything with gin."

He grins. He's cute, around my age, clean-cut with glossy dark hair. He gives a flirty wink when he says, "Sure thing," and turns away to mix something.

I take the moment to regroup.

Until a presence at my side has me smirking to the polished mahogany bar top.

I turn my smirk on Elethior.

He's in another expensive, sleek black suit like he wore at the awards brunch. His hair's braided down his shoulder this time, the shaved side showing the faintest shadow of hair starting to grow back. He's glaring at me, but he doesn't get a chance to speak before the bartender comes back over.

"Here you go, handsome," the bartender says, sliding a drink to me.

I take it; it's less liquid courage, more liquid lidocaine at this point. "Thanks. You're a lifesaver."

The bartender winks again, and my ears heat, but I'm in no state to see if that was a real wink or an *I'm in customer service so I flirt for tips* wink.

It's an open bar, but I throw a few bucks down.

Steeling myself, I turn back to Elethior, my shoulders straight, chin up—

—when his disdainful nose curl stops me dead.

His eyes swing to the bartender, back to me.

"What?" I ask.

"Your *date* last night didn't go well, then?"

I cringe. "Excuse me?"

He kicks back the rest of his wine unsteadily, and I get the feeling that's not his first glass.

But—wait. I'd told Elethior I had a date last night. That's what he's talking about.

I laugh. It's shockingly real and feels like a life raft in what has been my emotional state the past twenty-four hours.

"What's funny?" Elethior's suspicion is sharp. "So help me, if you pull any stupid stunt here, I'll—"

"Chill, Tourael. If you haven't noticed, I've refrained from doing anything that could be considered remotely unscrupulous all week. Don't I get a reward for that?"

I bat my eyelashes and take a sip of what turns out to be a gin and tonic. To be an ass, I slide my tongue on the rim of the glass.

Elethior's eyes glue to my mouth.

He looks dumbfounded. Struck silent and frozen.

And maybe a little . . . hungry.

Two things hit me at once: how I stripped off my shirt in front of him before the awards brunch. And now, whatever this is.

Both those things gather in the base of my stomach and burn, but a smoldering burn, nothing painful, just intent.

I slam my glass on the bar. "Actually, I need to talk to you."

He drags one hand down his face. "Gods damn it," he hisses, and I don't realize he's saying it at himself until his voice raises when he's speaking to me again. "No. That's what I came to say—you have other people you can mingle with. Other donors. You're not squirming your way over here."

I glance behind him, to the group he'd been with. The blonde woman is still there, veritably holding court with donors. "Why?"

"That," Elethior says, his teeth gritting, "is my cousin. And given how vocal you've been about all things *Tourael*, I'm not risking you foaming at the mouth mid-conversation with her. Go torture some other donors."

My grin is satanic. "But tonight's about schmoozing with *all* the donors. It'd be rude not to meet your family, Elethior."

I step past him, but I have no intention of getting farther than it takes to mess with him.

He grabs my arm and I go immobile.

I *never* go immobile.

I react.

Usually violently.

So to stand there, and *let* him hold on to my arm—my brain is a Ferris wheel, spinning, spinning, every seat empty.

I stare down at his long fingers on my white shirt.

"Let me go." My voice is rough.

His fingers spasm. But he releases me.

My eyes flip up to him, mutinous—

"Elethior," his cousin calls out. "Is that your new partner? Aren't you going to introduce us?"

Alarm bursts through my cocky anger.

I don't want to meet his cousin. Don't want to play nice with another Tourael. I'd have happily ignored her if Elethior hadn't made a point to tell me *not* to intervene, but I'm tangled up in both my desire to do the opposite of whatever he wants me to do and the deep-seated revulsion at the idea of being near his family.

The group around his cousin is watching us now. We're only two yards away, separated by a few people who come up to the bar.

Elethior's eyes stay on mine in silence, and I can practically see the thoughts taking shape in his head, warring with how he can get out of this, but what reason do either of us have to refuse?

His jaw flexes. "Of course," he calls back to his cousin.

He starts to grab my arm again, thinks better of it, and recoils, flexing his fingers. When he turns toward the woman, I find my voice again.

"Wait. I—I do need to talk to you about this whole . . . *thing*." I wave between us.

I need another second of not being over there. A second to unclench my fists and center myself and other calming shit Orok preached at me before I left the apartment.

Maybe it'll kick in.

Anytime now.

I note the color staining Elethior's cheeks. Damn, how tipsy is he?

"There is no *thing*," he snaps. "Remember? We're presenting individual projects."

"Yeah." I scratch the back of my neck. "About that. I've had a change of heart—"

"*Elethior*." His cousin has one eyebrow lifted, a finger tapping on the bar.

"Behave yourself." Elethior leans in, smelling of that rich wine he had. "I'm serious. Pretend you have at least basic people skills."

"Fuck off," I hiss back at him, but I paste on a smile as we move down the bar.

His cousin's group peels away at some unspoken command, so we have her full attention. Up close, she's older than Elethior, half elven like he is, with shorter pointed ears than a full elf would have. She's definitely related, though, with the same dark eyes, but her hair is so bright it almost hurts to look at. Her sleek scarlet dress is as expertly crafted as Elethior's suit, her ears, neck, and fingers set with glitzy jewels. Money, money, blah blah blah; I should text Crescentia to get her protestors over here.

I hold out my hand. "Sebastian Walsh. I'm sure Elethior's told you all about me."

She smiles amicably. "Arasne Tourael. And no, he hasn't."

I'm momentarily struck when I realize I don't know where she fits in the Tourael family tree. What branch is she a part of? Weapons manufacturing? Military?

A thought settles like a stone in my gut.

Is she a part of Camp Merethyl? I don't recognize her. Gods, my dad would love that—if Elethior has direct connections to that camp and my making good with him *could* smooth over the ripples I caused in dropping out.

My dad being happy annoys me, so I cling to that emotion. Annoyance. Frustration. *Anger*. There's nothing else churning beneath my surface, nothing else trying to drown me.

"You're a donor?" I ask, purposefully fishing.

"I am," she says through that expert amicable smile. "I also keep an eye out for up-and-coming young wizards who might find a home in any of our research and development properties."

I choke down relief. The Tourael family is massive; they all deal with magic defense, but they *don't* all have their hands in Camp Merethyl. Many of them do totally innocent things, like design weapons and fund dangerous spell research.

Arasne lets a pause linger, clearly expecting me to fawn over her, which is likely the usual reaction upon learning she has hiring power at high-paying jobs.

I give a one-shouldered shrug. "Neat-o. I've got a job lined up with the Clawstar Foundation."

She tenses, presumably at the mention of a nonprofit in direct opposition with what she's recruiting for. But she recovers and says, "Congratulations," with no inflection.

Elethior flags the bartender. Another glass of red wine is put in front of him and he grabs it.

"You drinking that Do Men de la Something-Candy?" I ask.

He and Arasne both gawk at me.

"Pardon?" she questions.

I smile innocently. "Some fancy wine Elethior was going on about."

He sets the glass on the bar and pinches his nose. "Domaine de la Romanée-Conti."

"*That's* how that last word is pronounced?" I paste on fake shock. "Do Men Dally with Roman *what*? Sounds like—" I make a circle with one hand and stick my finger through it repeatedly. "But whaddya expect of the Romans, ya know?"

Unveiled revulsion flashes across Arasne's face as she realizes what an imbecile her cousin is working with.

My smile is set in iron. Utterly unbreakable. Yeah, lady, I *am* that dumb.

"It's—no. It's not that." But Elethior doesn't pick up his glass again.

I think, I *think,* he's trying not to laugh.

Of all the reactions he's had to my antics, he's never laughed. Not even *at* me, and that's not what this feels like.

It's as if . . . he's in on it with me.

I'm not sure I like it.

Arasne regains her composure. "Elethior has been tight-lipped about how the project is going. Perhaps you can enlighten me as to why he has nothing to show for his first week?"

Elethior's humor dies and he looks pleadingly at her.

My hackles go up. They were already up. They go up higher. I'm wearing an Elizabethan neck ruff of hackles.

"He has plenty to show for his first week," I say to Arasne. "We both do. I'll admit, it's slow getting used to conjuration after coming from evocation, and vice versa with Elethior. But we're making great progress, and we have a solid foundation to get into deeper research in the coming months."

Elethior and Arasne gawk at me again.

Elethior in surprise.

Arasne in distrust.

Her eyes go to slits, lingering on my tie.

"*Great progress,*" she parrots. To Elethior, "How much progress should we expect from you, truthfully? If you are being forced to work with someone who will never amount to anything beyond magical tech support."

My jaw drops. Oh, *nice*. We're taking off the gloves, are we?

But as I open my mouth, inhibitions fully shucked, Arasne rounds on Elethior like I'm not here. To her, I might not be; she's decided I'm insignificant. Good.

"You know the family's expectations," she hisses.

The family. Like they're the mafia.

"It's bad enough you were unable to secure the grant for just *you,*" Arasne continues, "but you come to this cocktail party empty-handed and unprepared. This is not the behavior we expect, Elethior. This is not up to our standards."

Elethior stands there and takes her verbal assault, his eyes pinned over her shoulder.

Pieces shift around in my brain, lock together, and I'm not liking the picture they form.

"And now *him*." Arasne turns up her nose at me, and I bat my eyelashes. "This is the visage your partner presents? Perhaps I should have a conversation with the grant committee. If they insist on combining two projects, we can find a more suitable partner for you."

My pretense shatters. The idiotic blankness. The disdainful smugness. In its place comes the marching step of the anger that's been my biggest crutch.

"I'm not going anywhere," I tell her.

Arasne's eyes darken. My focus drops to her hands, but one is holding a glass of white wine while the other is unmoving at her side. No magic, no spells. She's just regular ol' mad.

"That's not up to you," she shoots back.

"Like hell it's not," I say. "I'm not going to roll over and step aside because *the family* wills it. I can't be bought and I won't vanish easily, and you can bet your ass that I'll escalate any fight you bring my way."

"You prove my point." Her scowl flicks back to Elethior, who's gone pale. "If *this* is what you've been forced to work with, no wonder you haven't accomplished anything. I'll speak to—"

"No," Elethior says.

I blink at him.

"No," he says again to Arasne. "I don't need your involvement. I have it handled."

Arasne's anger vanishes. She's suddenly compassionate, saccharinely so, one hand cupping Elethior's shoulder. "You're making things unnecessarily difficult. We have an image to maintain, and I'd hate to think what would happen if that image were sullied."

There's weight behind those words. Elethior looks sick, but his jaw firms.

"I have it under control," he says. "I promise."

Arasne sighs in a way that tells me they've had similar conversations before. "I'll expect a better report at our next meeting."

She flounces off, a potent *or else* vibrating in her wake.

Elethior lets out a slow exhale, his eyes on the space where she'd been standing.

The very last thing I ever want to feel for him is *pity*. Or worse: empathy.

"So," I start. "She's a real treat."

His eyes flick to mine.

And he laughs.

Well, more like *sputters,* a strangled snort that gets stuck in his nose. My brows bend. "How much wine have you had?"

What was a mottled snort is now a full-on chortle and he mumbles, "You made a sex gesture at my cousin," before he cracks up all over again.

A few people are looking over at us now. More donors we have to mingle with, more committee members we have to impress. And my esteemed lab partner is having a wine-fueled breakdown by the bar.

I put my arm around his shoulders. "Okay, buddy, let's get some air, yeah?"

Elethior keeps one hand over his mouth but nods.

I weave us through the crowd, avoiding eye contact with everyone we pass so we don't get pulled into any more sure-to-be-disastrous conversations, and we make it into the foyer unscathed.

The windows on the heavy front doors show that it's lightly snowing now, and I wrestle my jacket off the coatrack. Elethior doesn't; he's in just his suit as he shoves open the door and jogs down the steps. I follow, only realizing once I come to a stop on the bottom stair that I could've *not* followed him, I could've stayed in the warmth of the foyer and let him recover on his own.

Facing the building, and me, he shoves his hands into his pants pockets, tips his head back with his eyes shut, and lets the snowflakes pepper his face.

"I'm not going to apologize for mouthing off to her," I say, establishing myself in this weird, amorphous pause.

I'm a step above where he's on the walkway, and it puts me

over him when he blinks his eyes open, snowflakes on his dark lashes.

I can feel kisses of cold on my cheeks and ears; I'm getting covered, too.

"I don't expect you to," he says.

"Well, good."

"Good."

I shiver and tuck my arms around myself and do *not* say *good* again. "Awesome."

Elethior cracks a smile. It's unsettling. He's smiled more because of me tonight than in all our interactions combined, and not in his usual condescending way.

"Davyeras got on my case for not cooperating with you." I exhale, and it displaces snowflakes on their path to the already coated steps. "And while I could be pissed that they all expected some brilliant breakthrough after *five days,* I get it. We should've gotten over our bullshit and worked together. So," I straighten my spine, "if you're sober enough to remember this conversation, I'm ready to get to work when we're back in the lab next week. If you won't remember, well, I guess I'll have to give this dazzling speech again Monday morning."

Elethior's lips cock. "I'm not drunk."

"Sure you're not, Chuckles."

"I had one glass. I'm not drunk. I—" He looks at the windows next to the door that show the blurry forms of the guests within. His voice gentles. "I've always wanted to speak to her like you did. Arasne's an insufferable, pretentious drone."

My eyes widen.

And then I'm the one losing it, laughing so hard my sides split.

Elethior watches me, one side of his mouth lifted in amusement, but it isn't at my expense. And I laugh more until, yeah, I can believe he's not drunk.

I take my glasses off, wiping my eyes and cleaning the smudges of snowflakes off the lenses, before I settle enough to catch Elethior's questioning look.

"I'm pretty sure I've used those words to describe you," I explain. "So to hear *you* say that about your own family is . . . really weird."

He shrugs. "Well, that seems to be the theme of most situations that involve you."

I hold his gaze, tongue working along my teeth. "If you're not drunk, then what do you say? We don't have to like each other. But we need to work together. Can you do that?"

He rolls his eyes. "I believe I was the one who originally tried to broach a truce, so yes, Sebastian. I can do that."

"Well, your attempt at forging peace between our warring nations crumbled, so I get credit for it being a success now."

Elethior's face hardens. Ah, *there* it is, a flash of our old animosity. Nice to see it isn't completely gone.

I grin triumphantly and hook my thumb over my shoulder. "Should we take this new united front back in and wow the Armani socks off those donors?"

The snow's slowing down, but he's still coated in flakes, tiny glittering specks of white.

He tips his head up to the sky one more time, and I recognize the gathering of strength, the frantic scramble to cling to resolve.

I'd be doing the same if I was able. But I don't show vulnerability around anyone other than Orok. Just grit my teeth, make an inappropriate joke, and compartmentalize my breakdowns for later.

"I suppose," he says, no small amount of reluctance in his voice.

My stomach sinks. I don't know why I care.

"Or," I say, "we could fuck off, and I can spell a ward over the door so everyone who leaves the party tonight after us gets hit with painful diarrhea."

Elethior arches an *are you serious* eyebrow.

He climbs the stairs to stand at my side, taller than me again. Asshole.

"Don't strain your abilities with such complicated magic," he tells me with another of his haughty smirks. "You'll need all your strength to keep up with me next week."

My face falls. "Dick."

He clutches his chest, walking backward up the rest of the stairs, leaving footprints in the snow. "*Ouch.* All out of insults tonight already? My, you really *won't* be able to keep up with me."

"I—but with the—oh, just." And I flip him off.

He barks a laugh and vanishes back inside, leaving me alone with the falling snow, wondering what the hell happened.

I guess Elethior and I are . . . not *friends* now, gods forbid. But . . . partners?

What is the world coming to.

I'm halfway home when I realize I'm not freaking out, and I should be.

Turns out Elethior absolutely has the power to get me punted off this project, he just *hasn't*; and not only that, he flat-out refused the offer in front of me. Add on the fact that we—gag—*bonded,* and I have no idea why I'm not vibrating out of my skin.

As I unlock the apartment door, I'm in desperate need of spewing this to Orok and figuring out why I feel so . . . okay with everything.

After Elethior and I returned to the party, the night went well. We mingled as a pair, fielding donor questions with vague reassurances that we're excited to see what the semester brings. We fed off each other rather instinctively, volleying responses like we'd rehearsed them.

I should be *livid* with myself. But maybe all that worrying about losing this grant put my hatred into perspective. Maybe I will be able to tackle this project from a place of maturity.

I open the door and almost shout a perky *honey, I'm home* before I notice Orok sprawled on the couch, out cold in worn blue sweatpants. He had rawball practice this afternoon, and I know he also had a shift with his call center job where he answers the non-emergency line for an adventure party—he doesn't take the *There's a griffon rampaging Center City* calls, more the *I found a nest of pixies in my garden and they won't stop hoarding all my jewelry* calls. His laptop and head-set are perched on the cushion next to him, and he's got a folder open on his bare chest and a few books and papers next to his feet on the coffee table.

I quietly unzip my coat, watching him twitch in his sleep.

And he worried about me pushing it too hard this first week.

There aren't any food plates in the nest around him, so I throw up a quick silence spell around our kitchen and dig out some left-over drunken noodles from—I sniff them—four days ago? Five? They're probably fine. The noodles are little chewy even after I use a warming spell on them, but I carry two bowls to the couch along with bottles of water.

I watch him for a beat, but he doesn't appear to be having a nightmare.

"Hey," I say and kick his knee. "O. You—"

He jackknifes awake.

The folder flies off his chest, one arm winging up in a shield, the other bracing on the back of the couch.

"Orok!" I fumble the bowls and waters but manage to set them on the coffee table, then crouch until his eyes lock on me. "Orok—hey. You're awake. You're safe. It's Seb, O."

His shoulders heave, arm staying up as consciousness slides over him.

"Seb," he says, eyes meeting mine.

"Yeah." I force a smile, heart skittering and aching. "You're good, okay? You're safe."

His arm drops as he does, slumping back against the couch, the heel of one hand digging into his forehead. "Did I—"

"Just scared the shit out of me. My fault, though. I should've let you sleep."

"No." He scrubs his face and pins me with a look as I rise up out of my crouch. "It's not your fault. It's *never* your fault."

My eyes go involuntarily to his chest and the jagged white scar that sits along the seam of his left shoulder. Seeing it always pierces something deep inside me, my own scar to match his, but internal.

I can still hear the sound he made because of that wound. It wasn't a scream, wasn't a shout; something guttural beneath that, the shriek a person makes when they don't have time to recognize they're in pain.

Clarity brings my thoughts of Elethior into proper focus.

It doesn't matter how weird tonight was; nothing's changed, except for now, I'll be able to do my project. Elethior's still Elethior and I only trust that he also wants to work.

There's no need to dig into the psychology of why tonight didn't make me freak out.

"Want to talk about whatever dream you had?" I offer, even though I know the answer.

"It wasn't a dream," he says. "It was . . . emotions. It's not like I have full Hollywood blockbuster nightmares set at Camp Merethyl."

I hide my shudder by grabbing our dinner and shoving a bowl at him. "That's a movie no one ever needs to make."

He forks up a noodle and holds it toward me in a mock toast. It's shaking. "Hear, hear."

Mid-bite, he pushes away his laptop, headset, and the folder he launched off his chest so I can plop onto the couch next to him.

We eat in silence.

He's still trembling, likely from cold as his sweat dries, but also from the crash after waking up like that.

I hate when he gets all mother hen on me though, so I bite down on my need to baby him and instead grab the folder he shoved aside.

"Weren't you the one who told me not to work so—wait, the Hellhounds?" I reread the word spread across the front.

It isn't a folder for a class; it's a promo kit for the professional rawball team based in Philadelphia.

I flip it open, and it's full of info about the team, stats, and history—along with the benefits and bonuses for players.

My eyes go huge and I gape at Orok. "What the—"

He shovels in the last of his food. "It's nothing. They're going to be scouting at a few games and sent those packets ahead. We all got one. It happens every year."

I bend my knee on the couch so I can face him, but he isn't looking at me.

"Did you get an offer to play pro rawball?" I ask straight-out.

He rests his bowl in his lap and lays his head back against the couch, eyes fluttering shut. "No."

I set the folder on the coffee table. "Are you lying to me?"

Orok pops his eyes open. "No, Seb."

"That'd be pretty sweet. The pro team, not lying."

"I didn't get scouted. It's—" His eyes shut again. "It's nothing, okay?"

No, it's not. There's tension vibrating off him and I can't figure out why.

"It's not nothing," I say. "If you got scouted. If you—"

"But it's not the plan." It comes out as a whisper. Pained, almost.

My heart, already bruised to all hell by the way he woke up, squeezes. "Fuck the plan. Fuck *your mom's* plan. You think she wouldn't be happy about you playing pro rawball? That's suitably *tough* and *Urzoth-y.*"

Eyes still shut, he reaches out, misses once, then grabs my knee. "Stop. It's not that. It's—a recruiter came by practice this week. Talked to me. But she talked to a few of us. That's it, okay? It got in my head."

I thread my fingers with his. "Why did it get in your head?"

He doesn't respond right away. His hold tightens on my hand and he rolls his head to the side before looking at me. Something ripples across his face as his grip on my hand starts to hurt.

"It's all ending," he whispers, so low I almost don't hear the way his voice cracks.

"What's ending?"

He pulses his hand against mine.

My shoulders bow. "O. C'mon. If you haven't been able to get rid of me this long, it's not going to change when we're done with school.

No matter what, you're stuck with my handsome mug in your life."
I give him a flat, wide, cheesy grin. "And you know I'm locked into
Philly after graduation. Clawstar's HQ is here. Getting recruited to
the Hellhounds is a *good* thing."

"You're sure we shouldn't enroll in the doctorate program and
keep our heads in the sand a bit longer?" he asks, too serious for my
liking.

We'd talked about this when we planned for grad school. Neither of us has need for a doctorate, and honestly, I'm pretty sure he
doesn't need his master's.

He's only here to stay close to me.

"Do you want to go pro with rawball?" I ask gently.

"I want," he starts, half mumbling, "to go back to sleep."

Stubborn asshole. "If you fall asleep on the couch, I will levitate
your big butt upstairs and hurl you into your bed."

He grins but throws it into a pathetic whine. "No, Seb. Carry
me." He pokes my arm.

"Ow." I rub the spot, and as I gather our dinner stuff and stand,
he follows me up, scrubbing awareness into his face.

"Wait—your party," he says. "How'd it go?"

I made peace with the guy whose family tortured us for four summers straight.
"Fine. Weird. But fine."

Orok grimaces, fighting a losing battle with staying awake on his
feet. "That's cryptic."

I deposit the bowls and water bottles in the sink as nonchalantly
as I can. "I gotta inject some sense of mystery into our relationship
or you'll get sick of me."

He shoots me an amused look before plodding up to his bedroom with a warbling yawn. I follow, hitting the lights and activating
our security wards.

By the time I'm upstairs, Orok's face down across his comforter,
bedside lamp on.

"I should make you brush your teeth."

He scowls with his eyes shut. "Noooo, Mom; I'll do it in the
morning, I promise."

I swat his head and click off his light. "Night, dumbass."

He grabs my hand in the dark with the same constricting desperation as he did downstairs.

We've lived together for six years. Roomed together at Camp Merethyl before that. He's been one bunk or door away for more than a quarter of my life, and maybe that's why I'm not worried about things changing after we graduate. I can't imagine any future where he's not close.

He doesn't say anything now, just keeps hold of my hand.

"You want some company?" I try. He doesn't always.

Another stretch of silence. Then a grumbled "Yeah."

"Give me a sec."

It doesn't take long to throw on sleep pants and a T-shirt and fumble through my night routine, then I'm back, tossing my glasses on his side table and crawling into the space Orok leaves me in his queen-size bed. He's going to squash me by morning.

He flops onto his side, facing me, still above the covers where I huddle under them, and his hand seeks out mine on the sheet. "Thanks."

Don't thank me, I want to say. The same way he reassures me it isn't my fault.

I settle into his pillow. "Tomorrow's the day: we're officially going to have your therapist help us work through our codependency issues."

There's no heat in it. We've made promises and threats like that before.

"She'd love that," he mumbles. "She calls you my security blanket."

My throat pinches, but I force out, "A *blanket*? Hardly. A high-end cashmere sweater at least."

"We are, though." Orok yawns again. He's fading fast. "To each other. Security."

"Well. I mean, yeah." I stiffen. "This is probably crossing a line then, right? One of the first things she'd tell us to stop. This, I mean." I pat his bed, ribs contracting. "If this isn't helping you, I should—"

I start to get up, but Orok grabs my shoulder and thumps me back onto the bed.

"Go to sleep," he tells me.

The worry eases. A little. "Your therapist will be so disappointed in you."

I can hear his smile when he slurs, "Shut your mouth, Seb."

Chapter Six

Dagger hail's a pain in the ass, but it doesn't have shit on that one horrible summer where a warlock got pissy and unleashed a plague of dire mosquitoes.

Dire mosquitoes.

They were the size of chihuahuas.

So though it means traffic extra sucks because everyone has to dodge yard-long spears of ice plummeting from the sky, I happily embrace the dagger hail, and most everyone around me does, too. The *plunk, plunk, plunk* of shards rebounding off the bus's force shields doesn't faze anyone.

By the time I get to the lab, I *am* a bit annoyed by the hail, since it meant I had to keep a personal force shield up on the walk from the bus stop. My first day working under this tentative truce with Elethior, and I'm going in tired. But he likely had to keep up some kind of shield, too, so odds are he's in the same boat.

I push into the lab and don't find him out of breath and sweaty. He's standing by his clusterfuck of a workstation, thin blue strands of energy forming a web between his splayed hands.

I stiffen.

He scowls in concentration as he reads something in the spell he's cast.

The door thuds shut behind me. The distant *plunk*ing of the ice shards immediately vanishes thanks to the lab's soundproofing.

Elethior acknowledges me with a slight flick of his eyes to the side. All he asks is, "How did you do this?"

I don't have to answer him. We have a professional truce; I owe him nothing else.

I clench one hand and cross behind him to deposit my bag on my desk. "Genetics. I wake up looking this good."

"Yeah, that's obviously what I meant." He turns from his analysis spell to give me a quick once-over.

Or what he clearly *meant* to be a quick once-over.

But his eyes shoot to where I'm peeling off my hoodie. My T-shirt is caught on the hem and I can feel both rise up, a gust of cool air brushing across my bare stomach, making my abs tighten.

Elethior stares at that line. That revealed skin.

It itches. Prickles right where my stomach runs along the edge of my pants.

I release a noise. A gasp? A grunt? I want it to be an offended *ahem*, but I know it's too soft and breathy for that.

Elethior whips back to his spell. Those stupid lines of scarlet flare across his cheekbones, racing back so even his pointed ears turn vivid red against the silver metal of his piercings.

I can make him uncomfortable very, very easily, turns out.

But I don't take advantage of that. It doesn't *feel* like discomfort. Not really.

Oh, gods.

You know what? It's cold in here. Think I'll keep my clothes fully *on* today. Maybe come in tomorrow wearing a hazmat suit, normal laboratory fashion.

I jerk my hoodie and T-shirt down, pulling until both stretch below my component belt.

"I meant," Elethior swallows roughly, "*my ward*. It's—gone."

He claps his hands so the analysis spell falls, and he stares at the space over his desk, seeing nothing, *trying* to see something, with the same bewildered frustration as when he was trying to see Nick.

"You didn't just break it," he says. Does he sound . . . awed? He reaches out, fingers moving over where the barrier was. "It's—gods, it's like you neutralized the particles around it, too."

I busy myself pulling my laptop and supplies out of my bag, ignoring the dread ballooning in my chest. "Maybe your ward was unstable. I did a simple breaking spell. On principle of the fact that I'm offended you assumed I'd go through your shit."

One pierced eyebrow goes up. "There's no way that was a simple breaking spell. What did you do?"

I slam a book onto my desk. Bad enough I lost control at all, but doing it where Elethior could find the evidence and pester me about it—

"You want me to explain a ward-breaking spell to you, the mighty Elethior Tourael?" I ask.

He doesn't rise to my baiting, still more confused, intrigued, than annoyed.

One arm bends as he scratches the back of his neck, tattooed bicep flexing under his black T-shirt. "I'm trying to figure out what happened. I'm going to have to cleanse this area before I do other spells here."

"Well, if there's any fucked-up magic, it was from your wonky-ass barrier."

His arm falls with his expression. "I see we're diving straight into hostility, despite what progress we made on Saturday. Forgive me for trying to have a calm discussion about *wonky-ass* magic happening in *our* lab."

I deflate over my desk, fists pressing to the wood.

It was my dumb fault he even *has* weird magic to fixate on, and I sure as hell won't be making that mistake around him again.

"You're right," I whisper to my desk. "I'm sorry."

Elethior's quiet for a beat.

A beat so stretched out that I glance over to see if he teleported away.

His eyes glitter.

"Did you just," he licks his lower lip, "say I was right, *and* apologize to me?"

I drop into my desk chair, face hot again, and fiddle with my hoodie's sleeves. "We're on a fresh start, right?"

He's grinning. Smug-ass bastard. "Uh-huh."

"Get that look off your face."

"I can't help it. This is the look I get when an apocalypse is looming."

My mouth lifts in the barest smile that I quickly smother. Screw him.

I wave at my books and laptop. "Can we get to work, or are there other things you'd like to accuse me of? The dagger hail, perhaps?"

His eyes zip to the window, where beyond a slight ripple from Bellanor Hall's activated shield, we can still see spears of ice stabbing into the Quad.

"Fine. *You're* right." He sneers at me. "Thinking you did any powerful magic is giving you way too much credit. It had to be my ward."

I exhale relief before realizing, *insult.* So I turn my exhale into an aggrieved sigh.

Elethior reaches back to grab his overstuffed notebook. He wheels his chair to my workstation and sits, notebook open, pen in hand. His component harnesses are pinched tight around each thigh and the leather creaks as his legs spread.

He waits.

I turn on my laptop and swivel my chair to face him.

And *I* wait.

He waves at my desk. "Feel free to get started. Wow me with your evocation wonders."

I snort. "Um, *hell* no. *You* get started. I'm not spilling my project to you before I know what you're working on and whether this partnership is viable."

That eyebrow today is sharper than the dagger hail. "I don't think you understand how this is going to work. You're still the one who has the most to prove—"

"Oh, fuck all the way off."

"—because *you* are the reason we wasted all of last week working solo. And before you prattle on with what I'm sure will be a commendable speech displaying the versatility of the word *fuck,* I'm going to need you to tap into that earlier *You're right, Elethior, I'm sorry* energy. Because I *am* right."

It would be so easy to make each and every one of his piercings turn molten and sizzle right through his face.

But I'm not *reacting* anymore. I'm not leaping to defensiveness. I can *do* this. I *have* to do this, and not everything needs to be an explosion.

My eyes bore holes in the wall over my workstation.

"How do I know your family won't steal my project?"

I push the question into our lab, let it nestle alongside the silence after Elethior's too appropriate dressing-down.

His chair squeaks as he shifts. "What do you mean?"

"I mean—" I hiss out a breath and shove my glasses up my nose. Everything in my body feels inelastic. "I mean, what's to stop your family from snatching up our work under the guise of *whatever a Tourael does belongs to us* and slapping a patent on it, then carting it off to wreak untold havoc with *my* research?"

Nothing in my tone is accusatory and I offer more of an olive branch when I force myself to meet his gaze.

He watches me, eyes darting between mine, back and forth, his face drooping as he realizes I'm being serious.

But if he says, *Well, sucks to be you. I'm turning over everything to them no matter what,* can I do anything? I need this grant. Need to complete this project for my degree. Need all of that to keep my Clawstar job.

This massive lab is suddenly very, very small.

"Never mind," I mutter to my laptop. "Whatever you say, I have no other choice. So—my project."

Numb, I click open the document with all my plans.

"My family won't touch a gods-damned thing we do here."

I'm blinking at him before his words fully process. "What?"

He leans forward, eyes intent, a focus laden with promise that silences me. "I'm playing nice with them until I graduate, but once I'm out, I have no intention of working for any of the companies my family has their hands in, and I sure as hell have no intention of letting them patent my research. Our work—*your* work—is safe from them. Through me, at least."

That noise isn't the dagger hail; we can't hear it in here. It's my pulse *thud, thud, thudd*ing in my ears.

I can't sort through my thoughts for several seconds, and in those seconds, I stare at him, waiting for the wink and the laugh, the punchline.

Elethior smiles, apologetic. "You don't believe me. Well, believe at least that I gave you a huge bit of control. You could tell my family what I said and create problems for me. Hopefully, in some way, this helps even the power imbalance?"

My eyes widen.

Holy shit.

He could be lying about not wanting to work with his family, or laying out yet another game of chicken between us.

But his eyes are on mine, unshrinking, *vulnerable,* and I feel a prickling on my skin, the hyperawareness of sensation, the brush of my clothes and the firmness of the chair and the static space between his legs and mine.

"My plan for my project was to release it for free online," I say. My mouth is dry, tongue sandy. "After graduation. No patents, no copyrights. I have a job lined up with a nonprofit that does that sort of thing, so I was going to use this as a way to reaffirm their choice. We're only supposed to see how evocation and conjuration overlap, but if our projects end up being tied together, that could mean your project getting released, too."

I expect him to recoil at the idea of releasing any spell for free. The Tourael will come out in him, and he'll balk.

But he shrugs. "I have no problem with that. Even if we don't get concrete conclusions by graduation, our research will still make a good stepping stone for others."

My eyes narrow.

Is he mocking me? But he looks sincere.

I shift toward my desk, scrambling for grip in a brain that suddenly feels polished smooth. "Sure. Yeah. Sounds like a plan." I straighten my already straight laptop. "That's all light-years away. But my—my project."

Elethior's chair squeaks again, and out of the corner of my eye I see him slide down in it. He's fidgeting with his pen, tapping it on his notebook, his knee bouncing.

"I'm studying a way to cap energy pulled from components during spells rather than a wizard having to rely on their own concentration to ration amounts," I say too fast. Familiarity cancels out the strain, and my shoulders relax as I fall into something I know. "A safety net thrown over every spell so wizards don't have to worry about unnecessarily draining components."

He's writing something, and he nods. "It's irritating to always have to allot focus to ensure the correct amount of a component is used."

I barely restrain an eye roll. "Yeah. Irritating." I idly scroll as I talk. "I've been poking at this idea for months—well, longer, but I fine-tuned it for the grant proposal. The biggest problem I keep running into is that having one rune or equation that could be thrown into a larger spell is complicated, because every spell is too unique, with different components and amounts. I'd have to factor the energy demands of *every* possible component for *every* spell into the safety net so it'd adjust to whatever's being used, which would make it massive and impractical."

"And when you thought we'd be able to get away with working solo"—he peeks up at me with a *told you so* leer, and my hands clench—"what was the schedule you were aiming for?"

I spin my laptop to show him the calendar I created.

"Research for the first few weeks," I explain. "Develop at least three different theories. Test those theories. Fine-tune based on the results. Run more tests." An anticipated sub-step: scream in frustration a lot. "Develop a conclusion and overall analysis, then write it up."

Elethior rolls his chair closer to my screen. It puts him right next to me, his rich, earthy cologne nebulous in the air.

His thigh touches mine.

Warmth blazes from the base of my neck down to my lower back and I rip my leg away.

He doesn't seem to notice. He's studying my calendar, making a few more notes.

"What are *you* working on?" I ask. Damn these silences straight to hell.

Elethior grins at his notebook and kicks my desk so he rolls a few feet away. "The energy between a conjurer and their conjured item. But I have an idea. I'd like you to *hear* my idea before you bite my head off. Can you do that?"

My glare flattens. "Lose the condescending tone and yeah, I can."

"I think we should focus on your project first. We can both tackle research so we—"

"*Woah,* no way. It's your turn to tell me what you're working on. What do you mean, a conjurer and their conjured item?" That's all Davyeras said at the awards brunch, too, that Elethior was working on *the limitations of the energy connection between a conjurer and their conjured item.*

Elethior sighs, stands, and walks his chair back to his desk. The dismissal has me shoving up from my own chair and crossing into his workstation, even though it means kicking his gym bag out of the way.

He squares off toward me like he's prepared for a fight. "We should start with our combined focus on your project, at least for a week or so. It'll let us figure out how to work together before we take on too much. Email me the research you did for your grant proposal, will you?"

He scribbles something on a piece of paper, rips it out, and hands it to me before tossing his notebook on his desk.

I take the paper. It's his email address and cell number.

My back cramps. "Um, *you* email me the research you did for *your* grant proposal, and we've got a deal."

He's perfected the disappointed, exhausted sigh thing. "No."

I roughly pocket his email. "*No?*"

"No. *As I said,* I wanted you to listen to my idea before you take my head off. We should start with your project. We'll get familiar with working together on it, *then* I'll bring my project into the mix. Yours has merit, and I want us to—"

I black out. One minute, I'm standing a respectable distance away; the next, I'm right against him.

"You're not taking my project, Tourael," I snarl.

He huffs through his nose. "I'm not *taking* it. We should focus on yours *to start.* Gods, I *told you* not to bite my head off—"

"We're working together. Which means figuring out how conjuration and evocation interact in *both* of our projects and doing what the committee wanted us to do, so when we have our check-ins, we can tell them more than *Elethior's being a great assistant for me.*"

He rolls his eyes. "Like fuck I'll be your assistant. And, again, I didn't say *forever.* Just until we get our sea legs with not wanting to kill each other, which we're doing a bang-up job of so far."

"And my project's the guinea pig?"

"Honestly? Yes."

Rage is lava-hot, scalding every fiber, every nerve ending. My hands lift, fingers curling, not because I want to hit him, but because, okay, I *do,* but I won't; and I want to cast a banishment spell and shunt him back to the Fae Plane, but I *won't.*

I told him about my project. Only Orok and a few of my professors know the details; my parents know about it in a vague sense because I was obsessed with the concept when I was younger. It's like Elethior took this knowledge and shoved it carelessly into his disorganized clutter of a notebook, and it cracks me like glass, a shatter spiderwebbing through my torso.

"You pretentious piece of *shit!* You coerced me into telling you about my project and now you're holding it hostage?"

Elethior sucks his teeth, annoyance heavy on his face, which grates on my already raw nerves like sandpaper. He has no right to be annoyed by me; it isn't *his* research getting used as a test dummy for cooperation.

"Not everything is a manipulation," he growls. "And right now, you're proving me right in being cautious about us taking on too much at once."

"Then we should've decided on parameters *before* you had me tell you about my project, and we should've decided whose to go in on *together*. This isn't collaboration; this is you being a narcissistic control freak."

His head jerks to the side, nostrils flaring. I watch his chest rise and fall before he crosses his arms over that black T-shirt.

"You're right," he says softly.

I jolt back. Then regroup. "I know I am."

Elethior faces me again, chin lifted. "I'm sorry. I shouldn't have decided on our plan of action without your input."

My mouth drops open.

At my surprise, Elethior's eyes sparkle, but his steady mask holds. I snap my jaw shut.

"Now." He tips his head, black hair falling over his shoulder. "After this little . . . interaction, do you honestly believe we're ready to tackle both projects at once?"

My body thrums with the need to move, to do *something*, all that anger festering in my muscles like poison. I groan, take a step away, come back, and groan again.

"Screw you," I growl.

He grins. "We'll work on your project and see how evocation and conjuration play together with that. We have three weeks until our first check-in; that gives us plenty of time to figure each other out."

I glare one more time, trying to read him for any weak spots. There are none, as usual.

"Whatever," I grumble like I'm twelve. "I'll send you my research and let you know what reading I was planning to do. You can take half of it. If there are any conjuration resources you think would supplement, would you mind, O great one, mentioning them before we delve in too deep?"

Elethior sits again, slowly looks up at me, and positively *beams*.

"Are you admitting that there are valuable things to be learned from conjuration?"

I hold my ground—I *have* to stop letting him bait me so easily.

"I am, actually." I march back to my desk. "That's the point of this grant now, right?"

"Aw," he throws at my retreating back. "I'm proud of you, baby boy."

Don't cuss at him.

Don't curse him.

Don't *anything* him.

I sit primly. Perfect posture. I'm downright *elegant*.

After I fire off an email to him with all *my* research, I sort through the components I have in my belt. I always keep a wide array of things along with a few prepared vials.

I find what I'm looking for and toss an appreciative nod to the dagger hail that's still going strong outside, thanking it for the inspiration.

Elethior's back is to me as he scrolls through what I assume is my research on his phone.

I ready the components, mutter the incantation, and send the spell skipping merrily across the lab.

Frost creeps up the bottom of his chair, freezing the wheels, the rungs, the base, until—

He rockets up with a yelp, only his chair is frozen to the floor and can't roll away. Which makes him bang his thighs into his desk and flail back onto the now ice-solid seat of his chair.

Elethior stills, hands splayed, ass no doubt a little *chilly*.

"Sebastian," he barks, still not facing me.

"Oh no," I coo. "The evil witch-king must be after you. Should I call an adventure party?"

He sits for one more beat before he rubs a hand over his left shoulder. Through his T-shirt sleeve, there's a faint blue glow.

The ice vanishes.

My brows pulse. "You have a counterspell rune tattoo?"

Chair freed, he spins enough to look at me and lifts one of his arms, showing the ink swirling across his skin. Even from here, I spot a few other runes now, camouflaged with intricate snaking ivy and grayscale flowers.

Magic tattoos supposedly hurt a helluva lot more than regular tattoos; bits of components are woven in with the ink and the whole process involves a constant, steady stream of magic imbued in the art. I never let myself look too closely at his tattoos before, but—

Woah, pump those brakes. Not *let*; there was no *letting*. I simply did *not* look too closely at his tattoos. Why would I have wanted to?

I lurch away, scowling at my desk.

"Pouting doesn't become you," he says.

"I'm not *pouting*. I'm *focusing*." I point at my laptop. "As should you. Stop distracting me. *You* should wear the hazmat suit."

"I should—what?"

Breath gets trapped in my lungs.

That was not a thought he'd been privy to, wearing a hazmat suit to avoid uncomfortable situations, and saying it out loud has a nightmare-level realization cannonballing into my mind:

Am I *attracted* to Elethior?

Oh.

Oh, *fuck* no.

I have a fairly masochistic personality, but that's taking self-flagellation too far, even for me.

"Nothing," I fumble. "Never mind. Just—shut up and get to work."

Where I expect a quip about how I need to be more mature, he hums.

"Fine," he says. "Game on."

He faces his desk again.

Leaving me stupidly slack-jawed.

I frown at the back of his head. "Game on?"

"Yes," Elethior says. "I told you before that I was never involved in your ill-advised pranks, but if you insist on bringing that nonsense into our partnership . . ." He trails off and looks at me with a too-pleasant smile. "You started this. But I'll finish it."

Heat creeps across my face. Not rage this time. Something . . . definitely not rage.

I swing back to my desk. "Get to work, Tourael. We have *my* project to do."

His stifled laughter sounds tinny in the big lab.

It's not a huge sacrifice to work on my project. I'm still in the early stages, so we silently—separately—spend a few days ensconced in reading and note-taking. I hammer out things to try based on said reading and note-taking—only I have to, *get to,* share it with Elethior.

I wheel my whiteboard in front of the window and start a list of potential evocation spells that can be used as jumping-off points for my safety net idea. I'd ordinarily put it in a document on my laptop, but we're *collaborating,* and I'm vehemently pretending I'm not now overly aware of Elethior in the lab.

Gods-damned brain had to go and fuck up my already fragile truce with him by realizing, *shit,* he does have nice arms.

Thursday morning, before he's there, I stuff his desk with kindergarten workbooks. He hasn't reactivated a protection ward. Sucker.

He gets in while I'm scribbling a new idea on the board.

"Sebastian."

I roll my shoulders under the huge sweatshirt I borrowed from Orok. Not a hazmat suit, but it'll do. "Yes, partner dearest?"

Elethior's quiet for a beat, like I tripped him up, and I grin at the board before turning.

"Is something wrong?" I ask.

He swings around in his chair and holds up the five children's workbooks I'd shoved in the clutter of his desk. "I have no need for evocation texts, but you're sweet to think of me."

I cap the whiteboard marker a bit too hard. "I'm surprised you found them in your—" I gesture at his mass of *stuff* that has, against my warning, crept over into my workstation. I kick an offending item: a grocery sack containing a bag of chips and other snacks. "For gods' sakes, Elethior, the demarcation line, warfare, the collapse of our tentative peace—"

"Hey!" He shoves up out of his chair. "Don't crush it."

He grabs the grocery sack and pulls out a—not a bag of chips.

A thing of dog food?

He checks a few other items, a container of dried fruit, one of birdseed, before he decides they're unharmed and slides the bag closer to his workstation.

Okay. I got nothing.

When he dusts his hands off and straightens, I must have a perplexed look on my face.

He blushes.

Those two stripes, perfectly level on either cheekbone.

Orok's hoodie is way too thick; sweat drenches my torso and I curse myself up and down and all around.

"They're, uh—" Elethior rubs the back of his neck, flexing that gods-damned bicep. "They're for Nick."

He might as well have yodeled for how much it derails me. "What? What's for Nick?"

Elethior motions at the bag. "The food."

"Is for Nick."

"Yes."

"My fox familiar. *Nick.*"

"Despite the absurdity of naming your familiar something so mundane, *yes*. That Nick. How many other Nicks do you and I have in common?"

"We don't even have *that* Nick in common because he's *my* familiar. Why are you buying my familiar food?"

Another awkward shift. "I figured it would serve as an apology to him for the way I reacted to his presence." Elethior's face gets the teensiest bit self-aggrandizing. "It's not his fault his owner is a stubborn asshole who thinks invisibility is *funny*."

"I told you." I sit on the edge of my desk. "He *likes* being invisible. An ex-girlfriend got pissed at me and cursed him, but joke's on her, because he was *thrilled*. Despite your low opinion of me, I am capable of at least *basic* spell work, so of course I undid it. But there's nothing in the world more heartbreaking than a depressed fox, and it fucked with our wizard-familiar bond. So I put the curse back on him; he's happy, his invisibility has the added benefit of freaking people out, and everyone wins."

Elethior's lips part in disgust. "Your ex-girlfriend cursed your familiar?"

"Hence the *ex* part. Apparently I can be a workaholic and she felt I neglected her for my junior year course load. But let's loop back—you bought my familiar food?"

His blush deepens. "I looked into what foxes eat and bought a few things for the next time you summon him. Again, as an apology."

"You bought my familiar food." My lips curve into a grin. "You bought Nick *snacks*."

Elethior translates my smile with an exasperated huff. "Laugh it up, Walsh." He trudges back to his desk. "You've found yet another source of control over me. I've got a soft spot for animals, what can I say? Fuck off."

"What's your familiar?" The question's out of me like a rock from a slingshot. I'm smiling still and my chest's all tight and tingly and I think maybe it's some kind of cardiac event? Surely it's not from Elethior. Buying snacks. For Nick.

Elethior toys with a pen, seated at his desk, his back to me again. "A desert rosy boa," he says. "Named Paeris." He looks back at me. "You know, a name *worthy* of a familiar."

His expression becomes a challenge, daring me to mock him, a Tourael, for having a snake familiar. The jabs create themselves.

But I kick the toe of my Converse against the tile. "*Zootopia*."

"Excuse me?"

"*Zootopia*. The movie? That's where his name's from. Nick, the fox."

Elethior's confused gaze widens until he snorts.

I throw my eyes skyward. "Don't—"

"You named your familiar after a character in a children's movie?" He laughs again, rubbing the skin over his nose. "You would. Of course you would."

"I'm leaving your *snake* business alone, so you don't get to mock me for Nick's name. Besides, I was drunk, and it seemed fitting."

Elethior chuckles one more time but waves his hand in surrender. "Fine. It's added to our truce."

His smile is too soft.

I knot the sleeves of Orok's hoodie around my hands.

"Good," I say.

"Good," he repeats.

"Excellent." Fuck. "Can we—" I wave at my whiteboard. "And, I'd like to point out, you've contributed *no* ideas to my list. Maybe there isn't anything useful to conjuration after all."

Granted, I've only added *one* idea to my own list—a rune that softens the severity of any lightning spell; figured something's gotta be in there about affecting multiple spells with one single spell—but still.

Elethior doesn't echo my thought, though it's clear on his face. "There's a spell I've been researching by a conjuration wizard in the twelfth century. Kojyngilla. She used it to braid several spells into one, but I'm still trying to work out if her spell was successful or if it's something historians recorded but was never tested." He lifts one of the kindergarten workbooks. "But now, I've got all these extra assignments on my plate. I mean, I have to write the alphabet several times. And, oh, there are coloring sheets for each letter, too? I'll be here all night."

He smiles at me. *Smiles.* Not smirks, not grimaces.

"Good. Okay. Thanks. Perfect." Too many monotone words in a row but my hands can't burrow any deeper into Orok's sleeves, and running out of the room isn't an option.

I sit back at my desk and grab my phone, tapping frantically on the screen. This conversation is over and I am very, very busy.

My dad tried to call me again. He left a voicemail.

My body already feels like it wants to claw out of itself, so I delete it without listening to it. Honestly, it's nice to have something to do with my hands so I'm not pretending to be distracted.

Elethior turns back to his desk when it's clear I'm done interacting with him. But with every passing second, I *feel* the memories of joking with him, of him smiling at me, of all this *bonding* we're doing. We hop-skip-jumped right over professional and into camaraderie, and no part of me is okay with that.

He was only supposed to be another greedy, power-hungry Tourael.

He wasn't supposed to buy treats for my *fox*.

I drop my phone, pull out one of my own books, and research nothing that sticks in my brain.

Chapter Seven

The next day, Elethior's stolen all my pens.

I check my desk for more, and he's cast a darkness spell inside the drawers so there very well might be some in there, but I can't see them.

He played a prank on me. *Elethior,* king of *maturity,* played a prank *on me.*

I can feel him at his workstation, reclined in his chair with his feet on his desk, watching for my reaction.

A tremor starts in the center of my palm.

I slam the drawer closed, leaving the darkness spell intact, and fire up my laptop. "You get that research done about Kojyngilla?"

Silence is thick in the air. Another abyss that tugs on me, beckons me to fall.

His feet smack against the floor when he sits upright. "Yeah. I did," he says, voice stiff. "It's worth testing. I can add it to the board."

He stands to do that.

I throw myself out of the chair. "No, I got it."

I wince. I'm being a dick. But I write his idea on my list, bringing us to a grand total of . . . two. Awesome.

I'm not sure what I'll say to him when I turn around, but the awkwardness is taken away from me as a faint buzzing vibrates from his pocket.

He pulls out his phone and glances at the screen, back up at me——then does a double take at his phone.

The energy shifts. An undeniable narrowing.

His face pales and he answers, shoving the phone against his ear. "Hello?"

The responding voice is too low for me to hear, but I catch a caring tone, and it's obviously someone Elethior recognizes; his eyelids flutter.

"It's fine, Martha. I'm at school, but anytime, I told you. What happened?"

A better lab partner would step out, give him some privacy.

But I'm drawn closer to him, especially when his eyes stop moving and go glassy.

"Is she conscious?" he asks, and his voice cracks.

Martha responds.

"Yeah," he says quickly. "I'm on my way."

He hangs up, staring down at his phone again in a stupor.

Then he's in action, grabbing his jacket off his chair. It gets caught on the leg and makes the chair roll toward him, but Elethior's looking at his phone, typing with one hand, unaware that the sleeve is tangled; he's shaking, I don't know how he can even read whatever he's writing on his phone.

"Elethior—"

"I have to leave. I have to—*gods damn it*." He yanks his jacket and the chair slams into his knees with an audible crack.

Elethior buckles and curses but tries to free his jacket again. It's still stuck, and he lets out a frustrated, heartbreaking cry.

I'm in front of him. My hands are on his upper arms. "Elethior. Stop. Look at me. What do you need?"

He hears me. Enough to meet my eyes, and I see him catch his breath.

"My mom," he whispers. "She's at a care facility. That was one of her nurses. She's—" The muscles in his brow jolt. "She had a seizure. I don't—I have to go."

He tries to step around me, but I don't let up my hold on him.

"Elethior, *stop*. Okay, you need to get to her facility. How are you getting there?"

He grunts in connection and looks back down at his phone. "That's what I was doing. My car. My driver—I was texting my driver. Shit." He mutters the last word to himself and tries to text again, his hand less shaky now.

I disentangle his coat from the chair and pass it to him before grabbing my own.

He frowns at me, at my coat.

"Making sure you get to your car. Where's he meeting you?"

Elethior puts on his coat, his glassy eyes flicking agitatedly, like there's something he's trying to find. "Um, behind the building. He'll be there in five. I need—"

"What else? You've got your phone, your wallet?"

He nods and spots the whiteboard. "We're supposed to be working."

"For fuck's sake, Elethior." I hook his arm and haul him toward the door.

He goes without a fight.

I drag him from the lab and through Bellanor Hall until we topple out in the rear parking lot. There are a few potholes from the dagger hail, and construction crews are hard at work on them. The sky is clear and bright blue, a jarring, too-cheery backdrop for the way Elethior's still pale.

A car pulls up. He stares at it, not making a move to get in.

"This your car?" I ask.

He winces and seems to now realize we're outside.

"Yeah." He's holding his phone in one hand and flexing the fingers of his other.

I open the car door for him. "Is there anyone you can call? Someone to be with you?"

His eyes meet mine, and I know before he has to say anything. I think I knew the moment the energy changed back in the lab.

"Get in." I hold the door wider.

He folds himself into the car.

I nudge his calf with my foot. "Scoot."

He obeys on autopilot and it isn't until I'm plopping into the seat that he spins on me.

"What are you doing?"

"Going with you." I shut the door and pat the seatback in front of me. "We're good."

The driver maneuvers out of the parking lot, jostling over black-top rubble.

Elethior's gaping at me. "Wha—why?"

I sit back with an air of nonchalance I sure as hell don't feel. My palms are sweating and tension wraps in a thick band across my chest, squeezing slowly.

But hey, this car's nice. Like, *really* nice. Plush seats, leather, probably.

"Who would you call to be with you?" I ask. The black upholstery on the roof of the car is fascinating.

Elethior's quiet. For too long.

He says *nothing*. Not one single name.

He has friends, right? I've seen him at parties with people. And yeah, Arasne was an asshole, but the Tourael family is huge—surely there's someone in his lineage who isn't a prick?

I swallow the implied answers he gives me to those questions. If I let them linger, they'll choke me.

"You're not going alone," I tell him. And I do look at him now, through a forced, overly confident smile. "Okay? This isn't a thing you do on your own."

He gasps like he hasn't breathed since he answered his phone, and when he exhales, it's in a self-deprecating huff.

"Fantastic," he mutters. "This is how you want to be spending your day."

"Well, this sure as hell isn't how you want to be spending *your* day."

His eyes are still glassy, and that worsens until his feeble attempt at a shield disintegrates.

"She's been having seizures on and off the past few months," he whispers. He taps his palm on the seat as his jaw works. "They're trying to work out a new medicine for her. But they haven't figured it out yet. And each seizure she has—"

He stops talking.

Leans back against the seat and pinches the skin between his eyes.

That band of tension around my chest clamps painfully, leaves me winded.

He inhales another gasping, anxious breath before he lowers his hand from his eyes and works his tongue against the inside of his cheek.

"Thank you," he says to the back of the driver's seat.

I plant my elbow on the door, curling up as far from him as I can get in this admittedly spacious luxury town car.

So. This is happening.

Casually accompanying Elethior to where his mom might be—

Nope. Not gonna think that.

It takes about twenty minutes in stop-and-start traffic before the driver pulls up outside a building not far from the Center City neighborhood, a sign out front declaring it the Blooming Grove. Elethior's been glued to his phone but Martha hasn't called again, which is good, right? Although, she knows he's coming, so she wouldn't want to deliver bad news via phone call.

The moment the car stops, I pop open my door, climb out, then bend back over, knowing Elethior won't have moved.

As expected, he's still staring down at his phone, tugging on a strand of his hair.

"Hey," I say. "We're here."

Elethior startles.

The driver has the stoic, I'm-used-to-working-for-people-with-money thing down pat, because he has almost no emotion when he says, "I'll wait here."

But he looks back at Elethior and adds, his voice tempering, "For however long you need."

It's unnecessary, since that's the guy's whole job, but Elethior manages an unsteady smile. That smile transfers to me, and freezes.

"He can take you back to campus," Elethior offers, nodding at the driver. "You don't have to, um, come in. This is enough."

I step back onto the sidewalk. "No. Get out of the car."

"Sebastian—"

"Get out of the car, and don't make me say it again. If I *do* have to say it again, I'll call you a dumbass, and decorum frowns on calling anyone a dumbass in a family emergency."

He smiles.

It's small and real.

The cold winter wind is the reason I can feel my face reddening.

Elethior peels himself out of the car and pockets his phone. He looks up at the building, a four-story stone façade right against the sidewalk. It's . . . pretty. Pretty in a *this is definitely a care facility in a city but we worked with what we got; ignore the sterile feeling and the metropolis vibes and focus on these ornate buttresses* way.

Elethior heads for the stairs by the front door, his movements automatic. I follow, watching him closely, my muscles wound to spring to any action he might need.

We stop by the doors, and after a beat, a buzzer sounds before they *whoosh* open. A security camera above catches my eye; they must've recognized Elethior.

We step inside a reception area. There's a desk off to the right before the space opens into a hallway, the white paneled walls and polished wood floor at odds—one feels appropriately bleak and clinical, the other cozy and nice.

A middle-aged half-elven woman sits behind the desk, and she looks up with a smile full of recognition and sympathy.

"Thio," she says. "Martha's waiting—she's in with your mom and Dr. Chrosk."

Elethior comes to an abrupt halt. His hands clench and unclench at his sides, and I watch from slightly behind him as his mouth opens, closes, everything about him grasping and unsure.

"Is she okay?" I ask for him. "His mom?"

Elethior makes a noise like a muffled whimper. Like—relief. That I asked so he didn't have to.

The receptionist looks at me, then Elethior, and her smile softens. "They've got her stabilized. She's a fighter, your mom. Why don't you go on in and talk to Dr. Chrosk?"

Elethior sags forward so much I worry he'll collapse right in half, so I grab his arm and hook it with mine again, the way I hauled him out of the lab.

"Which way?" I ask the receptionist. I catch her name tag now that I'm closer. Nithroel.

Nithroel gestures to the right. "Down the hall, room—"

"I got it," Elethior says quickly and jerks out of my hold. "I'm fine, Sebastian."

He walks away, shoulders bunching, and I'm left with my mouth hanging open.

"Don't take it personally, hon." Nithroel's sympathetic smile widens. "We see a lot of stress reactions here. It's not you."

It shouldn't be me, I want to say. It should be a friend or a family member, not his *lab partner.*

Elethior's gone now, down the hall Nithroel indicated; he didn't wait for me. I only came so he'd have someone here if his mom wasn't okay, and his mom *is* okay, so . . . I should go?

But as I stand in indecision, wondering why tension is still gripping the daylights out of me, Nithroel slides something across the desk. Two visitor passes.

"He's here so often, we usually let him right on through, but give that to him, will you? And pin yours to your coat or shirt."

"Oh. Actually, I'm not sure I'll—"

"You're the first person he's brought here." That smile of hers is too analytical. "I'm sure it was hard for him."

"It's not like that," I tell her. "I'm only here . . . it was bad timing."

"These things never have good timing." Nithroel pushes the badges closer. "Room 125."

I look toward the hallway again, my brow furrowing.

Gods damn it.

I scoop up the badges, clip one to my coat, and hurry down the hallway.

The door for room 125 is open, all the others shut and quiet. I steel myself before ducking inside.

The room is long and narrow, with a raised bed surrounded by medical equipment. That's where the similarities end between a hospital and this space; the rest of it is a forest.

Plants are everywhere, potted trees and vines tendrilled around the ceiling, rainbows of flowers in vases on every free surface. The walls are painted a rich hunter green and a brown leather sofa sits opposite the bed next to a sturdy oak table and chairs. A short book-shelf is stuffed not just with books, but sculptures and picture frames and knickknacks, and the air smells of blossoms and greenery, a quick hit of wilderness in this care facility.

Elethior's next to the bed, talking with a halfling woman in a lab coat; so, doctor. A human woman in pink scrubs is taking vitals from the person on the bed.

His mom is human, with straight blonde hair cut in a bob around her sunken face, eyes shut. Her chest rises and falls stutteringly.

The nurse turns to enter data into a tablet on the bed when she notices me, clocking my visitor pass with a patient smile. "Are you lost?"

Elethior glances up, his face flipping through a few complex emotions. Like he thought I'd left. Or expected me to.

I hold out the other visitor pass to him. "Nithroel said something about a SWAT team rappelling from the ceiling and arresting you if you're caught without a badge."

The nurse flicks her eyes between me and Elethior.

Elethior's lips form a thin line. He takes the badge. "Thanks."

"Is she—" I'm not sure what to ask, how to ask it. My shoulders ache with holding still.

"She's okay. No lasting effects," Elethior says. He looks at the doctor. "Right?"

The doctor pats Elethior on the arm. "We'll get her medications balanced so this stops happening, and for now, we're keeping her under a tight watch. She'll likely be out for some time, but you're welcome to stay, as always."

Elethior's staring at his mom, gripping the frame at the foot of the bed.

The nurse—whose name tag says Martha—holds the tablet to her chest. "She likes to give us all a good scare. Don't you?" She drops a fond smile on Elethior's mom. "Has to keep us on our toes, this one."

I blow out a long exhale. She's fine.

She's fine, and I forced my way in here, into something incredibly private for Elethior.

I back up a step. "Okay. I should—"

Martha smiles at me, that same perceptive smile Nithroel had. "Thio, aren't you going to introduce him to your mother?"

Oh. *Oh.*

Oh no.

I shake my head as Elethior pivots sharply from the bed and marches for the hall. "Sebastian. A word?"

Yeah. Several, probably.

He cuts out of the room and I follow, hands bunched in my pockets.

We stop to the side of the open door and my head lowers, eyes on his boots.

Before he can speak, I grind out, "I'm sorry."

Silence.

I force my gaze up, braced to find him glaring at me—

But he's frowning.

"Why?" he asks.

"I thought you needed someone with you, but I'm intruding. I'll catch a bus back to campus." Fuck if I'm going to use his car now. "I'm . . . I'm glad your mom's all right."

I get two steps away when his hand wraps around my arm.

Like it did at the cocktail party, it freezes me, no fight or flight, no reaction other than complete inertness.

We're both trapped in that inertia for four full heartbeats. I hear them, feel them in the base of my jaw.

"I won't be here long," he tells me. "Enough to sit with her some. Then we'll go back to school. If that's okay?"

We'll go back to school.

Testing the weight of each word, I nod at the room and ask, "Do you want me to—"

His hand spasms on my arm and I think I pushed too far, misread what he was saying, but he releases his hold.

"Come on," he says. "I'll introduce you."

This thing has hurtled so far over any boundaries that I'm not sure we'll ever find our way back, and everything Nithroel and Martha implied tells me that accepting this would be . . . significant.

Elethior and I are working together. That's all.

It *isn't* significant. It won't be.

"Sure." I wince. "But—I don't want to wake her up?"

Elethior's smile is sad. "We won't wake her up. She doesn't . . . even when she's awake, she's—" His face falls. "We won't wake her up," he repeats.

I bite my lips together until pain stabs down my neck. "Ah. Then, yeah, of course."

Of course. Like any of this is assumed.

He heads back into the room and stops at the end of the bed. The doctor and Martha are still taking readings, but they flash us encouraging smiles when I stand next to Elethior.

The bookshelf is behind us. All the photos are of a younger Elethior with his mom—her arms around him as they smile at the camera, both of them covered in what's probably flour and laughing in a kitchen; a selfie where they're wearing hiking gear. Her eyes are bright and clear, and his are, too.

There's no one else in any of the pictures.

Elethior clears his throat and I whip around. He's looking at his mom, not at me, didn't even notice I'd snooped on his photos.

"Mom," he says, his voice thick. "This is Sebastian Walsh. The lab partner I was telling you about. He—"

"You were telling your mom about me?"

His eyes roll up to the ceiling as a smile bursts across my face.

"*Complained* to her about you, more like." He arcs his eyes around to me. "Shut up."

"I didn't say anything." My grin, though, is speaking volumes.

Martha suppresses a chuckle.

After a heavy, put-upon sigh, Elethior waves at the bed. "Sebastian, this is my mom. Dr. Rebecca Holmes."

Holmes. Not Tourael.

"And Martha." Elethior waves at the nurse, then the doctor. "Dr. Chrosk."

I smile at them before looking at the woman on the bed, still sleeping.

"Hi, Dr. Holmes," I say. "It's nice to meet you."

Martha coos but covers it by clapping her hands. "I'll have Nithroel get you boys some tea, yes? Take a seat, we won't be long finishing up with her now."

She scurries out of the room to Dr. Chrosk's amused headshake.

Elethior obediently sinks down onto the couch, one arm spread across the back, the other propped on the armrest and cradling his jaw.

I sit on the edge of the couch and have to physically restrain myself from bouncing my knee. "Once they're done with her, I'm going to set the record straight, just so you know."

He tips his head.

"Whatever lies you've told your mom about me," I explain. "I'm going to tell her the truth. Can't have her thinking I'm as terrible as you've no doubt said."

Out of the corner of my eye, I see a stunned smile light Elethior's mouth. He watches me in silence, that watching turning to studying the longer it stretches, studying turning to unspoken words I don't want, can't handle.

My heart hums, making it hard to get a full breath, so I lean back against the couch and nudge my shoulder where his hand's nearly resting on my neck.

"Contain your manspreading, Elethior," I grumble.

A pause.

Then he chuckles and lowers his hand into his lap.

When Monday rolls around, Elethior and I work in silence as thick as it was when we were actively ignoring each other. Only now, it's sluggish from an added strain of politeness.

It's all from me. Elethior's matching me, and what I'm forcing up are mile-high walls.

Days pass, and there are no more pranks. No more jokes.

I ask how his mom's doing; he tells me she hasn't had any more seizures but doesn't elaborate, and I nod and get back to work.

Soon, the whiteboard is full of scribbled ideas, none of them promising. We use some of our grant money to ship in research on a few ancient conjuration wizards Elethior comes up with. I pour myself into books I haul over after stints at my library job, pushing the limits of caffeine with how late I stay every night. Elethior mimics me again, but not like he's trying to one-up me; this is like he's gauging my reaction for something.

Which pisses me off.

He's not even *fighting* me on our sickening civility. Is this what he's wanted the whole time? For us to blandly shuffle around each other, working in anemic silence? Fuck him. Fuck him for being okay with this boring-ass dynamic.

And fuck me for being the one to implement it and stick to it.

Can't be friendly with him. Can't hold him at a distance. Can't drop the grant. Can't *escape*.

My mom texts for updates about *your project with that Tourael. Your father and I are so proud.*

And dad keeps calling. He doesn't leave more voicemails. Just lets the missed calls every few days be enough of a disturbance.

Clawstar checks in. Nothing threatening or passive aggressive, a simple *How is your project going, Mr. Walsh? We're looking forward to working with you!* But I still send back what is probably a too-thorough email explaining how I've been advancing my project and that I'm making the most of this grant and see, you haven't made a bad choice in giving me the job.

I'm pretty sure my blood content is 85 percent caffeinated beverages by the end of the week.

This semester is going to kill me.

I trudge into the lab Friday morning, bleary-eyed, clutching an extra-large drip coffee with a quad shot of espresso, which is apparently my regular order now.

Elethior's already here, dressed in his usual tight T-shirt and fitted dark jeans, his hair swept into a messy knot at the back of his head. He doesn't look ragged or like he hasn't been sleeping, which is good; it means his mom is okay, if he's here and not frazzled.

He's also standing in front of my whiteboard.

Writing on my whiteboard.

It's *our* project now, but that's still been *my* whiteboard, and only *I've* been writing on it. Only *I've* been touching it.

He hasn't noticed me, his cell phone pinched between his ear and shoulder as he writes, tracing the same rune over and over with progressive intensity.

"Yes," he says sharply. "*I told you—*"

His eyes connect with mine and he stiffens.

"I have to go," he says into the phone, and whatever's said in farewell makes his eyes roll in a grimace. But he clicks off and stuffs his phone into his pocket.

My gaze flicks to that pocket in question.

His cheeks pinken. "Arasne," he grumbles.

"Anything concerning?"

Elethior shakes his head, tongue pushing against his teeth in exasperation. "No. Her usual invasive pressure. Irritating, but—"

"Okay. Good." I shove my bag and coffee onto my desk, stomp over to him, rip the marker out of his hand, and give him my best sleep-deprived, at-the-end-of-my-very-last-wit glare. "Don't touch my stuff."

Elethior blinks in surprise. I'm making eye contact and that was *almost* banter, if not for the way I'm holding strong in my offense. This is more direct interaction than we've had all week.

He snatches the marker back. "Before she interrupted me, I was putting down an idea I got when I was cooking dinner last night."

I grab the marker again. "Then tell me, and *I'll* write it down." Boundaries. I have strapped myself to boundaries, and by gods, I'll let the bulldozer of stubbornness squash me flat before I give up this very, very flimsy grasp on the last vestiges of my sanity.

Elethior tosses his hands up. "You know what? Fine. You write it down. Write: *measuring cup.*"

I lean in to the board.

Then stop. "What?"

He crosses his arms. "Measuring cup."

"Repeating isn't an explanation."

"If you'd let me write it down, I would've written an explanation, too."

"So, again, *tell me,* and I'll—"

"I'm allowed to talk to you now?"

Oh, *fuck* no.

He's not going to point out our weirdness when this is the exact weirdness he once pushed for, all mature and collected.

My jaw clamps, muscles bunching near my ears. "What's your idea, Tourael?"

He holds long enough that I think he won't tell me.

"The research I was doing on Kojyngilla," he says. "Her spell to braid several pieces of magic together wasn't one spell; it was several variations that she used depending on the other spells she wanted to combine. That's a common idea in a lot of conjuration work, having variations on the same spell to fit different wizards. Since the conjurer is the source of energy, we make room for differences from person to person."

I lower the marker and look at him, listening.

"And it got me thinking, how it's like cooking," he continues. "If a recipe calls for two and a half cups of an ingredient, you wouldn't make a two-and-a-half-cup measuring device. You'd use a cup and a half cup, and double up the cup. Same for your spell." He waves at the whiteboard. "You can create baseline energy caps for different expectations. Wizards could select the combination they'd need for their individual spells, but *you* would only need to create a handful of variations rather than shove thousands of options into one single-use spell."

My face slackens.

Holy shit.

I use the sleeve of my sweater to scrub a clean space on the whiteboard and scribble out his idea.

A handful of general capping spells of different sizes rather than something that targets the exact amounts of everything.

Oh my gods.

Oh my gods.

It's so dumb. So dumb and so obvious. Why didn't I see it? I was going too big with the idea, trying to get it to fit *perfectly* in every spell. But it was never about fitting the safety net to every single spell; it's about fitting each spell *to the safety net*.

I stumble back from the board, my body vibrating like a hummingbird having an anxiety attack. "Oh my gods."

"We'll have to test it," Elethior says, staring at my chicken-scratch handwriting like it wasn't his profound idea. "We'll need to develop a few variations on it, but—"

He turns away from the board with a smile.

That smile plummets off. "Sebastian?"

I'm shaking. Gods, I'm shaking; haven't stopped shaking since—since the cocktail party, with him out under the snow and the way the individual flakes stuck to his eyelashes, and how he'd told his cousin not to kick me off the grant.

He might've given me a way to cap spells so no one has to risk draining their components.

Elethior Tourael might've given me what I've been wanting for six years. Since—

Is that all you've got?

My vision goes spotty and I throw the marker on my desk, start pacing. We haven't tested this idea yet. It might not work.

"Sebastian?" Elethior steps into my path. "Are you—"

I bump into him. That solid chest and the smell of green plants and flowers. Those stupid lip rings—

They're warm.

They're warm because they're pressed to his mouth, and his mouth is warm; and I know that because I'm kissing him.

I'm kissing him.

Neither of us moves. Just pillowy lips and metal rings.

Then he—then he *gasps,* sucks all the air straight out of my body, and it sounds so excruciatingly ardent.

His hands plunge into my hair and I'm not kissing him now; *he's* kissing *me,* eating at my mouth, and I let him.

He tastes *so good.*

Like mint toothpaste and berries and coffee; breakfast. Like the overwhelming diaphanous cloud of his cologne, invading my senses with springtime as he licks into my mouth, all velvet tongue and those sharp piercings. The kiss whips through me in a furor that weakens my knees and excises a noise from me that I've never made before, a rapturous moan.

"Fuck," Elethior growls against me. "Sebastian, *yes.*"

We're kissing.

I'm kissing Elethior.

My lungs close up and I shove away from him, I *leap* away from him.

This isn't—this didn't happen. Oh my gods, *this didn't happen.*

"No," I say to his fiasco of a workstation, *not* looking at him. "No, *no.*"

Then I do the only thing I can possibly do in a situation like this.

I snatch a vial off my component belt, turn myself invisible, and run from the room.

Chapter Eight

I've created a self-destruction infinity loop: What happens when the stupid thing I do is the catalyst that makes me want to do stupid things? Do I keep doing the same stupid thing over and over for eternity?

Not that I'm going to go back and kiss Elethior again.

Oh my gods, I kissed Elethior.

Then turned invisible.

And ran.

And left all my shit in the lab.

Which I can never go back to.

Because *I kissed Elethior.*

Of all the ways I feared losing this grant, *kissing my lab partner* was not one of them. But I have to drop out now, right? I have to drop out of the grant, probably the whole university, and move. Change my name. Join a druid commune.

What the *fuck* was I thinking?

I know Orok's at practice; they have their first spring season training game on Sunday. I veer across campus, and the moment my invisibility spell wears off, I check over my shoulder like I'm on the lam. But I don't see Elethior coming after me.

I get to the rawball field and find a configuration I vaguely recognize as one Ivo was talking about at dinner a few weeks back. Stone towers, endless pits, a thin river of lava cutting down the side, all courtesy of the team's artificers, usually students from the engineering school. Players are stationed on top of obstacles and on the ground, all shouting encouragement at someone I can't see downfield, but blasts go up there, magic bursts of arcane blue.

The coach floats above the field, held aloft by a levitation spell, and she blows a series of whistles. "Dunst—you polymorphed too soon. Monroe, Rodayne"—oh hey, Orok and Crescentia—"nice hustle, but you came in too late. Everyone, run it again!"

The players scurry into other positions, and after a beat, another whistle blast sets them into motion.

A handful of people watch from the stadium seating. It'll be mostly filled on Sunday; even for a training game, there'll be an outpouring of school spirit for the Manticores. For now, I take one of the lowest seats, hunched over, hands stuffed in my pockets. But the longer I sit, watching the team run drills, the more I realize . . .

I don't feel that panicky.

Even though I'm still rather exhausted and can't remember the last time I had real food, I'm not as jittery as I'd been only an hour ago. I'm not blacking out with the drive to feel something else as a counterbalance to feeling too much, and what I *am* feeling is—okay? Foolish. Embarrassed. Dumb. But I'm not freaking out, and I think I only ran out of the lab because I *expected* to freak out.

Why am I not freaking out?

The coach calls a water break, and as players pour off the field, most heading for the metal benches stacked with towels and water bottles, Orok takes off his helmet and spots me, his eyebrows popping.

He snatches water from his duffel bag, jogs over, and plops on the seat next to me.

"What'd you do?" he asks, guzzling half the bottle in one go. He's drenched in sweat, his practice uniform covered in grass stains and what has to be remnants of a magic blast.

"Who says I did anything?"

"You're watching my practice." He motions at the field. "You've either had a complete personality change and taken a sudden interest in rawball, or—" He twists to eye me, then looks at his teammates by the benches and groans. "You're not still trying to get with Crescentia, are you?"

I blanch. "What? No. That was months ago, and—how do you remember that? You were shitfaced. But no. I'm not here for—for *that*."

My tone warbles. I am here for *that,* sort of. Just not involving Crescentia.

All that calmness, all that *not* panicking, screws up tight. I can't get my throat to work right.

Orok's eyes narrow in concern. "Seb? You—"

"I kissed Elethior," I whisper. It barely comes out at all. A hiss of sound, and I sit there, frozen, reliving that moment.

The softness of his mouth.

The contrasting bite of his lip rings.

The way he'd groaned. The clench of his fingers in my hair. How he'd seemed *relieved* I'd kissed him, like he'd . . . like he'd been wanting it.

My knee bounces hard and I watch Orok. His reaction is all that matters.

He stares at me, his eyes round, his lips parted.

"It was fucked up," I say, and here comes the panic, racing in like a mudslide. "It's a complete betrayal of everything that happened, and I'm sorry. I'm sorry. Gods, say something?"

The water bottle crinkles in his grip and he downs the rest of it before carefully screwing the lid back on. He's studying me in a way that feels too levelheaded. He's always been too mellow, and I need him to be *mad at me*.

Orok cocks his head. "You like him?"

"I—what?" I flinch. "He's a *Touruel.*"

Orok rolls his eyes. "That's your hang-up, not mine. All I know is, you've been talking about this guy pretty much nonstop. For someone you claim to hate, you spent a *lot* of time going on about those treats he bought Nick."

My face burns. This isn't how he should be reacting.

"*I kissed Elethior.* You're not—you should be angry with me. I fucked up. Again."

His face collapses. He looks heartbroken for some reason, and before I can figure out why, he shifts to face me fully and grabs my shoulders.

"You are not a fuckup, Seb," he tells me. He sighs, hands lowering to his lap. "I'm kind of hard on you, aren't I?"

"No, you're—I mean, I need it, right? I appreciate you looking out for me. Gods know what I'd get up to without you reining me in."

Orok scrubs angrily at his chin. "That's it, though. You don't *need* it. You have issues, but you're not broken. You can make choices and do things without my voice in your head questioning your motive. You liked kissing him?"

His coach blows her whistle, calling the players back. Orok doesn't move.

My heart thunders, a roiling storm in my chest, in the curve of my wrists.

You liked kissing him?

No. Elethior's . . . *Elethior.* He's infuriating and pretentious and everything, *everything,* that pisses me off.

"Yes," I whisper.

Orok grins. "Did he kiss you back?"

My face burns so hot it aches. "Yeah."

"I know you might not believe it right now," Orok says, "but this wasn't a fuckup. You like the guy. You kissed him. *That's* what it is. Simple."

"*Simple?* This wasn't—it *wasn't*—we can't—"

"Tell ya what." He knocks my shoulder with his fist. "After the Manticores secure what's sure to be an embarrassingly elaborate win on Sunday—"

"So humble."

"—we'll hit the party circuit with the express intent of finding a way for you to blow off steam. What you're *not* going to do is spiral out and punish yourself, okay? And if you thought you'd get that from me, that I'd berate you for this, well, too damn bad. You kissed someone you're interested in, and he kissed you back. Like I said. Simple."

He stands, and I stare at the spot he vacates, numb.

"Oh." Orok flattens the empty water bottle. "Speaking of voices in your head, your dad called me."

I whip an appalled look up at him. "What? What'd he want? What'd you tell him?"

"Nothing. I didn't answer. But he left a message saying how he wants to talk to you, and could I be the voice of reason and get you to call him?" Orok's face falls, that heartbroken deflation again. "But I don't have to be your voice of reason, because you're perfectly capable of making your own choices, Seb. And I'm sorry you feel like you have to question yourself."

"It's not because of you," I say softly.

He smiles, just as soft, just as unconvinced.

When he gets a few steps away, a mundane detail clicks in my brain.

"I left all my stuff in the lab."

He glances back at me, one brow lifted. "And?"

"And I can't go back. Not—not yet." I plaster on an utterly pathetic, wincing smile. "Can you go for me after practice and rescue my shit?"

Orok rolls his eyes up to the clouds. "Urzoth, give me strength. Yeah, I'll go."

"Love you."

He bats his hand as he jogs back to the field.

And I sit there in a stupor.

I hadn't expected him to support me. He was going to tell me I'd made a mistake. That I *am* spiraling again, that it's unfeasibly dumb to fuck around with your lab partner, especially when said lab partner rattles your heapin' helpin' of emotional baggage.

But if he doesn't think this is a bad thing.

Maybe . . . maybe it's not.

I scoff at myself.

I'd rather this be one of my fuckups. Then at least it'd be something I know how to deal with.

That Sunday, the Manticores *do* secure an embarrassingly elaborate win, prompting all students to set off celebrations that serve the dual purpose of both distracting me and hiding me. Surely, in the hordes that take over every bar, dance club, and restaurant within a ten-block radius of the stadium, Elethior won't be able to find me.

He emailed me, though. Once. On Friday night.

Sebastian,

Don't avoid me. We need to talk.

—Thio

Thio. Like we're *friends.*

See? This is what I need distracting from.

Orok landed a massive number of saves during the game, ever one of the team's best players, so I let his fame sweep me up and carry us to Prismatic, a club near the river. We used to frequent it in undergrad, but the shine of dancing all night wore off when grad school barged in with what is, quite frankly, an unreasonable demand on our time.

The club lives up to its name with a myriad of flashing lights spasming constantly, some magic, some not. Music throbs through the converted warehouse that gives a grunge vibe beneath the rainbow-hued illuminations. One full end is a bar with multiple bartenders scurrying—sometimes flying—around, pouring drinks called things like Guardian and Poison Cone and Fairy Lights. I'm almost certain the club owners pump pixie magic into the air, because the whole place always feels a *little* wobbly even if you haven't had anything to drink.

The club is already packed, but Orok's teammates drag us to one of the VIP areas where we're given champagne that glows a faint shimmering pink.

"Fae Plane champagne!" declares a cheerleader for the Manticores.

I pass my untouched flute to Orok. With the heaving lights and thudding music and swelling noise of such a tightly packed crowd, my limbs itch to move.

"Gonna dance," I shout into his ear.

He stops me with his elbow. He's in simple jeans and a corded brown sweater, which is going to be soaked in no time thanks to the heat of so many bodies in here, but he's never been one for club clothes. Not like the skinny jeans and silver crop-top tank I'm wearing; I even swapped my glasses for contacts, though I hate the way they feel, but they make dancing easier. Plus, it lets the eyeliner I swiped on pop more, and I roughed up my hair in that lazily messy way that'll still work once I'm doused in sweat later. We're going all in on blowing off steam, baby.

"You good?" Orok asks over the music.

"Not gonna drink. Just dance." I know better than to indulge in two vices at once, especially in my current emotional state.

The fact that I'm not that far gone is reassuring.

I'm getting over the whole kissing Elethior thing already, look at me go. By tomorrow, I'll be able to apologize for making things weird, and we'll carry on with our work.

"Good," Orok says, "but that's not what I meant."

I give him an excessively bright grin and pop both my thumbs.

He starts to say more when Ivo appears next to him. "Shots! Shots!"

Orok smiles good-naturedly before powering back both flutes of champagne, raising the empty cups like trophies, burping loudly, and bellowing, "MANTICORES, BITCHES!"

The entire VIP area *howls.* "Feel the sting! Feel the sting!"

I slip away with a laugh, ducking past the VIP ropes and weaving through the regular tables. Most of the people are students, some still decked out in Lesiara U gear, but my focus is on the dance floor.

Until a body blocks my path.

Well, two bodies.

I stumble back. The guys look familiar, but—

Ah. They're from the Conjuration Department. They were part of some pranks last year, but I was always more focused on their ringleader.

Who told me he wasn't, actually, involved in any of the pranks.

My shoulders go back with renewed interest. In the unsteady

light, it's hard to pick up distinguishing features, but both guys are taller than I am. One's human and wearing a Manticores T-shirt, holding three shots that fizzle and spark, and the other's half siren with bright blue hair and a sheen of teal to his skin.

Blue Hair smiles. He takes my arm, presumably to pull me closer to talk, but *nope*.

I yank away without hesitating.

His smile turns slick. "Haven't seen you poking around our lab this semester," he says, leaning in to be heard, and I eye him warily. "Does that mean Conjuration wins the feud?"

I honestly haven't thought about the interdepartmental feud in weeks, since the grant declared it *ended* and the focus of my own personal rivalry has been all up in my space. I also hadn't pieced together that since Elethior claimed he wasn't heading up the Conjuration Department's pranks, that meant someone else *was*.

I roll my eyes, and I can't believe *I'm* the one who's exasperated by all this. "The rivalry's on hold, didn't you get the memo? Though I guess your overlord didn't pass on the directive."

Blue Hair laughs. And touches my arm. *Again.*

I flinch away. *Again.* "What are you guys, freshmen?"

It has the intended effect.

Human scowls. Blue Hair's nose curls. "Seniors," he says.

"Ah. Great. I've been engaging in a prank war with baby undergrads."

"*Seniors,*" Blue Hair enunciates.

"*Babies,*" I shout back. And I wave my hands, trying to bat them aside. "Move, children, I have better things to do with my night."

But Blue Hair plucks a shot from Human's hand and holds it out to me. "Fine. Let's drink to the truce, then."

Are these the masterminds who've been plotting against me all these months? Though, it tracks—they fucked up the Evocation Department's spell components and generally enacted shit with no concern for the actual ramifications.

My eyes go to the shot, then back up to Blue Hair, who's smiling sweetly.

"If you think I'm going to drink anything you hand me, then you need to apologize to the university at your graduation and refuse your diploma."

Blue Hair's humor vanishes. Human glares at me, but my focus is on Blue Hair and the way his head slants forward, his pupils widening.

"Drink the shot, Sebastian Walsh," he tells me, and at the base of my neck, I feel the slightest fizzle of magic. It's immediately countered by the wards I always throw up around myself.

Fury lances through me.

Okay, playtime's over.

I glower. "Are you trying to *enchant* me into—"

A hand reaches out and seizes Blue Hair's shoulder. He swings around to—

Oh, fuck me.

Heat burns across my face even though Elethior isn't looking at me.

He snatches the shot from Blue Hair and sniffs it. The top's still sparking with tiny bursts of gold glitter, and one hits his nose, making him recoil.

Elethior holds the shot up to Blue Hair. "I interrupted. Here you are. Bottoms up."

Blue Hair hesitates, his eyes flashing to me. "Nah, it's for—"

Elethior's smile is flat. "Take the shot, Aqeanoe."

Even in the flashing rainbow colors, Aqeanoe—I prefer Blue Hair—pales. "I—"

"Unless there's some reason you wouldn't want to?" Elethior pushes. "Unless you attempted to *poison* a fellow student?"

"We're not on school grounds, man," says Human.

"Wow." I slow clap. "Really making a good case for the Conjuration Department's superiority. Why would our location matter if there was nothing wrong with the shot?"

Human's mouth slams shut and Aqeanoe scowls at him. "Dumbass," he snaps. Then, to me, "You shut up. This isn't—"

Elethior's grip on his shoulder must pinch tighter. Aqeanoe

staggers and winces. "Don't finish that thought. Take the shot or leave."

Aqeanoe grimaces at Elethior. Holding eye contact, he accepts the shot and downs it.

I chirp in surprise, but before I can get out a word, Aqeanoe's teal skin is covered in purple and gold stripes. Lesiara U's colors.

That's . . . that's it?

That's not even a good prank.

Aqeanoe tosses the empty shot glass aside. "There. Fuck, dude, you ruined it. Gods, you've always been a killjoy."

"This stupid rivalry is *over*." Elethior's volume doesn't seem to be due to the music; his brows are low, his eyes irate. "Lay off. Oh, and you're done here—Prismatic doesn't tolerate spiking drinks."

Elethior waves behind Aqeanoe to a security guard. I hadn't noticed him, but he folds out of the crowd with a snarl, orc tusks thick and shoulders pushing several feet wide.

Aqeanoe and Human protest, but the security guard corrals them away.

A disbelieving scoff bursts out of me and I scrub a hand over the back of my neck. "Holy shit. Is that how you see me? Gods, tell me I'm at least a *little* more respectable. I mean, I have subtlety. I have *standards*. I have—"

Elethior shifts in front of me, taking Aqeanoe's place, too close, too towering.

It's significantly less uncomfortable from him.

I make the obscenely stupid mistake of meeting his eyes.

I can still taste him. Mint and coffee and the external layer of his cologne teasing the edges of my senses. I can still feel *all of it, everywhere,* the kiss remembered in parts of my body that weren't complicit in it. The inside of my elbows. My eyelids.

"Are you all right?" he asks, bending in, his loose hair curtaining us on one side. His eyes run over my face like he's searching for injury or upset.

My tongue touches my lip. Feels one of the places where his piercings pressed to my skin.

He tracks the motion. Lingers on it.

My hand is still behind my neck and I tug it down to fist at my side. "Fine. Yeah. Thanks. But I—" Pride zaps up my spine. "I didn't need your help. How are you here?"

One side of his mouth cocks. "Your friend told me you'd be here."

"Who?"

His looks toward the VIP area.

Realization hits me in a drawn-out groan.

Orok, who I sent to get my stuff from the lab because I was a big coward.

Orok, who must've seen Elethior there, and they *talked about me*.

Orok, who used to be my closest friend, but is now dead to me, RIP to our relationship. We had a good run.

"Great." I suck my teeth. "Well, have a nice night, I'll be—"

I try to step around Elethior.

He matches me, blocking my path. "We need to talk."

"No, we don't." I wave at my ears. "Can't hear you in here anyway. So—"

I step to the other side.

He matches me again.

"Why?" I stop fighting to get past him, breathing hard. "We could show up tomorrow and get back to work. That's all we have to do. Work. We don't have to talk about it. *Ever.*"

"But what if I want to talk about it?" He's breathing hard, too. Chest heaving with the beat of the music, drums plummeting lower as the same lyric is repeated in a skittering stop-and-start, *Move with me, move—move with me, move—move with—*

I don't respond. Can't. My jaw deadbolts.

"What if I want to talk about it," he repeats, "because I can't stop thinking about it?"

A flash of orange light cuts across my vision, followed by a sharp flare of blue.

I shake my head. Shake it again, and hold up a hand to push against his chest, get some space.

Gods, he's wearing a black mesh short-sleeve button-up. It lets me feel the skin beneath, the rough abrasion of his chest hair, the heat of his body. And I can see his tattoos through the fabric, swirling across his shoulders, down his pecs.

The light shifts, a wash of magenta, and *kill me now*, his nipples are hard.

My head won't stop shaking, negating everything. "We don't like each other."

He doesn't respond for a beat. I manage to tear my eyes away from his chest to look up at him, and he's studying me like I'm one of his research books.

Then that analysis is gone, and he's smirking, the cutting, self-important cockiness I hate.

"I don't think liking each other is a prerequisite for that," he says.

For some reason, that sets my entire body on fire. An instantaneous frisson that scours my muscles, my nerves, the part of my face where I can feel his breath bathing down on me.

"You're unable to see beyond me being a Tourael?" he asks. He's so, so close to me.

I nod.

"Well, good," he tells me. "I'm unable to see you beyond a smartass, low-level evocation wannabe who would rather bother real wizards with childish antics than apply himself."

There's something wrong with me. Which is not a new revelation. But I've drilled down into a previously untapped vein of wrongness. My fingers tighten where they're still on his chest, tugging the fabric of his sheer shirt, pulling him closer, just *pulling*.

The music rises, and the lyrics roll, *Move with me, move—move with me, move—*

The beat drops. A cry goes up in the fall and bodies thrash harder on the dance floor.

My lips part and I'm sucking in his exhales, my eyes wide and unblinking on his.

It's the pixie magic. The slightly off-kilter sway of being in a club. It's the stress of this semester and the impending threat of graduation and all the hatred I let have space in my body finally breaking me.

I hold Elethior's gaze, giving my grip on his shirt one firm tug, before I let go and step past him.

This time, he allows it.

I cut around the remaining tables and push onto the dance floor, wiggling between people who are lost in the music and lights and effervescence of the night. We're all free here, equalized in the fantasy of escape, and my emotions crank to only simple extremes.

I'm sweating already, can feel it beading down my spine, in the palms of my hands. The song is all synthesizer and swelling drums, throbs that climb my legs, vibrate my thighs, settle in the base of my stomach.

My hands go up, and almost immediately, fingers ghost down the undersides of my biceps, over my armpits, along my sides, to settle on my hips. Every place he touches sparks so strongly that the club won't need their light shows—we can create pyrotechnics on our own.

"Is this okay?" The way he asks, forehead pressing to the back of my head, voice a muffled croon against the music—my body twitches with resistance.

"Don't do that." My arms jerk down, head angling to the side. "That's not what this is."

Elethior mimics my stiffness, but he doesn't peel his hands away from my hips. "Then what are we doing?"

"Using each other."

His fingers clamp my hips more firmly. I hiss, but it isn't bad.

It *should* feel bad.

It should feel like standing on that collapsed bridge behind the grocery store when I was younger and wondering if the levitation spell would fail; but it feels like the final time I did that, when I turned away instead of stepping into the abyss. When I chose to be safe.

He feels . . . *safe*.

My heart's been going at a sprint since he appeared beside me, so it's got nowhere to speed up under the wash of panicked adrenaline, and it all churns together, confusion and fear and *wanting*, such heady, dismantling *wanting*.

His voice is mostly tremors as he growls into my ear, "You want me to use your body, Sebastian?"

I don't trust what'll come out of my mouth, so I nod.

No thinking here. Just feeling.

Feeling those fingers conform to my hip bones.

Feeling my ass against the solid wall of his pelvis.

Feeling his face alongside my head, feeling his breath dust across my collarbone, feeling, *feeling*—

We sway with the music. Exploratory at first, finding the rhythm with the crowd, with each other.

The song builds and we let it take us faster, faster. The bass crashes and we jump with the other dancers. One of his hands leaves my hip to splay against my bare stomach and I loop my arm around his head, holding him there as I grind on him shamelessly. I'll be mortified by this in the morning.

Or maybe I won't.

Maybe I don't have to carry this with me. It doesn't have to be anything more than what it is now, an outlet. We don't like each other and don't have to. This is a safer detonation than screaming at each other. Although, not gonna lie, that's pretty hot, too.

The energy of our dancing changes. Nothing on the surface, no new song, no new moves; but the rock of my hips against his takes on a new gravitational pull, directing us in a wordless, fluid reorienting.

My heart goes sluggish, slowing everything to the frame-by-frame shuttering of my head dropping back against his shoulder.

His hand climbs my stomach. All the air leaves my lungs in a punctured groan that he has to feel, the rumble of it; he moves his hand up under my shirt, sliding between my pecs until he's gripping my neck and the lights go scarlet.

The beat falls again, but we miss the jump.

He's holding my body to him with his hand on my neck and fuck it if I'm not a boneless, compliant mess.

On the next swaying grind of my hips, he cants into me, letting me feel he's as hard as I am, and the knowledge skitters across my sweat-slicked skin like a gust of wind. Goose bumps erupt everywhere; I shiver in their attack.

My lips part, eyes pinched shut like I'm in pain. I am. It hurts, and it *doesn't,* and that hurts, too.

His fingers spasm on the pulse point in my neck. I turn my head and I know his face is right there. I can taste the heat on his mouth.

Our lips touch, a scratchy brush.

His thumb will leave a bruise under my jaw, and we hold there, panting into each other's mouths, bodies pressed together, limbs tangled. We're not dancing anymore. Just—just *gasping,* miring in each other.

Kissing Elethior Tourael should be as catastrophic as the worst thing I've done.

And it is.

But it's not a *bad* catastrophe, and I never knew, never *fucking* knew that calamities could be wondrous, too.

This isn't one of my self-destructive episodes. This isn't something I'll regret.

And I'm going to keep it that way.

Gods, I think it's been going on for a while.

Quakes rock from my ankles to my neck, oversensitized, overwhelmed.

I twist into Elethior, disentangling his arm from under my shirt, his fingers from around my throat. I press my mouth to his ear, push down against the thudding of his racing heart under my palm.

"We should talk," I say, unable to catch my breath. "But not here. Come home with me?"

He leans his head against my lips. Strokes his fingers over the bare, sweat-glossed skin of my lower back.

And nods.

Chapter Nine

Elethior's car is waiting outside the club.

I don't make any smartass comment about it, just give the driver my address and sit otherwise quietly in the back seat.

Elethior stares out the opposite window, hand over his mouth, body immobile.

It's barely past ten when I check my phone. Another message from my dad, this one a text I ignore; I swipe to Orok's thread and let him know I'm heading home. With a guest. I don't tell him who, but if he's the reason Elethior knew to show up at Prismatic, he'll figure it out.

The car stops in front of my building and I'm out the door like a shot. Elethior follows me wordlessly, we're both practically running. Up the stairs, two flights; I stumble to the door, digging my keys out of my pocket with quivering hands.

Elethior presses behind me. Like he did on the dance floor. Body molded to mine, our coats blocking most of the contact now, but I know what he feels like against me, and that knowledge is unendurable.

Get in the apartment. Get in there and lay ground rules and *be responsible*—

"Sebastian," Elethior says into the back of my neck, my own name scalding my skin.

I get the key in the lock, twist, deactivate our security wards with a dismissive flourish, and shove inside.

The moment the door closes behind us and I pop on the lights, I take a trembling step back, putting the kitchen counter between us. "Just—wait. Stay there."

He hesitates, paused in stripping off his coat.

One side of his lips lifts in amused confusion. "Am I rabid?"

"Maybe. I don't know if you've had all your shots."

A laugh falters out of him, and he finishes taking off his jacket, hanging it on an empty hook by the door.

Gods, that sheer shirt in bright light should be illegal.

He takes a step closer to me. "Sebastian—"

I move back, bumping into our dining table. "Wait. Stay. Stay— right there."

There's about four feet between us and I feel every bit of it broken down into inches, centimeters, millimeters, atoms.

Elethior wings up an eyebrow and holds his hands in surrender.

"We need to talk," I say.

"I agree."

"This—this could be messy."

"Yes."

I glare at him. "Really? *This* is how we come to nonconfrontational understanding in our lab partnership? Our first check-in with Davyeras and our advisors is this week. What are we gonna tell them? 'Hey, turns out the secret to rectifying interdepartmental differences is horniness.'"

Elethior's grin widens.

I scratch my hands through my hair in agitation, my coat still on, the heat of the apartment making me too warm, but *fuck* if I'm going to be standing here in a crop top with him yet.

"Is that what you wanted to talk about?" he asks. "Our check-in meeting?"

"Yes. No. Kind of? It's a factor." Gods, I can't swallow, saliva filling my mouth. "We should, uh, come up with some ground rules. Addendums to our truce."

Elethior sticks his thumbs in his pockets. "What ground rules?" He's talking cautiously. Scientific, almost.

Makes this easier.

We're lab partners, adding a new dynamic to what is, at its core, a professional arrangement.

"We don't let it interfere with our projects," I say. "They take precedence."

"Agreed."

"If either of us decides we want to stop, we stop, no questions, amicably. We'll be mature about this."

Elethior's eyes light up, and I expect him to go, *Can you be mature? About anything?*

But he says, "Agreed. Can I add one?"

I grunt.

"Not in the lab. We both have full apartments off campus. We don't need to screw around at school."

I'm hit with the image of Elethior pressed up against me while I stand at the whiteboard.

It's not a bad image.

At all.

"Agreed. Not at school. Nope."

His smirk returns. Crawls back across his face like it never left.

He eats up some of the distance between us, stepping a foot closer.

I don't snap at him to stay back.

"What else?" he asks.

"Um—" My mind goes to mist which is quite a feat in and of itself. It's usually *so loud in here.* "What else what?"

He takes another step. "Limits?"

Limits. Limits for—

Another foot closer. I can smell him. Floral and greenery and— maybe that smell is on me now. His cologne. On my skin.

He stops. Close enough to touch.

"You told me to use your body," he says. Without music to dampen it, I can hear every facet of his growl; ripples and rough edges, it serrates along my spine in a delicious shiver. "How do you want me to do that? Or, more importantly, what do you *not* want me to do?"

"Uh—pain," I rasp out. "No hitting or spanking or anything."

His fingers lift, and my lungs clench shut. He pinches the zipper of my coat, pulls it down, unlocking it tooth by tooth until he works the thing open and pushes the warm material off my arms.

I shiver again, not sure I'll ever be able to stop.

"Same," Elethior says. "Another of mine is that I don't share.

Even if this is only physical, I won't be fooling around with anyone else. And I don't want you to either. For safety reasons, and because I'm a possessive fucking bastard."

His hands brace on either side of my hips where I'm still against the table, and Elethior leans in, caging me to his body again, but facing him is a whole other inferno. Our eyes connect and fire ignites, the coarse drag of a match followed by the flicker and sizzle of a flame's first sparks.

I swallow fully, throat clicking. Oh look, that feature's back online.

"Ah," is my very educated response. "Yeah. Sure. I, uh, I haven't been with anyone in—" I think back. "A few months." Okay, *few* is an understatement. "Since before I got tested, and I was negative then, so."

Elethior cocks his head. "What about the date you had?"

The what I what?

He studies my confusion. "The date?" he asks again. "Before the cocktail party?"

I snort. "That wasn't real. I was fucking with you."

He looks unconvinced. "And that bartender?"

"What bartender?"

"At the—" His face turns red. Those stripes right along his cheekbones. "At that same party. He was—he seemed—" His eyes roll shut. "But you did leave alone, so forget I—"

My smile is slow and wicked. "Gods damn. You *are* possessive."

Even then.

Before we'd started anything remotely close to *this*.

It's on the tip of my tongue to mock him. To ask, *How long have you wanted me, Tourael?*

But it crumbles in my mouth. The teasing, the humor.

How long *has* he wanted me?

Has our every argument been foreplay for him?

Has our every argument been foreplay for *me*?

Elethior looks at me again. "But it's the same for me. I haven't been with anyone in months, and I'm negative."

"So we'll be—" I cut myself off, the word *exclusive* settling next to the half of me that told him to stay back.

My fingers rise to grip his shirt like they did at the club; it's muscle memory already.

We're laying boundaries for what could too quickly become a mess. But it feels like we're tiptoeing close to it *already* being a mess, and I'm fighting hard not to shove him aside and go invisible again.

I must have my emotions smeared across my face. His eyes soften, and one hand cups my jaw, his thumb sweeping over my cheek. Paired with that look in his eyes, I can't move, trapped in stone by *Elethior Tourael* looking at me like—

Like—

Like I'm something important.

"We can stop," he says. "We don't have to do this."

He could so easily make it a challenge, another game of chicken, but he doesn't. His tone is open and warm and muddles my thoughts.

My grip on his shirt firms up and I push back, locking my elbow so he's away from me about a yard. "No. Not stopping. Give me a sec? Bathroom."

I dart around him, race up the stairs, throw on the upstairs light, and dive into the bathroom.

I hang there in front of the sink and stare at myself in the mirror.

My eyeliner's smudged, hair sticking up all over, skin sheened, and crop top twisted. I don't move to fix anything, my mind racing back over the situation and forward over what's to come.

It's just physical.

Just sex.

With Elethior.

My heart's reaching speeds previously unknown to mortal man. But this is *good*. We're handling this like adults. *I'm* handling this like an adult.

I watch myself, waiting for the collapse, for the freak-out.

The only thing that comes is a breathless huff of laughter. I'm . . . okay?

I'm okay.

I'm going to have sex with Elethior Tourael, and I'm okay.

Why . . . why do I keep not freaking out with him?

And what am I doing up here if I'm all right?

I frantically wash my hands and splash water on my face, then shove out the door.

But as I cross the upstairs landing, my skin prickles, and I jerk to a halt unconsciously.

Magic's being cast.

It shunts me into alertness so fast I stagger, scrambling for what vials I could fit in these jeans. I didn't wear my component belt, but that doesn't mean I went out defenseless.

Adding to my surprise is that my first thought isn't *Is this Elethior?*

Before I can formulate a counterspell, my dad's on the landing in front of me.

I got all my looks from my mom. Complexion, height. Dad contributed nothing, towering at well over six feet, broad and bulky with an eternally stern expression and once-brown white hair neatly trimmed in a military cut.

He's slightly translucent, glowing, auras around him pulsating blue.

This isn't him; it's an astral projection.

A grimace seizes me.

I didn't reactivate the security wards I keep around the apartment.

"What are you doing here?" I'm holding a vial of components to activate a fireball and I keep my voice down, praying to all the gods that Elethior doesn't hear.

Dad folds his arms over his chest. "I'm done letting you ignore us. You won't respond to any of my messages—"

"So you astral project to me? At *ten o'clock at night?*"

Oh my gods. If he'd astral projected ten minutes later, once Elethior and I were—

Nausea burns in my stomach.

"What should I have done?" he barks. "Continued to let you drive this wedge between us? I knew you'd be home now."

The stairs creak.

My ribs ache with the deep, panicked breath I shove into them. "Dad, *quiet*—"

"I've stood aside while you've treated us disrespectfully for years, but this ends now." He plants his hands on his hips. "You're going to drop this victim act. I need to know that once you graduate, you'll be making something of yourself. How much damage have you done to your career already? You're still working with Elethior Tourael?"

Alarm has me stumbling closer to him. "Dad, *stop*—don't—"

"If you're willing to treat your own family so disdainfully, how are you behaving around him? Have you told him who you are?"

"Dad—"

"Like it or not, the Arcane Forces is a part of you. It's a connection you can use to improve your partnership with Elethior. Your project—it's that safety net spell, isn't it?"

He knows about my project generally, the way I'd go on about it when I was younger. After I started at Camp Merethyl, but before I realized I couldn't trust him anymore.

Gods, that ache is one of the many that never heals, and I rub at my chest as if that'll stifle it.

There was a time when I thought he'd help me develop this safety net spell. When I thought he'd help me with everything. He loved spell work as much as I did and he was this powerful, decorated soldier—he'd help me fix this.

He'd *help*.

"Yes, but—"

"Good. Sebastian, *use this*. Tell Elethior where you got the idea. Connect it to Camp Merethyl."

All the blood rushes from my head to my toes in a scalding tidal wave, leaving me swaying.

One of the training courses everyone undergoes there involves sharpening your focus in component control. That's where he thinks the idea came from: a simple first-year training course.

Get out, get out, GET OUT.

"I'm not talking to him about that." I speak through my teeth, hands in knotted fists, the fireball vial clenched so tight the lip bites into my palm. "I don't need—"

"I wish I could say I'm surprised you haven't brought it up, but this is precisely how I was afraid you'd been behaving. You're limiting yourself, *again*. You're sabotaging yourself, *again*. I can no longer stand aside and watch you—"

"No one's asking you to watch. That job application must be ramping up, huh? You're worried my new BFF might report to his family that Colonel Walsh's son really is a screwup, and it'll reflect badly on *you*."

Dad's used to people kowtowing to him—his soldiers, my siblings, my mom. Even me, usually. But every once in a while, I surprise him. Every once in a while, I remind him that I did inherit something from him: his anger.

"How *dare* you speak to me that way," he bellows. "You ignore my calls and ignore your mother's attempts to reach out, and I come to you, offering to extend a—"

He's gone.

I blink, but his astral projection has vanished.

Movement yanks my focus, and I see Elethior, two steps down, his hand on his counterspell rune tattoo.

"Didn't think you'd mind," he says. "Figured I was returning the favor from you snapping back at Arasne."

A pause stretches, and in it, he tries a cautious smile.

I freeze. Ice, from the tips of my hair, down the knobs of my spine; my fingertips go numb.

He heard.

He heard everything.

I shove the unused fireball vial into my pocket so I can clumsily go through the hand gestures of reactivating the security wards.

Stupid, *stupid,* why didn't I reactivate them as soon as we got inside?

Because I didn't think my father would be this determined to speak to me. Didn't think he'd *astral project to me.* Didn't *think—*

"He's worried about a job," I mumble. Excuses gush out of me. "That's all he's ever worried about, getting ahead, appearances. That's all that was."

"Sebastian."

"*No*." I hate how my eyes burn. Hate even more the look of *sympathy* on Elethior's face; I want to scrape it off. "Don't say anything. Don't *fucking* say—"

"You went to Camp Merethyl."

A gut punch. Lungs deflate forcefully. Stomach crumbles and I arch forward, hands on my knees, unable to breathe.

I don't want to know if his immediate family is involved in it. I don't want to know how close he's connected to that camp. *I can't know.*

Elethior comes the rest of the way up the stairs until he's on the landing in front of me, but I don't straighten up, glaring at his dark jeans.

He makes a low, pained sound, the sound of details making sense. "And your father is—"

"Colonel Mason Walsh." I speak the name to Elethior's shoes, still bent in half. "US Arcane Forces. He's in the running to take over Camp Merethyl."

"And he thinks your connection to me will bolster his chances?"

I finally peel myself upright, watching his face carefully.

I nod.

"I don't have anything to do with that camp," Elethior says. He sounds like he's pleading.

Breath whooshes out of me in a trembling gust and I want him to say it again.

But I also need him to stop talking and *leave*.

"My immediate relatives are part of research and development," he continues. "Camp Merethyl is a different branch of the family, and I haven't spoken to anyone about you or your father. I don't plan to."

"Stop," I beg him. My eyes shut, lashes damp.

"I've never been there," he keeps going. It's strung with his own tautness, winding through him the same way my anxiety is winding through me, tighter and tighter, gearing up to snap. "My family has had its hands in it for generations, but none of them send their children there, and if that doesn't say everything there is to say about how cruel and objectionable the methodology is—"

"Then don't say anything else." My fingers arch into claws and scratch, scratch at my arms. "Then *shut up*."

"My family is tied to a lot of fucked-up legacies, but that one? Gods, that one involves *kids,* and if you endured any of the atrocities they—"

"I said *shut up!*"

I'm on him, flinging my body at his, hands fisting in the collar of his shirt and heaving him around until his back slams into the wall beside my bedroom door.

He grabs onto my wrists but doesn't fight me off, gaze locking with mine as I rattle in gasps and pretend my eyes aren't welling, pretend my head isn't spinning, pretend I'm not *drowning.*

His heart pummels against my knuckles pressed into his chest.

"Shut up," I say again, pitifully, and I'm kissing him.

Three days. It's only been three days since I kissed him—earlier tonight was barely a kiss, not like this—and the moment we connect, it's oxygen after being submerged, it's something I *missed.* How could I have missed it? I've kissed plenty of people and never craved it *as it was happening,* never felt it trigger some otherworldly hunger that possesses me in a rage.

I release his shirt to clamp my fingers around his head and pull him down to me, our lips clashing, mine trying to devour tongue and teeth. He meets me in the furor and isn't that dangerous? Shouldn't one of us keep a handhold in reason? But he sucks my tongue into his mouth as he shoots his hands up under the back of my shirt, arching my body to his, and freefalling together is safer than anything else I want to do. Safer than anything else I *would* do, so I jump.

I bite across his jaw, the skin smooth and tasting faintly of sweat and shaving cream, until I get to his neck, to those black ink swirls. His hair hangs down and I rake my hand through it, twisting the strands around my thumb and fingers and jerking so his neck bows.

"Sebas—*fuck*," he cuts off when my teeth graze the highest line of ink, a spiked vine that swirls up to his ear. I can feel the ridges of the tattoo under my tongue, slightly raised against his skin, and it's another thing I add to this churning storm of need—I'll need to do this again, and again, and—

His hands fumble my belt, faltering every time I lick and suck a new spot on his neck. He thumps his head back against the wall with a frustrated groan, and in a whirl of forearms against my chest and weight shifting, I'm the one with my back slamming to the wall, I'm the one with his height towering over me, pinning me in place.

"Bedroom?" he asks, lips ramming against mine in more bite than kiss.

I scramble at the knob next to me and he's hauling me in before it's all the way open, my shoulder smacking off the edge of the door. The blinds are cracked so streetlights haze the space yellow, but that's the only light, and it's enough; we don't need to see much beyond the few inches in front of our faces.

Laundry and towels clutter the floor; I haven't straightened up in a while, but the bed's made, and we topple onto it. Or *I* topple onto it, thrown by Elethior gripping my waist and tossing me in a rush of movement he doesn't give me any time to absorb before he's crawling up my body. Shoes slip off, I get a few of the buttons on his shirt free, but he's after my neck now, payback for the way I bit and sucked at him, and I lose all conscious thought beyond *fuck yes, fuck yes* as he laves his tongue up and down my throat.

I rock my hips into his, hardness rubbing on hardness and I'm disintegrating in lewd, frantic whimpers, the air between us damp with our exhales.

"More, need more." I work at his shirt again. My fingers have lost all coordination and I'm ready to rip it off when he sits back on my hips and looks down at me, eyes taking me in, every inch.

"You're so hot," he moans like it hurts to say. "And seeing you all desperate for me—"

"I'm not desperate for you."

He grins. "So I could leave now, no harm done?"

My hands scramble at him; I'm pretty sure I scratch him trying to hold him here. Not that I think he'll leave, but I *am* desperate, and his smile goes triumphant.

He hangs there, one breath in, one out, watching me, and the pause has a cry twisting up in me. I don't want to pause. I don't want to stop. I don't want to *think*—

He puts his thumb on my lower lip. His face transforms, all teasing gone, and he looks at me like *that* again. "Can I suck you off?"

My brain shuts down. No one's home, forward the mail, hire a plant-sitter.

But that *look* on his face.

I want him to look at me like he wants to eat me, not like he wants shit I can't give.

"Gods damn it." I clamp my fingers into his sides, up under his shirt, hoping I bruise him. "Not like this. Stop it."

He frowns. "Not like what?"

"Like—*sweet*."

His frown is baffled. "Is that another rule? I can't be sweet to you?"

"No. You can't. That's not—"

"—what this is," he finishes. He licks at his lip ring, thinking, *stop thinking*—

Then he leans down, and I arch up to kiss him again, intending to go ferocious, but he slams his hand around my neck and pushes my head back into the bedding. Not cutting off air, not pinching; just his grip there. Heavy. Secure.

I stop moving and gape at him.

His lips curve into a grin, and there's that ferocity, the quirk of his eyebrow, the spark of control in his dark eyes.

"I know you're sensitive right now," he whispers, feeding me the words.

I thrash, not really wanting to escape; my body reacts to that word, *sensitive*. He pushes at the tendon in my neck with his thumb and I moan.

"I know that was a lot of personal shit you never expected to have to share with me."

Another whine, another helpless buck of my hips, but he clamps his thighs around mine and keeps us from rubbing against each other.

"It makes us even now, though, yeah?" His voice roughens, deepens, his own vulnerability flaring up.

His mom at her care facility. Me, seeing behind his curtain.

Elethior's giving me a lifeline, and usually, I'd grab it.

But I don't think I need this lifeline. Not as much as I should.

My eyes go half-lidded. "Yeah," I manage. "We're even."

He grins, viciously pleased. "I'll help you forget, I promise. I'll fuck you so good you won't remember your own name beyond me calling you *baby*. But I can do that and still respect you, so look into my eyes and tell me you want my mouth on your cock."

I'm a mess.

We're still clothed, and I'm a mess.

Whining, writhing, fingers futilely pulling at his wrist where he's holding my neck.

"Elethior—"

"Say it." He holds my gaze with the same intensity he holds my neck.

Fuck him. Fuck him *so much*—and in any other situation, I'd refuse. He doesn't get to tell me what to do.

But he's bent over my body, barely touching me; my pulse is thundering under his fingertips and I *need him*.

"Please," I break down. "Please suck me. Just—touch me or *something*, Elethior, *please*."

His expression goes reverent, not like I babbled incoherent pleas, but like I spouted off some epic sonnet.

"The way you beg," he groans and thrusts his body back onto mine, grinding our fully clothed dicks together, and I don't care about anything else. Nothing exists outside of us, a wholly new spell we've created where all interplanar life ceases to function because the sensation of his body on mine shames everything else out of reality.

He kisses me, and I trill in the back of my throat, an onslaught of relief from the ecstasy of hips and mouths and movement. His lips trail down my neck again, he shoves my crop top up to climb the peaks and descend the valleys of my chest.

He pops the button on my jeans. I arch my back and his fingers hook in the waistband.

"*Fuck*," he growls before my jeans are even pulled down.

I try to get up on my elbows, really I do. I cannot be in this much of a jellylike state yet, it's embarrassing. But all I manage is to lift my head and look down at him, and he's got his eyes shut, his shoulders bowed forward.

"What?" I pant. "What's—"

"You're not wearing anything under your jeans."

I grin. "You thought I was? You saw how tight they were, right?"

"Oh, I saw." His eyes flip open and pin me in place with ardor. *There,* that's what I want; destroy me with a look, take me apart piece by piece, leave nothing behind.

I dump kerosene on that energy. "Maybe I'll go bare under my pants every time we're in the lab. Or maybe I'll wear jockstraps. Or thongs—would you like that? Doesn't matter though, does it? We won't be fooling around in there, so you'll never know what I'm—"

He wrenches my jeans so they're around my thighs and gulps me down in one vibrating snarl.

I cry out, head thrown back, body going lethally taut. He's relentless, brutal, works his tongue and throat in punishing tandem, pumping his head and swallowing. His lip rings drag with every pull, hard bites of metal contrasting the soft pressure of his mouth. I croon to the ceiling.

My fingers find their way into his hair and I clench hard, those silky black strands sweeping across my stomach, his own fingers gripping my thighs, leaving bruises there, too. The thought of having his fingerprints, proof and ownership, gathers that sparking, living heat low in my belly.

"I'm gonna—'lethior—" I can't even say his full name. Can barely make words at all.

He rises off enough to say, voice hoarse, "Come in my mouth, baby," and *oh my gods*.

One more pump of his head, one more fierce contraction of his throat, those lip rings digging in, and I'm coming with a full-body shout, liquid fire washing through my veins in a self-contained blaze. My shoulders contort and my back bows off the bed, and he works me through every ripple, swallowing and groaning.

I go boneless on a ragged, wet gasp.

He keeps me in his mouth with an almost painful suction. I whimper at the oversensitization—but he's humping into his hand. His lips fasten to my head, suckling, and I squirm at it being too much, but watching him get lost in his own desire with me still in his mouth, I thrust helplessly, half-hard again so fast I go dizzy.

"*Elethior*," I sob, and he finally releases me to bury his face in my groin and muffle his shout, his body quaking and twitching as he comes in his palm.

No pause, no lingering in the glow—he shoves back up and his mouth on mine now tastes like me.

He'd made me half-hard, but I'm fully ready again, and I rub myself on him brazenly. His jeans are open, and I can feel him against me, skin to skin in an eye-rolling slide.

If I thought I'd made some embarrassing sounds before, they've got nothing on the way I mewl at his cock coming to full hardness against mine. We got off, we should be done; it was mind-melting, *it should be enough*—but we're kissing like we're starving still, open-mouthed and scraping, and he's making noises, too, husky growls and symphonic cries.

"Shit, Sebastian—need you to come again, need to see it." Elethior takes us both in the hand that he came in and he uses his own cum to jack us.

It's the hottest fucking thing I've ever seen.

Him, bent over me, propped on one arm, his other hand straining as he works it, face shuttered in desire that's borderline agony; I'm right there with him. I don't know what hurts more, the need or the pleasure itself, but I thrust up into his hand and anchor my fingers around his neck, our noises now grunts and breaths.

There's no gradual build. Coming this time is like buckshot, dozens of pieces here and there and there, peppering my body inside and out. I arch and shudder, trying to escape the ambush of *so much, too much*; every nerve is unscrambling, every receptor rupturing. I'm vaguely aware of Elethior following me over the edge with a cry that I swear rattles the walls.

He drops down on me, both of us breathing too fast, hearts racing each other's, chest to chest. His face is in the curve of my neck and I feel his lips part, dragging roughly on my skin so goose bumps flurry over me.

Half-dead, I fumble on the side of the bed until I grab something from the floor—an old shirt—and shove it between us. We both make a valiant attempt to clean up, and when I go to pull my jeans back up, limbs shaky and head in that perfect, tingling fog of wooziness, Elethior stops me by peeling my pants all the way off.

I'm still in my crop top. He's still dressed, his jeans gaping open, cum stains on his black mesh shirt.

He tugs down my bedding and shoves me under it and I'm dazed, so I let him.

But when he crawls in next to me, I try to sit up. "What're you doing?"

He loops his arm around me and eases me against his chest. "Aftercare is part of it. I'll be gone by morning."

I'm shivering again. I don't know when I started, or if I've been shivering the whole time. But each one shakes and shakes until my teeth chatter and I don't know why.

Elethior tightens his arms around me and I grip on to him, something solid as my body deals with the aftereffects of—

He knows about Camp Merethyl.

He made me come harder than I ever have in my life.

Fuck, the way he kisses me.

My brain is still malleable, and I convince it not to spiral, not yet. Wait until he leaves. He'll slip out and *then* I can fall apart, *then* I can figure out how all this makes me feel.

Elethior strokes his fingers up and down my spine. He's so warm. Soon, I'm not just gripping on to him. I'm outright snuggling him, my face pressed into his shoulder and my arm draped across his chest.

I'm not shaking anymore.

Gods, this feels nice.

Everything's back to being fogged and woozy, and the last thing I remember is Elethior's lips on my forehead, and his voice, low and rumbling: "Sleep, Sebastian."

Chapter Ten

I fell asleep with my contacts in.

Eyelids welded shut, I grope in my bedside drawer for eye drops, and by the time I've doused myself in them, pried my contacts out, and found my glasses, it hits me.

I'm alone.

The sequins on my shirt scratch my palm as I rub at my pec, but the motion doesn't soothe the sharp ache that pinches behind my rib cage.

Sunlight's easing through my window, and I blink around my room, looking for . . . some sign, I don't know. A shift in the fabric of the universe. A rip, a destruction, a *change*.

Elethior and I hooked up.

And he held me until I fell asleep.

I don't know when he left. I don't remember anything after passing out, and how did he manage to stay conscious following back-to-back orgasms? Especially orgasms like *that*. I still feel sluggish, relaxation fighting hard to keep my muscles lethargic and weighed down.

He said he'd leave before morning, and he did. That's good. It keeps the delineation clear—a hookup, period.

But in the swelling light of morning, with blankets pooled around my waist, it isn't the sex that flares across my memory.

It's—

Camp Merethyl. His assurances. All those things he said. *Look into my eyes and tell me you want my mouth on your cock. What about the date you had? And that bartender?*

Get out of bed. Get out of bed and shower and *function*. It's Monday and I had a hookup and *that's all it was*.

I throw a towel around my waist, shuck my crop top, and stand in the hall outside my room.

Orok's door is closed.

Elethior was only at the club last night because Orok told him we'd be there.

I mean, you can't argue with the results, but still, I cannot let such a slight go unaddressed.

Which is a *way* better focus for all the energy that wants me to fixate on last night but *fuck that shit,* I'm going to torture my best friend instead.

Growing up in a house of wizards, you learn certain tricks early. Especially when your siblings are significantly older than you; I think that's where my tendency toward pranks comes from, an ingrained sense of survival.

So imbuing rocks with low-level noise spells? Child's play.

Hiding those rocks around Orok's room while he's passed out and hungover? *Psh.* Don't insult me.

Waiting until he texts me good morning so I know he's up, then triggering the spells to activate when I'm on the bus, and all seven rocks start simultaneously screaming, "*You are dead to me,*" in the most cackling, fiendish voice I could crank out of the spell? The least of what he deserves.

And I set up one rock to scream-sing the chorus from Chappell Roan's "HOT TO GO!" on repeat, and that one I hid under a deflection spell, so he ain't never gonna find it.

By the time I'm stepping onto the bus, Orok's calling me.

I answer, and before I can speak, I'm bombarded by the shrieking spell voice in an overlapping discordance along with the faintest upbeat bop of how *you can take me hot to go*—

"Fucking hell, Seb," Orok brays into the phone. "Make it *stop.*"

"That's a hard no after you *betrayed me* and *salted the earth on which I live.*"

The guy I sit next to on the bus pops an eyebrow but pretends to be engrossed in his phone.

"YOU ARE DEAD TO ME, YOU ARE DEAD TO ME, YOU ARE—"

There's rustling, and at least two of the voices stop.

"How did I betray you?" Orok asks. Shuffling joins the hodgepodge of background noises. Another screeching voice cuts off.

"How was Elethior at Prismatic?" I reply.

"Ah." Orok coughs.

"*Ah?* Ah? You don't sound remorseful. Hence your new surround-sound speakers."

"You sent me to get your shit out of the lab," Orok says. Something thuds; he curses. A few more rocks quiet. "He asked where you were. He seemed honestly upset about you running off. Sorry, about you *turning invisible,* then running off. Smooth move there, Casanova."

"I will lodge a shrieking rock up your ass."

The guy sitting next to me stands abruptly and motions to get around me. "Uh, gonna—"

"No, I'll move. I'm sorry." I get up and shove myself into the alcove near the rear door. To Orok, I hiss, "You told him where I'd be last night."

"To be fair, I only told him we'd *probably* hit Prismatic after the win." Another rock shuts up. It sounds like there's only one more "*YOU ARE DEAD TO ME*" along with Chappell Roan telling Orok to raise his hands and body roll.

"Shit, Seb, where'd you hide them?"

"Hang up and do a seeking spell. It's your punishment."

"For trying to get you out of your own way?"

"Yes. No. For—" I rest my head against the bus door's window. It's grimy and disgusting and gods know what I'm letting soak into my skin.

"Under your dresser," I mutter.

Orok coos triumphantly. "*Thank you.*"

"*YOU ARE DE—*" It shuts off mid-sentence.

But Chappell's still going. "*H·O·T·T—*"

"*Seb.*"

I sigh. "On your bedside table."

"There's no rock on my bedside table."

"Cloaking spell."

"*Asshole.*"

"Yeah. A bit." I scrub a hand through my hair as Chappell Roan stops.

"Thank *gods*." Orok blows out a huge breath in his now silent room. "My head is killing me."

The bus rattles and hits a bump.

A memory surfaces: my mom showing up before winter break.

"You're making a habit out of letting people pop into my life without telling me," I accuse him. "I'm not sure I like it. Are you conspiring with anyone else to leap out at me? My grandmother? An elementary school nemesis?"

Orok huffs, but it sounds like he's wincing. "No. I'm not conspiring with anyone else. I wasn't *conspiring* with—no, I'm sorry. I should've told you I talked to him."

"Or you should've *not* talked to him."

"So he isn't who you texted me you were taking home? And that wasn't him creeping out of our apartment last night as I was getting in?"

My neck heats. That heat climbs, hits my cheeks, my ears. "The outcome of your meddling cannot be used to counteract the treachery of the meddling itself."

"*Thank you, Orok,*" he badly mimics my voice. "*I got laid because of you, Orok. You're the best wingman ever, Orok.*"

I usually push back. I usually keep the banter going.

But my mouth dries.

Orok allows that silence for a beat. "You're trying to make it something complex when it's not. *He is not his family.* You can like him. You're allowed to like him."

"I don't like him," I say. "What we've done is just physical. That's where it stops."

That's where it *has* to stop.

If I think beyond that, it all falls apart.

Like how we're lab partners, and no matter what happens, we're committed to working together for the next several months, and we can barely do that when only animosity is involved; but adding in other feelings? *Ohhhh* boy, actual murder, violence, implosions.

Or how he *is* part of his family regardless of what Orok says, but . . . it's honestly easy to forget that. Too easy. And that's a betrayal of myself, isn't it? Forgetting who he is, what his family's done. I can't let that go. I *can't* forget.

This is too messy. I'll call it off. I'll walk up to Elethior at the lab, give him a firm handshake, and say, *Good game, buddy, but we can't take to the field anymore.*

My brain comes up with a very sophisticated counterproposal, which is Elethior's growly *Can I suck you off?*

Great. Now I've got a boner on the bus.

Orok brings me back to the topic at hand when he asks, "You both agreed that it's just physical?"

I shrug though he can't see me. "Yes."

Well, *I* laid that boundary, and he didn't push back. Is that what he wants?

"And you'll be okay with that?"

"Why wouldn't I be?" I frown at the passing city streets. "You told me to trust myself. Elethior and I laid boundaries. We know where we stand. It's—"

"*Seb.* I just asked if you'll be okay with it only being physical."

My brain stutters. "I—why wouldn't I be? We're going in circles."

Something squeaks on Orok's end and I can imagine him lying back on his bed. "I'm not sure you're ready to hear what I think yet."

My heart launches up into my throat, panic frying my nerve endings. "I told you, I have this handled. I'm thinking clearly, I'm in control. I promise."

"That's not what I meant. I meant I don't think you'll *hear* what I have to say, and that's fine. I know you're doing better. This lab partnership thing with him has been messed up, but you've handled all of it. I think you're only freaking out because you're not freaking out. But what I will say"—his exhale scratches across the phone—"is that you should be gentle with yourself. Don't compartmentalize this so much that you get lost in the boxes you've locked yourself in. Trust that you can handle more. That you can handle *real*."

"You and your armchair psychology. Or bed psychology, as it were."

"Have you meditated today?"

"Oh look, it's my stop. Gotta go."

The bus really does stop, and the doors really do open, and I really do jump off, but I don't hang up.

Orok still sees a therapist occasionally. I did for a while, but there were only so many times I could be told the same stuff Orok gives me—*Try centering techniques, Your anger is a defense mechanism, Strive to be calm*—before I lost my mind. It works for Orok and I'll be forever grateful he has that option, but it did nothing beyond piss me off more.

I rub at my chest like when I woke up, trying to push away the ache that starts again.

"I want to be better," I whisper. "I'm afraid I will freak out, and I don't want to."

Orok hums, and there's a smile in his voice now. "That's the first time you've ever said that. You usually choose your anger."

Do I? I mean, obviously; I know I do. But I don't want to *not* choose it. Anger isn't all bad. I just don't want it to control me.

Anger has protected me, but I'm tired of it being the dominant thing I feel.

Why have I pole-vaulted this emotional crossbar now? Why *today*? I'm not dumb—I know my night with Elethior rattled me, but two orgasms are hardly cause for an internal breakthrough.

It doesn't feel like I came to this conclusion in one night though, like a light switch has been thrown on because he was such a good kisser. It's been more . . . gradual. I've had ample opportunities the past few months to fully lose my shit, and I haven't. Over and over, I've *seen* that I've been getting upset, and I've refrained from doing anything I couldn't take back.

Most of the time.

It's a process.

The sun's been rising bit by bit; I've been living in an in-between not-dawn, not-morning. But the sun *is* rising, and I think I see it now.

"Thanks, O," I concede.

He huffs. "You're welcome, jackass."

By the time I get to the lab, I've decided to call off hooking up with Elethior. It's the responsible thing to do.

Until I step inside, and see him standing by his desk in ass-hugging dark jeans and a faded gray band T-shirt, his hair tucked behind his ear and a pen in his mouth.

Son of a bitch.

My brows pinch in a whimper I'm thankfully able to stifle.

Elethior looks over his shoulder, notebook open in one hand. His eyes connect with mine and widen slightly, his body going still like he's worried a sudden movement will make me sprint out of the room. Considering I did that the last time we were both here, it's a fair concern.

I cross to my workstation and deposit my bag and coat on my desk, gaze on him the whole time.

"Whatcha working on?" I jut my chin at his notebook.

His eyes drop down my body. I forewent smothering myself in one of Orok's hoodies; seems a moot point now. I'm wearing a blue Henley with tight whitewashed jeans, my brown leather component belt, and faded Converse.

I'd wondered if Elethior had noticed I'd been cocooning myself in oversize clothes, but he's at least noticing the *lack* of oversize clothes now, the way his eyes follow the trail his hand took as it snaked up to my neck last night.

Call it off. End it now. Stick out your hand, Sebastian, and say these words: *It sucks, but there'll be no more sucking.*

Elethior eases the pen out of his mouth.

Those lips.

Fuck.

By the time his eyes lazily make their way up to mine, an hour might've passed. Two. It could be the next day. My heart's veering onto a runaway course and my hands twitch so I pocket them and lean against my desk, feigning nonchalance.

"What are you working on," I ask again, but it comes out gruff, a cover question and we both know it.

He plays along. "We'll start testing that theory for your project this week."

My gaze zeroes in on the way he grips his notebook to his chest, the veins that swell in the back of his hand, vanish under his tattoos.

"Yeah," I say.

Then I hear what he said and I jolt back to awareness with a painful lurch.

"Wait—no. We worked on mine, we got some progress, we didn't kill each other; now it's time to bring in your project. We need to make some actual steps toward combining our work before the check-in on Friday."

Elethior catches my tone with a resigned smile. "I'm guessing I shouldn't ask how you slept, then."

Better than I have in weeks, but I woke up and you were gone.

My cheeks burn. "I'm serious, Elethior. That was the agreement, we'd start with my project, then—"

"Thio."

My words trip over themselves, tongue flicking against my teeth. "What?"

He shrugs. Totally *chill*. "I've had your dick in my mouth. Figure you can call me Thio now."

How hot can the human body blush and not get internal third-degree burns?

Don't think about last night. *Don't think about last night.*

But I subtly shift how I'm standing, hating how easily my nerve endings flare though I have a very logical reason to be talking to him that has nothing to do with *my dick in his mouth.*

His eyes snap to my crotch and a self-satisfied smirk tugs one corner of his lips, rings flashing.

Then *he* blushes. Two stripes, perfect lines.

And I remember what I said, how he wouldn't know if I was wearing anything under my jeans.

I'm not today.

What were we talking about?

"Shit." I rip my hands through my hair and put my back to him. "We're going to start on your project. Tell me about your project."

Heat. Heat's against my back. The smell of cut greenery.

He crowds in closer to me.

"Sebastian. Look at me."

I don't tell him to call me *Seb*. This isn't tit for tat. And it definitely isn't because I like him calling me *Sebastian*, the way his tongue folds around my whole name.

A frustrated snarl builds and I stay facing my desk. I am not a flower and don't need to be drawn to his sun. "No. We need to have more to present to Davyeras and our advisors this week, and I want us to start on your project before we get too far into any experiments. We have a good amount of funding, but spell components aren't cheap, and I don't want to waste anything if it turns out we could've doubled up on testing. So talk."

His heat retracts as he steps away from me.

I exhale a long breath.

"I'm studying the limitations of the energy connection between a conjurer and their conjured item," he says with no inflection.

I face him, arms still crossed. "Well, that tells me absolutely nothing."

Elethior—*Thio*—goes to his workstation, dumps his supplies on his desk, and sits in his chair, swinging it around so he can look up at me. A good few feet of padding stand between us again. My breathing ratchets up, body hating that space and desperately needing it all at once.

"How much do you know about conjuration?" he asks.

My glare flattens and I move toward him. "Enough to understand what I'm sure is a concept you believe to be beyond my feeble human brain's aptitude."

He smirks. It blows into a wide grin.

"Even so. I—" His hands twitch where they're resting on his lap. "Could you back up?"

I'm standing an inch away from him. Between his spread legs. But he's rattled, so I don't move.

My turn to smirk. "No. Even so, what?"

His face shutters, darkening as his hands fist. "Baby boy, you keep standing there, I'm going to pull you onto my lap."

It was a huge mistake to hook up.

Just, like, an enormous mistake.

But we're in it now. We're barely treading water in the aftermath of our stupidity typhoon.

"I'll move if you tell me about your project."

He grimaces. "We should go over some basic conjuration ideas this week while we test your theory. Give you a foundation in—"

"I don't need a basis in conjuration," I cut him off. "Why won't you tell me about your project?"

"It's not that," he counters. But it's *absolutely* that by the way he adjusts on the chair.

My shoulders bunch. Gods, swinging from pissed at him to horny over and over in such a short timeframe can't be healthy, can it?

"What, we'll report on Friday that what progress we've made is me going over freshman conjuration bullshit?"

Thio points at the shelf over his desk where the kindergarten workbooks sit. He's got them displayed like trophies.

I roll my eyes. "That was a *joke,* asshole, and you know it."

"We're on to something with the measuring cup theory," he tries. "The fact that you and I are working on your project with conjuration theories should be enough for our check-in meeting."

My gut sinks. Plummets right through my toes, leaves a hole in the floor.

"When did you decide we needed to test my theory first? After you heard my dad last night?"

Thio's eyes widen. It might be in revulsion, but my brain says I was right, I hit on why he's going back on our agreement: he heard my dad tie this project into Camp Merethyl, he knows how fucked that place is, and he *feels sorry for me*.

Rocks settle in my lungs, gravel and weight. "Fuck you for—"

Thio grabs my arm and yanks me forward.

I'm already off-balance, so I topple into him, and he deftly grips my thighs and tugs until I straddle him.

"I'm not doing this because of what I heard last night," he tells me. "Believe it or not, despite your massive ego, not everything is about the almighty Sebastian Walsh."

I try to shove away and he holds me tighter, fingertips bruising me again, and I *hate my body*, the traitor; everything stings where it touches him, everything *broils* in the best, most toxic consumption. But that fire is in my chest still, too, anger and shame warring for dominance, and I buck.

His chair skids but he holds on to me; I'll definitely have bruises.

"*Stop!*" he shouts. "You're not the only one whose project *hurts!*"

I don't exactly go limp, but I don't keep trying to shove away. My body's rigid and my thighs strain where I'm pushing myself up so I'm not fully seated on his lap. I don't say anything, staring down at him, lips parted.

His eyes lock on mine and we both feel his words, the threads they weave around us.

My legs give out and I fall down on him. He takes my full weight with his arms constricting even more. Not holding me down; holding me *to* him.

The same emotion emanates from us both: uncertainty. How did we get here, how did I go from yelling at him to sitting on his lap.

So we don't react to it. Can't. If we acknowledge it, it'll shatter.

"I'm trying to disconnect a conjurer from their conjured item," he tells me, his voice a feather brush of noise in the disappearing space between us. "Typically, when a conjurer summons an item, they're connected to that item. If the item gets destroyed or used up, the conjurer is hurt, too. It isn't excessive for most things—like with fire, small flames make the conjurer woozy. But for bigger things, it can be incredibly dangerous."

That's not how it is in evocation. Since we create something new, the energy draw is entirely from components, which means evocation wizards go through *insane* amounts of components. Conjurers use components, too, but only to trigger the initial spell, so their required amounts are typically less.

Thio stares at me for another second. Two. And when his tongue darts out to lick his lower lip, I hiss in a breath like I can feel that roughness on my skin.

His eyes slip shut, pinching at the corners. "I'm working on a way"—his voice is all business, but low—"to disconnect a conjurer from their conjured item. To make it so a conjurer can summon something, and not be energetically bound to it."

My brow furrows. "But—where would the responsibility be?"

"Where is the responsibility with evocation-created items?" He looks at me. "Why does there need to be a responsibility with conjured items?"

"The responsibility in evocation is in the amount of components needed. Would you increase the components in conjuration spells? Are you . . . are you trying to invent evocation?"

"I'm trying to use conjuration spells, but have the option to disconnect the energy link. That's one of the issues I'm working on: what to use as a source of energy if not the conjurer."

"The conjurer *should* be the source of energy with conjuration. You're taking something that already exists. You're stealing it. Especially if you conjure something tangible, like weapons or gems—those things *belonged* to someone else."

"The majority of conjured items are elemental, and you know that," he says. "Fire, lights, water. Like with evocation. Rarely does a wizard conjure something like a diamond necklace, because the components alone needed to cast that spell would be astronomical. And there are required additions to spell work so you don't take an item actively being used by another person."

I'm fighting not to jump to defensiveness and typical *conjuration is theft* arguments. This is important to him, but I'm still not seeing why, and my jaw works as I think through my response.

"If you disconnect conjurers from their summoned items," I start, "wizards will misuse it. They'll summon cursed items and subject innocents to them. They'll—"

"There will always be people who misuse spells," he cuts me off. "We can work in fail-safes to ensure abuses are limited, but are you saying we should only create spells with evil people in mind? That the world should operate to contain bad, not reward good?"

He's not getting defensive either, and it's fucking with my head. This whole thing is. We're wrapped around each other, and we're having a calm discussion.

"The costs should be weighed against the benefits. And in this case, I see a helluva lot of costs."

He hums, quiet for a beat, before one side of his mouth cocks. "I don't expect to figure out a way to fully disconnect conjurers. It's a huge topic that far more talented wizards than me have failed to solve."

"But you're going to try."

"I'm going to try," he echoes, "because it was my mother's research topic when she worked at DaylarTech. Do you know it?" At my hum of negation, he continues, "It's one of the research companies Arasne recruits for. I'm being primed to take over a position of leadership there. It's been my family's plan for me since I was a teenager: conjuration undergrad, then a Mageus in Conjuration, and get slotted into a department head job while pursuing my Doctorate in Conjuration."

He could be reading a dictionary for all the emotion in his voice. No excitement, no passion.

My hands flinch around the back of his neck. When did I loop them there? I don't know how to respond, but I don't have to. He keeps talking, his gaze unfocused over my shoulder.

"They've had other requirements, too. Goal posts on the path to being a *respectable Tourael*. The Mageus Research Grant was one of them."

His gaze slides to mine.

That's why he went after the grant. Because his family *required* it of him.

There's something in the way he's watching me. He's bracing, expecting me to explode, and he looks like he wouldn't fight it at all. Like he knows he deserves any reprimand I dish out, how he doesn't *need* this money.

I choke off my response.

Why is he playing along with his family like this? From what I know of him, he doesn't seem the type to do anything he doesn't want to do. Why is he obeying them?

Thio's eyelashes flutter and he regroups, shoulders leveling. "But the topic of the grant research project—that I chose on my own. And I picked my mom's topic because—" He pauses. "She met my father and married into the Tourael family shortly after she started at DaylarTech. She's . . . idealistic. Believes that what she did there helped the world. And sometimes it did, but . . . she developed some dangerous shit, too, shit that *hurt people*." He bites one lip ring, trying to convince himself as he says, "But she isn't a bad person, Sebastian."

I nod rather than speak. If I open my mouth, I'll remind him that this isn't what we do. We don't *share* shit like this. It was an accident that I even met his mom.

"The last project she worked on." His face grays. "She was trying to disconnect a conjurer from their item, and it came after a series of failed projects. You don't fail in my family. Even those who marry in. *Especially* those."

I stroke the back of his neck, like I'm soothing him.

"One of her first tests went . . . badly. No one could figure out what happened. But she was overworked and exhausted and stressed. *That's* what happened. My family is so cutthroat that even after being married to my father for almost eighteen years, she still felt she had to prove herself and push beyond her own limitations."

My face collapses as his goes detached.

"After the accident," he swallows, the tendons there straining, "my father went back to the Fae Plane. I haven't seen him since."

"How old were—"

"Seventeen."

Electricity seizes my muscles.

Seventeen, and alone in a family set on weaponizing every ounce of magic. Seventeen, and watching his mom get battered by that ambition.

Eighteen, and dropping out of Camp Merethyl because there's no side of this machine that doesn't destroy.

"I moved in with some relatives until I started at Lesiara U." Emotion breaks across Thio's face again, imploring and raw. "The intention behind their plan for me was to make up for my mother's failing and my father's abandonment. For our unit of the family to not be a *lost cause*. And I've gone along with everything they've demanded of me, I've played the good Tourael, because—" A tight swallow. "Because my mom got a settlement for the accident, but that money ran out after the first two years. My family's been footing the bill for her to stay at Blooming Grove ever since. They've made it quite clear that her continued support is contingent upon my . . . *amalgamation* into a Tourael company."

Horror streaks through me. "They'll stop paying for your mom's care if you don't work for them?"

His lips pinch. "I'm an *investment*. Arasne's my main babysitter, so to speak, and I play along, but when I saw the opportunity to expand on my mom's project, to do something for *me* in all of this?" He shrugs. "I won't involve her research directly, though. That'd give my family an avenue to claim any results I get."

"After you graduate," I start, choosing my words carefully, "you said you aren't going to work for them."

The ghost of a smile passes over his face. "I'll need some kind of high-paying job to keep up with my mom's payments. But luckily, my family has a lot of enemies willing to fork over money for me, so my plan is to get a job with one of their competitors."

I recognize what it is to have no self-preservation; that slightly wild yet sad look in Thio's eyes. He doesn't want to work for any Tourael competitor, he just needs the money. He doesn't *want* any of this beyond taking care of his mom.

What does *he* want? If he could choose. What would he do?

Stupidly, I open my mouth to ask him. These questions aren't mine to ask and his answers aren't mine to hear, so when his fingers pull on me again, defying the way matter occupies space by drawing me impossibly closer to him, I pretend I'm relieved to be cut off.

"I'll do what I need to support my mom," he continues, "and it'll be a big, final middle finger to the Touraels, so they'll know. They'll know I'm her son, not theirs."

My lungs cave in but I quickly inhale, forcing them to stay inflated, to keep the ache away.

"Why didn't you ever say you hate your family as much as I do?" I whisper, too pitiful for my liking. But I feel like my foundation with Thio has been decimated in the last few minutes. Everything I knew about him went from immovable stones to quicksand.

He shrugs. "I didn't know why you hated them, just that you did. I may not have chosen this path on my own, but that doesn't mean I don't take pride in the work I produce; and you were an immature little twat who kept fucking with my lab."

I roll my eyes. "I never *damaged* anything beyond—"

His finger pins my lips together and I give him a look that lays out, in no uncertain terms, that I *will* bite it off.

He grins, and it does something to that strain in my chest. Makes it quiver and ripple.

"Damage or not, you were a nuisance," he says. "For all I knew, you hated my family because of their war efforts, which is fair. But I refuse to take the blame for my entire family's sins, and I don't owe anything to people who expect me to."

I lick his finger and he recoils with a smirk that says, *You little shit.*

One piece doesn't fit, though, and I hate asking it.

"Are you still good to release our work for free after we graduate?" I try not to let my own desire mar the question. "I'm not sure we should encourage people to detach conjurers from items, but we can cherry-pick what we share—if that's still something you want?"

Thio draws a circle on my lower back, his smile soft. "Yeah. That could do a lot of good."

"You wouldn't want to patent your research and take it to

whatever enemy company you go to? It could be an attractive bonus for them."

"I won't need anything to sweeten the deal with a rival company. The mere fact of me being a Tourael will be enough. Plus, I don't think we'll get very far in my project, in *her* project, not enough to patent anything. Whatever we do end up presenting will be mostly *your* project, and something tells me you wouldn't like me to hand your project over to a Tourael competitor, no matter how much it'd piss off my family."

His eyes sparkle, but the reality is sinking in slowly, what the enormity of his project means: it will be me sharing credit for my project with him at the end of the semester, unless we make massive leaps in his project. I hope we don't; it's way too dangerous.

But the measuring cup theory was his idea. At this point, my project *is* largely his project, too.

Which should, hopefully, appease Davyeras and our advisors.

I'll still get to release it for free like I wanted. Nothing about my planned future is changing. And yet, possessiveness churns in my stomach, and I shift restlessly on his lap.

"Yeah. Let's not give it to any big corporations," I manage.

"It's bad enough you have to share it with me at all." He finishes the part I don't say aloud.

My jaw bobbles open, but he pushes it shut with his knuckle.

"I get it," he says. "I do. Hell, I've been dragging my feet telling you about my project because I don't want to share it. The fact that yours might come to something, and mine will probably be a dead end, but I'll get credit for yours? I'd be livid at me, too." He inhales sharply, his eyelids pulsing. "You have a lot of very valid reasons to hate me."

I do. Even more now.

He's only in this grant, in this program, because of his family, not because he *wants* any of it. Weeks ago, that would've been enough to have me screaming at him until my throat bled.

But now?

My lips press to Thio's forehead.

I hold there, second-guessing this reaction.

He exhales. With the warm gush of his breath comes a susurrating whimper.

I kiss his temple. His eyelids, tissue-thin skin. His cheekbones, his jaw; getting hungrier, frantic.

His whimper blasts open in a greedy snarl.

He catches my mouth and our kiss is an attack, bodies rocking in the chair, hands in hair and a bomb goes off, emotional detonation.

We fucked after my dad brought up all my stuff and now we're barreling toward another go-around because of Thio's shit, and this was supposed to be mature and healthy, wasn't it? We laid *boundaries*.

I peel back, panting, my hand on his neck this time so I can push him away. "Your rule," I gasp out. "In the lab. Can't."

Draw a line. See it there? We can't cross it.

I can be rational. I can be mature. I *hate* myself for it, but I can be, I *have* to be—

Why do I want him so much? This level of need shouldn't be possible. It's eating up my insides in the same napalm-laced firestorm he always used to trigger in anger, and there's nothing too different about the consumption of these flames, except I *want* them so badly now, and that wanting is fuel, too.

Thio's breath shudders and his gaze is on my swollen lips. "Yeah. I—you're right."

"Be easier to believe if you'd stop looking at my mouth."

His eyes zip up to mine and he smiles. "It's a nice mouth."

I'm still on his lap, his arms around me. It hits me, what this is. Why I keep shying away from moments like this.

Intimate.

It's intimate.

Far more than getting off together. Even more than kissing.

This is so messy. This is such a *fucking* mess.

"Okay." I talk fast. "I'll do for your project what you did for mine, start going through evocation texts for anything that might apply. We can also see if what works for my project works for yours, since they're both dealing with energy limitation. Send me what you have for your project, research and papers and shit, and I'll get to work familiarizing myself with it."

"Sebastian," he whispers.

I clamber off his lap and he lets me go. But I put my back to him, straightening my glasses, smoothing my hair, *resetting*.

We're hooking up.

That's it.

He told me about his mom because he needed to explain why this project means so much to him.

That's it.

But he told me while holding me. Like he needed that connection. And that word is corporeal inside me now, *intimate,* a parasitic growth.

"We should start pulling together a preliminary report for Friday's check-in," I continue and face him, but I don't look at him. "Detailing how we're using both evocation and conjuration, and what progress we've made."

He clears his throat. "I'll keep moving on the best ways to test the theory for your project. We can reconvene after you've read through my materials and figure out if there's some overlap—if not, I say we run one or two tests for your project while exploring options for mine."

"Yeah. That sounds good."

He pulls out his phone and types. "Just sent you my project materials."

My phone vibrates behind me. Thio gives me a less forced smile and turns to pick up a book at his desk.

When his back is to me, his shoulders bow.

I open my laptop and pull up the materials he emailed.

We work in silence, doing what we came here to do, but it's off-balance, and I can't figure out if it's because I let things go too far . . . or they didn't go far enough.

Chapter Eleven

We're back in that state of professionalism.

For the next few days, we work around each other, talking only to share ideas or ask about progress. We don't discuss our hookup Sunday night or how we decided we'd be fuck buddies but haven't taken any further steps toward that, and I think some of the energy that swirls around us is sexual tension. But neither of us makes a move or invites the other to his apartment; is it another challenge? Horny chicken?

It doesn't have that challenge feel though. The way Thio watches me, concedes to me in our conversations and interactions—is he waiting for me to initiate it? Since he initiated it the first time. And I've been nothing but hesitant from the start, so yeah, it makes sense he's hanging back, letting me be the one to confirm that I do, in fact, want this.

Oh gods. We'll be waiting forever.

By the time our check-in meeting rolls around on Friday, it isn't a surprise that my knee's bouncing while Thio and I give Davyeras, Thompson, and Thio's advisor the spiel we came up with.

In a conference room in Bellanor Hall, we ensure they know that Thio and I are working *together* now, and how we're incorporating conjuration ideas into my project while I'm starting to do the same for his. We talk about our future plans, and when I'm midway through a run of word vomit about potential tests we'll do, Thio kicks my foot to get me to stop fidgeting.

My face heats. "Um, yeah. That's where we're at," I finish. Then realize we should've had more flare, maybe? I spread my fingers and give them jazz hands. Because that's collegiate.

Thio drops his chin to his chest with a soft moan.

But Thompson is smiling across the long table. "Very good, Mr. Walsh. Mr. Tourael."

Davyeras hums agreement, looking far more pleased than he did at the mixer a few weeks back. "Indeed. This is the progress the committee has been hoping for. And what would you say has been the most beneficial tool towards your reconciliation?"

"I—" *Do not say sex, do not say sex.* "We—"

Thio glances at me, and my thoughts must be clear on my face, because his eyes bug out.

"We—" he starts, then his mouth hangs open, and I swear I can see the same words rolling through his head: *Do not say sex.*

Yeah, not so easy to answer that question, is it?

But I think about Thio counterspelling my dad. Telling me about his family. Introducing me to his mom.

"We realized we have more in common than we'd expected," I say softly.

Thio's face relaxes, a smile tugging the corner of his mouth.

I catch myself the moment I start to lean forward, like I'm going to kiss that spot.

It's been four days since Thio and I have so much as touched each other. And that's entirely because I've been overthinking it; he's following my lead. He's giving me the reins and I can't decide whether I like that.

I slam back in the chair, posture straightening, to see Davyeras and the advisors making notes and nodding at each other.

Next to me, Thio clears his throat and runs a hand through his hair. Is it me projecting, or can I feel more body heat coming off him than normal?

He noticed I leaned toward him while looking at his mouth.

I clear my throat, too.

Davyeras smiles to his notepad. "I'm glad to hear it. That'll come in handy for our Founder's Day challenge."

I frown. "Uh—what? Why?"

Thompson grins. He's got the same energy as a mother trying to convince her child that going to the dentist is, in fact, like going to an amusement park.

"You and Mr. Tourael, along with myself and Dr. Narbeth"—Thio's advisor—"will be competing in teams of two. The Founder's Day coordinators heard about this grant and thought it'd be a great draw, along with the ever popular student-versus-professor head-to-head." He winks. "You'll have to take it easy on us old-timers."

Thio winces, but recovers and asks, "What's the challenge?"

"Oh, that'd hardly be fair for them to give us time to strategize, would it?" Narbeth says as he closes his leather folio, and Davyeras and Thompson follow suit. The tension in my muscles goes out, knowing the check-in meeting is over, and we didn't fuck it up. "We'll find out what the challenge is the day of. I've been told we're to wear clothes we don't mind getting messy."

Thio stifles another low moan.

My smile is more than a little stiff. "Fantastic."

Davyeras, Thompson, and Narbeth file out of the conference room with wishes of good luck, leaving Thio and me to gather up our materials.

Which we do.

In that professional silence again.

Only it's strained more now, drawing between us like fishing line, tangling us up, too, tighter; I'm losing feeling in my extremities.

Just say . . . *something.*

Gods. Why isn't this simple? It *should be* simple. I'm overthinking it. I need to talk to Orok—no, fuck, any more talking to him about this and he'll have to start charging me by the hour.

A knuckle raps on the door and I look across the table while hooking my messenger bag over my head. Thio's gathering the printouts we made of our planned schedule, so he doesn't turn right away.

I don't recognize whoever is at the door. But—he's familiar? Short and compact, with receding brown hair, pale skin, and pointed ears.

"We're clearing out. The room's all yours," I tell him, assuming he's come to use the conference room after us.

But the guy gives me a cold, flat smile and tugs the hem of his beige suit coat. "Ah. I was rather hoping you both could stay a bit longer."

At the guy's voice, Thio whips his head up, papers clutched in his hands.

His entire posture changes. What tension had been brewing between us is nothing compared to the crystallizing brutality that takes him now, his jaw hardening, face blanking. He's shutting down. Shutting *out*.

"Myrdin," Thio says. "What are you doing here?"

The defensiveness in Thio's tone has my spine popping upright. My eyes go from him to this guy, Myrdin, my gaze narrowing.

Myrdin's cold smile doesn't change. "Arasne expects a report."

Arasne. He works with Thio's cousin?

My mind fits together a missing piece: I *have* seen this guy before. He was at the grant award brunch, sitting at Thio's table. Making sure, I know now, that Thio lived up to their Tourael standards to determine whether his mom gets the care she needs.

I curl my hands into fists around the strap of my messenger bag.

"And I'll see her at our lunch meeting next week," Thio says through his clamped jaw. "You didn't need to show up here to—"

"She heard your first check-in for the grant was today," Myrdin interrupts, pulling a tablet out of his jacket pocket. He starts tapping on the screen and poises over it, like he's waiting to take notes. "She has been . . . less than pleased with your updates and wants a recap of the presentation you just gave. Which shouldn't be hard, should it?"

Thio deflates, his focus dropping to the table as his knuckles go white on the stack of papers he's clinging to.

"Fine," he relents laconically, an inevitable exhaustion sweeping over him.

I can't immediately tell why I hate seeing him like this. But it is that, *hatred*, and a sharp, ravaging "No" cuts up out of me, drawing both Thio and Myrdin's attention.

"We have, uh—" I fumble, eyeing Thio. "That thing. We have to do. You don't have time for this now."

There is no *thing*. It's the end of the day.

Thio briefly gives me a look of gratitude, but it's resigned.

Myrdin's head tips. I swear his nostril curls, but he resets and smiles that flat smile. "This won't take long. Provided you are both forthcoming in the details of this project."

Confusion has me shaking my head. "Both?"

"What?" Thio frowns at Myrdin.

Myrdin sighs impatiently and lowers his tablet. "Yes. *Both.* The family is concerned that this partnership will not bear the fruit we expect, and as such, Arasne has requested that you both begin reporting your progress. Until such a time as we can be assured of your success."

My body goes numb. Inside and out.

The Touraels want me to start reporting to them, too.

I stand there, gawking at Myrdin, some part of my brain screaming at me to react, but I can't.

Until Thio slams the papers onto the conference table.

I jump at the impact, my heart restarting in a painful hammer against my ribs.

"Myrdin," Thio barks. "Leave."

Myrdin startles, too.

"You had no right coming here," Thio tells him, redness rising across his face, shoulders arching like he's one wrong move away from leaping over the table and tackling his cousin's go-between. "I will see Arasne at our regular meeting next week, where I and I alone will tell her what she needs to hear to satisfy the terms of our arrangement. This? You showing up on campus? You barging in, demanding Sebastian report to her, too? This *does not happen.*"

Myrdin blusters. I swear he'd clutch pearls if he was wearing them. "You are making this out to be something it isn't, Elethior. This is so unlike you."

Breath hisses through the seam of my lips.

Stop being so dramatic, Sebastian.

I look at Thio. Fuck Myrdin. My whole focus is on Thio, the vehement scarlet on his cheeks and the rage in his eyes and the way he's barely clinging to decorum.

"Leave," Thio says again. No, he *commands* it, the walls rattling with the force of his shout. Somewhere beyond this conference room, I hear a passerby gasp, but I can't look away from Thio.

Myrdin huffs and there's rustling; he must put away his tablet. "She won't be pleased."

"She never is." Thio shoves back from the table. "And Sebastian is off-limits. To you. To Arasne. He isn't part of this. Do not approach him, do not speak to him. Do you understand?"

Holy shit.

Myrdin mutters something else. I don't know what. I don't fucking care what he says.

Thio's radiating fury and I'm hypnotized.

Then we're alone.

I only know we're alone because Thio turns his focus to me.

A crease forms above his nose. "I don't tell Arasne anything about our project. And I won't. I tell her what *I'm* working on, but only in terms of how it affects conjuration, and I keep it vague anyway. That's why she's being so persistent; I'm *withholding*, and—"

"Drive me home."

That crease smooths flat. "Pardon?"

"You get chauffeured to and from school in that fancy private car. Right?"

His eyelashes flutter in bewilderment. "I—what?"

"Actually, it doesn't matter; it'd just have been easier." I adjust my messenger bag and hand him his leather jacket from where it's hooked over the back of his chair. We're leaving. Now. "But however you get from school to home, don't. Don't do the home part, I mean. Your home. Instead, take me home. To my home."

Fucking hell, I'm bad at this.

Thio accepts his coat from me and realization dawns in the parting of his lips.

It only takes a second for all the other emotions on his face—anger and shame and grief—to get packed away.

He steps closer to me, eyes glinting. "What are you trying to say, Sebastian?"

"I'm trying to say that I fucking want you. Right now. So take me home. I mean, not like to *stay*, but take me to my apartment and come in. For a bit. For—"

Aaaand that's where my mouth chooses to finally shut up.

Thio's eyes fix on mine with such intensity I'm worried when I look away, it'll hurt.

I can smell his cologne. It's muted after a day in the lab then this meeting, earthy freshness mingled with the smell of chalk from when he'd practiced a few runes.

Without saying a word, he steps back, gathers his stuff from the table, and angles for the hall.

"You coming?" he throws over his shoulder.

My sigh of relief is worryingly loud.

Orok's got rawball practice this evening, so I let us into the apartment—and reactivate the security wards, fool me once—and the moment my bag hits the floor, I'm on Thio. No decorum. No walls. No hesitating. I fucking need him after not having touched him since Monday. And after . . . I *need* him, and I let that need overwhelm me, become a flash point.

Thio's right there with me. We didn't say a word the whole way here but he's shaking now, the drop in adrenaline probably; he yelled at his family for me.

Fuck.

His hands clamp my head and hold me in place so his tongue can invade my mouth, and I fight back, shoving him against the closed door and biting down on his lip. His moan is hoarse and desperate and has me scratching my hands up under his coat and shirt, seeking skin, ready to write sonnets to the rise of his stomach, the coarse hair leading up to the swell of his pecs, the pebbled mounds of his nipples.

I tug one of his lip rings between my teeth and he's already half blissed out, but I pull back long enough to dig a vial out of my component belt and hold it up. "You trust me?"

Thio's gasping, flushed, and he studies the vial. "What is—"

"Trust, Thio."

His eyes narrow, then roll. "Gods help me. Yeah, yes, I trust you."

"Good. Because it's my turn."

Then I'm sinking to the floor, unzipping his pants, and taking a quick sip of the vial.

It's an emergency potion I carry in case of electrical outages. A big dose causes massive currents, can jumpstart pretty much anything.

But a dash of it across my tongue?

An instant sizzle flutters through my mouth and I swallow, stretching the magic down my throat in the barest coating of fizzing, jumping shocks.

He showed me no mercy Sunday night, and I return the favor now.

His dick's bigger than mine, longer and thicker, and while that pings the barest dredges of my competitive side, I channel it into relaxing my throat and taking all of him.

That, coupled with the tingling, sparking sensation from the potion, has Thio's head thunking back against the door.

"Holy *shit*," he whines, squirming, helplessly thrusting himself deeper into my mouth as his jaw gapes, fingers knotting in my hair, knocking my glasses askew.

I moan around him, wanton, self-indulgent, and pump my head, working him with my hand, too. His taste, the salty musk of him, the scent of his cologne even here, like he sprays it on his naked body—*fuck*, my jeans are too tight and my coat is swelteringly hot, but I'm caught up in Thio's broken sounds of need and the way he rolls his head forward to look at me.

My eyes tear and my vision blurs. He's unraveling because of me, *in* me, those stripes on his cheeks gone to deep, vivid red, his pupils wide in his dark eyes.

He's unfairly stunning, coming apart like this. All the sharp lines of his features, all his harsh edges become cliffs I want to bungee jump off, see how far down I can fall before the rebound snaps me back up. He's the plummet and the catch and the rise again all in one, and kneeling at his feet, the world orients around him.

"Sebastian," he wheezes, and I swirl my tongue in his slit, feeling the jumping shocks in the tip of my tongue so I know he's feeling them here, too. He hisses and shivers, his eyes glassy as they dart all over my face. "Gods, you're wicked. Fuck—your lips stretched around me like that. Shit. Gonna—"

I suck long and hard, head bobbing, and as he comes down my throat, I distantly wish we were back at the lab. The soundproof walls would trap the noise he makes, a cracked cry that sticks against his tongue, a chewed-up *Fuck, baby, yes,* and I want nothing more than to be sure I'm the only one who hears it. It's *mine,* and I get where his possessiveness comes from.

This isn't just messy.

It's a full-on environmental disaster.

Geiger counters will pick up radiation here a century from now.

In the aftermath, I rest my forehead against his thigh and he slides his fingers through my hair.

"C'mere," he whispers, and I'm hard and definitely want him, but I feel as wrung-out as he looks. I rest there, breathing, trying not to think, the last bits of the electric potion fading so my tongue's left with ghost sparks and vibrations under the taste of him.

I shiver, head to toe, muscles bunching in my shoulders and straining across my back.

He helps me to my feet and gets me off into his hand. We're both panting after I come, and I want to ask him to stay. To hold me until we fall asleep. To wake up at 2 A.M. and suck each other off again and fall back asleep sweaty and sated.

To talk about how bad it is that he told off Myrdin for me. Will he face any repercussions for that?

"I can pick you up Monday morning," he gasps.

"Yeah?" I nip lazily at his mouth, palms flat on the door on either side of his head. "It's on your way?"

He grins. "No."

A kiss. Soft and so sweet it makes my toes curl.

I don't have it in me to tell him to stop. *That's not what this is.*

Gods.

What *is* this?

"Mm," he moans against my lips. Then, pulling back, "I'll be here at six on Monday."

I give him an appalled look. "You sadist. *Eight*."

His smirk is too satisfied. He did that on purpose. Jackass.

I get him a towel so we can clean up, and I realize as we do that neither of us took off our clothes, not even our coats. It really was utilitarian. Just a hookup.

Thio kisses me again, tongue dipping into my mouth one more time. "See you at eight," he tells me, then he's gone.

Halfway to school Monday, with traffic moving at a standstill beyond the tinted windows, I ignore his condescending smirk.

"If I'd picked you up at six—"

"Like you've ever gotten to school that early."

"Rush hour traffic isn't nearly as bad at—"

"*Thio*."

He grins. It seems to delight him to no end, the simple act of me saying his name.

I should go back to *Elethior*. Or *Tourael*. Scrub that line in, make sure we know where the boundaries are.

Eyes on me, he pulls a handful of items out of his pocket, does a quick spell, and a wall of black rises between us and the driver. The windows are already tinted, so we're cocooned together.

My heart kicks up, body jumping—no, *cannonballing* on board with the light in Thio's gaze, the way he tongues his lip ring.

"Your turn to use a spell for sex, huh?" I point out.

Thio smirks. "If you want it to be for that."

"Your—um, driver," I say. He can't see us now, but—

Thio's smile heats up. "Spell muffles sound, too. Plus, he's paid very well by my family to not care about anything but the road."

The reminder of who is funding this vehicle should be a bucket of cold water all over this energy. But it's vindicating knowing the Touraels paid for this pretentious car, and I'm going to have sex with Thio in the back of it.

I'm on his lap before any lucid part of my brain can stop me.

This time, we're both quick to strip off our jackets, and as the car continues its glacial crawl across the South Street Bridge, Thio and I devour each other like it's been weeks instead of days.

Each touch doesn't alleviate, it only exacerbates, fuel on fuel on fuel, burning me up until all I am is pure, unfiltered need.

Need to make him feel good.

Need to expunge these flames inside of me somehow; they'll blister right through my chest if I don't.

We end up in a sloppy sixty-nine, elbows and knees propped on the wide car seat, windows fogging, hips thrusting and moans staccato, racing each other and drawing each other out. It's frantic and messy and perfect.

After we come within seconds of each other, I try to lay on the seat next to him only to topple inelegantly into the footwell.

Thio busts up laughing above me.

I swat his knee. "Dickhead. Help me up."

He complies. I move to tuck myself away, but he does it for me, then takes care of himself before hauling me back to straddle his lap.

I'd first sat here out of brazen need, but now it's an echo of him holding me in the lab and telling me about his mom, and every muscle previously relaxed by my orgasm wrenches tight.

Thio's eyebrows flinch together, a wince.

He dusts his lips across my forehead. "We're almost to school."

His arms go slack so I can move off him.

I should.

I don't.

I can feel his smile, the way it curves on my skin when he pushes his face into the crook of my neck.

We fall into a routine.

Thio picks me up in the morning. His driver, a dwarf named Hordon, doesn't let us know that he definitely knows what we're doing behind the barrier spell, gods bless him. The poor guy must be going through a ton of air freshener to keep the back seat from smelling like sex all the time.

We get to school and spend the day in the lab. I trek to the library for my job or off campus to eat with Orok. Thio occasionally heads out for stuffy meals with Arasne or calls with Myrdin for *updates* on his progress. Those always throw him out of sorts, so I've taken to summoning Nick afterward, where he spends a few hours curled on Thio's lap, getting fed pieces of dog food like grapes at a Bacchanalia feast.

There's no repercussion from Thio yelling at Myrdin, not that I can tell. I asked Thio once, and he shook his head and cooed at Nick how *his daddy is cute when he worries.*

I'm not worried. Or cute. Fuck him.

Thio and I always end up leaving for the day at the same time, and three of the five days, Hordon takes us to my apartment. The other two days, Thio says he can't give me a ride, and when I find out it's because he's going to visit his mom at Blooming Grove, I hop in the car anyway.

Which is how we spend a few hours a week with Thio's mom, having dinner with her in the garden courtyard or playing checkers in the game room while she sits next to Thio. Even though she doesn't respond to what we say, occasionally she'll lean her head on his shoulder with a contented hum or pat his arm.

I don't hear from my dad anymore. Mom keeps up her usual stream of asking how I am like nothing happened.

My replies were already almost nonexistent, but it's harder to respond when I expect every text to be news that my dad got the job.

I focus on Thio instead. On the stories he tells about stuff he and his mom did before her accident. On the way she'll make eye contact with him, and he lights up like a supernova.

I expect Thio to drop me at home and leave after our evenings at Blooming Grove, but even those end with him following me up. Orok's practices keep the apartment empty on the weeknights, which is good, because we never get farther than the kitchen.

Does Thio kiss me longer the nights after Blooming Grove? Does he linger more, make it almost agonizingly good?

The only time we don't see each other is on weekends, but *gods,* that separation turns Monday morning into fireworks, prompting

us to find *really fun* uses for spells that create a temporary extra hand
or generate warmth on certain focused body parts.

Orok mocks me for my distracted energy one Sunday, but I
quite pleasantly remind him that I'm having sex twice most days.
To which he says, "Low blow, dipshit," and steals the leftover tacos
I'd been saving.

But seriously, I'm having sex *twice a day*.

I'm saving a ton on bus fare.

And I can still barely focus when Thio's in the lab.

Every eye contact, every brush of our hands, every time he's
standing too close or not nearly close enough—it's all something I'm
aware of, and that awareness eats up my attention like acid. What's
the solution? *We're having sex twice a day.* What more does my body
want? Sure, we're keeping it to hands and mouths and that's more
than satisfying, but something tells me that even if we went further,
it wouldn't quench this greed.

Thio's no help. I swear he stands too close on purpose. I catch
him dragging his nose near the skin on my neck and I glare at him,
but he grins like a little fucker. I bend down to grab the marker I
dropped, and I catch him checking out my ass with his lower lip
between his teeth, and he pops an eyebrow and *pats his thigh* like I'll
hop to and plant myself there in an obedient heap.

Which I *don't*.

Because we're in the lab.

Where we said we *will not fuck around*.

We map out experiments to run on my project and brainstorm
things to try with his, but nothing overlaps. Our lab space becomes
cluttered with more than his mess; we've got books on conjuration
and scrolls from the dregs of the library on the oldest forms of evocation, and we've started sorting through piles of components to fit
in our tests.

Working together is . . . fluid. Ish. He'll reach for something, and
I'll already be handing it to him. I'll say, *Maybe we should look up—* and
he'll have a book open to the page that lists the thing I'd been about
to say.

But there'll be times when he insists on using a pure crystal rod for a spell we're testing the safety net idea on, even though the standard way to do the spell is with a glass rod. The spell needs a light-refracting component, and we're not sure if the equation we've come up with for the safety net addition will *work,* so why waste expensive materials?

Thio concedes to me, and we use the glass. But when we run the test and it turns out, hey, the safety net equation *is in fact off* and the original spell destroys the glass rod, he insists it wasn't the equation, but the use of glass instead of crystal, and I should *stop being such a cheap-ass.*

An added benefit of knowing him now is the realization that he's not arguing to be pretentious or superior—he's fighting for control because he's terrified.

Terrified of his mom's accident repeating itself.

I don't know how to process that knowledge. It feels like something I shouldn't know, something forbidden. So I suggest we add more protection spells to our next test. Which is reasonable, right? Meeting him halfway.

But Thio keeps on about me being stingy over our components, only instead of me storming out when I can't stand the sight of him anymore, I shout at him to shut up and call Hordon.

We close the lab early.

Head to my apartment in infuriated silence.

Then he hate-fucks my throat until we both come all over my kitchen floor.

The weeks until Founder's Day and spring break fly by—until one day, we get off on the way to school like normal, but it does nothing to bank the fire, even less so than usual. Hordon drops us behind Bellanor Hall and Thio and I are both strung taut, breathing like we raced to school. The energy between us *aches,* a bruise in the ether. Maybe we should see a doctor? Maybe we've caught something. A lust spell gone wrong.

We get into the lab, and the minute the door shuts, Thio's shoving me against the wall.

"Sebastian," he growls, and he sounds *pissed*, but honestly, I am, too. *What is this?* "Why can't I get enough of you? Why the *fuck* can't I stop wanting you?"

I don't know. *I don't know.* I almost whimper it, dolefully.

He bites his way down my neck and I tear off his jacket, wanting to rip his black T-shirt in two, but I stop with my hands fisted in the fabric, my chest heaving.

"Your rule about the lab. Thio—back up. Not in the lab."

But he doesn't move. Stays right up against me, his teeth in my neck, the bite sharp and making my eyes roll back.

"I rescind it," he says. Laps at the bite mark he left.

"Rescind—?"

"That rule. The no-fucking-in-the-lab rule. I rescind it. Agreed?"

We can change the rules?

The rules can change.

It rings in my head. A fire alarm. Smoke's gathering, churning—I nod frantically. "Agreed."

The components in his hand barely register before he murmurs a spell. My wrists are lifted and slammed back against the wall, held in place by invisible force shields.

Adrenaline spikes, stays high and roiling as Thio grins deliciously. "Good?" he asks.

Need ribbons through me. "Oh, *fuck* yeah."

Chapter Twelve

CAMPUS-WIDE SECURITY ALERT: All students, faculty, staff, and visitors attending the Founder's Day activities are being directed to avoid the southwest corner of the Quad where the Nomadic Order of the Enchanted Beast Pet Adoption Event is being held. An adventure party is on site following the reported escape of an infant basilisk.

As of this alert, three Nomadic Order staff and four hopeful adopters have been petrified, and the basilisk remains at large. Authorities recommend all Founder's Day guests have anti-petrification spells on hand. More updates as they become available.

"Aw, there he is!" I walk backward with the group, snapping about a dozen pictures on my phone. "My boy's all grown up."

Orok shifts his rawball helmet under his other arm and rolls his eyes. The Manticore logo is emblazoned across his purple jersey with a smaller patch stitched on his shoulder, the symbol of Urzoth Shieldsworn. Not every player has a patron god, but there are more than a few patches scattered throughout the forty-person rawball team as they make their way in full uniform out of the stadium. Their designated Founder's Day charity game against a local kids' group doesn't start for several hours, but the players are scheduled for photo ops in a massive booth across the Quad.

Founder's Day goers stop to ooh and ahh at their procession. Someone shouts, "Feel the sting!" and a number of players chant it back.

Players and fans alike do not appreciate it when "Feel the sting" is followed up with "of going raw." Ask me how I know.

The whole of Founder's Day is in full swing all across campus, with gold-and-purple bunting covering every surface imaginable. Booths

line most walkways, selling food, drinks—including the aforementioned Founder's Day punch, which I give a longing glance at—and
university paraphernalia. Guests are out in droves, mostly students
and faculty, but also people from the surrounding city who take advantage of the festival-like atmosphere. There aren't carnival rides or
stuff like that, and most of the events are Lesiara U—themed—does
any young family care about professors competing against students?—
but the overall energy is bubbly, carefree fun.

I scroll through photos. "Look at you in your fancy costume.
Such a handsome—*ow!*"

Orok hauls me into a headlock without slowing his pace.

"Wait!" I wave my phone helplessly back toward the stadium. "I
need to go that way—my event starts in, like, ten minutes."

"No," Orok says simply. "You called our uniform a costume. If I
don't give you some kind of punishment, the whole team will."

"I'm sorry. I forgot how delicate you rawball players can be."

Orok squeezes me tighter. I smack his arm, but he doesn't let up.

"Okay—" I wheeze. "Uncle, unc—"

My phone buzzes in my hand. I look at it absently.

And see my mom's name over a text notification. In the preview
window, the words "*. . . Camp Merethyl director.*"

I go limp.

Orok glances down at my change and lets me go. "Seb?"

His teammates continue around us when we become inadver-
tent obstacles in the sidewalk.

I swipe open the text.

MOM

Your father has officially
been named the next Camp
Merethyl director.

It would mean the world if
you could call to congratulate
him.

Emotionless, I hold my phone out so Orok can see.

"Shit," he mutters, and if he says more, I don't hear it.

My dad's going to be the director of Camp Merethyl.

My father is going to be the one running that place. *That* place.

It's fine.

It's fine.

I think those words over and over, an endless loop weaving into a life raft that might carry this weight for me.

"Seb—" Orok touches my arm and I cringe away, hard.

Are my eyes tearing? No, it's . . . allergies or some shit.

"It doesn't matter," I snap. "He'll run the camp. Nothing'll change. He'll find whole new generations of wizards to—"

My throat closes.

Eyes burning, jaw tight, I focus on messing with my phone's camera settings. "Smile, O. One more picture."

He watches me a beat longer.

Then, deadpan, flips me off.

I spit a laugh, so grateful for it, and Orok manages a smile, too.

"Aw, that's a keeper," I say to the picture. "You probably shouldn't pose like that when you're taking photos with festivalgoers, though."

Orok leans over my shoulder to look at it. He huffs another laugh.

Then threads his arm around my waist and gives me a side hug. "Let me know when you want to talk about it."

Muscles cramp across my shoulders. I pocket my phone and lean against him, his rawball padding dense and uncomfortable on my back.

"Don't you have fans to torment?" I shove him. Playfully. Sort of.

He grunts and trots off. And it isn't until I watch him slump away that I realize maybe *he* wants to talk about it. He's known my dad for years, and this is a blow to him, too.

I mean—it's not a blow. It's not *anything*.

I turn on my heel and head up the sidewalk. Most people are moving around me, but one person stays fixed in place, and I pull up short to avoid slamming into them.

Thio.

Seeing him slants reality. Makes me question if maybe reality *was* slanted, and looking at him is what it feels like to be level.

He takes me in from head to toe. Per Thompson's suggestion, I wore clothes I don't mind getting messed up—old jeans, a T-shirt I don't particularly care about, my grungiest pair of sneakers, and I swapped my glasses for contacts. The weather's cool but tolerable without a coat, and I have my component belt, but that's easily cleaned.

Thio's similarly dressed, but his version of trash clothes are well-worn designer brands that fit him like a second skin: a black T-shirt and black jeans with holes in random places that let the straps of his component harnesses do really, *really* lovely things to his thigh muscles.

My eyes get stuck there. On the way the leather straps bite into the skin I can see through one of the rips in his jeans.

We should've blown each other before this. But Orok and I took public transport in together rather than Thio picking me up, which was fine at the time, but now?

I pretend I'm adjusting my component belt but, nope, I'm adjusting something quite different.

Thio's smiling by the time my eyes make it back up to his. "You ready, partner?"

"Yup. You hear what it is we're doing?"

Whatever this challenge, it'll let me scorch through my mom's text. Melt it right out of my mind.

My chest thrums, twists sharply.

It's fine.

We fall into step, heading toward the stadium. Our mystery challenge is at the rawball field until the charity game.

"Not a clue," Thio says. The crowd pushes us together, our arms brushing as we walk.

His fingers stretch against mine.

He doesn't take my hand, though. That would be—*nope.*

"You two are close?" Thio nods behind us.

To where Orok had his arm around my waist.

I stop in the middle of the sidewalk again. People pass us when Thio matches me, and I study his expression, bracing for accusation. It wouldn't be the first time, and it's usually what people jump to in regard to me and Orok.

But Thio looks . . . interested? Like he's honestly curious.

"Yeah. We're close," I say, testing the waters. "We've known each other most of our lives. He's important to me."

Thio smiles, and it's kind of sad. "You're lucky. He seems to care about you a lot."

They've only met twice, barely: once in the lab when Orok went to get my stuff, and once when Thio was doing the walk of shame out of our apartment.

Thio turns to resume heading up the sidewalk, but I grab his arm.

"Wait. What's this?" I point at his face.

"What's what?"

"*This*. This—*coolness*. You were jealous of a bartender I talked to for two point three seconds, but you aren't jealous of Orok?"

Thio blinks. "I don't get that vibe between you two." His head cocks. "Should I?"

"Gods no."

"Okay then."

"You don't think it's weird?" I'm still bracing. Still . . . confused.

Most of my exes had some issue with Orok. His, too, with me. And a few hookups would either get squirrelly and duck out, or assume we were down for a three-way. Which, *fuck* no. And if it wasn't that, it's been weirdness from other people, like how Ivo and Crescentia assumed we were together.

But Thio looks at me with that bittersweet smile. He wars with himself, decides on something with a flicker of his lips. "Every friendship or relationship I've had has been fucked over by my family somehow. Fame seekers who wanted what the Touraels could do for them, or people my relatives planted to manipulate me, or friends bribed to leave because they weren't *good enough* to associate with me. So to have the kind of friendship you have . . ." He shrugs, forlorn. "You're lucky, like I said. To have someone you can count on."

I'd been pissed at his family when he only had me to help him during his mom's seizure. That anger surges to life again, and I include now all those assholes who could've been friends with him, could've had him in their lives, but chose Tourael fuckery.

For a second, we stare at each other, and all the crowds, the smells of fried festival treats, even the escaped basilisk we're supposed to diligently watch out for—they vanish.

What would the fallout be if I kissed him here?

Why do I *want* to kiss him here? To claim him, now, in public.

To remind him that he's not alone anymore.

I pause too long.

His weak smile hardens, then fragments.

"But whether or not I'm jealous doesn't matter, does it?" he asks. "Since that's not what this is between us. We only agreed to be physically exclusive."

My heart kicks hard against my ribs. It rocks me backward, awareness shuddering through me like a shot of tequila. I can feel it everywhere; it's corrosive.

"Yeah. Right. We should head on," I say, and start back up the sidewalk.

Thio's next to me, both of us silent.

He doesn't want this to just be physical. I don't think he ever has.

Would it be so terrible if it were more?

Yes, part of me immediately screams. Yes, it would be so terrible. I don't *do* more—more means letting him in. More means he'd be someone I'd tell about my mom's text. *Hey, my dad's going to take over the place that fucked me up.*

It's not fine.

It's not fine at all.

We reach the stadium. After giving our names to security, we're let out onto the rawball field.

The field has been divided in half by a huge concrete wall

painted in purple and gold stripes. On either side are identical set-ups: various obstacles, boulders and block walls and stairs that lead to nowhere, all of it done in the same purple and gold hues. Everything on each side is centered around a platform embellished with the Manticore logo.

"They're being too subtle on the school spirit theme," I mutter at Thio. "They really should try harder."

He glances at me but doesn't pick up the banter. Our gazes linger, his softening.

I don't want to hurt him.

The realization that I probably *am* hurting him by insisting on these boundaries digs a pit in my chest, and that more than anything has my breath coming out in a forceful push.

I need to talk to him. Figure out if this arrangement is still working for him. That's appropriate, right? That's a mature reaction to what's been a very reasonable, structured arrangement. We're both adults. And we've already established that the rules can change.

But what if I ask him if this is still working, and he says no, he wants more?

"Mr. Walsh!" Professor Thompson emerges from the same door we came through. "Mr. Tourael! We're ready to start, if you'll join us on the field? Ah, but leave your component harnesses and all spell ingredients aside. We're not to take anything in with us."

I trip. Internally, externally; my thoughts catch and topple all over, and I whip toward him so fast I lose my footing and my knee buckles. Thio catches me, his hand gripping tight around my upper arm, and I'm grateful for the sting of his fingers.

"What? We're going in unprepared?" A dozen other questions gather, but I choke them down. "I mean, I thought we'd be casting spells for this challenge?"

"We are," Thompson says. "We'll have everything we need. Components will be provided for us; that's part of the challenge. Now come, come—we'll hear all the rules in a moment."

He walks off to where Thio's faculty advisor, Dr. Narbeth, is standing at the end of the divider wall, facing the crowd that's gathered in this side of the stands. The hum of conversation echoes through the stadium, dozens of people watching us, most in Lesiara U clothing, a sea of purple and gold that ripples and heaves.

A shudder walks through me.

In the front row, decidedly *not* wearing Lesiara U clothes but instead another boring-ass beige suit, is Myrdin, looking like he sucked a lemon.

My eyes flick from him to Thio, who shakes his head in fatigued acknowledgment that yeah, Arasne sent her spy to watch.

"I'm surprised Arasne cares how you do at this challenge," I say, lips numb.

"It's a public event; I'm *representing the family*." His brow furrows. "You okay?"

He's still holding my arm.

I don't want him to let go.

I shrug out of his grip and take off my component belt, my fingers ungainly. "Yeah. Fine. Just hate the unknown."

Thio huffs a laugh. "What, you? A control freak? Never would've guessed."

The way I roll my eyes and mock-laugh is strained.

I set my component belt on one of the player benches that runs along the short wall blocking off the stands from the field.

My hands are trembling as I let it go. Anger wafts up in a sweeping cloud, filling in the spot where fear tries to go.

One of the therapists called it PTSD.

But it isn't. I'm *fine* and this is a dumb school event; my mom's text means *nothing*.

I head out to stand next to Thompson and Narbeth. They're dressed down as much as I've ever seen them, and it's always odd seeing suit-wearing professors in sweatshirts and jeans.

Thio removes his component harness and takes a place next to me. We face the crowd as Narbeth throws up a volume spell and begins speaking, his voice projecting:

"Thank you for coming to our first ever Evocation versus Conjuration departmental challenge! For those who don't know me, I am

Dr. Rydel Narbeth, and I oversee the Conjuration Department here at Lesiara University."

The crowd cheers.

"Instead of pitting Evocation against Conjuration," Narbeth continues, "we will each be competing in teams of two, comprised of both an evocation wizard *and* a conjuration wizard. In order to cast any spells, teams will have to fight for their components—"

Everything fades out. Narbeth's voice. The crowd's responses.

My eyes go to where my belt sits on the bench, fingers clenching at my sides, wanting to reach for components I don't have on me now.

I'm defenseless.

Your father has officially been named the next director of Camp Merethyl.

My mom wants me to congratulate him. It'd mean *so much* to him.

Congratulations, Dad. Congratulations on overseeing the thing you chose over your son. The thing that you let break *your son.*

It takes everything in me, every flicker of resolve I pretend I've built over the past six years, not to sprint over and grab my component belt.

Thio elbows me gently.

"Sebastian?" His voice is low. Narbeth's still talking, going over rules I should probably pay attention to, but I can't; air is a burr in my throat and it won't go down.

I'm seeing things through a funnel. All other details are muffled and muted.

I need my component belt. I *need* it. I—

Thio's fingers clamp around my wrist. "Sebastian? What's wrong?"

His fingers on my skin. Focus on that. I look down and see his knuckles turn white. I want him to squeeze tighter, squeeze and squeeze until he rings my wrist in a bruise and the only thing I feel is him.

This isn't Camp Merethyl.

This is a stupid school competition.

A breath goes in on a choking gasp.

Thompson gives me a concerned look, but he quickly refocuses when Narbeth claps and shouts, "Let the challenge begin!"

Narbeth and Thompson jog off to the right side of the field and vanish behind the divider wall.

Thio and I stay where we are, his hand on my wrist.

"We can leave," he tells me. "We can go. I'll make up an excuse."

He doesn't know what's wrong but he'd fuck all this off for me, no questions asked, even with Myrdin watching.

My entire body sways toward him.

"No." I extricate myself from Thio's hold, barely aware I'm doing it, and walk toward the left side of the field on autopilot. "What, uh, is this competition? I missed what Narbeth said."

Thio keeps pace with me. "Screw this competition. What's going on?"

"Nothing. I'm fine."

Thio's lips part, a soft huff. "Sebas—"

Fury races through me, chewing me to pieces. "Not now. I said I'm *fine*, Elethior."

I want to suck it back. Peel off the extra letters that immediately erect a barrier between us. He gave me his name and I went and shoved it back in his face, and the way he looks at me, with a recoil he can't hide quickly enough, jabs into me.

My mouth hangs open.

This isn't what we are.

This isn't what we are.

This isn't—

You had such promise, Mr. Walsh. This was wasted on you.

Only it's my dad saying it now. My dad standing over me and Orok. My dad walking away as I begged, *begged* for it to stop.

I can't breathe, and for once in my life, I'm not angry.

Well, not *just* angry.

I'm devastated.

Thio waves at our side of the field, resignation hollowing his features. "The competition—components are hidden all around our side of the arena. We have to get what we can to cast whatever spells we think we'll need. First team to defeat the spitting ooze cube wins."

My head twitches. "A—*what*?"

A smile touches the corner of his lips. "You really weren't paying attention. A spitting ooze cube. There'll be one on both sides, in the center platform, and the first team to successfully restrain or defeat it wins."

I never thought I'd be so grateful for a weird monster. It derails my brewing storm and I rip a hand through my hair. "A spitting ooze cube. What the fuck."

Thio continues into our side of the arena and takes a position behind a short purple brick wall. I follow him and crouch down, the crowd able to fully see us, but we're blocked from the center platform.

"Wait." My head twitches again. "Aren't ooze cubes usually acidic?"

A buzzer sounds.

Thio and I both arch up to look over the wall as a ripple of arcane blue energy falls across the Manticore platform.

A hefty ten-by-ten square of hazy purple Jello-O-like material appears.

"Competitors!" a voice echoes over the arena. "Begin!"

"We're graduate students," I say, voice flat. "Graduate. Students."

Thio chuckles. "Then this should be easy."

The cube makes a truly repulsive squelching noise as it shifts one of its sides parallel to the wall we're behind. It must have some noise-sensing abilities; barely a beat passes after we finish talking before a wad of purple goo launches out of the cube and smacks into our wall.

We duck as chunks of goo spray into the air, a few wads dripping down onto my bare arms. They don't burn, thank gods; it isn't an acidic cube, then. Just a *spitting* one.

"I see a component box." Thio points up at a staircase to nowhere beside the cube. Sure enough, a small wooden box sits precariously on the edge of the top step.

Now that he's pointed one out, I clock others around our arena, at least half a dozen. The sides of the boxes have symbols painted on them, denoting what they contain: phosphorus, iron, glass, silver, gems, herbs, and more.

"What are you thinking?" I ask, ducking another gelatinous loogie.

Thio's quiet for a beat, studying me, and I think he might keep pushing, until he says, "I can teleport it away." A common conjuration spell. "We'd need chalk, a diamond, copper wire, and iron. I can see two of those component boxes from here."

"No way. I'm not dumping this thing on some unsuspecting person. I can encase it in a force sphere." An equally common evocation spell. "Chalk, iron, glass, a silver disk, and a ruby."

He smiles wryly. "That's one more component than my spell needs, so it'd waste time."

"But your spell would *dump this cube on some random person*. No."

"I wouldn't make it some random person. I'd drop it on *our competitors*." He points at the main dividing wall, beyond which Thompson and Narbeth are working against their own cube, but we can't see their progress.

An evil smirk spreads across Thio's face, and I can't help it: I grin. Gods, it feels good.

And it seems to surprise the hell out of Thio, who leans toward me, his smile shifting from demonic to intent—

Only he straightens up. Above the wall.

The next chunk of ooze cube blasts him in the side of the face.

He goes down with the force of it, but immediately pops up onto his knees and scrapes goo off his face.

"*Fuckinghellgodsdamnit,*" he curses, sucks in a breath, then again, "*Fuuuuck*—this shit is *cold.*"

There's goo all in his hair, plastering it to the side of his face, and dripping in globs down his shoulder, his chest.

Laughter grabs me. I can't fight it; I'm sputtering as Thio wipes purple goo out of his eyes and his annoyance dissolves in a smile.

"Laugh it up, Walsh. Wait until it's your turn."

"Oh, I don't plan on getting hit."

"Hm." Thio scoops another chunk off his shoulder and flicks it on my jeans. "Let's test that confidence. I'll take the left side, you take the right. The chalk and diamond boxes are on my side, the iron and copper wire are on yours. First one back without being cubed gets a blowjob."

My jaw pops open and blood rushes to my cheeks.

He beams at me, knowing he's distracted me even more, and I want to kiss him so damn bad.

"And *go!*" Thio takes off, leaping out from the wall and barrel-rolling behind the next closest obstacle, a wooden door.

I glance over the wall, note the cube lurching and gurgling in Thio's direction—it's staying on the platform at least—and don't give myself a chance to hesitate. I bolt out from the wall, duck under a segmented open window, then copy Thio's barrel roll behind a boulder.

Oh hey—a component box. This one's marked with a symbol for herbs, and even though it isn't one of the things we need, I keep it.

Three consecutive globs of goo launch from the cube, hitting the window I ducked behind, the wall, and somewhere on Thio's side.

The stairs to nowhere have the box for the iron at the top, and the bottom step is only about two yards from this boulder.

Tucking the herb box to my stomach, I hobble-sprint in a squat for the staircase. The side closest to the cube has a wall at least, and I make it to the first step before the cube propels a chunk of itself at me. It plops against the side of the staircase, splashing goo across my shoes.

I'm not counting that as a hit.

I clatter up the staircase, keeping pressed to the wall because the other side is a sheer drop to the field.

Shouldn't we have had to sign a waiver to do this?

The top stair hangs precariously over the cube's platform. I stop before it, watching the cube spit several rounds of projectiles around the field, hitting things at random.

Thio's across from me, creeping through what looks like the first floor of an abandoned house, clutching at least three boxes. He's grabbing as many as he finds, too.

The cube spits at him, and I dive for the top step, snatching the iron component box and flinging myself backward as the cube gurgles and fires at me. This chunk hits the step and sprays into my hair, but I miss the worst of it by hurling my body halfway down the stairs in a cumbersome topple.

The crowd makes a noise—a cheer? A gasp? It's hard to tell.

My heart's already thumping with the running and ducking, but it lurches painfully as I catch my breath against the staircase wall.

Anxiety still prickles across my skin, makes me want to dig at my forearms.

I need to get the copper wire. Thio said it was on my side.

Go.

Focus on that.

I scan the area from my elevated place on the stairs. A few more boulders are scattered around the staircase, more walls, a concrete sphere—ah, there. A box is wedged next to the sphere, and I can see the symbol on it for copper.

Movement out of the corner of my eye turns out to be Thio, nearly back to our wall.

I curse but clutch the boxes and clatter the rest of the way down the stairs to make a run for the sphere.

Halfway there, a downright *frigid* projectile lobs onto my side, sending me careening to my knees with a yelp.

Shivering, I scrape it off and army-crawl my way to the sphere, grab the copper box, and haul ass back to the main wall, cover be damned.

Thio's already there.

Which means he has a front-row seat for the chunk of cube that hits me in the back.

I wheeze but stagger to safety behind the wall next to him, where he's wearing that way too smug, way too satisfied grin I hate. Used to hate. Not sure I ever did hate.

"I win," he says.

My answering smile is only a little exasperated as I dump my armful of boxes between us, into the pile he's already made with his. "Well, I like making you come apart in my mouth. Who's the real winner here?"

His cheeks are already red with exertion, but he bites one of his lip rings, and I don't want to be here. Don't want to be doing this challenge or using a lot of energy to not think about so many things. I want to be in the back of Thio's car or in my kitchen—no, I want to be in a bed because we haven't had that since the first night, after the club. I want a bed and a locked door and I want him naked and spread out for me.

That becomes the bright light in my tunnel, the only thing I see: getting out of here.

I tear through the boxes. "Diamond, copper wire, iron?"

Thio follows suit. "Yeah. I grabbed chalk and sulfur, too—the chalk will be good. If I can draw a teleportation circle, I can get the coordinates of the location more exact. Do you—Sebastian?"

The boxes are wood. No clasps. The lid just pops up.

I've got the iron one open.

It's empty.

The copper wire box had its component in it. I check the herb box I grabbed—it's full of vials stuffed with various herbs.

But the iron box.

I stare at it. Flip it upside down, checking the hinges—more wood—even the base.

It's empty.

There's no iron.

My back tenses muscle by muscle. Rising up my spine, panic comes like a tide until my hands quake so badly I drop the empty box and it clatters against the others.

Thio grabs my forearm. "Okay, Sebastian, what is going on?"

"The iron," I hear myself say. "The iron's gone."

"I don't give a shit about the iron. *Look at me.*"

I can't.

Unclench your fists. Stay grounded. Come back into your body.

I look up and see Thio.

And then my eyes shut, and I see that scar on Orok's shoulder.

Is that all you've got?

Orok's screaming. He's screaming and there's blood everywhere—

But it isn't Orok this time. It's Thio. And it's my father's voice echoing through the room, telling me there's only one way out, *this* way out.

I'm panting, nostrils flared and fingers clawing into the grass, dirt and rocks biting under my nailbeds. My eyes open again but everything's gone red.

Fuck this challenge.

Fuck playing by the rules.

They want us to defeat that damn cube? I'll defeat it. I'll obliterate the ever-loving shit out of it, and it won't matter that there's no iron, it won't matter what they ask me to do; *I* choose how *I* use my own power.

I snatch the box of sulfur Thio got. It's all I need for several fire-based attack spells.

"Sebastian!" Thio grabs my arm and I try to jerk away but he holds on tight; I'd wanted him to bruise me earlier, he is now.

"*Stop,*" he tells me, face halfway between furious and concentrating, like he wants to spring to action right alongside me but he's staying present because—

Because I'm *not*.

"Stop," he repeats, and seizes the back of my neck. "You don't want to tell me what's wrong? Fine. You want to be angry? That's fine, too. But use that anger, Sebastian. I might've thought you were an immature nuisance once upon a time, but you're *not,* and I know you're smart enough not to do something dumb right now."

No. I'm not.

I'm the kid who did stupid shit because I couldn't handle anything that happened.

I'm the guy who doesn't think and makes a mess of everything and no one takes me seriously, *no one ever took me seriously*; so I embodied that, I embodied it so much I forgot how to be anything else.

But . . . I'm not just that. Not anymore. I haven't been that guy in weeks. Months, maybe.

My grip releases.

The sulfur falls between me and Thio.

I'm still panting, shoulders heaving, but my anger is parting like curtains over a window and there, there's that dawn again, the one that's been rising, the one I can't always see. But I feel it now, and it's warm and clear and safe.

Thio sees me coming back. "Now, there's no iron. How do we fix that?"

He's asking me directly, giving my brain a more immediate problem to solve.

We need iron for the spell.

How do we get it?

My body twinges, but I shake my head, shake it and shake it, no, *no*. Another way. He isn't talking about that. *There has to be another way.*

What other components do we have?

Herbs. Herbs—

"I can summon Nick," I mutter, my lips trembling. "I can—I can have him—" My eyes meet Thio's, a burst of lucidity. "Can we use any components on the field? Not just on our side of the field?"

A slow smile spreads across his lips. "You know, they didn't clarify that."

"So everything's fair game?"

He shrugs.

"I can send Nick to steal the iron from over there." I point at the dividing wall, behind which Narbeth and Thompson are working on their own spells.

Thio's face blows into a wide grin. "Go for it, baby."

I pick up the herb box and he starts sketching out a circle on our wall. The cube's still spitting at us, but most of it seems to be hitting the wall itself or patches of grass on either side.

Thio's face bends in concentration as he draws some conjuration runes.

"Have dinner with me."

He stiffens. Glances over his shoulder. "What?"

"Have—" I twitch. "Have dinner with me. A . . . a date."

Gods, I'm flayed open. This morning has done nothing but peel back my layers until all I have left is pathetic neediness, and I know it's painted on my face.

Thio lowers his arm, chalk pinched in his fingers.

I've seen him smile so many times. So many different flavors of it, I could write a thesis on the dozens of ways Elethior Tourael's lips move.

But this smile? It puts all the others to shame. It's joy and relief, it's ecstasy and an unspoken, vibrant *finally*.

"Tonight," he says through that smile. "I'll pick you up tonight at seven."

I start to agree, but— "Wait, *I* asked you out. Shouldn't I plan it?"

Confidence sparkles in his eyes. "Fuck no. I know exactly what I want to do with you. *To* you. Let me?"

I should fight him more. Just, like, set a precedent for not being a huge pushover when he goes all—*him*.

But I nod, pretty sure there are heart emojis circling my eyes. "Okay."

He beams. "Good."

"Good—oh no, gods, we aren't doing that again."

He laughs. And nudges the herb box in my hands. "Call Nick so we can win this thing and get out of here."

But I don't move. Not yet.

"I'll tell you," I say. "I want to tell you."

Everything. All of it.

It's another shock how much I mean it, how easily I make that promise.

I should have explained what exactly I want to tell him—but Thio's face softens.

This smile is small yet overwhelming.

"Whatever you want, Sebastian," he whispers. "You can tell me whatever you want."

I summon Nick. And not long later, my invisible fox plops a chunk of iron into my palm.

The boxes aren't latched. I could've dropped the iron at any point in my mad dash across the field.

It doesn't matter.

Thio's going on a date with me.

He finishes the teleportation spell. Our cube vanishes, and after a pause, there's a loud, wet plop from across the wall, followed by aggrieved shouts.

The crowd cheers, a roar that cocoons us in white noise as Thio turns to me.

"Looks like we won," he says with a breathless grin.

I return that grin. Feel it through my whole body.

We won?

Yeah.

I'm pretty sure I have.

CAMPUS-WIDE SECURITY ALERT: The missing infant basilisk from the Nomadic Order of the Enchanted Beast Pet Adoption Event has been safely recovered and all affected parties have been de-stoned.

After her daring exploits, during which we are told she assisted in the recovery of a stolen wallet and prevented a fire on the second floor of the Herbology building, the infant basilisk is no longer available for adoption, and will instead be trained to become a guide basilisk for the visually impaired.

Have a happy spring break!

Chapter Thirteen

I stay to watch Orok's charity game while Thio vanishes—to avoid Myrdin's approach, but mostly with mysterious promises that he'll have everything ready when he picks me up tonight. I'm told to *dress nicely.* Which I'm not sure is warranted, given my plans are for whatever clothes I wear to end the evening on someone's bedroom floor, but hey, that *is* the point of an actual *date,* isn't it? To do more than have sex?

Why did I think this was a good idea?

Oh. Because I like the guy.

Probably more, and for longer, than I'll let myself believe.

The kids' group Orok's team is playing didn't come to mess around. Most are high school age, maybe fifteen, sixteen max, but they're out for *blood,* and by the second half, I catch more than a few winded *holy shit* glances between Orok's teammates. The overall vibes are still in good fun. The kids secure a win by one point, and the Manticores cheer and congratulate them with honest excitement.

Security lets me back onto the field and I jog over to the player benches while Orok sprays his face with a water bottle.

"That loss wasn't intentional, was it?"

He glances around, notes only his teammates nearby, and bulges his eyes at me in disbelief. "You see that one rogue get past me to swipe the ball from Crescentia in the third quarter? Where did he come from? Gods, kids these days. They're ruthless. Our future's in good hands."

"All right, Grandpa." I pat his shoulder pad. "Glad you're such a good—"

A woman approaches us, her blue hair pulled up in a sleek bun, eyes a translucent aqua—a siren. She's dressed in a sharp business suit with a leather folio clutched to her chest, immediately making me feel more than a little underdressed in my goo-stained clothes; magic could only clean ooze cube loogies so much.

She stops next to us, and Orok's face pales.

"I've been looking for talent in the wrong places," she says, nothing but camaraderie in her tone, the same pleasantly surprised energy the Manticores show as most mingle with the kids now, exclaiming over them.

But Orok nods tightly. "Yeah."

That's all he says.

I look back at her to figure out why he's being weird and clock the logo imprinted on her folio: the pro rawball insignia.

"She's the recruiter?" I guess. Then, to her, "You're the pro rawball recruiter?"

The woman holds out her hand, and I take it. "Savasea Corruguna. It's reassuring, at least, that Orok has told you about the opportunity." Her eyes sparkle, not from using magic, just in friendliness, and she looks up at him. "Is it too much to hope that that means you've made a decision?"

Orok's mouth bobbles. "Uh. Not yet. No."

It's my turn for my eyes to bulge comically, but he doesn't look at me as Savasea pulls a card out of her folio and extends it to Orok.

"I'd love to talk more before I leave town next week. Give me a call, would you?" She winks at him. "Try not to lose my card this time."

I translate that. "She's asked you to call her before and you *haven't*?"

Orok snatches the card and closes his hand around it, his face cherry red. "I—" He sighs. "Yeah."

I huff at Savasea. "I promise I raised him better than that. He'll call you this time." I bat his chest with the back of my hand. "Won't you?"

Savasea seems amused by me, more so when she realizes I'm on her side. "Thank you. I'd appreciate that."

Orok remembers basic manners all at once. He gives her a smile and blows out an apologetic breath. "Thank you, yes. I will call you. It's just . . . a lot."

I'm practically bouncing in place. *What's* a lot? What's she offered him?

"I understand," Savasea says. "I'm happy to answer any questions you have."

Orok's smile is truer. "Thanks. I'll call you."

She leaves, not heading off to talk to any other players, I note.

Oh my gods. She came for him. To a *charity game,* not even anything official.

The moment she's a respectable distance away, I grab Orok's arm tight enough to sever arteries. "*What was that about,*" I ask, but it comes out as a high-pitched shriek.

Orok hangs his head. "A recruiter. It's noth—"

"If you say *it's nothing,* I swear to the gods—"

"Seb."

I try to rein myself in. His eyes hold mine imploringly.

"You got recruited?" I ask, voice lower. Maybe no one else knows. How would his team not know? If she's been around practices and games.

But how did *I* not know about this offer? How did Orok not tell me?

I don't let the stab of hurt unsettle me. Too much.

"Not recruited," Orok counters. "I'd still have to try out. And it's crazy competitive. But—"

"O." I squeeze his arm more gently. "This is a big deal. You're gonna call her, right?"

He bites his lip.

"O."

"Yeah, I'm gonna call her," he says, but it's lacking several degrees of conviction. He sniffs before his lips twitch in a smile that's—sad? "I'll call her," he says again, more firmly.

I grin. "Good, you oaf." I shake his arm. "This is *good.*"

His happiness brightens. "Maybe. I dunno."

"*I dunno,* he says." I punch his chest. "Well, *I* know that the Hellhounds will be lucky to have you."

There's that sad smile again. He can't still be worried we'll lose touch after graduation?

Yeah, it'll be a big change. But not all changes are bad.

The weight of my mom's text in my phone makes my pocket heavier. I'll delete it the first moment I get.

"Hey." I take his hand. "I'm not going anywhere. We'll get through this phase of our lives together." I smile through a wince. "You're not the only one taking steps like that. I have a date tonight. That I initiated. With Thio." I wince again. "Did I mention I initiated it?"

Orok throws his head back with a cackling *whoop* before he loops his arm around my shoulder and hauls me into his side.

"About time." He laughs into my hair.

But his grip on me stiffens, all his muscles seizing. It sets me on alert.

"I wasn't sure either of us would ever be able to make a connection beyond our trauma bond," he whispers.

I push back. "It's not a trauma bond. And besides, it's one date. A *first* date. It isn't a . . . *connection*."

"Uh-huh. Sure it isn't. What time's he picking you up?"

"Seven. But why—"

Orok's smile is so big his teeth glint in the afternoon sun. "Good. I'll make sure to vet him thoroughly tonight."

My face falls.

I won't be able to rely on Orok having rawball practice to keep him out of the apartment.

"Well." I swallow. "Shit."

Orok's grin is evil. "Trial by fire, baby. He wants you, he's gotta go through all of this." And he waves his hand across his body as he gyrates his hips.

I'm sure tonight'll be fine.

It is not fine.

Not only is Orok home, but a dozen of his teammates also toppled back here with him, and now Orok's drunk, along with Ivo and several other members of the Manticores' defensive line, all of them playing potion pong—a slightly riskier cousin of beer pong with mild low-level spells in the cups instead of alcohol.

One of the other tanks got a weak flight spell and is currently hovering against our ceiling.

Someone else got a potion of fire breathing and is drunkenly, frantically searching on his phone for the antidote because he'd been mid–trying to flirt with a cheerleader, and now every time he talks he spits a column of flames. His friends aren't helping because they're having too much fun laughing at his expense.

It's in the midst of this chaos, with me standing at the base of the stairs and considering downing an invisibility potion so I can sneak to the door unnoticed, that the doorbell rings.

Music had been playing, but that shuts off. Conversation, ribbing each other—it all flatlines.

An apartment full of Manticores looks at me.

Orok told them I have a date tonight.

All their heads simultaneously swing left, then back to me, and they clock that every single one of them is standing between me and the front door.

The doorbell rings again.

In perfect mimicry of a Wild West standoff, none of us move. None of us blink.

My fingers twitch at my sides, but I didn't wear my component belt—I have a few things lodged in my back pocket though. Will they do me any good?

Best to run for it.

I bolt forward, but Orok and his teammates react like a gun went off, and I'm quickly thwarted by my attempt at running offense against a group of people who are trained to hold off far bulkier people than I am. I end up trapped behind a wall made of Ivo and the guy who took the fire potion, both looking too smug as Orok reaches the door first with three other players.

He swings it open and puts on his best *who the fuck are you* voice. "Can I help you?"

Thio looks so good I briefly forget I should be struggling to get out the door. He's in dark jeans with a chunky silver buckle on his black belt, and a short sleeve knitted black T-shirt shows off most of the ink on his arms. Gods, I bet he smells good, too.

His hair's down and swept over his head, and his lips quirk as he takes in his greeting party of four physically intimidating assholes, one still hovering up by the ceiling.

Thio spots me behind my own two assholes before his head tips in question.

"Can I *help* you?" Orok snaps at Thio again, this time folding his arms over his chest. The terrorizing effect is lost when the rest of the people with him do the same thing, to the point I think they must've rehearsed it; but no, they're all sharing one drunk brain cell that collectively went, *Be scary, make self big.*

Thio sticks his hand out to Orok, amused but playing along. "Elethior Tourael, here for Sebastian Walsh."

Orok lets Thio's hand hang for a stretched-out beat in which he thrusts his jaw forward.

He finally shakes Thio's hand. Hard. "Orok Monroe. It's nice to meet you when you aren't creeping out of my apartment with mysterious stains on your shirt."

Thio's eyes round.

"Okay, that's enough of that." I try to shoulder my way around Ivo and Fire Breather—Kenneth, actually—but they move to block me. "Seriously? Orok! This isn't—"

Kenneth opens his mouth, his eyes bloodshot, and before he can say anything and exhale fire all over me, I whip up my hand.

"If you singe even one hair on my head, I will resort to magic-user stereotypes and turn you into a newt."

His mouth shuts.

And his lower lip juts out.

"Oh, for the love." I pull a vial of components for a cleansing spell from my back pocket. "Here. Mix it in some water. Drink it. And start bringing your own counterspells to parties."

Kenneth takes it with a happy mew, his lips firmly shut.

Ivo snorts. "Softy."

Over their shoulders, Orok is still doing his best to look terrifying. Thio's expression is even more terrifyingly blank. I'm hard-pressed to figure out how this is going to go down, which side I should be leaping to defend.

But Thio smiles. "Your stats are impressive," he says to Orok.

My confusion forces out a strangled cough. "What?"

Thio looks at me but points to Orok. "His stats. He's one of the best defensive tanks we've ever had."

Orok glances back at his teammates with a lip pucker of approval. "He's a fan. Stand down."

The group immediately clears. Music starts back up, Ivo and Kenneth cut back to the potion pong table, and I hurry to the door, my face scrunched.

"You know his rawball stats because—?"

"I . . . go to Lesiara U," Thio says, like it should be obvious.

"And you watch rawball games?"

"Yes."

"On purpose?"

He smiles. "Ah. Not a fan?"

"I'm not *not* a fan," I allow, and Orok elbows me hard enough I puff out all the air in my lungs.

"Don't lie to your date, Sebby. That's rude," he says in a fatherly, chastising voice.

Thio's amusement sharpens. "I'm guessing I shouldn't have bought tickets to the Philly Hellhounds training game for our date tonight?"

Silence reigns. Me, in horror, trying to figure out if I can date someone who likes rawball; Orok, in a drunken delayed reaction, piecing together whether Thio's joking about the tickets, and if he's *not* joking, whether he could weasel in on our date; and Thio, watching me, bright eyes glittering.

Orok breaks the silence with a barking laugh and throws his arm around me. "I like him, Seb. Don't fuck it up."

I shrug him off. He has a habit of mussing my hair, and I managed to tame my curls tonight. I don't want my clothes wrinkled either, a bright blue crewneck sweater that makes my eyes pop, brown pleated pants, and even my nice leather shoes—sorry, Converse, sometimes I gotta cheat on you.

"Well." I kick the kitchen floor. All things considered, this wasn't as awkward as Orok threatened, so I resolve to get out while I'm ahead. "Don't wait up."

But Orok grabs my arm as I step away. Thio, who'd turned for the hall, stops and meets his eyes.

The party's back in full swing behind us. Someone takes a potion that makes them refract light like a disco ball, so we're bathed in flashing silver specks, but the energy between the three of us dips.

Orok's expression toward Thio is severe, and I lift my other hand, start to step between them, when Orok says, simply, "Don't hurt him."

It's a plea. It's a command.

I've had relationships before and gone on dates plenty. Orok's messed with a few of them, playfully threatened people, but that's where it ends.

This protectiveness is . . . new. Why?

My usual wall-building thoughts stack up in my head like bricks. *This is just a date.* Brick.

It's still something simple and easy. Brick.

Whatever Orok's picking up on, about this being different, he's wrong. Brick.

The wall wobbles. Teeters. Topples right on down, even before Thio steps back across the threshold.

"I won't," he promises with a smile, one as vulnerable, somehow, as Orok's plea. "It took me most of the semester to get him this far. I don't plan on hurting him or letting him go."

The noise I make is somewhere between a wheeze and an undignified whimper.

Orok and Thio both look at me, then back at each other, and the serious moment is broken when they share a grin. At my expense.

I free myself from Orok's clutches. "If you're done discussing my dowry, we're off."

"Two grand," Orok says too quickly. "I'd also settle for a new gaming system. Dealer's choice."

Thio pretends to consider. Or, at least, that'd better be fake consideration. "Done."

"Two grand?" I squawk. "Fuck you both, my virtue is worth more than that."

Orok laughs in a way that's just the word *wah* shouted really loud. "Virtue. Right."

I wave Thio to leave and follow him into the hall. But as I shut the door behind me, I lock eyes with Orok.

Thanks, I mouth.

He winks.

Then points in the direction of Thio and makes a complicated series of perverted hand gestures I interpret as *tap dat ass.*

I slam the door.

Thio's leaning against the wall next to the stairwell, swinging a set of keys around his finger.

He looks wildly amused. "I passed the best friend test?"

"That's not an accomplishment. Orok has a terrible bullshit radar." I nod at his keys. "No Hordon tonight?"

"Nope. I'm going full proper date with you. Pick up at the front door, interrogated by the father—"

I'm on him, pressing him into the wall, hands fisted in the sides of his shirt.

He does smell good. Like the deep part of a forest after it rains, lush greenery and warm springtime, but something else, too; garlic, maybe? Spices? I bury my nose in his neck and he hums contentedly.

"I need to get this out of my system before you drive us anywhere," I whisper against his skin.

He shivers, hands going down to grab my ass. "I don't know about you, but I've stopped believing there's a way to get this out of my system at all. I'm pretty sure you *are* my system now."

My lips trail up the side of his neck, tongue following the curve of his jaw. I rest my mouth over his and close my eyes, but he's still consuming me. Scent and touch and taste and the stuttered gusts of his breath.

"You've wanted me all semester?" I ask into his mouth. No way I'm going to let that comment to Orok slide. Not when Thio's said stuff like that before. Not when he didn't back down from Orok's *interrogation,* and does seem to be legitimately unthreatened by our relationship.

Thio threads his fingers up the back of my hair. I swear I can feel the warmth coming off his cheeks from his blush. "Yes."

"Even when we hated each other?"

His forehead rests against mine and he drags his hand around to cup my jaw. My eyes are still shut. Can't look at him. Can't see whatever his face is doing as he says, "That's part of what drew me to you at first—you so obviously hated the Touraels. And it wasn't the usual type of hate we get; it was—" He falters and goes silent. "It was personal. I know now. But I knew you wouldn't be a pushover like everyone else. I knew they wouldn't be able to manipulate you." He pauses. "Plus, you're insanely hot."

I peek at him, doing my best to look sardonic. There's a crash of emotions battering me apart, fighting to be felt, to be acknowledged. "Ah. My prejudices and virulent sex appeal are the only reasons you're with me. The truth comes out."

He smiles. "*At first*. But now?"

A kiss on my cheekbone, trembling.

"Now," he says again. Like there's a lot more waiting behind that *now*, more he doesn't want to say. Not yet.

I swallow, my body overheating in this chilly stairwell.

"Now," he says again, more resolute, "I'm going to take you to my apartment, where I made you dinner."

I pull back with a goofy grin. "You made me dinner?"

He looks deservedly proud. "And I'm going to wine and dine the fuck out of you. I haven't had many good things in my life that my family didn't ruin." He interlaces his fingers with mine. "So this? I'm going to do this right."

Gods help me. Someone, somewhere, surely there's a god up there who'll step in and prevent me from melting into a useless, babbling puddle of myself. But no such luck; I'm a doe-eyed goner. A sappy, lovestruck—

Woah.

Big word.

Big, scary word.

I look down at Thio's hand in mine.

I'm going to do this right.

On the challenge field, I'd decided that, too. Hell, pretty much from the start of this, when we were hooking up, I made myself adhere to doing things right. The *healthy* way. The way with boundaries and communication.

I promised I'd tell him what happened. And I know, if I want this to be something more, something *solid*, that he needs to understand that part of me; and there's no way he can do that if I don't tell him.

I probe that decision now, have been all night. Is it still something I want? That's the real test of this being different. If I can nudge that bruise, and want to push forward even with the pain.

I kiss him. Just lips and breath, gentle nips and unspoken secrets.

"Let's get to this wining and dining, mister," I tell him, and he happily obliges.

Chapter Fourteen

So. Thio's loaded.

Which, I knew, but there's *you have a car and a driver* knowing, then there's *you have a penthouse apartment with a private elevator that lets off IN YOUR LIVING ROOM* knowing.

I stand in the middle of said living room, jaw unhinged and not trying to hide it. Floor-to-ceiling windows show the Philly skyline tucking itself up at night, city lights twinkling in lieu of stars we can't see. The two-story walls are white, which should look stark and cold, but the furnishings are black leather and reflective chrome, so the overall effect is sleek and—yeah, still cold. Even with a fireplace going, flames crackling and warm.

It's not the furnishings that make it sterile; it's so *clean* here. None of the messy chaos that plagues Thio's workstation at the lab. So though I know he lives here, heard the doorman greet him by name, saw him put his key into the elevator, it doesn't *feel* like his home. It feels like a hotel.

The living area pours into a kitchen with a huge island dividing the space, the black marble swirled with veins of brown. Dishes sit on the edge, all covered, but they scent the air with garlic and sharp tomatoes. A dining table stretches behind the leather couch, and two places are set along with a bottle of wine and a vase of roses.

He bought me flowers.

For some reason, it's the roses that render me speechless and I'm more than a little annoyed at the way my eyes sting.

Thio tosses his keys into a bowl by the elevator and rubs a hand through his hair. "So. Um. Want a tour?"

I realize I've been quiet for a solid minute, standing there motionless.

I feign adjusting my glasses to cover wiping my eyes. "Do I need a ticket?"

Thio's lips quirk. "I'm sure the tour guide can fit you in."

"I dunno. A place like this?"

I spin in a circle and spot a statue beside the fireplace. It's metal and shaped like a . . . horse? No. A dragon? No clue. But it's taller than I am and looks like it belongs in a contemporary art museum, not someone's living room.

"Good gods, Thio. This is—"

"A lot." He pulls at his hair again. "I know. It's the family's. I'm staying here while at school."

"Ah." Another slow circle. Oh, there's a chandelier. Why not? It's the size of my bed. I let out a whistle. "Damn. I get it now. Why you play along with them."

I roll my eyes shut in a cringe.

"I'm sorry." I turn to him, but his face is unreadable. "I didn't mean—I know you're not doing it for perks."

He smiles, a wince. "I know."

I look at the time on my phone. "Three minutes into this date, and I've killed the mood. A new personal record."

Thio smiles for real this time and reaches out. I close the remaining distance, and the moment our fingers touch, a mushroom cloud bubbles in my stomach.

He sighs like he feels it, too. Like me being close is something calming.

"I like that you call me on it," he says to our conjoined hands. "It's keeping me focused on what matters. Getting out from under their thumb. Being able to support my mom on my own. I—" He hesitates. "I started figuring out who I need to contact. For after graduation."

His silence is heavy, so I rub the back of his hand, watching goose bumps ripple up his arm.

Thio arches his gaze up to the cathedral ceiling. "I know I need to put plans in motion, but I don't want to risk news getting to my family. The moment I take this step, the moment I officially reach out to any of their competitors . . ."

"It's a bell you can't unring. I get it."

He's stiff, the telling of this not alleviating his stress, but seeming to make it worse. The reminder of the responsibilities looming.

"What would you do?" I ask, gently brushing a piece of hair by his face. "What do you *want* to do, I mean? If you could. What's your dream job?"

Thio gives me such a perplexed look, it's heartbreaking.

"What would make you happy?" I try again. The question is a crowbar, and the way Thio's biting the inside of his cheek is a locked chest.

"Sebastian—"

"I'm saying, maybe there's a way to incorporate something you want to do into this. Maybe it isn't self-sacrifice or bust."

Thio twists our hands to thread his fingers with mine, holding the knotted tangle to his chest. His expression shutters, like he's reached the max of his sharing abilities tonight, and normally, I'd let it drop. I'd pivot the conversation to something safe. But tonight *is* different. I want to know. I want to know everything.

I keep my eyes on his, eager, and he looks away with a low sigh.

"I always liked helping people," he whispers. "The nurses who've cared for my mom especially—they've all been great. That'd be nice, I think. To actively help someone."

I smile.

That's what I want, too. The reason I'm doing everything I can to keep my upcoming job at Clawstar. To replace the bad in my life with active good.

I have no idea if there's room for anything like that with the competitors he's focused on reaching out to, but his tone, his posture, the tender look of longing on his face—

I squeeze his fingers. "You shouldn't give up on that. If that's something you want. I bet your mom wants that for you, too. For you to be happy."

Thio's eyes are watery as they shift over mine. Back and forth, back and forth.

His silence lasts so long I know I overstepped.

Shit. Am I guilting him into doing this? That's not what I meant—

He seizes my mouth in his.

The kiss is brutal. I don't try to assert dominance, just give it all up to him with a helpless moan as his tongue invades my mouth.

"Thank you," he says when he lets me up for air. "I haven't had—" A swallow, the scratch of it loud. "I haven't had many—fuck, Sebastian." He leaves kisses like breadcrumbs he'll pick back up later as he works his way down my neck. "How did I find you?"

The words tattoo right where his lips are, at the intersection of neck and shoulder. The world goes evanescent, attention whittling to sensation only, and that sensation is a falling open.

He tries to pull at my belt, but I'm somehow conscious enough to constrict my fingers around his wrists.

"Dinner. You made me dinner."

"Mmhmm."

"And you bought me flowers."

I feel his smile. Feel the stretch of his lips against my skin. I shiver.

"Yes."

"I want to eat this dinner you made me next to those flowers you bought me."

A bite on my neck, one that has my knees wavering, his arm banding across my lower back to hold me to him. He's hard and I am, too, and if I grind on him once, twice, well, that's not *my* fault, is it, when he's gasping in my ear like that?

"Dinner," he growls, hoarse.

He steps back, smooths out his shirt, and blows a long exhale. I'm sure I look just as disheveled, touching my kiss-swollen lips.

Exasperation is scrawled all over his features.

"Sit." He points at the table.

"Barking commands at me. So chivalrous."

His chin tips down. Prickles race up my spine, fizzling at the base of my neck. Warning, instinct; gods, it's delicious now.

"Sit at the table, Sebastian," he tells me. "Or I'm going to fuck you over the back of my couch, and we'll never get around to eating."

My breath catches. Doesn't just catch; it's fully reeled in, vanishing above the surface, leaving me down below in cool dark water and utter stillness.

I'd hoped that was where tonight would end up. We haven't taken that step yet, not as fuck-buddies, but now? I didn't know if it'd be on the table.

Apparently it's on the back of the couch.

And hopefully his bed.

Possibly the shower.

Fuck.

I take the seat he indicated, the one closest to the flowers at the head of the table, and watch him over the island as he sets about re-heating food with an easy warming spell. I point at the wine bottle, and he nods, so I pour us each a glass as I note his television across the room.

It isn't a television. It's a tank. A reptile tank? With stones and logs, a light, dishes for food and water.

And on a log, curled up in a tight oval, is a pink snake.

"Um. Thio?"

Ceramic clatters as he moves a lid. "Yeah?"

"Your familiar. What is it again?"

His eyes dart to the tank and he grins. "Ah. That's Paeris."

I watch him sort out food for a minute, waiting for his explanation. None comes.

"You have a magical creature," I say. "Living in a reptile tank. Like a *pet*."

He ladles something out of a baking dish. "You know very well he could go back to the Familiar Plane anytime he wants."

"What if you need him for spell work?"

"Summoning him from here is the same as from another plane." He shrugs one shoulder. "He's happy here."

I chuckle into my wineglass. "And you gave me crap for letting Nick be invisible. You're as whipped by your familiar as I am by mine."

Thio rounds the island and places two plates on the table, one for him, one for me, before taking the seat next to me.

I lean over the plate and inhale savory heaven. "What *is* this?"

Thio elegantly puts his napkin on his lap. Meanwhile, I'm already snatching up my fork like the uncultured mess he for whatever reason is attracted to.

"Rotini with grilled chicken and a sun-dried tomato parmesan cream sauce," he tells me with a dismissive wave, and I pause to give him a dry look.

"Oh? Just that? Sound less impressed with yourself. Like using sun-dried tomatoes isn't some *Top Chef* fancy business."

Thio beams, cheeks pinking; I want to kiss them.

But the siren song—siren scent? Siren scent-song?—of the pasta is screaming at me. I shovel in a bite.

And moan.

Gods, do I moan.

It's tart and creamy and cheesy, savory and sweet and *fuuuuuuck*.

"*Holy shit*," I mumble around my mouthful. "Where did you learn to—*how* did you—"

His smile could power the city. "You like it?"

"You can *cook*." I take another bite. "Oh my gods. If there'd been any question about whether I put out on the first date, you can assuage your worries. I will. Done and done."

He laughs, eyes catching the chandelier light, and he looks so damn happy. I *feel* so damn happy as our gazes connect over the table. The moment stretches, warping and extending until the bulk of his apartment fades into darkness; only his face is illuminated in light we generate. Our own chiaroscuro reality.

I stab a piece of chicken, but I just push it through the sauce.

I'd wanted it to come up naturally in conversation. I'd wait, and let it happen. I've never told anyone else before, not since I went through it, so I expected to get derailed by resistance and want to put it off, but—

But I want to tell him. I *want* him to know. It feels easy.

Everything with him has felt easy.

And it's frightening, bone-rattlingly *terrifying*.

Thio frowns when I don't keep eating.

"Orok and I went to Camp Merethyl together," I say in a rush. "So a lot of this . . . what I tell you, know it's my story, but it's his, too."

Thio lays down his fork and puts his elbows on the table to lean toward me, immediately attentive.

I should've waited until after we ate.

But he takes my hand, plays with my fingers, and doesn't say anything, letting it be fully in my court.

The only reason I don't scratch at my forearms is because of the grip he has on my hand.

I blow out a breath, staring at the roses. Dark, rich maroon. "We started there the summer after freshman year of high school. It was a proud moment for us both—my family's all into the military, his is all into the god Urzoth Shieldsworn. We were going to do our four summers in their training program, then graduate and go off to the Arcane Forces. Fulfill both our various family expectations."

Thio knows all about that weight. I don't have to explain.

My knee bounces. "We got there, and there's a test they make you do. A placement exam. They put you in one of five levels based on your skills. It's—"

"Five levels?" Thio's fingers throb on mine. "I've only heard of four."

My lips pull up, but it isn't a smile. I wonder if he can feel the way my heart kicks into overdrive, the thudding of my pulse in my fingertips.

"That's what my father said. *Sebastian, the Walshes have been going to Camp Merethyl for generations,*" I mimic his deep voice. "*We'd know if there was a secret fifth level you claim to have gotten placed in. Don't make up stories.*"

Thio's head tips. "The camp didn't inform your parents of your progress? You were a minor. Don't they have to get approval for things?"

"At Camp Merethyl, I wasn't a minor. I was a soldier. My parents signed the same waivers as everyone else's. And in those waivers, there's a whole lot of legalese about safeguarding the proprietary training programs that Camp Merethyl uses, blah blah blah; basically, you sign away your right to know what they're doing to your kid."

"How—" Thio hesitates. "How are people okay with that?"

I drop back against the chair, shoulders hitting it hard. Thio doesn't let go of my hand; he adjusts to the edge of his seat so he can stay in contact.

"The people who graduate from Camp Merethyl go on to be some of the most powerful wizards in the world. So what if they come home at the end of the summer with scars and stories of abuse and neglect? It's all in the name of *toughening them up*. That's how soldiers are made. Even at *fourteen*."

My voice gets too loud, knee bouncing, rattling the table.

Thio squeezes my hand. "Sebastian. You don't have to—"

"I do." My eyes lock on his. "I really do."

He studies me, my wide eyes, my quivering tension.

I scrub a hand down my face, willing the words to uproot with the least pain. "My family all graduated from Camp Merethyl. Well, not my mom, but my siblings, my dad; his side. None of them believed me when I told them Orok and I had been selected for an elite training level. I was also, well, *me*; scrawnier then than I am now, and I was always good at spells, but the physical side of things? No way. Why would *I* have been chosen?"

My throat closes. I clear it, try again.

"There were ten of us in that fifth level. The camp dropped us in the middle of the Appalachians, no supplies. Told us we had two days to get back to camp, or we'd forfeit all meal tickets for a week. They'd refuse us food and water regularly, in an effort to train us not to need it. Sleep, too; we'd get woken up every hour for two days straight, one day off, and repeat. They taught us fighting styles, hands and fists, and with weapons, too, but padding? Blunted training weapons? No. If you bled, no meal tickets. That wasn't far off from what the *normal* training levels endured; wilderness training, combat. Just not as . . . brutal as what we had in that fifth level. I told my parents what they were doing to us, and my dad said I was exaggerating."

Thio's watching me. I can feel it. But my gaze isn't here anymore, I'm only grounded in his touch.

"Orok and I were paired up from the start. We were all in pairs. Anything we did, we had to do together, or fail and lose meal tickets, water tickets, sleep tickets—yeah, after the second summer, we had those. They controlled everything we did at every moment of the day, all in an effort to *hone our skills*. But these tests, the things they taught us and had us do—they were about how far we could push magic. How much we could test the limits of spells on the elements, on our situations. On ourselves.

"The only reason I got through those summers was because of Orok. He was there, enduring it with me." My lungs quake, hurting. "He made me feel like I wasn't crazy. The things I told my father were being done to us *were* happening, and I *wasn't* lying. It was real."

I'm up and pacing in a tight line behind the chair before I realize that means releasing Thio's hand, but I'm in motion already.

"The last summer." My fingers go to my arms under my sleeves, scratching. The pain flares, centers me. "We knew it'd be bad. We'd spent the previous summers getting screamed at, doused in freezing water, beaten when we complained, left for nearly dead in all manner of places, starved and driven to insanity with sleep deprivation, all while doing things with magic that left us drained emotionally, physically—but we knew, this summer? It'd be worse. Orok and I promised we'd watch out for each other. But we still—gods." I shove my glasses up my nose. It doesn't clear my vision. "We still wanted to make our families proud, ya know? Orok's were pushing the doctrine of strength; mine were impatiently waiting for the last Walsh to prove he wasn't a whiny little bitch. My brother's words, not mine."

Thio's standing. I don't know when he moved. His arms are loose at his sides and his head shifts as he tracks me across his dining room.

"Somewhere during the first weeks," I say to the floor as I walk, turn, walk, turn, "the other pairs of fifth-level students—soldiers—vanished. I don't know what happened to them. If they dropped out, or if they . . . but it was just me and Orok. In that mythical fifth-level training program. The instructors focused all their attention on us. Said we were the future of wizardry and a whole lot of other bullshit as they pushed us and pushed us and we obeyed, because—because we were *kids*, we were scared *kids*, and no one ever believed us anyway."

I stop. Stop walking. Stop digging at my arms; they ache, feel bruised.

"Our final test," I whisper, "was before graduation. Before all *their* hard work paid off—the instructors'. We were an experiment; that was why no one had ever heard of a fifth level. There hadn't been one. We were the first. A test of an elite type of training, pairing up wizards for remote, risky missions. The program had been about testing the limits of magic and forging a bond between us. Well, Orok and I had certainly bonded. We thought we could handle whatever final thing they threw at us, then it'd be over, *it'd be over*."

My hand goes to my forehead, and I take a couple of deep, steadying gulps of air. Get it out. Get the words out.

Get out get out GET OUT—

"They put us in a sealed, empty room. Used scrying magic to communicate with us. Told us there was a ward on the door. Told us to break it." My eyes meet Thio's. He hasn't moved, watches me, hands still loose, ready. I'm not. "We didn't have any components. They'd yanked us out of bed in the middle of the night. We were sleep-deprived, hadn't eaten in two days. But they told us to get out of that room. How do you do a spell when you have no components?"

I'm asking him.

Thio frowns. "You don't."

"Wrong. To break a ward, what do you need?"

Thio knows I'm pushing him toward something but he can't see what yet. And I hate that I'm doing this to him. That there'll be a before and an after.

"Chalk to draw sigils, and iron from a lock," he says.

"No," I snap. "No. You only need iron to break a ward. It being from a lock is semantics. It isn't *required*. You can force the spell to work through it, like with chalk and drawing sigils; it just helps you focus. But you don't *need* any of that. You only need iron."

He looks appalled. As he should. "That isn't how magic is done," he hisses, not at me, at the situation. "That's—there are *rules*. Forcing magic to use components like that could damage the wizards who do it or result in the spells recoiling dangerously—"

He cuts himself off. I know he's thinking of his mom, how her experiment recoiled; but that's how dangerous magic can be. That's how volatile. And now here are two instances of the Touraels being behind the advancement of magic, whatever the cost.

"Where can you get iron," I whisper, "if you're trapped in a room without any components? Just you. And your partner. Where can you get iron?"

His face drains of color.

"They'd been testing us for years," I say. "Leaving us in barren places, telling us to do this spell or work out this problem with whatever we had on hand. Forcing us to use what we had available, in the most extreme, stark situations. They called it an ouroboros partnership. It was why we were paired up. Every wizard has most of the components they need—if they have access to a person."

Thio collapses back into his seat. "No. That kind of magic is illegal. *Highly* illegal. Not even necromancers use human remains in spells."

"It isn't human remains." The words come and I'm separate from them. "Not if the person's still alive. Not if they give it up willingly. An ouroboros, symbiotic; a snake eating itself. That's why they had us work on our bond, so one of us would be willing. The instructors rationalized it—it wasn't crossing legal boundaries if it was a new form of wizardry. They were sculpting an exclusive type of arcane soldier."

I don't need to pace anymore. I don't even need the numbing pain of scratching at my arms. I go limp, staring at Thio.

"Orok and I both refused to do that to each other to get out of that room. Then they started pumping in water. *Your parents signed the waivers,* they told us. *Accidents happen.*"

Pathetic.

This was wasted on you.

No one else could handle this program either. Are you going to let this be a failure? You could change the rules of magic. You could be a pioneer. The first ouroboros partnership.

You had such promise, Mr. Walsh. Mr. Monroe.

I touch my shoulder. The place where Orok dragged his nail through his own skin, tore it open. *Use it, Seb. Fucking do it!* As frigid water lapped at our thighs and we shuddered head to toe.

His blood was sluggish. Because of the hypothermia, the malnutrition. I had to drag it out, focus on the iron in him and *pull.*

Tears drip down my cheeks. I scrub them away with my thumb and cut my eyes up to that massive chandelier. That massive chandelier that the Touraels paid for, in this massive apartment they own.

"I got us out," I tell Thio. "And while Orok was in the infirmary, unconscious from blood loss, and the instructors were congratulating me on doing such a good job, I told them I was done. I wasn't going to graduate. I wasn't going to be their elite wizard pet. They . . . did not like that."

I smile at the memory of their shocked faces, how they were unable to comprehend why I'd say no *now,* when I was done. Why I hadn't *voiced concerns* years ago.

I had. Over and over. To them. To my dad.

Gods, I'd been so certain he'd save me after that first summer. I'd *known* he'd help.

My smile grows. Grows too big. I'm bent double, laughing at things that aren't funny.

"And then that stupid iron box," I wheeze to the floor. "At the challenge today? We had to leave our component belts, too. And the iron was missing. The *iron.* I probably dropped it, but gods, Thio. I was back there and they were making me do it to *you* now, and I—"

He's sitting perfectly still in his chair, eyes wide, face deathly pale.

I'm on my knees in front of him before I can process why. My hands rest on his thighs, and I look up into his face.

"I dropped out of Camp Merethyl," I tell him. "I dropped out and became the disgrace of my family, and they think I'm an immature screwup who couldn't cut it as a real wizard. Now my father is going to run that place—"

Thio jolts. I hadn't told him that yet.

"He got the job, he's going to be the next director, and—and part of me is glad for it. He'll have access to the records, won't he? He'll see what they did to me. He'll *know* that I wasn't lying. That it happened, *he let it happen,* and it was *horrific.*"

Thio stays silent, not reaching for me.

Oh, gods.

Does . . . does he not believe me either?

The idea is more sickening than I anticipated. That he'll scowl and echo one of the things my father has said. *Don't make up stories, Sebastian. Do you need attention that badly? No one would pervert magic like that, certainly not at a place as esteemed as Camp Merethyl.*

I dig my fingers into Thio's thighs. "Say something. Say—say anything, please."

"Who?"

My shoulders go rigid. "What?"

"Who was at the camp?"

His voice is—I can't figure it out. Angry? No.

He's *irate.*

Redness rises up his neck, hits his face; his eyes are murderous, his jaw tight.

"Which of my piece-of-shit family members were part of that program?" he asks through his teeth. "Which of them did that to you?"

My mouth opens. Nothing comes out.

He believes me. He's not dismissing it. He's not putting it on me.

Thio grabs my hands. "No, never mind. You've told me enough. I can find out on my own. You don't need to do anything else, okay? You—"

"Thio—"

"They'll pay for this, Sebastian," he swears to me. His eyes are wide and manic in their fury. "Everything they've done. Everything they *do*. They won't get away with this. I'll make them *pay for this*."

Tonight has ripped open wounds and I feel every single one all at once. Gashes here, cuts there, a laceration in my chest; my heart beats and hits it.

"No," I say. "Going up against your family for this is a move you can't undo either, like getting a job with their competitor. You have too much to lose."

"I've lost *everything* to them already." He's practically yelling. I flinch. "I won't lose—"

"This isn't what I need from you."

That pulls him back. Settles him, one slow blink at a time, until he frees a palm to cup my jaw.

"Shit, I'm sorry." He kisses my cheekbone. Lingers with his nose pressed alongside mine. "I'm sorry, baby. What do you need?"

He believes me.

That's all I need.

I lock my lips with his, licking into his mouth, and it isn't healing, it doesn't erase what I told him, what truths I shared. It just makes them bearable.

That's what I've done since those summers. I can't erase the trauma; I find what makes it endurable. I learn to live around it.

And kissing Thio? Being with him?

Is the most riotous kind of living.

"Take me to bed," I plead.

Dinner's mostly uneaten next to us, gone cold, and I wince at it. My appetite's shot to hell now, but . . . he made me dinner.

"I mean, after we finish—"

Thio hauls me to my feet. "It'll keep."

Chapter Fifteen

Thio's bedroom smells so strongly of him that I'm shunted into an aphrodisiacal cloud. It buffers the sharp edges of the transition, dinner to revelation to desire.

I take a beat to note the room—gray bedding, dark gray walls, a soft light Thio dims via a switch near the door. This space would be as cold and impersonal as the rest of the apartment, if not for the plants bearding the edges of the room. That's why it smells like him here, not the burrowing in of his cologne, but the hearty abundance of plant life, potted trees and flowers. Like his mom's place at the care facility.

This room is more lived-in, clothes spilling across the floor, a stack of books on a dresser, the barest suggestion of the mess Thio scatters all over our lab.

He stops a few feet in front of me.

"What do you need?" he asks again, breathless, respectful.

Not this.

I cringe, and he catches it, his face pulsing in confusion before his eyes shut.

"Sebastian," he whispers. "I'm not sure I can continue to be impersonal. That I can put the space you need with—"

"That's not it." I sit on his bed. "I—"

That's a lie. That *is* it; my instinct is to throw up a boundary. Especially after something like what we just did, me being so voluntarily candid, with no flicker of deprecation.

If I make a mockery of things, if it's light and unserious, then everything's fine. It's proof I'm not hurt because, look, I can joke around, see? I don't need gentleness because only broken people need gentleness and *I'm not hurting.*

But this does hurt.

And when I think we've reached the bottom of the pain Thio

and I will inspire, no, there's more, sublevel after sublevel of vulnerability.

I've never gone down this deep. I won't know my way back up.

I reach out, fingers quaking. "Thio."

His eyes open. He takes my hand, and I pull him to stand between my spread legs. His fingers on my cheek catch tears I'd forgotten about, wipe them away with sure movements.

"Let me take care of you," he implores. "Please."

No, I don't need that; no, I'm not broken; no, I'm fine.

My jaw clenches against all my self-preservation, and I nod.

He leans down, cradling my jaw in his palm, and offers me a kiss. Slow, velvet swipes of his lips, each brush reverent. It doesn't build, doesn't push faster, stays the same until I surrender to its constancy. That constancy becomes its own evolution; my inhales get ragged, my hands find Thio's shoulders and grip on.

More, part of me cries out.

This, another part says. *This, forever.*

He peels off my sweater and motions for me to move higher up the bed. I lie back on his pillows and he grabs the hem of his shirt, whips the whole thing off one-handed.

My eyes pop. "Oh."

"What?"

"Oh. Just *oh.* An unremarkable exhalation of sound. Oh, it's Friday. Oh, it rained a few days ago. Oh, a hot guy did the one-handed cross-body shirt-stripping move. No biggie."

He prowls toward the bed. There's no other way to describe it. It's a *prowl,* his eyes darkening, shoulders tensing—this, I know what to do with.

So when he says, "Just a hot guy, huh?" in a teasing voice, he's going along with my energy shift. Making it light, making it easy.

He crawls over top of me, holding himself up on hands and knees.

I lay my fingers on his hips; even that minimal contact is electric. "No."

His brows pull together. "No?"

I dig my fingers against his skin, mouth dry, heart overtaxed already. "Not just a hot guy. My—"

Everything I told him in his dining room was terrifying.

This is . . . excruciating.

Thio takes one of my arms. Angry red scratches run up from my wrist; they're almost always there. He presses his lips to those lines, peppering kisses over the physical proof of my anxiety.

Pressure, from both pain and comfort, squeezes my throat.

"Do you want me to say it?" he whispers. "What you are to me?"

I shake my head again. No more talking. I'll ruin it, or it'll open too wide and eat me whole.

Thio doesn't agree, doesn't do anything to say he understands. But he tells me by the way he moves those kisses to my mouth, agonizingly sweet again, and taps whimpers out of me in no time. He's whimpering, too, and seems to lose control of the kiss; it stops being gentle, teeth crushing together, tongues and delving fingers and our bodies grinding.

I need to feel the expanse of him against me. I haven't felt that yet. Suddenly everything we've done is the worst kind of *not enough,* morsels that have barely sustained me and underneath it all, I'm starving.

I work his belt and pants open and shove them down. He kicks his shoes off, loses his clothes, then we're twisting in a lurch and I throw him onto his back. I rid myself of my remaining clothes and lay my body out over his.

Skin connects with skin from head to toe, warmth shuddering through me in cresting wave after cresting wave and I hold there on him, hips gyrating, the two of us breathing frantically.

"Want you," he says into those breaths. "Want you so damn much."

Still can't speak. Don't trust myself. Too many words want to come, words I can't say; if I strip any more bare, I'll turn inside out.

I slide down his body, tracing his tattoos with my tongue. I owe him something, after the Founder's Day challenge; he got back to the wall with the components first. Even if we hadn't made that bet, I'd be salivating for him.

I lick one nipple until the hollow of his throat throbs with a stifled moan. I watch it beat, beat, hips canting to the drums. His fingers tangle in my hair and knock my glasses askew; I rip them off and toss them onto his nightstand. I can see fine up close, but if I couldn't, he so vibrantly dominates all my other senses that sight is a distant concern.

I continue down, mapping his body, rememorizing it from all our hasty blowjobs and fumbled, chaotic interactions.

Yes, sweet is frightening. It's real and foundational.

But gods, it's *good*.

So good, the noises he's making in these gradual, syrupy touches. The way the muscles in his abs jump when I coast my lips down his defined V. His eyes lidding and bursting back open because he wants to watch but also can't stay present in the onslaught.

By the time I take him into my mouth, he's shaking all over and so am I.

"Sebastian," he gasps, and I answer with a long, thorough suck that has him hissing. "Sebastian." Just my name, some filthy prayer as I drag my tongue through his slit.

He slaps at his nightstand, wrenches the drawer open, and a container of lube plunks onto the mattress next to me, followed by a condom.

I pull off. Look at the condom, then up at him.

We talked about our test results the night we hooked up the first time, but if he wants to use protection, that's fine. Probably for the best; hey, I get to keep one barrier in place today.

He's panting, but he comes through the haze enough to say, "I wasn't sure if you wanted to use it?"

I shake my head and pause, waiting to see if he wants to.

With absolutely no hesitation, he snatches the condom and frisbees it across the room.

A laugh sputters out of me.

"No magic either," he says. "Just you. Just want you."

Gods.

I crawl back up, kissing the hell out of him through my smile. He tastes like rich red wine and happiness.

"You gonna fuck me, Tourael?" I ask between kisses, and he groans, our dicks sliding together in increasingly frenzied pulls.

A click, a curse; his hands vanish from my body to figure out the lube before he's guiding my mouth back to his and slippery fingers brush over my ass. I groan now, and when he circles one finger around my opening, my lips pop off his with a muddled grunt that gets lost in the pillow next to his head.

"Good?" he whispers, one tip easing in, easing out.

"So good." It's been a while, but it's *him,* and that's all I'm aware of. Thio easing a finger knuckle deep, pulling out. Thio gliding two fingers in this time, working me open. Thio pushing kisses to the sharp joint of my shoulder and smoothing his other hand down my back, whispering reassurances and promises and "You're so tight, baby; you'll feel so good wrapped around me. I'm gonna make you fly."

I keep myself propped over him, but my body's swerving and twitching, each drag of his fingers disconnecting wires and I'm short-circuiting.

"Thio," I beg, already well past the point of caring. "Thio—enough, I'm ready."

I grab for his dick, add more lube, and start to sit back on it when he locks his leg with mine and flips us again, him over top of me, grinning like a fool.

"No way." He grabs my ankle and hooks it over his shoulder. "I'm taking care of you, remember? This is my ride. Buckle up."

"Buckle—?" I laugh again.

He laughs, too, laughs as he's fisting his cock to line up with my hole. Laughing as that laughter fights a losing battle with a keening sigh, then nothing is quite funny, but it's still sweet somehow, sweet and intimate and so hot I'm incinerating from the base of my stomach, up and out.

He pushes through the first tight ring, slides all the way in with a rhythmic thrust. Everything whites out, awareness going static at the tidal wash of fullness, pressure; my breath is lodged in my throat along with a needy, slurring plea. He stays still, letting me adjust.

I grab at him, spearing my hand into his long hair, pulling him down into focus. "Move."

"Yeah?"

"Fuck yes."

He pecks my mouth. "You didn't say please." But he's as winded as I am.

I laugh again; has it ever been this *fun?* Gods, it's breaking my heart and filling in the cracks all at once.

He moves, still seated deep, hips doing art as he rolls his pelvis and hits that spot inside me. My head throws back, mouth opening noiselessly.

Teeth in my neck, stabs of the best pain all the way up to my ear.

He stills again. "Say please."

"Oh my *gods,* you bastard."

"Yes. Say it."

I lock my legs around his back, heels digging into his spine, and wiggle unsuccessfully; he's got me pinned. No amount of whining or thrashing does a damn thing, and that sense of fullness is taunting, a ship there on the horizon.

Sweat pours off me, every nerve wound so taut I fear what the snap will bring.

"Please," I relent, tugging at his arms, his neck. "Please, Thio, fuck me. *Fuck* me, own me, ruin me—"

He kisses me to silence. Eats the last few garbled words. "Oh, I'll ruin you," he tells me. "But you're mine, so I'll always put you back together again, too."

His hips jerk away, almost all the way out, and slam forward so brutally I shout. He doesn't give me a beat to brace myself or prepare for the next wave; it comes and comes, seismic thrusts that trigger earthquakes across my skin, goose bumps so sensitive they ache.

I moan his name, moan it until it becomes a sob, and I know as I reach for my dick that he isn't going to let me. He grabs my hand and puts his mouth at my ear and snarls, "*Mine,*" and it doesn't matter that he stopped me from touching myself, I almost come on that hair-trigger word.

He pulls out without pretense and flips me over.

I go, ass in the air and fingers groping for the top of his mattress as he impales me again, nailing my prostate with each hard drive, interstellar light playing in fragments across my eyelids.

The sheet pops off the corner of the bed. A pillow goes flying. I'm scrambling, clinging to fabric, seeking leverage, seeking gravity. Every thrust shoots me further into orbit, the air thinning.

"Thio," I whine. "Thio, *please*—"

He pulls out again. I all but scream and claw back for him, but he grabs my torso and heaves me up until I'm sitting on his bent legs and he's slamming up into me.

He has his hand around my neck, holding my back to his chest, the way we were at the dance club. I writhe like there's music now, bouncing on his cock, swaying to the firing beat of our own pulses.

"This ass." He digs his forehead into my shoulder. "You're too good. Gonna make me come. You want that? My cum in you. Filling you up. Gods, Sebastian—wanna mark you, wanna come inside you."

If I had a semblance of control over my brain, I'd be mortified by the sounds that undulate out of my mouth. Wails and "Yes, gods, Thio, I want it, please—"

He grabs my hips and stabs so deep within me I swear I can feel him in my throat. It stops me from moving and my head falls back against his shoulder, hands grasping at his hair, at his fingers where they bruise my hips.

"Not yet," he tells me. "Don't want to come yet. Okay?"

No, no—the need to come is stifling me. It's a clamp on my neck and pleasure-pain radiating through my chest and down my thighs, *no.*

I whine again, and nod.

Ruin me.

He maneuvers me off the bed, bends me over, and fucks me face-first into the mattress.

The moment either of us gets close, he pulls out and changes the position.

Him holding me against the wall.

We drop to the floor, and fuck there, too.

Then back on his bed, me riding him, gods, so close, *so close*—

He shoves me away, my head bouncing off the foot of the

mattress, and I barely have enough grip on reality to bark out a raspy *fuck you* before he's driving back into me, the two of us half hanging off his bed.

His lips are everywhere; mine are, too, biting, sucking. What's bruise and what's shudder, what's kiss and what's teeth? This stopped being something tangible; we're stratospheric now, rocketing through outer planes and star-speckled multiverses.

His hand finally wraps around my oversensitive dick and I strangle down a scream. I'm coming on barely one tug, orgasm detonating in the pit of my stomach and rolling off eruptions that annihilate all last ties to anything substantial. There's only pure beams of light, the salty taste of sweat on his neck, the tectonic shift caused by this destruction.

One last determined thrust, and his shout chokes off in an intensity that doesn't allow sound. Bleary, I watch him, soaking up the way the tendons in his neck stand out in stark contrast, those red stripes on his cheeks near neon.

I lean up and kiss one of those stripes. The other.

He catches my mouth in a retreating kiss as he pulls out of me. I only have a moment to wince before he's dragging me away from the edge of the mattress and shoving my knees up to my stomach.

"Wha—" But no question comes, just pathetic gasping, and I look down to see him staring at my hole.

I can feel his cum leaking out of me. That's what he's looking at.

He's been a predator before, but it was only a part of him, a flicker of could-be.

The rabid look on his face leaves nothing hypothetical about what he is now.

"So hot, baby," he snarls and bends to lick a long stripe through the crease of my ass to my balls, dipping his tongue into my hole as he passes it.

Electrocution. A full-body lightning strike.

It's hypersensitive but I'm begging, *sobbing.* "Please, please, *Thio.*"

He attacks, licking and sucking. I writhe and he hauls me up to him like his own personal feast, tongue arrowing into me, messy and dirty and gods, I think I could come again. But it's too much and too good all at once, and when my cries change in pitch, Thio shifts to bathing the insides of my thighs in open-mouth kisses. Each one slows more and more until it's worshipful, intimate, everything he wanted this to be, boiled down to lips on quivering skin.

I don't know anything else until I feel his chest rising and falling under my cheek. He moved us, tucked us under what parts of his bedding remained on the mattress. His arm is tight around me, both of us wrecked.

He coasts his fingers through my hair. "You with me?"

"No," I grumble. "Summon me back to earth. Not sure where I ended up."

A chuckle reverberates in my ear.

His hand moves down, stroking, soothing, and he stops at the small of my back, fingers toying over the swell of my ass.

"Are you okay?" he whispers. "Did I go too rough? Too—much?" There's uncertainty in his tone.

I look up at him, resting my chin on his chest because I can't find the strength to hold my own head up.

"It was perfect," I manage. Then I attempt a glare I'm sure falls flat. "Sadistic, with the edging. But perfect." My face heats. "All of it."

Thio grins, his own cheeks red again, too. Gods, those stripes. "My sadism ends now, I promise. How about a shower, then we eat?"

I groan and bury my face in his armpit. Even that smells good, his sweat and cologne and deodorant; just *him*.

"You said no more sadism," I mumble.

"I did."

"Then don't make me move."

He chuckles again. "We can eat dinner in bed."

"Can we shower in bed?"

"Sadly, no one's developed a spell for that yet."

Another groan. "What is the point of magic?"

Despite my protests, we get to the shower, which is huge, and luxurious, and I'm instantly okay with having left the bed for it. Thio washes me thoroughly, and that washing turns to touching turns to creating our own steam to rival the water. We get each other off again in a soapy, leisurely grind.

And back in bed, naked, plates of reheated—for the second time—pasta balanced on our knees, Thio and I lean against each other and eat and talk about nothing. All the heavy shit has been said and done; now we get to prattle on about shows we've binged and that gaudy statue in his living room and how Paeris and Nick will get along.

The food is still phenomenal, and with our empty plates stacked on his nightstand, Thio pulls me back against his chest.

His hand drifts through my shower-damp hair, and I flutter in and out of consciousness, absorbing the warmth radiating off him, the warmth we generated that seems to linger. It's been nonstop heat with him from every angle, fighting and fucking, constant infernos and explosions. It should be exhausting, or feel like a warning. Something this tumultuous can't sustain itself, can it? Something that does nothing but burn can't last.

But I come back for that burn. My own fire was destroying me, and I keep getting close to his fire because I need a better warmth.

"Sebastian?" Thio asks into the soft glow of his bedroom's low lights.

I moan, half asleep.

"I'm in this," he whispers. His hand in my hair, his other arm around my waist; they both tighten. "You don't have to say anything. What you told me tonight, about Camp Merethyl—I want you to know how seriously I take it. I know it was no small thing for you, and this, you and me, isn't small for me either."

He gave me an out. I could stay quiet and drift off in his arms and call this night the best of my life.

"I'm in this, too," I say.

Now it's the best night of my life.

His fingers draw shapes on my hip and I know he's smiling. Grinning, probably, all dopey and shit.

"Shut up," I mutter.

His snorted exhale is hot on my bare shoulder. "Never. You like me."

I can't wrestle down my smile. He really has ruined me.

One last, mumbled confession slips out. "You make me happy."

And I fall asleep with his lips pressed to my forehead.

The first half of spring break, we barely leave Thio's apartment. It isn't until Orok texts asking for proof of life that Thio makes the executive decision to put clothes on, because *I won't give your best friend reason to think badly of me.* Which, damn, that's downright honorable of him, so we end up hanging with Orok and some of the rawball team.

Thio fits. With Orok, and Orok's sporty circle of friends. They're quickly laughing along with a joke Thio told or buying him a drink because he beat them at axe throwing, and even Crescentia gets over her prejudice. I can only watch in disbelief at incontrovertible proof that I've somehow attracted another people person into my inner circle.

I can't believe he doesn't have his own established group of friends; he's so easy to like. Charming and engaging. I'm not at all too proud to admit I latch on to his side on most of our excursions. *Gods damn,* he chose me? *He* chose me, and he holds my hand or idly plays with my hair or smiles down at me in a private way between us.

We visit his mom at the end of the week. The care facility staff seems to have figured out her medicine; she hasn't had any more seizures, and her eyes are clear when we sit with her in the courtyard. Thio tells her what we've been doing—the PG version—and her focus drifts as he talks, to the weeping willow we're seated under, to the lilies blooming by the pond in the corner, to—me.

She stares at me as Thio talks about how we went axe throwing. I smile, not sure how much she's aware of, if she remembers me from our other visits.

She touches my hand. It's fleeting, barely a brush of contact, but my eyes prickle.

I still haven't heard from my dad since his unsolicited astral projection visit. My mom stopped her usual harmless *how are you* texts, probably because I didn't *congratulate* my father on his new job. This silence between us feels . . . conclusive. Like this was the last straw.

The effect of them giving up is that they've *given up*. And now neither side of our already rickety bridge is passable.

I don't know what to do about that. Why I find myself glancing at the text thread with my mom in case I missed something.

I'm dating an incredible guy who for whatever reason is obsessed with me. I have Orok. My parents have finally stopped hassling me about my failures. I'm on the downslope to graduation, set to finish up my project in a few weeks. I have the Clawstar job locked in, so I'll be able to get protective spells to people who need them.

For the first time in my life, I have everything I've ever wanted.

If I'm feeling uncertain, it's because I'm not used to being happy. If I'm feeling like this perfectly clear, brilliantly bright day is forecasted for a storm, it's only because I've never had stuff to worry about losing.

If all this joy has me holding Thio tighter at night, it's only because that's what you do when you like someone. You hold them close.

And wait for the dread to let you take a full breath again.

Chapter Sixteen

A good chunk of that dread gets slapped silly when Thio and I return to the lab and neither of us lets the new dynamic of our relationship alter the preestablished dynamic of our working partnership.

Translation: he immediately pisses me off.

I swear to the gods, I'm practically beaming through that first argument. Something about still being able to yell at him and have him get mad at me, too, helps the fuzzy edges of our expanding relationship come into clarity. Yes, we're sleeping together every night, but in this lab, we're still Sebastian and Elethior and *fuck* if he's going to get away with taking point on a test for *my* project.

But this anger is his insecurity coming back out, his fear of what happened to his mom—and now, his fear of what I told him about my own past.

Instead of letting the argument barrel on, I kiss him, hot and heavy and anxious.

And there's that dread again. The bruising throb of *This can't last. This is too good. You're too broken to handle this.*

We're both broken, though. And our jagged pieces don't exactly fit together, but we know how to move around the sharpest points of each other's, how to adjust and make space so no one bleeds.

We spend a week setting up extra safety precautions before we do more tests. During that, I still try my best to find evocation solutions for Thio's project, but he's right; it's too big. Too complex. We don't have a hope of solving it, let alone making any headway, and I can't be too upset about it, what with how dangerous it would be for conjuration wizards to be able to disconnect from what they conjure.

Even though Thio's project won't be a big part of our final presentation, we're still incorporating conjuration ideals into mine, and that pacifies Davyeras, Thompson, and Narbeth at our next check-in. They're excited we're running tests and thrilled at the measuring cup concept we're trying, even without Thio's project.

A little over a month until we're due to present our joint paper, we run a test on my spell safety net. It's small, a cap to limit component drain on a low-level ice spell. The spell requires a cup of water and one gram of quartz; we're trying to take that amount from a full, solid pound of quartz. That's the safety net rune we've come up with, one that should automatically pull a gram of a material component, then stop. No focus needed from us.

We set it all up. I summon Nick for a boost, and he sits at my side in a sharp purple beret. Thio has Paeris wrapped around his arm for his own boost, and he activates the security measures and gives me a thumbs-up from the side of the room. He's watching everything, checking wards, monitoring the components. It's a simple test and we've *done* simple tests before. I don't know why this feels big.

I draw the evocation circle on the center marble dais with the added safety net rune. Murmur the incantation, tugging on my connection to Nick for an extra controlled swell of magic.

The spell triggers.

The block of quartz vibrates, and Thio and I both watch as a chunk vanishes from the top corner before the water freezes solid.

Neither of us moves. For one minute. Two. Watching, waiting for a rebound, for the magic to decide it didn't like our new rune and go haywire.

But nothing happens.

It—worked?

Our eyes lock.

My face hurts with my smile, and Thio's grinning, too.

"Again?" I ask, winded; my heart thinks we're sprinting around campus.

He nods, giddy. "Again."

"That last glass of champagne was a bad idea."

I verify that statement by tripping on the warped carpet outside my apartment, a warp I've successfully stepped over every day for several years.

Thio catches me, sputtering laughter, and rolls us until I'm trapped against the door. His eyes darken, and it flips all the switches in my body, every single one. Heat here and my own internal fizzy bubbles rocketing through my veins there.

"No," he says against my jaw, nipping at the skin in a slow ladder-climb of bites up to my ear. "What was a mistake were those awful gin drinks you ordered."

I scoff. "Excuse you, gin is never a *mistake*."

"It tastes like old lady perfume."

His teeth on my skin and the fuzzy-headed fog from the alcohol are working against me in perfect sync, so I almost forget we're talking, almost forget we're still in the hall.

He'd picked the restaurant, somewhere to, and I quote, *celebrate both of us being brilliant.*

There's a rune now that prevents wizards from draining their components.

We've run test after test the past two weeks, with six variations to account for six different component amount requirements, and the safety net rune works every time.

Knowing it exists, knowing it *works,* heals something inside me. No, not *something*; I know what it heals. I can tell eighteen-year-old me that there's a way to stop it now. What they made me do to Orok. I didn't use an evocation circle then, I didn't use runes at all, but this is a start—it'll lead to figuring out a way to incorporate safety nets into incantations, into every part of a spell, until that protection is ingrained in magic.

I grip the lapel of Thio's jacket and rock up against him.

"You're the one who chose that pretentious bar," I manage. "They had the high-end gin, so I had to—"

His phone vibrates. It's in the front pocket of his jacket, so I feel it hum between us.

He drops his forehead to my shoulder with a groan before pulling his phone out, glancing at the screen, and clicking it off.

Fingers still locked in his jacket, I stiffen. "Arasne?"

"Yeah." He shoves it back into his pocket, avoiding eye contact.

She's been calling on and off all evening. For several days, in fact; since Thio's last regular meeting with her about a week ago, right after our second check-in with Davyeras and the advisors.

She wanted details on our project.

He only told her about the conjuration side of things, which is next to nothing.

He's so close to getting his degree, to finding a different job, to being *free* of his family—but they're suspicious. They *know* how unhappy he is.

"Do you need to call her back?" I whisper.

Thio finally looks at me, lips quirking up. "Fuck no."

"Thio—"

He kisses me, effectively shutting me up, but the questions I don't get to ask churn in my belly and make me grip him tighter.

Thio maps my face with his lips, down my jaw. He fastens his lips to my neck and sucks and *fuuuuck*—okay, sex won't solve everything, but it sure as hell will distract him, won't it? Big sacrifice on my part.

"Keys," I moan, head thumping against the door. "Let me get my keys."

The door opens.

Did I open it?

Dizzy, I look over my shoulder.

To see Orok, his face . . . grim.

He hasn't opened the door all the way. Enough that I can see his head and half his body.

Does he have someone here? We almost went back to Thio's place, but mine was closer, so—

My grip on Thio clenches tighter and he releases my neck to look behind me.

"Sorry." Thio winces. "Did we disturb—"

"You weren't answering your phone," Orok says. Not accusingly—but he is upset.

My brain's moving through about half a bottle of champagne and two elaborate gin-and-blackberry something or others, so I squint at Orok while still tangled up in Thio.

Why would he care about Thio answering his phone?

Oh gods. Did Arasne talk to Orok? Did she do something to get to us through him? No, that's insane—right?

"What phone?" I ask. "Whose phone? Thio's?"

Orok sighs. "Your phone, Seb. Your parents are here."

Okay. Now I *know* I had more than half a bottle of champagne. There's no way he said that. There's no way that's *true.*

Thio straightens immediately, processing what Orok said faster than I am. "What? Now?"

He nods, eyes flicking from Thio to me. "You need to talk to them," he says, voice low. "They're—just get in here."

And he closes the door. To give me time to compose myself.

Which would take years.

My parents are here. They came to see me.

I'm still facing the closed door. Thio hooks his fingers under my chin and turns me to him. "Hey. Are you okay? What do you want to do?"

My instinctive reaction is to cover up what's happening with a joke and brush it off, but he already knows. He knows about my dad, all of it.

"Come in with me?" I haven't let go of his jacket. Not sure I can. How quickly he's become a lifeline.

"Of course," he says. Then, "Are you sure?"

"You don't have to." I cringe. "I don't know why they're here. It's probably about my dad's new job, and if so, it's—it's not going to be pretty, so I understand if you'd rather—"

He kisses me. Pillowy lips and the soft lick of his tongue against mine.

"Let's go in," he promises.

I droop, forehead to his, for a breath.

It's been a month since Mom texted about Dad's job. And radio silence between all three of us since.

This isn't good.

No hesitating. No running. Get it over with, and move on.

Get it over with, and ignore the shit out of it.

I scramble for the doorknob behind me, shove it open, and push inside.

My parents are on the couch. Orok's perched in a dining room chair he dragged over, arms folded, discomfort screaming from every strained muscle.

Dad's in his usual business-casual button-up and slacks, and Mom's in a nice sundress. They're here, not a projection.

But my dad looks *rough*. His shirt is wrinkled, his hair flattened but not brushed.

These facts filter through my disbelief and I frown at them.

Thio closes the door behind me.

Not two seconds after it shuts, Mom leaps from the couch, runs into the kitchen, and hugs me.

Her shoulders shake, her grip death-tight around me, spots of wetness seeping into my shoulder.

She's crying.

There's not a scrap of alcohol left in my body, suffocated by a barrage of sensation that tightens around me as immovably as my mom's arms. Dread rises to the forefront, corrals everything else, and asserts dominance over the way I stare at my father and can only think, *Oh gods, no.*

I go rigid. Arms out at my sides. Heart flatlining, impossibilities trying to take shape in my head, but I don't let them. Can't trust them.

Dad scrubs his hands on his knees, his eyes bloodshot, like maybe he hasn't been sleeping.

My gaze tracks to Orok, who analyzes my dad, my mom still hugging me, before looking at me with broken-apart exhaustion.

"Sebastian," Dad says, and coughs into his fist. "I hope you don't mind us coming. We—"

He notices Thio, who steps up beside me.

Dad goes silent, looking at me in question.

His demeanor is throwing me off. He's cautious and careful and I almost do an identification spell to be sure someone with actual emotion hasn't taken over his body.

"This is Thio," I introduce, dazed. "My boyfriend."

Thio's head whips toward me.

That's the first time either of us has used that word.

And it had to be *now*, of course. When I can't feel the importance of it.

Mom peels back from me and digs in her pocket to free a packet of tissues. As she dabs at her eyes, she turns to Thio with a polite smile and extends her hand. "Hi, Thio. I'm Abigail, Sebastian's mother."

He shakes her hand. "It's nice to meet you, Mrs.—"

She sucks in a breath. Of recognition.

And drops his hand to gape at me, her brows coming together in utter—horror?

"This is *Elethior Tourael*," she states.

Unease itches the back of my neck. "Yeah?"

"*Tourael*," she says again, and gods, the utter irony. Months ago, she'd stood in almost this exact spot and said that name reverently, thrilled I'd be working with a *Tourael*.

Now she's looking at me in disgust, glaring at Thio with all the rage I once showed him.

It adds another layer of confirmation about why they're here.

I step in front of him, hands in fists. "What do you want?" I demand it of her, and my dad, who hasn't moved from the couch.

"Abby," Dad says.

She sniffs and bites her lips together, but retreats to the couch.

Dad stands once she sits. Like they're taking turns.

"We have some things we'd like to discuss." Dad eyes Thio. "In private?"

"He's not going anywhere," I say. "Whatever you think you're going to get from this, I promise, it won't—"

"Sebastian," my dad says. "Give us five minutes. That's all we ask."

He's towering over the room like he always does, a massive force of presence. But it doesn't feel threatening this time.

I don't know what impact this will have but I know I don't have the resiliency to endure it.

Or.

Maybe I do.

Thio touches my arm and I immediately link my fingers with his.

Dad's eyes glisten. It's a fist wrapping around my heart, squeezing where it's gone stationary, restarting it.

"We know," he whispers. "About Camp Merethyl. About the ouroboros project."

Mom muffles a sob into her palms.

I don't look at her.

I'm looking at my father, and for the first time in . . . my whole life, probably, he *sees* me.

It's appalling. Insufferable.

I'd wanted this. Didn't I tell Thio that? That I wanted my dad to get the job. He'd have access to the records, and he'd find out. He'd know. He'd know all my secrets, all the secrets I never wanted to keep from him. Things I *tried* not to keep from him, and he told me I was lying. He told me I'd misunderstood. *That isn't what happened, Sebastian, don't be dramatic.*

I thought I wanted this. I thought I could handle this.

I turn to Thio, eyes blurring.

"Take me to your place," I beg him. "Now. Please. Let's go, now."

I'm crying. When did I start crying? Fucking hell, *I don't want this*—

Thio cradles my cheek. "Okay, baby. Let's—"

Dad steps around the coffee table. Orok hasn't moved, his eyes on the floor, and he's slumped in his chair.

"Wait," Dad says. His voice cracks, and I'm undone. "Sebastian. Just—wait."

My eyes pinch shut, but I don't move, and Thio doesn't make me. He loops one arm around me and I rock into him.

"We're so sorry, son," Dad tells me. "*I* am sorry. We—the things I learned, I—"

He stops. I'm not looking at him, my eyes still closed so I don't see what his face does, but I can *hear,* and he sounds shattered. There's rustling, the squeak of couch cushions; I think he's sitting again, and that makes it easier, somehow.

"You should know." His voice is stronger, but there's still a choked-off quality to it. "I turned over everything I found to the Mageus Military Police. I doubt, however, that much will come of it, given how many people within the ranks have benefited from Camp Merethyl."

"They won't believe you." I pop my eyes open and glare at him. "Will they?"

It's targeted, and it hits, my dad flinching against the cushions. Mom has her hand in his, gripping tight.

"There will still be an investigation," he tries. "There will still be—"

"*Nothing*. There will be *nothing*, because no one will hold them accountable. You're asking people in positions of immense power to admit they fucked up, *and that will never happen*."

I'm shouting, words echoing off the apartment walls. I stepped away from Thio at some point, too hot now to be near anyone. It's burning me up, the fires that have always eaten away at me; this is their final inferno, the finishing blaze.

Dad sits up straight again. "It's a step forward."

I laugh. Bitter, cackling. "That's why you've come? To get credit for doing the bare minimum *six years too late*? Where the hell were you when I came home from camp every summer malnourished and *ill*, and you told me I needed to beef up before next year? Where the *hell* were you when I had to rip blood out of Orok's body? I could feel his heart slowing down; do you have any idea what that's like? I could *feel him dying*. I came home after that and you told me I was a failure. *Where were you then?*"

A sob gags me and I bend over, hands on my knees, gasping to the floor, crying so hard my body aches. Orok's head is in his hands, fingers arched against his hair. No one else moves, no one reacts, all of us trapped in the inescapable cage of the pain emanating out of me. I don't know how to stop it. I don't know how to cap it.

I loved my parents. I loved my *dad,* this larger-than-life man I trusted and admired. I loved them both, and I still do, and I *hate* that I can't hate them. That this hurts so bad.

Dad stands slowly. Still crouched over, I scowl up at him.

He's crying, too.

I've never seen my father cry. Not at funerals. Not for anything good, even. But he's crying now, tears dripping down his cheeks as he watches me.

"I know," he croaks out. "I know I made mistakes. I can't—" He takes a beat, eyes flipping to the ceiling, back to me. "I can't fix what I did to you. To you both." He includes Orok, who's still folded in on himself. "But I can start from here, and do the right thing. I didn't just involve the Mageus Military Police. I spoke with my lawyer."

That yanks me upright. "You did *what*?"

"In hypotheticals," Mom adds, her face blotchy. "We haven't opened anything official yet."

Dad nods at what Mom said. "We got information at this stage. But he said we have plenty to go after—" He side-eyes Thio, sucks his teeth. "To go after the Touraels who own Camp Merethyl. He reviewed the camp's bylaws, and even with the . . . restrictive terminology in the forms they had us sign, he said we are well within our rights to sue them for gross abuse of magic, at the very least."

Exhaustion's appearance is swift and violent. Maybe I am still tipsy, the alcohol bypassing drunkenness and shoving me right into pure, unfiltered fatigue.

Dad's offering me justice.

It was all I'd wanted, any of those summers. For him to step in.

For him to save me.

I can't speak. Can't move. Can't figure out how I'm supposed to react to what he's offering.

"Give him time?" Thio asks behind me. "To think it over."

Dad glances at Thio again. He doesn't look as murderous as Mom did, but he's still hesitant, like he's about to question why I'm dating a *Tourael* when Dad now knows what *those Touraels* did to me. When Dad himself offered to sue Thio's family.

"Of course," Dad says. "Take your time. We—" His inhale is shaky. "We want to fix this going forward, Sebastian. Whatever it takes. Whatever you want."

"Are you keeping the job?" I don't know why that's the question that digs its way out of me.

Dad's smile is fragile. "No, son. I turned over the information to the Mageus Military Police and stepped down."

Tension releases. A small knot of it, somewhere deep in my stomach.

There are still dozens of other knots. Other sources of distrust and pain that are years old.

But I sink into myself, shoulders bowing.

Mom rises. "We're staying at a hotel in town for another night, if you want to talk. But after, we'll be back home, and still—anytime you want to talk, please, we'll be ready."

I shrug. It's all I have to give at this point.

Mom kisses my cheek. Dad pats my shoulder; I think he might want to hug me, but he doesn't.

Our dynamic has been etched in stone for almost a decade. I'm the disappointment; he's the enemy. I remember how it was before, how it was to smile at him and love him and *trust* him, but the memory is faded and blurred, like a dream turning to wisps the more I try to hold on to it.

The door shuts behind them.

Thio moves. I'm being pushed to sit on the couch and a bottle of water is put on the table next to me; I see Orok has one now, too. Thio's saying something quietly to him, and Orok nods.

Then Thio's next to me on the couch, his arm around me. "Sebastian?"

Everything my dad said rolls over me at once and pain lances through my chest, gouging from the base of my throat straight down into my gut. I whimper at the force of it.

"It's too much," I say, pathetic and pained, and I bend into Thio, clinging to him, grounding myself in him.

"I know, baby." He strokes my hair. "Don't decide anything to-night. Let's go up to bed. We can—"

"If I'm suing your family, would you still want to be with me?"

His hand flattens against my head, holding my face into his neck.

"If you're suing my family, would you still want to be with me?" he returns quietly.

I rest my forehead on his sternum, absorbing as much of his scent as I can, each breath relaxing another muscle, another, until I'm boneless.

"Orok?" I ask, voice muffled in Thio's chest.

"Here. Alive. Barely." He gulps from his water bottle. "What the fuck."

I laugh. It grows, crushes me, and I twist out of Thio's hold to scrub my hands over my eyes, dislodging my glasses.

When I can see, Orok's sprawled back in his chair, face gaunt.

He holds my gaze for one unspoken moment.

By the third summer, we didn't have to speak to communicate. It was better not to, better not to let slip anything the instructors could use as ammo. Every time they'd announce a new challenge, I'd look at Orok, and he'd convey the full weight of his fear and exhaustion and steadiness in his eyes, in the pulse of his brow.

I'm here. I'm terrified but I'm here, and we'll get through this together.

"Thio's right," he whispers. "Not tonight. This is—" He tosses the water bottle onto the table and stands. "I'm going to the gym."

I flick my eyes to the clock on the microwave. "It's almost ten."

"And it's open 'til midnight. I'll be back. I need to—"

He stops. Hands opening and closing at his sides.

"No matter how long it's been," he says, attention on the floor. "It's like I'm a kid again."

He looks at me, and I know. No matter how thick the scar tissue, the wound beneath is always raw.

More tears well and I wipe them away, unable to speak.

Orok uses the sleeve of his shirt to wipe his own eyes and heads to the door to grab his keys.

But he doubles back, bends over me on the couch, and plants a kiss on my forehead. "It's gonna be okay, yeah? This was probably a good thing."

I snort. "Take your therapizing and sweat it out at the gym."

Orok holds his fist out to Thio.

Head cocked curiously, Thio bumps it.

"I'm so glad his stubborn ass is someone else's problem now," Orok tells him.

"Hey," I manage, head lolling on Thio's shoulder.

Orok smiles at me.

We'll get through this together.

"If you can't sleep tonight," I tell him, "wake me up."

His smile widens into a snort. "So I can cuddle between you and Thio? Tempting, Seb. Really."

I kick his shin. "I'm serious, O."

Orok's face does something complicated. A shift, a hard sniff, and he nods. "I know you are."

He leans over to kiss my forehead again.

"Love you," he whispers.

"Love you too."

He leaves with a parting wave.

Silence blankets us in his absence.

Thio traces the shell of my ear. "Don't factor me in," he says.

I rock my head toward him, reactions muffled, delayed.

"If worrying about me is what ends up holding you back in any lawsuit," he expands. "Don't factor me in."

I sit up so I can see him better. Exhaustion is dominating my movements now, each blink too slow, reality blurring at the edges.

But his meaning hits me with a jolt of worry. "You don't want to be a factor?"

Thio runs his thumb along my chin. His expression is hardened, like he can see a resolution coming, and it's inevitable.

"I'm saying if your only holdup is me, don't let it be. I don't care what fallout would come from my family—you have the chance to do something. To stand up against them, to stand up *for yourself.* Few people get that chance." He inhales sharply, exhales long and re-signed. "It would break my heart if you held back from that because of me."

I lean into his hand. "I'd wait until after you graduated. Until you got a job, and were secure. I wouldn't—it wouldn't be anytime soon."

"Are you considering it, then?" His tone is tentative. Unsure. Hopeful?

Yes. No. I don't know.

My dad believes me.

An ache thuds across my head and I wince.

"Distract me. Please. I don't want to think about it anymore."

Thio's demeanor changes. Shifts to the situation, to what I need.

He's always doing that, adapting to me like a chameleon, and I should feel guilty for how often he slips into that role. But right now, I'm choking, and he's turning into air for me.

He tugs on the collar of my shirt. "We could talk about how I just met your parents."

A weak smile pulls over my mouth. "Yeah. Well. I met your mom before we were even dating, so."

"And you introduced me as your boyfriend."

Thio's pupils dilate, and my face warms.

"You liked that, huh?" I ask, raspy.

He nods, possession intensifying in his gaze, in the set of his shoulders.

I try to lean into him. To kiss him, or crawl into his lap. To utter a bunch of mushy bullshit that'd make saying *my boyfriend* sound dull by comparison.

But all I do is teeter, and then he's bringing my head to his lips and pressing kisses to my eyelids.

"Now, I'm taking my boyfriend to bed," he tells me. "And we're going to sleep."

"That's not fun."

"I dunno. Falling asleep with you in my arms?" He peels me off the couch; everything's half dream already. "Sounds like the perfect end of the night to me."

For two people who built a relationship on screaming at each other, Thio's good at saying things I can't argue with.

Chapter Seventeen

It's dark when I wake up.

The clock on my nightstand is blurry without my glasses, but I barely make out that it's after two in the morning. Which explains the groggy pressure weighing down my limbs, and I roll onto my back, sluggish, thoughts held at bay by the in-between of being only half awake.

I'm not sure what woke me up at first. I hold my breath, listening for Orok, but there's no moaning or telltale signs of him having a nightmare.

After a long stretch of stillness, I relax into the bed.

Next to me, Thio's still asleep, curled toward me, a strip of his face illuminated yellow-white by a streetlight blade that slashes through my curtains.

The previous night tries to come back to me.

But what overwhelms the kick of anxiety, what pushes it down and levels out my heart rate, is Thio.

My lips find his, a brush of contact, something to settle me back into sleep.

But he stirs under me.

His lips rise to mine, the brush turning to a hold, mouths connecting.

He pulls back and his eyes glide open. Dark pupils, sleep-drenched in that shaft of light. We stare at each other, heads nestled close on his pillow; everything is quiet and sleepy and we could slip back into unconsciousness.

I don't know who moves. It's a shared collision, we're both at fault.

We're kissing again, my hand on his neck, his on my waist, fingers waking up. A pull, blankets coming with me; I roll on top of him, cradled between his legs, rocking against him as our kisses create humidity and we're still half asleep.

Thio moans, and I curse that we went to bed in boxers.

Another thrust, our hard cocks dragging against each other through two layers of thin fabric, muted but so good. Everything with him is so *good*.

My mouth goes to the spot on his collarbone I know makes him shudder, and I work his body into just that. He reaches between us to shove down his boxers; we kick and wriggle until we're naked and somehow the blanket stays over my shoulders, tenting us in. The smooth, precum-slick glide of our bare dicks against each other has me concaving my body over his and whimpering.

His legs go back around my waist, crossing so his ankles rest in the divots on either side of my tailbone. I find the lube in my nightstand, but as I reach back to prep myself, Thio grabs my hand and guides my fingers to his hole.

The muscles behind my belly button twist viciously. "Thio—"

"Yes," he says, and it disintegrates into a moan as he pushes one of my fingers around his rim. "*Please*."

I take over, no part of me still drowsy. Every nerve is inexhaustibly awake, memorizing the hitch of Thio's breath and the already blissed-out gloss to his eyes in the darkness. I circle my finger around him once, twice, the lube warming in the friction, each pass making his body do this convulsive twitch that intensifies until he's begging again.

"Please, Sebastian," he says and I eat it down, sucking his tongue as I delve my finger into his body.

His whine? Delectable.

I increase to two fingers, three, rocking and smooth, and then—

A crook of my fingers, and Thio's stomach arches off the bed, head digging back into the pillow and exposing his long, inked neck.

"Fuck me," he begs, fingers hooked in the ridges of my spine and pulling. "Fuck me, please, baby—"

Always. Anything. Everything.

My fingers curve again and he breaks apart in a keening wail I quickly suck down until we're back to quiet gasps and slick, moving skin. More lube, my cock aching and rigid, driven to the very edge of insanity by Thio giving me this, coming apart for me.

I notch at his entrance and his eyes crash to mine, half shadowed in the blanket over my shoulders. The air is thick with the smell of sex and the muted notes of Thio's cologne and as I push inside, neither of us says anything.

My hips hit his ass and I collapse over him, arms coming under his shoulders; I'm as close to him as I can possibly be and it isn't enough. He grips my cock in the best strangulation, so tight and hot I can feel the muscles in his walls quivering as he adjusts to me; his body is conforming to mine and I want the imprint to last forever.

That possessive drive jerks my hips deeper, back out, deeper again. I need to change him from the inside the way he's altering me at a cellular level.

No words still. No pleas or warnings or admissions.

Just the air disappearing. Thio sucking on his lower lip. Me finding some kind of ascension between his legs. I don't know how much time passes, what outer planes might have shifted to make room for our orbit.

I can feel the beat of blood in his body, in mine, I'm not sure what's his pulse and what's from me. His dick's trapped between us and I focus on rolling my hips to drag across it so his jaw slackens and his fingers fist my hair.

He comes with a bright cry, eyes bursting open to latch on to mine like he can drag me with him in the pleasure wave. And he does; my own orgasm rips through me in a fervor, relentless and brutal and he's kissing the moans from my lips.

It's still early. The fog of orgasm shifts everything dreamlike again, and as our kisses slow, I fight through the haze to clean us off before we tangle up in bed again.

My head on his chest, his fingers card through my hair, slower and slower until he's asleep again, the *whoosh*ing inhale and exhale of his breath a lulling, symphonic rhythm.

The calmness of this moment has my chest cramping tight.

He faced my parents' ridicule without flinching. He made sure Orok was okay, too.

I *need* Thio to be happy. I need him as happy as he makes me, as supported, as *safe*.

In the low light, I look up at him, watching the interplay of sleep and dreams smooth out his features.

Powerlessness was my driving force behind studying magic. Because we have all this potential literally at the tips of our fingers, so there should never, ever be situations where we're small and weak and acquiescent.

But there are. With Arasne, with his family, and I can't do a fucking thing to fix it. Can't get his family off his back; can't pay for his mom's care; can't intervene in any way that'd help. I'll be here next to him like he is for me, a firm hand on his back, a shoulder to lean on, but there should be *more*. There has to be something else I can do. Something else I can give him, the way he's given me—

An idea sizzles through me like a lightning strike.

I can do one thing. One of the first things he gave me: his research topic.

That topic is the only thing he's gotten to choose on his own. He doesn't want his degree or the life path his family set him on, but figuring out his mom's topic?

Yes, it's a huge concept, and yes, it's dangerous. But it's too late to incorporate anything new into our main project anyway, so if I found something, it'd be just for him; and I don't have to give him a complete solution for it to have an impact. We've both set aside his project to focus on the measuring cup theory with mine, but I can dive back into his and dedicate the attention to it that it deserves. That *he* deserves.

What good is living in a world with magic if I can't use it to make him happy?

Three weeks until our final presentation.

Four weeks until graduation.

I tell my parents that I'm busy with school and can't think about any lawsuits yet. And they, for the first time in my life, respect my boundary. My mom restarts texting me though, asking how I am. It isn't surprising how good it feels to have her messages filling my phone again, and I respond every time.

Back in the lab, Thio and I run more tests, adding various factors, recording the limitations—and as we work, I poke at Thio's project with deliberate focus. Every time I find something in evocation texts that I think will work, we try it; but nothing makes a dent at disconnecting a conjurer from their conjured item.

Thio shrugs it off. He never thought we'd make progress on his topic, so these failures aren't unexpected to him, and if he notes my new levels of ferocity in research he doesn't say anything. He's distracted on his own; when he comes back from his meetings with Arasne now, he's hollow, withdrawn. Not even Nick purring brings him out of the fog. He works in silence until we leave for the day, only to kiss me in the car on the way to his place like nothing happened.

"I just need to make it to graduation," he tells me. "Everything's fine."

I'm the fucking king of things being *fine*. And this? Not fine. Not at all.

He doesn't tell me what Arasne says to him at these meetings, only that he's trying to keep her appeased with mundane details of our project, but she has to know what he's planning to do after graduation. And she's not going to let him go easily.

Neither of us mentions my dad's offer, but I know Thio's waiting for me to talk about it the same way I wait for him to bring up his family.

We visit his mom and there are bruises under his eyes from lack of sleep.

Focusing on Thio consumes me those last weeks. I fall into a state of delirious work but Thio and Orok blame it on the end of the semester approaching fast. We're all stressed, we're all overcaffeinated and sleepless—but mine is half from writing up the safety net rune paper, and half from researching Thio's project in every free moment.

The days pass, and the grant presentation looms. We have our final check-in meeting with Davyeras and the advisors, where they give our last tests and concepts their approval. Thio and I put finishing touches on our paper and I think, maybe, there won't be anything for me to find, no great revelation I can offer him as a buffer against the stress looming post-graduation.

That's sappy, isn't it? I want to bring him a research solution on bended knee.

It's coming for Thio, his future, as unavoidable as mine; but his is the precarious column on which his mom's care is balanced.

I can't fix that for him.

But I can do this.

I can do this.

The day before our presentation, I'm due to meet Thio in our lab so we can officially submit our paper to the university's online portal. He had a breakfast meeting with Arasne, and I left his place early this morning to hit the library again—and it paid off.

Because now.

I stumble into the lab, letting the door shut behind me, and he's at his workstation with his laptop open. Lesiara U's assignment website is pulled up, and I know he has our paper loaded into the submission window already.

Around him, his hurricane of stuff is in semi-neat piles, his notes and clothing and food. We have to be out of here by next week, before graduation.

Thio looks up at me with an exhausted smile that doesn't reach his eyes. His smiles haven't, not in weeks, especially not on days when he meets with Arasne.

That ghost of a smile immediately breaks off when he sees me, and he launches up from his chair. "What's wrong?"

"I figured it out."

My eyes burn, I haven't slept since . . . yesterday? I know I tossed and turned all night in his bed. I'm shaking from an excess of coffee, my stomach aches, but I'm smiling, gasping; did I run here from the library? Maybe.

Thio frowns. "Figured what out?"

I push past him, pulling stuff out of my bag as I stumble to the whiteboard. It's my turn to make a distracted, chaotic mess, and I leave a trail of highlighters and loose papers. But I find the notes I'm looking for, unhook my bag and let it splat on the floor, and grab a dry-erase marker from the tray.

"Your mom's project," I say to the board and uncap the marker in my mouth, spit out the lid to the side. I copy the notes I scrawled in a twisting spiral around an already crammed paper—I've been spending too much time with Thio, he's all over me.

He steps up to the board. "My mom's—"

But he stops talking. Watches me write, scribbling out the theory I nailed down this morning.

It's my theory. Well, his theory, the measuring cup theory.

His mom was trying to disconnect a conjurer from their conjured item. But the energy has to come from *somewhere,* and since conjuration demands that energy come from a conjurer, the conjurer is, in theory, the component.

I don't absorb that. Don't let it affect me. It's different from what happened at Camp Merethyl, and this? This solution? Would keep conjurers safe.

I keep writing, sketching out the runes I altered to fit this idea. "The safety net runes? Instead of protecting any material component, they could also act as a cap *on the conjurer.* Once a threshold of energy has been drained from a conjurer, we can set it up to trigger the spell to disconnect, and the item will return to where it came from, protecting the conjurer."

I all but drop to my knees when I turn to Thio.

It isn't a perfect disconnect between a conjurer and their conjured item, but it's *something.* Something for him.

Thio reads over everything, his brow furrowed.

He takes the marker from me and rewrites one of the runes I made, adding other elements.

I see it, and frown.

"Or," he says, "the safety net runes could be adjusted to spread the energy draw among multiple conjurers, so it isn't reliant on only one person. The limits would still be in place; Conjurer A would be connected to the conjured item until they hit X threshold of energy drain, then it'd shift to Conjurer B, and so on. The conjured item wouldn't vanish, and—oh gods, Sebastian. This could work. This could—*oh my gods.*"

He scrawls out test equations next to the rune.

"Wait." I scrub my eyes under my glasses and splay my hands out. "That would—you can't force another conjurer to take on *your* spell. That's not—" I point at the board. At my original rune. He's not looking at me. "This is about *protecting* conjurers."

Thio mouths something to himself as he writes. Absently, he says, "My project's about the energy connection between a conjurer and their item. This way, the energy connection is dissipated among a group, and the item remains. It isn't—"

"It isn't about keeping the item; it's about protecting the conjurers."

"They *would* be protected. Once the threshold is reached, it'd shift to a different conjurer."

"But people could get hurt."

He turns to me. Excitement had been building in him, but it pauses now. "Hurt how?"

"You'd force other conjurers to take on the energetic responsibility of your spell."

"Of course not. They'd be *willing*. It wouldn't be through force."

"For now."

Thio sets the marker in the tray and faces me fully. "We'd work it into the rune that there'd have to be reception on both ends. It wouldn't be one conjurer doing the spell; we'd make sure it's fair."

I'm so sleep-deprived. Stretched thin over the past few weeks. I've been *feeling* more than I ever have before, too. Where I usually tamp that shit down, I've been swimming in nonstop waves of happiness. I let those waves carry me, wash me out to sea until I'm here, so far from shore, shaking my head.

Thio grabs my wrist. "Sebastian. Talk to me."

"This was for you," I say to the whiteboard. "Not—not something we'd release. It's just for you."

His head cocks until I look at him, and his confusion is clear.

"Why? Why wouldn't we release this? Not with our project, I get that, it's too late; but after. Your idea would work. If we can distribute the energetic demands of a conjuration spell, we—"

"Do you think it'd stay willing?" I twist my arm to my chest. He doesn't let go of my wrist, so we're pulled closer, his eyes locking on mine. "Do you honestly think if we released this, even in theory, that people like your family wouldn't figure out a way for a conjurer to select people at random to serve as their energy drains?"

Thio's face collapses in horror. He glances at the board.

"Shit. *Shit.*" He releases me to rub a hand roughly over his face. "You're right. It's—that's what they'd do."

My throat swells. "I wanted to give you some piece of what your mom was working on. Some result for her, for you. But any bit of this is too risky, isn't it? Gods, even trying to do it to keep conjurers *safe,* and—"

"And I immediately figured out a way to make it dangerous," Thio whispers.

He's staring at the board. At the runes that would, in theory, let a conjurer dissipate energy to other conjurers. It's the barest dregs of an idea, not fleshed out at all, but it's a seed.

And Thio's staring at it, his eyes tearing, and my heart cracks.

This isn't what I'd meant to do with—*fuck.*

"Thio—"

"Do you know what Arasne said to me this morning?" he asks, a brush of sound.

I don't. Of course I don't. He never tells me what she talks to him about beyond assurances that he's not spilling our project's secrets; and he never lets me come to those meetings with him. I've offered.

He rubs at his cheek, scrubbing away emotion, so when his eyes meet mine, he's almost composed. *Almost.* "She said the same shit she's been saying for too long. That the reason my mom had her accident"—Thio's breath is harsh—"and the reason she had so many failures in her career was because she isn't a real Tourael. And if I leave, I'll end up just like her. I'll waste away in obscurity because I have nothing substantial to contribute to this world."

His words, his posture, the empty, shell-like look in his eyes—it's agonizing, and I move toward him, arms lifting.

Only I stop.

Because—I've heard those words before. Why do I know them?

Thio keeps on, facing the board again, his eyes burning with ire, and passion, and *pain*.

"This could work," he says, gesturing at the runes. "I've read my mom's research. I've read *all* the research my family did on this topic. And this idea? They never came *close* to anything like this." His jaw bulges by his ears, cheeks reddening. "For all their resources, for all their finely honed methodologies, for all their *torture*, they couldn't come up with this solution. But we did. We're better than them."

"I know that," I whisper. Then, louder, "I know we're better than them."

He only half hears me. "We could . . . we could buffer it with protective spells. We could lock in the need for the spell to be willing, for it to work from two ends, not just one."

My lungs swell, refusing oxygen. "We're not releasing this idea. This isn't why I worked on it. I did it *for you*. To pay homage to your mom. Isn't it enough to know we have this theory? Why do you need to release it, especially if you know it's dangerous?"

He frowns, incredulous. "You thought you'd solve my mom's project and I'd be okay doing *nothing* with it?"

I wheeze at my own stupidity, the blinders I'd had on for him; but also, because he's pushing this. Because he *did* immediately figure out a way to make it dangerous, and he's still *digging* at it.

"I thought I'd give you a way to keep conjurers safe, and maybe we could work on it more, just us." I wrap my arms around my chest. "But if it means giving people a way to force others to be their components in conjuration spells? Then yeah, we shouldn't do anything with it."

"*Fuck*." Thio rips his hand through his hair but doesn't close the space between us. Doesn't touch me, and that choice widens the distance, pulls at the already taut energy of the room. "I'm sorry. That's—it isn't the same, though. It's *not* the same."

"I came up with a way to *protect* conjurers. That's what I thought the purpose of your project was—to keep magic users *safe*. Was I wrong? Is that not what you care about?"

"Of course it is," he says, teeth gritted. He's trembling, holding himself restrained.

"Then this shouldn't be—"

"Releasing this idea, solving what my family couldn't, rubbing their faces in how we did this *without* their methodologies—" He waves at the lab, all our work, every surface we've spent the past few months filling with research. "They pushed us and *broke* us, but they still *failed*. This idea redeems everything they did to us. *That's* how it's different."

Obscurity . . . nothing substantial to contribute to this world . . .

Oh my gods.

I remember now. Why I know those words.

"That's what you said to me," I gasp, eyes rounding.

Thio scowls. "What?"

"Before the grant banquet. In the bathroom. You said that to me—you told me I would die in obscurity because I have nothing substantial to contribute to this world."

He cringes. "I didn't—"

But his mouth stays open, nothing else coming out, no rebuttal.

"You said that's what Arasne's been telling you. For how long? *Months?* Probably longer. She's been beating you down like that to try to get you compliant in any way she can, and that's what you said to me. What she's always saying to you."

His face drains of color. He shakes his head once, a sharp, desperate snap. "I'm not them. I'm not my family."

I nearly fold right in half. "I didn't say you were. I—"

"*I am not my family,*" he cuts me off, anxious. Tears fill his eyes, hands in white-knuckled fists. "They almost *killed* my mom. Then I find out they almost killed *you*. I've been living for them, playing along with their sick games, accepting the hatred from everyone who sees them for what they truly are. I've been *obedient*. They've hurt everyone I love and *I just let them*."

Love.

Everyone I love.

Moving slowly, stunted, I step closer to him. "I know, Thio. I—"

"No," he growls and tries, *tries* to refocus, but he's feverish now, unhinging. "We need my family to know they failed. DaylarTech and Arasne and my immediate asshole relatives; and Camp Merethyl, too, and the Touraels who were involved, Colonel Vemir, Lieutenant Hana. We need them to know they hurt us, but they didn't destroy us. They *failed.*"

I gape at him. Something shatters, glass, maybe; no, it's internal.

"How do you—" My tongue scrapes the roof of my mouth. "How do you know those names?"

Thio's jaw shuts.

"I never told you who was running the ouroboros project at Camp Merethyl," I whisper. "I never told you their *names.*" Oh my gods. "Did you talk to my dad? Did you—"

"No, Sebastian, I didn't—"

"Then *how do you know those names?*"

His glare weakens, eyelashes fluttering. "I searched what members of my family were there at the time, and who were in positions to have been part of that project. What if it was someone I *was* closely related to? What if they were at one of the pretentious meetings Arasne has and I smiled and shook their hands and treated them *cordially,* while all along they were the ones who—" He pants, tongue pushing against his lower lip, and one of the tears he's holding back slips down his cheek. "The ones who *touched* you, and I didn't know?"

"Did you contact them," I ask, or try to; it's flat, lifeless.

Thio hesitates. Hesitates enough that panic floods my veins, replaces all the liquid in my body, before he says, "No. I'm not closely related to them. I shouldn't ever have to run into them. I wanted to be sure." Another pause. This one holds a dagger to my chin. "But—"

"*No.*"

"No one ever held them accountable. No one ever stops my

family, no one ever *does anything,* and I am sick of doing *nothing.*" His voice cracks, words echoing between choleric sobs.

He wants me to let my father sue his family, doesn't he? He hasn't told me that. We haven't talked about it since my parents came. But he *wants* that.

Thio's crying, splitting apart, and me?

I'm standing, dry-eyed, numb.

"I told you I didn't need that from you"—I can't feel anything, not my lips moving—"and you found out their names anyway, then *used those names in an argument against me.*"

Thio looks like I sucker punched him. "That's not fair. I was trying to—"

"I don't give a fuck what you were trying to do." I laugh humor-lessly, it throbs in my chest. "You don't see the irony?"

His desperation peels back. Confusion.

"I asked you not to do something," I say, "and you found a way to do it regardless. Just like your family would with this spell. They wouldn't give a *shit* how we came up with the idea, that we got it on our own without their messed-up approaches. They'd take it, and they'd abuse it, because *that's what Touraels do.*"

The wrong thing to say.

I know as soon as the words leave my mouth, and I see it hit him. The final tap on his already fracturing shell.

I see him break.

"*I am not my family!*" he screams, the words shearing his throat. "*Gods,* Sebastian, is that what you think of me? *Still?* When I fuck you, do you just think about Camp—"

He stops. Eyes wide.

I stop, too. His unsaid words beat against my skin.

And the words he said. *Everyone I love.*

"Sebastian," he says, shuddering, adrenaline releasing. "I didn't—"

I hold up my hand, palm flat.

Air jerks out of my lungs. I'd fold double if I wasn't already walking for the door.

"Sebastian—*wait.*"

He touches me now. Grabs my arm, tries to get in front of me. He's saying things, apologizing, but I shove him, *hard*.

Thio topples back into his desk with a rattling thud.

I'm not looking at him. The floor, I think. Something white and rippling.

Everyone I love.

"Stay away from me," I tell him. Beg him.

And I leave.

Chapter Eighteen

I'm back at my apartment.

Fingers knotted in my hair, a headache throbbing across my skull, I drop against the door.

What just happened?

I can't breathe. Out, at least; air goes in, in, damming against words, angry, stupid, small *words*.

One word.

Going around and around in my head.

Love.

Footsteps pad down the stairs.

Orok stumbles into the living room, screwing the heel of his hand into his eye, looking as exhausted as I feel. Maybe, impossibly, more.

He takes a few steps toward the kitchen before he sees me and jumps, startled. "Shit, dude, what are you doing here?"

"I . . . live here?"

He snorts. "Do you?"

And I suddenly can't remember the last time I was here when it wasn't to grab a change of clothes. Have I really been staying at Thio's so much the past few weeks?

I'm pushing at my chest. Pushing, pushing against my sternum. It *hurts,* it's cracking in half, why can't I hear the bone breaking? Why isn't my body collapsing from the pain?

It isn't pain.

Yeah, what Thio said hurt. But what this is, what I'm feeling, isn't agony from that.

I'm in love with him.

A breath finally goes out, a grasping, frantic noise.

Orok immediately straightens. "Seb?"

"I'm in love with him," I say out loud, testing the words. "Oh my gods. I'm in love with him."

Orok nods soothingly. "Pretty sure you have been for a while."

I know my eyes are bloodshot, know I look a wreck.

"Why is that a bad thing?" he asks.

Reasons clatter over themselves in their rush to get out first.

I don't deserve it.

I'll freak out and fuck it up.

"It isn't," I say instead. I *make* myself say instead.

And it forces all those reasons to evaporate like mist, like the insubstantial bullshit they always have been.

It isn't a bad thing that I love him. I *deserve* to love him.

What *is* a bad thing is that he's gotten so stressed out by his family that he said what he said to me.

How did I not see how much this was beating him down?

Or maybe I did. Maybe I knew, but thought he was handling it. Maybe I was so corrupted by my own stress that I trusted his smiles and reassurances because why wouldn't I? We've only been dating for a little over a month. We're still new and cautious and I couldn't have known he was hurting so much. Right?

Fuck that.

A month, two months, hell, two *days*—it doesn't matter how long Thio and I have been together. This is *real*. We decided *this is real*. And that means he should have told me how upset he was getting, and I should have *realized* how upset he was getting, but I was lost in my own issues, and *fuck that*.

I'm pacing across our kitchen, back and forth, Orok watching me, a considering, worried look on his face.

It rips me to a stop, my eyes running all over him, taking in his posture, his stained sweats.

He really is exhausted. Sunken eyes, with a crease between his brows.

"You're not okay either," I guess.

Recognition slams into me. Orok's been struggling, too. Not in the same way as Thio, and not in the same way Orok's usually struggling; this is different.

I haven't talked to him about my dad's visit either. About the lawsuit. He hasn't brought it up, and I thought we were both fo-cusing on surviving this last push until graduation. That we'd talk about it after.

But . . . whatever's wrong with Orok has been going on since before my dad's visit. The differences echo out over the past few months: Orok's deflection, he *let me* not be home practically ever.

Orok chews the inside of his cheek. Between one blink and the next, his eyes tear.

My stomach knots, desperately trying to build a retaining wall against the remorseful look he's wearing now.

I don't pry, don't push him, and we watch each other in silence until he shakes his head and lays it all out in a breathless rush.

"I got a contract. To play pro rawball."

I rock backward. "What? When? I—but, tryouts, I thought—"

He shrugs. "I was supposed to. But I kept putting off responding, and it must've scared them. They offered me a position straight-out. A full contract, Seb. The kind of money that—" He gasps, winded, like this news has been running circles in his head the whole time he's held it in. "In one season, I could pay off all my student loans. All *your* loans."

"You aren't paying my loans."

He ignores me. "And I'd be playing professionally, and I—"

"O." I cross the kitchen and squeeze his forearm. "You don't have to sell me on it. Are you happy? Do you want this?"

He nods.

"Well, that's all—"

"It isn't for the Hellhounds."

My fingers spasm on his arm.

Orok keeps his eyes pinned on me, fragile. "It's for the Chime-ras. In Vegas."

Vegas.

Nevada.

And I have a job here. In Philadelphia.

"That's—" *Far. Far away.* "Great, O."

I sound like I'm saying it through my teeth. Because I am.

I peel away from him and flex my hands, try again.

"Orok. That's—"

He takes a step toward me, a step back. "I've been thinking about this for . . . weeks. The recruiter, Savasea? She sent the official contract over a few days ago, but Vegas has been interested since the beginning of the semester—"

The beginning of the—

He's known that long? Known it was a possibility that long, at least.

"—and it's why I've been dragging my ass about it. But I'd have money. *Real* money. I thought, that'll be fine, I'll fly us back and forth whenever we want. Or I looked, and Clawstar has a branch in Los Angeles. That's crazy though, asking you to move across the country to be a few hours closer to me. You have Thio here, and I'll be traveling so much anyway, and *you'll* be working, and—"

He cuts himself off. Silence hangs. I loop my arms around my chest, holding myself together.

Orok sucks in a breath. "I kept thinking. Over and over. How it could work. I talked to my therapist, too. I—it's been killing me."

"You should have told me." It's killing me, too. And I want to say it's only because he felt like he couldn't tell me, but I'm not that selfless.

He'll be in Las Vegas.

And I'll be here.

"I wanted to figure out where I stood before I told you," Orok says. "Whether I wanted it. And if I did want it, whether I wanted it *for me*. I was worried I'd be doing it for my mom. Yet another thing I'm doing to please her. But it's not. I *want* this. I'm good at it. This could be . . . this could be big."

He smiles, easy and hopeful, and it brings a matching one across my face.

"You are good at it," I say. "You deserve this. So gods-damned much."

"And—" Another sigh. Another wounded look. "I was worried it'd break us. That's why I kept trying to figure out ways to make this"—he points between us—"work before I told you. But I . . . it won't work. What we are, how we are. When I go to Vegas."

I almost offer to go with him.

"No," I whisper. "It won't."

"It won't," Orok repeats, his eyes bloodshot. "I love you. You'll always be one of the most important people in my life. But you don't need me as much anymore, and I'm so glad for that."

My arms unwind from my chest. "I need you, O. I'll always—"

"But not as much." His smile wobbles. "Not as much as I've needed you. Not in the same ways. And I . . . I need to stop needing you. We've both been clinging to what's safe for too long, which is why—"

His eyes go to the floor.

"If you want to do what your dad said," he whispers. "If you want to go after the people at Camp Merethyl. I'd back you, Seb."

My chest lurches. "You'd be in the lawsuit, too. It happened to you, too."

"But he's your father." Orok looks back up at me with a one-shouldered shrug. "It's your family dynamic that'd be at the center of this. Although, I'd have money with this contract, too. To fund a lawsuit."

"No." I shove toward him. "This money, this opportunity, it's your future, and like hell are you going to use even a cent of it for anything from our past. If we do it."

Orok's smile is lopsided. "We will. I think we need to."

I want to argue. Deny it. We don't need it. It'll be messy and painful and dig up everything we've spent six years trying to forget.

But Orok takes my hand. "Watching you break out of our past this semester? Seeing you have a healthy relationship? Seeing you fall in love? It isn't enough to ignore what happened. We owe it to ourselves, now and back then, to *live*."

Tears pour down my face and I barely get out a whimper before Orok snatches me into his arms. He trembles against me, crying, too, a sloppy hug that keeps us both from collapsing.

"I'm going to Las Vegas," Orok says into my neck. "And I'm going to play pro rawball, and you're going to stay here and change the world at Clawstar and be dopily, crazily in love with Thio. We're going to be so happy, Seb."

I sob into his shoulder. "Gods, you oaf, *shut up*. I can't handle this. I love you, too, you absolute asshole."

Orok stills.

Then he *loses it*.

Great hiccupping rolls of laughter, his body heaving.

I peel back from him, my sobs turning to helpless laughter, too, and he snorts and cries; we're a mix of blotchy faces and snot and emotion.

We settle, end up on the couch, and I tell him what I said to Thio. What Thio said to me.

"You know he wasn't going behind your back when he looked into their names," Orok says. He's sagged into the cushions, body deflating. He'd been carrying the news about the Chimeras for too long.

I twist to frown at him. "But I asked him not to."

"You asked him not to get involved with them, and he didn't. But he wanted to know who they were. I get that. He wanted to make sure he isn't inadvertently nice to them, and after spending his whole life genuflecting to all those assholes? I can see how that was a last straw for him. Check your phone." Orok elbows me.

"What?"

"Check your phone. Is he trying to apologize?"

I pull my phone out of my pocket and tap the screen. My background is a picture of me and Thio, a selfie we took at a date I set up for us, an outdoor concert on the river. The song that'd been playing was folksy and sad, all about yearning, but in the photo, I'm beaming at the camera and Thio's grinning, his face pressed to the side of mine.

There aren't any notifications. But I haven't reached out to him yet either.

Are we letting each other cool off?

No. We *are* letting each other cool off.

I pull up his text thread. It's relatively empty. We're usually together, at the lab during the day or his place at night; we rarely have to text each other because we've made a habit out of always being near one another, and I hadn't realized how easily that habit reshaped my life.

I tap out a text to him.

THIO

I'll come to your place
tonight. We both have things
we need to say before
tomorrow.

Like *I love you. I'm so in love with you. I'm sorry I didn't see how much you were hurting, but we'll get through this together. Gods, please, let us get through this together.*

Before I can convince myself to toss my phone on the coffee table, three dots pop up. Then his response.

THIO
Not tonight. I'm sorry. I need
some time.

I sit bolt upright. Orok's beside me, so he reads Thio's response, and hums.

"He's only asking for time," Orok tries. "You both said some hurtful things. Him especially. He's probably kicking himself for what he did, and—"

"But he doesn't have to be." I stand and get halfway to the door—

—when Orok scoops me up and flops me back onto the couch.

"What the fuck!" I gawk up at him, *pissed.*

He points a threatening finger at me. "Do not go storming over to his place when all he asked you for was time. Didn't you just get angry when you thought he went against something you asked him to do?"

I scowl. "Fuck you and your logic, I swear."

"You're meeting him before the presentation tomorrow, right?"

"Yeah." We both knew we'd need to get ready in the morning at our respective apartments, so we always planned to meet outside the same banquet room where the grant award ceremony happened.

"Then meet him like normal, and *give him time*. Get your head together. Let *him* get *his* head together. Graduation, this project, jobs, his family, the lawsuit, *you*. Any one of those things would be overwhelmingly stressful on its own, but all at once? No wonder he's a mess. No wonder *you're* a mess. Sit your ass down and *breathe*."

"He doesn't have to be stressed about me, though," I counter. "And I want to help him with the rest. Neither of us has to be shouldering any of this alone."

Orok's smile is sweet. "I know. Make sure Thio knows that, then give him what he asked for."

One last glare at my supposed best friend, and I type out a message with quaking hands. This kills me as much as everything else has today.

> Okay. I'll give you tonight. But we're meeting tomorrow morning like we'd planned, and before we say a gods-damned word to each other, I'm going to kiss the fuck out of you.

I almost add *I love you*, but like hell will the first time I say that to him be via text.

Orok, deciding I'm not a flight risk anymore, sits back down and flicks on our TV to a pro rawball commentary show. I let it fade to background noise as I watch Thio's text thread, willing three dots to appear, willing *anything* to appear.

Nothing does. My message doesn't even switch to *Read*.

Fine. He wants time? He gets exactly—I do some quick math— twenty-two hours and seventeen minutes.

After that, he's mine, for the rest of our miserable lives, and he's just going to have to deal with it.

————————

Mr. Walsh—

On behalf of the Clawstar Foundation, I wanted to wish you good luck on your presentation today. The Mageus Research Grant is a very prestigious addition to your already impressive résumé.

We are all still tremendously excited to have you join our team, Dr. Zishi Zuarashi

I read over the email from my future boss three times before I realize what's missing.

Anxiety.

I'm not freaking out that I need to prove myself to her. I'm not going over all the ways I could fuck up the presentation and lose my job. Not a flicker of my emotions is spared for Clawstar, because as I stand in the hall outside the banquet room, dressed in my one nice suit like the last time I was here, I know I've got this. The presentation, our paper, all of it.

But Thio?

That's where my anxiety goes, rocketing right toward the knot in my chest that made my sleep erratic and my dreams muddled.

I don't like not sleeping in the same bed as him. I don't like not being near him, and maybe he was right, actually. About needing this time apart. It's helped me crystallize that realization I had yesterday, helped it grow from an idea to a concrete belief.

I'm in love with Thio.

Orok nudges me with his shoulder, dressed in his own suit, a dark, smoky blue. "Put your phone away. He'll be here."

I comply, giving him my fourteenth exasperated glare of the day.

Orok grins at my annoyance. "He'll be here. Hands."

My fingers stretch automatically.

The presentation's due to start in a few minutes. The banquet room has been set up with a stage at one end and rows of padded chairs lined in front of it, the hall and room already filling with people. Grant committee members, university board members, donors, professors, faculty. Even a few students, drawn by the topic of our research.

Arasne's here with Myrdin. They're inside, right in the front row, along with people who have to be Thio's other relatives. Those who run DaylarTech or who knows what Tourael properties, all come to make sure the next cog in their Tourael machine does what they expect him to.

I force myself not to think about them. Thio isn't going to get sucked up in his family's bullshit.

I scan the hall again, searching the faces of new arrivals.

He didn't respond to any of my texts this morning.

I bounce on my heels. My anxiety grows, swells up and out, pushing on my ribs, and—

He'll be here, Orok said.

No.

I don't think he will be.

I don't know where the thought comes from. It seizes me like an errant muscle cramp; one of my knees buckles, and I glower at everyone around me in business attire chatting amicably.

Orok catches my change of expression. Before he can ask anything, Dr. Davyeras comes rushing up the hall at a tight clip between a jog and a walk.

He spots me, and his shoulders sag in relief, which immediately sets me on alert.

In the time it takes him to reach me, I check my phone again.

Nothing from Thio.

Something's wrong.

"Mr. Walsh," Davyeras says. He smiles tightly, trying to look professional despite the flicker of panic in his eyes. "I'm hoping you can shed some light on the situation?"

"Situation?" But Davyeras is ushering me to the side of the hall, throwing pleasant smiles as people pass us to enter the banquet room.

"With Mr. Tourael." Davyeras lowers his voice. "Dr. Narbeth and the grant committee received unsettling letters from him this morning, and he isn't responding to our attempts to reach out. Given your close proximity to him, we were hoping you had insight into—"

"What letters?" My heart's in my throat. Orok followed us to the side of the hall and his bulk helps create an illusion of privacy, but he touches my arm, reminds me not to shout.

Davyeras eyes Orok, then me in confusion. "Mr. Tourael has re-signed from the program. He informed us this morning of his intent to withdraw from the grant as well as his degree."

Orok's hand is around my wrist, holding me in place. I'd run otherwise. Sprint right out of here and go find Thio.

"What?" I ask; nothing congeals. "What are you talking about? He isn't dropping out."

Davyeras seems just as confused. "Forgive me, Mr. Walsh, but we assumed you knew."

"I didn't know, because he *didn't drop out.*"

Davyeras pulls his phone out of his suit jacket. After a moment of tapping, he shows me his screen.

It's our paper. Thio's and mine. I scan the title, look at Davyeras questioningly.

"The paper was submitted last night," Davyeras tells me. "You are the only author listed."

My eyes go back to his phone. Under the title, it says *Sebastian Walsh.*

And that's it.

Yesterday, Thio and I were going to submit our paper together. We didn't. Because we were yelling at each other.

Thio submitted the paper on his own last night. After taking his name off it. After I said he was like his family. After he used Camp Merethyl against me.

Oh my gods.

He dropped out.

He couldn't take playing their games anymore, and he *dropped out*.

"I have to go." I shove Davyeras's phone back at him. "I have to—"

I expect Orok to be the one to stop me. But he releases my arm, and it's Davyeras who leaps in front of me, blocking my path.

"Mr. Walsh." His voice is clipped. "It is admirable that you care about Mr. Tourael. But one of you needs to present your research today, or the final requirement for your degrees remains incomplete."

Everything's overlapping.

Yesterday, Thio sobbing in the lab.

Six years ago, the voice that became my nightmares: *Are you going to let this be a failure?*

And right now, Thio's family sitting in that banquet room, expecting him to walk in and puppet himself for them.

They'll cut him off. They'll stop paying for his mom's care. He'll have nothing. No money, no support. And now, no degree, nothing to use in the fight to come.

Are you going to let this be a failure, Mr. Walsh?

Vibrations race up and down my arms, burrow into my lungs, dig into the bedrock of that new realization, *I'm in love with Thio,* and set off earthquakes, one after another.

I've had this emotion before. I've had it so many times over the past few years that I almost surrender to it out of familiarity alone. This is what precedes me doing something dumb, something I can't come back from: fear. I lash out to protect myself. I lash out because I'm terrified, and reacting aggressively is the best way I've found to reclaim the power they've taken from me.

But *this isn't the same as Camp Merethyl.* Thio dropping out now, me dropping out then. This isn't the same. Getting his degree wouldn't make him a toy for his family to abuse; it'd give him what he needs to break free.

I can separate these events. Similarities don't have to consume me. I can take a breath—gods-damned anger management techniques—and see through the haze.

I don't have to be reactive. I don't have to let it control me.

And that is far more powerful.

"He didn't drop out," I tell Davyeras, jaw wired shut. "He's not—tell Narbeth not to process anything yet. Thio isn't dropping out."

Not if this is his fucked-up way of atoning for what he said to me. And if this is what he wants, I'll talk to him, support him; but like *hell* is he not going to have the option to complete his degree, not when he's this close, not if I can help it.

Davyeras smiles, tentative. "No one is eager to see Mr. Tourael give this up, I assure you. I'll speak with Narbeth, but for now—" He glances at his watch and winces. "The presentation is supposed to start. I'll introduce you?"

"Yeah," I say, muscles still coiled to run. "Yeah, I'm good."

Davyeras lingers one more beat, nods decisively, and slips into the room.

In the past few minutes, the hallway has cleared. The seats inside the banquet room are filled.

And Orok's unmoved beside me, his eyes wide. "It's possible I was wrong when I told you to listen to him. You should *not* have given him time. He *dropped out?*"

"He's getting his degree." Certainty wells up inside of me. "And he can chuck it aside after for all I care, but he's getting it, because he's earned it. And maybe I should've raced after him yesterday, maybe I could've changed his mind then, but it doesn't matter. I'll find him after this, and we'll figure it out."

I'm furious. At Thio's family, at all the situations that forced him to this. I'm *livid*, but not at him, and not at myself, and not at Orok.

Thio told me once that if I was going to be angry, I should use it.

Well, I am.

It's giving me clarity and a target.

Within the banquet room, Davyeras's voice rings out. "Thank you for joining us today. The Mageus Research Grant has a long history of—"

"I can start looking for him," Orok offers. "Tell me where he might be."

He's poised, waiting for whatever I want to do. Always.

I'm going to miss him. I'm going to miss him so much.

"And this year's project," continues Davyeras within the room, "is an exciting collaboration presented by Mr. Sebastian Walsh."

The audience applauds.

I adjust my glasses, blinking away the rush of heat in my eyes, and throw my arms around Orok in a quick, fierce hug.

"Thanks," I say. "Check his apartment?"

Orok squeezes me tight. "On it."

He jogs up the hall, but not before tossing a grin over his shoulder. "Present the hell out of your project, Mr. Walsh!"

Head high, an unavoidable vibration in my hands, I walk into the banquet room, and the audience claps politely.

This research, this project, has always symbolized healing for me. I didn't think it was ever something I'd get, though. And it wasn't something I got, not all at once—I got it slowly, the smoothing of a scar there, the stitching together of a wound here. Part of healing is growing again, too, even if it risks those scars stretching, even if the skin breaks back open.

But I know I can heal now. I can look at the wounds and think, *You are not all of me.*

Gods, there's so much more to me. So many more fascinating, enthralling parts. And I can *feel* them, a feeling that takes my breath away as I climb the stage.

My eyes land on Thio's family, front and center. They're scowling, likely wondering where Thio is, why it's just me up here.

Resolve is strength. Healing is anger and it's sorrow and it's calm certainty.

It's peace.

Davyeras yields the podium to me. There's already a copy of my paper laid out on it. Only my name is typed across it.

I rest my fingers on that line, then look up into the watchful, waiting eyes of the audience.

"Hi," I say. The microphone squeals. "I'm presenting 'The Proposed Effect of Energy Limitations on Material Component Usage.' By Elethior Tourael and Sebastian Walsh."

Chapter Nineteen

After my presentation, nothing else matters.

Arasne tries to intercept me. I beeline past her, and she scoffs, offended.

I also dodge Davyeras, Thompson, and Narbeth until I'm racing out of the banquet room and sprinting through Bellanor Hall, slapping open the rear door and pulling out my phone.

Orok texted that Thio isn't at his apartment.

There's only one other place he'd go: Blooming Grove.

I check the public transpo app. Traffic's minimal right now, but it still estimates thirty minutes to get there, and I growl at my screen as I jog for the bus stop and mentally tally whether I can afford a rideshare—

"Mr. Walsh!"

I trip on the sidewalk and rebound off—Hordon?

Thio's driver.

I frantically scan the area. His car's next to the curb, but Thio's nowhere, and I don't even get out a question before Hordon's opening the rear door for me.

"He's visiting his mother," Hordon tells me.

"He's—did he send you for me?"

Hordon straightens his suit jacket, his face impassive. "Mr. Tourael's instructions were to deliver him to Blooming Grove despite our scheduled trip to today's presentation."

So . . . no.

One of my brows lifts.

"Given his change of plans over what I know is a very important event," Hordon continues, "intensified by the fact that he seemed . . . uncharacteristically upset, I delivered him to Blooming Grove and took my break early."

Hordon nudges the door wider.

Some of the tension unwinds from my shoulders, and I slump forward. "Thank you."

He shrugs, like it's part of his job, like it's no big deal that he came to get me when he sure as hell didn't have to.

"Wait right there!"

The door to Bellanor Hall bangs off the wall, and Hordon and I spin to see Arasne and Thio's family pointing at us, looking slightly winded; which, for uptight, rich assholes, is the equivalent of being completely disheveled.

"Mr. Walsh," Hordon says. "I do believe we should hurry."

I dive into the car.

He shuts the door and calmly rounds the hood as Arasne and her brigade storm toward us.

Hordon takes the driver's seat. Adjusts his rearview mirror.

"Seatbelt, Mr. Walsh," is the only warning I get before the dude guns it into a full one-eighty.

Tires scream over the blacktop, the engine bellows like a cave monster, and somewhere behind us—beside us? We're spinning—Arasne shouts about Hordon being fired.

"Um, Hordon, I think you lost your—"

"Seatbelt, please," he repeats as he tears out of the parking lot, expertly weaving into traffic.

I obey with a discreet click, unable to scrape off my grin.

We get to Blooming Grove in under twelve minutes.

Hordon squeals up in front of the main doors and I lurch against the seatbelt as he slams the brakes.

"Would you like me to get the door for you, sir?" he asks evenly.

I stay glued to the seat, one hand gripping the *oh shit* bar by the window.

"Nah, man." My voice is squeaky. "I'm good."

"Very well, Mr. Walsh."

"You got fired for us."

Hordon looks back at me. "I have driven the Tourael family for almost twenty-five years. And your Mr. Tourael?" Gods, I like that, *my Mr. Tourael*. "I suspect I would not have been driving him much longer anyway. This is as good a time as any to take an early retire-ment."

I pry my fingers off the handle and lean forward to squeeze his shoulder. "Thank you."

"I will be here when you're done."

I climb out of the car and leap up the steps to Blooming Grove. The main doors release with a gust of cool air, and Nithroel's got her arm stuck out over the desk already, a visitor pass in one hand.

"Courtyard garden," she says by way of greeting. "Martha's been trying to ply him with tea all morning."

I stagger to a halt in front of the desk, reaching for the badge.

Hordon. Nithroel. Martha.

I wonder if Thio realizes he isn't as alone as he'd thought.

Just like me.

Dad's face flashes in my mind. His earnestness.

My smile is soft. "Thanks, Nithroel."

She smiles back. "We're not sure what's happened, but—" She releases the badge to me. "Make sure he's okay, yeah?"

I pin the badge to the collar of my shirt. I'd shucked my jacket during Hordon's Fast & Furious impression down Broad Street, and I spear my fingers through my hair; it's probably a lost cause at this point.

"Of course," I promise her.

Blooming Grove is quiet this morning. I weave through the pris-tine halls, nodding at staff I recognize now, a few residents, too.

Outside, the courtyard is picture-perfect in springtime bloom. A massive willow tree dominates the space, with vibrant flower-beds framing the area and a pond nestled in the back corner. A few wrought-iron tables are clustered around, two other residents and their guests settled in them, but my eyes immediately go to the tree, to Thio's mom's favorite spot.

She's in a wheelchair, a blanket tucked around her lap, her head tipped as she stares up at the tree. Thio sits next to her, his back to me, one arm propped on the armrest to cradle his jaw, legs spread and knee bouncing.

Sweat breaks out across my palms, but I curl my fingers tight, release them, and make my way across the lawn.

The tree boughs rustle as I part them.

Thio glances up.

And shoves to his feet.

He's wearing the same jeans and T-shirt he had on yesterday, his hair in a bun that's unwashed messy, not intentionally messy.

The pinches of sorrow that've been grabbing me all morning convene at once, and I want nothing more than to hold him.

His mouth bobs open. "Sebastian. I can—"

"Just a sec. I'm here to see your mom."

He freezes, surprise knocking him off-balance.

I kneel next to her. Her eyes drift to me, away.

"Hey, Dr. Holmes," I say. "I wanted you to be the first to hear how the presentation went this morning."

Thio sucks in a breath.

"It was fantastic," I tell her. "Our research was well-received. *Our* research, because despite your son's misguided decision to drop out, I gave him credit for the paper anyway. The questions that the audience posed were all reasonable and expected, nothing that undid all our work, thank gods. So, once our paper is fully reviewed by the Mageus Committee, your son will graduate after solving your research project. That wasn't part of our presentation, but he probably didn't tell you: we figured out a solution to your topic because he's fucking brill—sorry, cussing—he's *brilliant,* and I know you're proud of him."

I finally look up at Thio.

His eyes are tearing, chest heaving in tight, apprehensive jerks.

"I'm sorry I said you were like your family," I tell him, still kneeling. It makes my words an offering. "That argument got out of hand, but I refuse to accept whatever penance you think this is."

"It's not penance," he says, brittle. "You were right. I *was* thinking like my family. I let them sculpt me. I let them pick so many elements of my life, and no matter what job I get with this degree, I'll be like them, won't I? I'll be working in industries like theirs, hurting people like they do. It was the only way I could think to stop what I saw happening."

"Quitting won't stop that because you *aren't like them*." I push to my feet. "I put you back on that paper because it's *ours*, whether you like it or not. Dr. Narbeth's waiting for you to contact him and rescind your withdrawal from the program, because everyone was fucking heart—gods, sorry." I wince at Dr. Holmes. "Everyone was heartbroken you'd do that. *You don't deserve that*. You deserve this degree, Thio. You've worked hard for it, and it's *yours*, and that's something your family can't take away or corrupt. Don't give up a powerful tool in your arsenal. You don't have to use it for anything that'll make you like them."

I close the space between us, finally touching him, taking his hands and pressing them to my chest.

"I know you've been trapped under them by yourself for a very long time." My voice is low but sure, more sure than I've been about anything. "It's daunting to face a threat like the Touraels on your own, and that's why so many of us turn to magic. Some conflicts are too big when it's just us. But it isn't just you anymore. Because I—"

"I'm sorry," Thio cuts me off, freeing his hands to loop around my neck, thumbs on my jaw. "I'm so sorry for what I said to you. I should never have looked up those names without your consent, and I sure as hell shouldn't have *said them to you*; and what I said about Camp Merethyl, too, I didn't—"

I kiss him. Let his apology fill the air between our lips and he moans into the contact, a fatalistic whimper heavy with regret, with need.

It stays gentle against the heat welling in my chest, how even one night of not being with him triggers greed. We're both gasping as our foreheads grind together; I wonder if Hordon will let us subject him to one more X-rated usage of the car's back seat.

"Let me in, okay?" I whisper into our space. "I know that's rich coming from me, but I will now, too. I promise. You're not bearing any of this alone anymore, and I'm not either."

He nods against me, grip on my neck pinching tighter, keeping me in this dimension.

"And you're graduating," I tell him. "Okay? You've done all the work. *You* did it, not your family, and whatever you do with this degree, *you'll* use it. Not them. Just because you have the skills to work in their fields doesn't mean you have to. I'll help you figure out what job you *do* want. But get this degree. Get this stepping stone. It's yours."

Thio winces, breaks with a panting gasp. "I love you so much."

I yank back from him.

He teeters, not letting go of me.

"You dick," I snap with no bite whatsoever. "I wanted to say it first. I *almost did* say it first, but you cut me off."

Thio grins. An unhurried, delighted smile, it bathes over me, settles the last of the worry.

"I win," he declares, eyes teary, and before I can get out more than an indignant huff, he's kissing me again, bending me nearly backward, our bodies slamming together and his tongue invading my mouth.

A throat clears.

Slowly, we shift to face Martha, her hands clasped against her scrubs, her head tipped in amused reproach.

"This is hardly the place, is it, gentlemen?" she softly scolds.

I try to disentangle myself from Thio, but he holds on, keeping one arm around my waist.

"Sorry," he says, not sounding sorry at all.

I elbow him, and he buries his face in my neck, inhaling, absorbing. His sigh of pleasure ripples out across my entire body, makes my neck arch, feline and supple.

Gods, this man.

Martha smiles. "I'm glad to see you've worked out your issues. But lunch is being served in the main dining room, and I know your mother will want to get a zucchini fritter before they're gone." She fiddles with a few settings on Dr. Holmes's wheelchair and pivots her toward the door. "Will you be joining us?"

"Yeah," I say, and Thio extricates himself from my neck to give me a look of such adoration my knees nearly collapse.

This is how it's going to be, then? Not a damn thing buffering this connection between us now. Nothing left to shield us or the outside world from the full onslaught of everything blazing in Thio's eyes.

Martha heads off with Thio's mom, and we linger for a beat under the weeping willow, a breeze playing a melody through the branches and elongated leaves.

"We don't have to stay," he tells me.

I pick at a spot on his shirt, right over his pec. "Hey, I like zucchini fritters as much as the next guy."

His arms lock around my waist and my eyes leap up to his. The smell of him surrounds me, greenery and flowers and spring, vibrancy and growth and *life*.

"I love you, too," I say.

Thio groans, bumping his nose against mine. "We'll eat fast."

"But, Thio," my voice goes up, intentionally bratty, "proper digestion calls for a patient, deliberate consumption of—"

"*Sebastian.*"

I shiver at his tone.

"Yeah, okay," I agree. "We'll eat fast."

I have Hordon take us to my apartment because I'm almost certain Arasne will be staked out at Thio's. He checks his phone as we veer through the streets—at a much more sedate pace—and his screen is cluttered with missed calls from her, and texts, and voicemails.

Thio toys with his phone, his other hand looped around my thigh where I've got him pulled against me, my arm over his shoulders.

"I should call her," he says against the hum of traffic.

"Why?" I put my hand over his phone and push it into his lap. "You're still graduating. You can keep playing along like you have been—"

"No." Thio sags into me, head against mine, eyes shut. "I'm done with them. That hasn't changed. I can't keep letting them think I'm okay with everything they are. Even if it means—" He shudders out an exhale. "I'll have to move my mom. I'll have to get a new place to live."

Hordon had a barrier spell up before we'd gotten back in the car, which I mentally filed as unspoken permission; Thio's energy was exhausted though, so I was more than content to have him in my arms.

But at the despondency in his words, I unfasten my seatbelt and straddle his lap, wanting to be the center of his focus and break through the dread swamping him. His eyes fly open and he grabs on to my hips, and there it is, a widening of his pupils, a repositioning of his awareness.

"This is what I meant, Thio," I say, fingers sliding beneath the bun his hair's in. "You're not alone. I'll help you research other places for your mom, somewhere affordable. Or—hell, I have a deep inner knowledge of how to make leftovers stretch multiple days, or how to navigate this city without a driver, or—" I shrug, cheeks hot. "I have a place to stay."

His eyes shift over mine, memorizing me, and he doesn't need to say anything. I can see it in him, feathered layers of adoration and relief.

"Only if you let me do something for you, too," he whispers.

I squint. "I haven't had a lot of successful relationships, but I'm pretty sure they don't have to be perfectly even in terms of—"

"Call your father," he says.

I lean back on his thighs, throat seizing.

He rises up, meeting my retreat, keeping our chests together.

"Move forward with the lawsuit," Thio continues. His lips brush across mine like saying the words so close softens their blow. "I know it'll be awful. It'll drag out things that'll destroy us both. But I'll be there for you, every second of it, every moment where you're taking back the power my family stole from you."

I scratch my fingers across his scalp, arch his head up, and devour him.

It's violent and eradicates the numb exhaustion Thio had been cloaked in, once and for all smashing through it.

We part on a shared, knifelike breath.

I nod.

My eyes shut.

I nod again, giving him as much of a promise as I can.

He surges back up, starving, tongue warring with mine and arms dragging me to grind against him. My hips roll and he lets out a hoarse grunt before he clicks his seatbelt, tilts his body to the side, and tackles me on the cushion.

The car rocks as Hordon turns and maybe we're close to my place, maybe we still have hours in traffic, but Thio's tugging aside clothes and leaving kisses and bites as he crawls down my body and time stands perfectly still.

He undoes my belt, works open my pants, and drags out my hard cock to the needy, grating whimpers I pour into the back of the car.

Thio looks up at me, his eyes thunderstorm black with their own hits of lightning, his lips distending as he sinks his mouth around me.

I brace my palms flat against the car door by my head and cry out, thrusting unconsciously. Neither of us has the fortitude to make this last or stop to pull up a teasing spell, not after everything. Thio answers my cry with all the ferocity that drives me wild, sucking hard and tunneling the base of my cock through his fist and dragging his lip rings on the underside of my head. Saliva leaks from the corners of his mouth, his increasingly desperate moans groping toward my disjointed sounds until they intertwine.

Sensation rockets through me, abrupt and forceful, an onslaught; I come and he swallows hard, never one to back off quickly, and I love that I know that about him. That I know he lingers in the afterglow like he can feel mine, too, licking and nuzzling; it's reverential in a way I want to shy from, but at the same time, he makes me feel like I'm worthy of it.

The car lurches to a stop and shifts into park as Thio's climbing back up me. He kisses me, wet and salty-sweet, and I reach down for the buckle on his pants when he grabs my wrist.

"We're going to go to your room, and I'm going to put a levitation spell on you, then fuck you until you come again," he informs me, and I can't do anything but moan like the hopelessly love-drunk nitwit I am.

Thio grins on my mouth, lets me feel the slow pull of his lips upward. He knows what that does to me, when he lets me feel his smile.

I shake my head in wretched self-loathing. "I hate you," I whine.

He brushes a lock of my hair from where it'd tangled with my glasses.

"No, you don't," he says with a teasing, arrogant smirk, and I got nothing for that.

Because he's right.

CAMPUS-WIDE SECURITY ALERT: All cultists who attempted to hijack the graduation ceremony and turn it into a demonic summoning have been apprehended. The ceremony is progressing as planned with extra adventure parties on hand and added measures in place to see that no ritualistic chanting or pentagram formations occur.

The official spokesperson for the Temple of Galaxrien Vossen has issued an apology, claiming the cultists did not "understand the full efforts one must go to in order to perform a successful demonic resurrection."

We have been assured by several adventure parties as well as the Temple that no one in attendance at the graduation is in true danger of Galaxrien Vossen appearing, especially since "this is not the correct date for his prophesied return."

Congratulations, graduates!

Chapter Twenty

Four Years Later

I found the ring in Thio's sock drawer.

Not the best hiding place, and I'm almost positive he *wanted* me to find it. It prompted me to check where I'd hidden mine, under a loose floorboard in front of our closet—and, sure enough, the ward I'd cast over it was broken.

So.

He knew I was going to propose.

I knew he was going to propose.

Thus began a small war of not outright telling the other *I know what you're doing* while doing the exact same thing.

Like we were watching a sappy rom-com, and at the part where one character proposed to the other with the glittering Eiffel Tower in the background, Thio nudged me and went, *What do you think? Would you want something like that?*

I thought he was joking. Until a Paris trip ad popped up on his phone while he was showing me a recipe he wanted to try for dinner, and he chucked that thing across the kitchen so hard it cracked his case. Didn't prevent me from seeing the prompt *Finish your booking now!*

Nuh-uh. *Paris?* First of all, we can't afford that; second, over my dead body is he going to propose like I'm the prize in this relationship. *He's* the prize. He's the whole damn jackpot, and I'm going to get down on one knee and proclaim how much I love this man and put my ring on his finger.

I started researching how to create a portal dimension. Nothing massive, something small and sweet for the two of us, maybe full of plants, junglelike.

But I must've left my laptop open, because soon, we were getting letters in the mail addressed to Thio from pixie skywriters asking if he'd reconsidered his proposal inquiry.

I thought, fuck it; he wants to play? We'll play. And I left literature around the apartment about druid-run tree canopy suites and their romance packages.

Which Thio responded to by asking if I had a fear of enclosed spaces—*what*—and mentioning how a coworker had gotten engaged on an Atlantis submarine cruise.

Before I knew it, seven months passed, and I barely thought of the trial at all.

Well. That's a lie.

But I didn't *spiral out* about the trial, which was, I suspect, Thio's actual reason for encouraging this rivalry: distraction.

And that makes it all the more important that I propose to him *first*.

Not in Paris, or a portal dimension, or on an elaborate trip; too expensive. Not via pixie skywriting or over a romantic dinner; too cheesy.

As I stand in front of the component supply cabinet at work, vacantly staring at the jars of chalk dust, I beat my fingers on the shelf and go over all my plans. Again.

I know, after today, this competitive back-and-forth will come to a head, so I need to execute my proposal before he does. As far as I know, everything's ready. Just waiting for my go-ahead.

But is it too obvious? Too simple?

I thump my forehead to the shelf.

Nothing's worthy of him.

Nothing's good enough for him.

My phone vibrates on my desk.

I jolt upright, cold sweat doing nothing to douse the frenetic energy that's been humming through me all day. I could complain about the call breaking my concentration, but my concentration's been nonexistent, and it's a spreading virus; a fact proven by the way my two lab techs simultaneously leap away from the data they were supposed to have been entering and break into action like they've been rehearsing for this moment.

"Everyone, *SHUT IT!*" Olayra screeches, and the half dozen sectioned-off research areas in this long lab immediately go silent.

Skogrin snatches my vibrating phone, wheels my desk chair over, and thrusts both at me.

Heads pop out of the partitions separating our lab spaces. In the middle of the room, the department lead, Dr. Zuarashi, comes to the door of her office with a tentative smile.

The whole of Clawstar Lab's attention is fixed on me.

And I'm staring at my phone in Skogrin's hand, my anxiety so potent it'll screw with whatever experiments are being run around me.

The screen says *DAD*.

Thio wanted us both to take today off. But I'd nixed that real hard, nauseated by the thought of spending all day pacing our small apartment. Turns out that's what I did anyway, only I swapped pacing our small apartment for pacing my small lab area, and now the phone's buzzing and Thio isn't with me.

No, that's good. I don't want him here. I told Dad to call me, not Thio.

I want the news first.

That shovels aside enough anxiety that I shudder in a breath and take my phone.

The pin-drop silence of the lab is suffocating. I want to glare at my colleagues for being nosy fuckers, but can I blame them? They've ridden this lawsuit with me practically my whole time at Clawstar, whether getting updates from me directly or through the clickbait news articles it generated.

FORMER CAMP MERETHYL STUDENTS SUING OVER ALLEGED MISTREATMENT

I don't know which word I hated more when that first headline popped up years ago. *Alleged* or *mistreatment*. But it's been four years of headlines way harsher than that, four years of public opinion shifting back and forth—*Are they telling the truth? Are they lying for attention?* Four years of waiting for the trial, then the actual trial itself, rehashing every detail of the summers that tried to break me, but I survived.

I *survived*.

And I'll survive this phone call, too.

Heart in my throat, I answer and shove it to my ear.

Skogrin and Olayra grumble, clearly upset I didn't put it on speaker, but I bat them away—they ignore me—and sink into my desk chair.

"Hey, Dad."

"Guilty."

One word. Not even a greeting.

One word, and I'm folding over myself, elbow on my knee and hand covering my face and it's a miracle I keep the phone pressed to my ear.

"What?" I croak, because I need—it isn't—

"The conviction came through," Dad says, and I can tell he's smiling. "They've been found guilty on thirty-four counts of negligence, misconduct, gross abuse of magic—do you want me to read the list?"

I laugh. It's watery; my eyes are burning. "No, I'm good."

"Are you sure? It's a doozy." He chuckles. "I might get it framed. Hang it in my study—"

"Sebastian!" My mother's voice. She's grabbed the phone. And she's sobbing. "Oh, sweetheart, I'm so happy for you. For you and Orok. Oh! We need to call Orok! Mason, have you called Orok?"

"I haven't—"

"Call him!"

"I will, but we're on the phone with your son *right now*."

I smile.

Because they're bantering, a dancing, celebratory arguing that's light and teasing.

Because my parents were like this when I was a kid, before Camp Merethyl wedged itself between us and all I got from them was disappointment and collisions.

I smile, because after four years of wondering if ripping out my deepest pain for the world to see would be worth a damn, I have my answer—but what's throbbing through my body isn't even in response to that.

Camp Merethyl and the people who ran the ouroboros project are being held accountable for what they did. Our lawsuit brought other allegations forward, and the rest of the partners who'd been in our training group—the ones who disappeared, who *failed out*—came with their own stories, their own evidence. With this guilty verdict, it isn't just me and Orok who'll benefit from restitution; with this guilty verdict, the money Camp Merethyl will owe us all now means they won't be able to keep running. They'll shut down.

It's over.

But that's not what I focus on.

Dad reclaims the phone. "We'll be up to celebrate this weekend, Sebastian. I love you."

But *that* isn't what I focus on either, how my relationship with both my parents is an entirely new beast. I can't recognize who we are to each other now versus the people who barely spoke for six years. I've even made up with my siblings, too.

No, what has me staying hunched over, hand in my hair, is the confirmation that I can do it now.

"We'll be celebrating more than that," I say.

At the word *celebrating*, my Clawstar colleagues let loose an ear-piercing cheer.

Dad chuckles into the phone. "We will, huh? You going to propose to that boy?"

Somewhere behind him, my mother shrieks. She *adores* Thio, especially since he switched careers and they've bonded over the highs and lows of nursing. Dad loves him just as much, and originally I thought my father's affection was his way of overcompensating with earning my forgiveness; but he and Thio really do get on, and I think it has more to do with Dad realizing Thio needed a family after the shitty way his treated him.

My grin stretches and I laugh, nearly disintegrating at the release of pressure, the *freedom.*

I'm almost certain Thio's been waiting until after the lawsuit verdict to propose, too.

Is that the real reason I didn't want to be with him today and had my father call me first?

Abso. Fucking. Lutely.

I shove up from the chair. Olayra and Skogrin are rejoicing with everyone else and the lab is buzzing with conversation and excitement now; I've started an impromptu party.

My boss nods at me from outside my lab area, reading the unspoken question on my face, *Can I dip out early?*

"Yeah, Dad." I wipe my damp cheek on my sleeve. "I'm on my way to propose to that boy right now."

Dad hangs up, promising not to let Thio know yet and saying that he's going to call Orok. We were already planning on getting together tonight, guilty verdict or not; me, Thio, and Orok. He's only been back in Philly for about two months since the Hellhounds snatched him from the Vegas Chimeras, and having him physically in the same city as me again, particularly on a day like today, almost makes me believe gods like his give a shit about us.

But we'll celebrate tonight. I'll let myself *feel* this verdict tonight when I see Orok in person and we can both take a breath.

For now, I have a boyfriend to turn into a fiancé.

Exuberant, so light I could float across town, I board a bus and text my coconspirators—a few of Thio's coworkers—in Operation: Proposal and give them the all clear to set everything into motion. They respond with thumbs-ups and I grin at my screen like a fool, eyes teary. I get a few odd looks for the way I sniff and laugh randomly, but hey, we've all seen weirder shit on the bus.

It's happening. It's really happening. All these months of tormenting each other with planning lavish proposals, and I'm *finally* going to see my ring on his finger.

That confidence lasts until I get two stops from Thio's work, and he texts me.

THIO
Did you hear from your dad?

Which isn't suspicious. He knows today's the day.
What *is* suspicious is the winky face emoji he sends after.
I shift upright, my work khakis slipping on the plastic bus seat, and glare at that emoji.
Why . . .
Why would he *wink* about that question?
Dad said he wouldn't call Thio. Could Thio have found out some other way? My coworkers all know. Did Skogrin text him? That fucker—
By the time the bus lets me off, my dad hasn't responded to my accusatory text and neither has anyone at Clawstar. Even Orok's gone silent, and I know he's glued to his phone today, too.
My eyes narrow, suspicion hot and demanding.
Fucking winky face.
I purse my lips and check that I still have his ring in my bag.
Thio is getting *proposed to today* if I have to do it in the middle of the street.
I power walk the block between the bus stop and Thio's work, flipping the ring box over and over in my bag's front pocket. The city emanates late summer heat like an oven, rippling rays making me sweat, but I'm blasted by the welcome chill of the AC as I duck inside the Harbor.
Orok used his pro rawball money to help us keep Thio's mom at Blooming Grove for a few months after graduation, but taking money from a friend stressed Thio out as much as taking money from his family. With help from Dr. Chrosk, we found the Harbor, and while in some ways it's a far cry from Blooming Grove—we have to provide the potted plants in Dr. Holmes's room ourselves, the horror—the staff here are every bit as caring. They welcomed

Dr. Holmes like she's their mother, too, and they welcomed *Thio* with just as much love, shepherding him through first a desk job here, then encouraging him to become an RN.

During the employee evaluation I had after Thio started nursing school, I told Dr. Zuarashi straight-out why I was suddenly so focused on healing spells. *That's all my boyfriend's studying now, too, and if I can figure out ways to make his life easier by creating new healing spells or streamlining old ones? I will.*

The attendant at the front desk is on the phone but flaps her hand excitedly at me and tips the handset aside. "It's all set," she whispers. "And he's on rounds, so you can sneak right on up."

I beam at her as I sign in. "You're the best. Send him up in ten?"

She bounces back and forth in a shimmy-dance. "This is so excit—yes, sir, I'm still here." And she's drawn back into her phone call, but she throws me one last grin.

As I slip into the elevator, I dig components out of my bag, the remaining pieces to activate everything I have planned.

There's no roof access via the elevator, but I take it as high as I can, head to the stairwell, and climb the remaining two flights to the roof.

As I reach the door, I'm already shaking head to toe, each quake jostling the need inside me, the need I've been suppressing the hell out of throughout this trial.

I want to be engaged to Thio.

I want to be married to him.

I want our forever, and I want it to start *now.*

The door's silent as I shove outside.

The afternoon sun is high and bright in a cloudless sky, a vibrant backdrop to the cityscape around the rooftop. I should be assaulted by the honking of horns and the shouting of pedestrians and the general chaos of Philadelphia, but it's . . . quiet. Which is one of the spells I set up, a sound-deadening bubble; and music's playing. Which is also something I set up.

But I haven't activated those spells yet.

I pause, door held open, brow furrowing.

A short brick wall rims the space, the lawn chairs for visitors pushed aside in favor of a picnic blanket.

Which is *not* part of my plan.

The red checkered pattern is set with food; by the smell, it's that sun-dried tomato cream sauce dish that never fails to let Thio get in my pants. A bottle of champagne perches next to a vase of bursting red roses.

Roses that Thio is currently crouched next to, fussing over, muttering to himself as he tugs one to lay in symmetry with the rest. He hasn't seen me yet.

This bastard is stealing my proposal.

I smirk.

Unluckily for him, I know my future fiancé quite well and anticipated something like this.

I hold the door open behind me for another beat, watching him.

He's in a set of navy-blue scrubs, so he must've raced up here not long ago; or maybe he just knows I like him in his scrubs. His long hair is braided back and twisted into a bun at the nape of his neck, tattoos slashing harsh black lines against his neck and arms as he carefully adjusts the vase.

There's a newer tattoo on the inside of his left wrist. It's one of the runes we created that stops a wizard from draining their components. He didn't get it as a magical tattoo, just the image.

He got it for me.

The wide-angled lens of this day contracts, bypassing the verdict, the lawsuit, proposing before he does.

Heart swelling, I let the door thud shut behind me.

Thio spins to his feet. He smiles, the corners of his eyes lifting, and a giddy laugh wants to burst out of me, that he still gets that look on his face when he sees me.

I cross the roof to him, taking in his setup with an appreciative whistle. "Well, damn. Whoever did this—" I motion at my ear, the lack of city noise, the music. "Pretty talented wizard. Nice romantic atmosphere."

Thio's smile doesn't waver, but his head cocks. "I . . . yeah. I am a pretty talented wizard."

Um. "What? I did this. I set up these spells."

He snorts. "I know when I do spell work, baby. I set this up a few minutes ago."

Oh my gods. He didn't steal the spells I set up; he just had the same ideas as me?

Well, *some* of the same ideas. It ain't over yet.

My grin is wicked, and Thio seems confused, but he's still smiling, too.

"And why, oh, why would you go to all this trouble?" I ask, making my eyes big, feigning ignorance.

He grabs my shirt and tugs me into him, into an onslaught of his cologne and the essence of him as he nips at my mouth. "Why, indeed? Brat."

"*Brat?* You're talking about yourself, right? Because there's no way you could know we have anything to celebrate, since I told my father to not call you with the news. However you found out was through dishonest means and doesn't count."

"Except"—Thio puts his finger on my chin—"*I* had your father call *me* first."

I scowl at him. "No, you didn't."

"He told me about the verdict two hours ago. When did he call you?"

"I—" I calculate. "Gods damn it."

Thio beams, smug in his victory, and I let him have this.

I like him happy.

"You're conspiring with my dad behind my back." I sneak my thumbs under his shirt, wanting skin contact. "Which is fitting, honestly, since I've been conspiring with your coworkers behind your back."

Thio's head jerks, wonder pulsing over him.

I activate the last spell.

Dozens of floating lights sparkle to life around us, delicate hovering flickers that coat the air. I made them green and spelled them to take the shape of ivy vines, so we're encased in our own secret fairy garden on this roof.

Thio gazes up at them, the lights shimmering in his eyes, enhancing his awe.

But his head snaps down, surprise mixing with love and hope and promise.

We hold in a beat of watching each other, absorbing the moment, the anticipation.

Thio moves first—he steps back and slides a ring box out of his pocket.

My pulse quickens at the sight, and I almost feel bad for stopping him.

Almost.

He's been with me through every fucked-up moment of this lawsuit. Through it advancing to trial, through my testimony and how I was basically catatonic for days after. He's been there as he was juggling nursing school and his job here. He's been there, even when his family tried to go after him for what I was doing. *He's been there.*

He starts to sink to one knee—

When he bursts up with a squawk.

Thio whirls around, rubbing his ankle, frowning at the picnic blanket. "What the—?"

By the time he's facing me again, I'm on one knee, my own ring box out and open.

"Thio," I say, shocked I can talk at all with the intensity bearing down on me, happiness as unyielding as a dam, like it's trying to force the question not to come too fast.

His lips part.

But he doesn't stop me. Doesn't fight to be the one to do it.

He just stares down at me, eyes tearing.

"I love you," I get to tell him. "I've loved you through thinking I hated you. I've loved you through figuring out how to rely on one another. I've loved you through not knowing why you love me at all. Every day, getting to love you remains the greatest honor of my existence. Will you marry me?"

Thio gasps a laugh, composure threatening to topple him sideways. "*Baby.*"

My nose scrunches in a smile. "Yeah?"

"That was—" He looks behind him again.

A plate of parmesan cream sauce pasta vanishes, bite by invisible bite.

"Nick," Thio realizes, and Nick rumbles, a happy little purr.

With a heaving breath, Thio faces me, his tongue working the inside of his cheek. He's exasperated but his eyes are sparkling, not just in the emerald lights that dance around us.

"Is that a yes?" I prod.

He opens the box he'd had in his pocket and shows me a silver band. "Of course it's a yes. I've wanted to marry you for years. It's why I told your dad when this lawsuit started that, regardless of how it ended, he should tell me the verdict first."

My brain slips right over his *yes.* "You've been planning to do this since the lawsuit started? For *four years?*"

He nods.

Heat crawls across my chest, up my face. "Why—" My tongue feels too big for my mouth, my throat closing over. "Why'd you wait?"

How did he wait, more like; I've only been planning this for the past few months, and even waiting this long was torture.

Thio's expression tempers, ineffably sweet. "Regardless of the verdict, I wanted the lawsuit to be behind us so we could count this as a fresh start. I wanted to be able to plan a future with you, for *you* to have that future, too, unmarred."

I shut the ring box and launch to my feet.

Thio teeters back in surprise, but I seize the collar of his scrubs and haul him into me.

"Propose," I say. "I want you to propose to me."

"But you—"

"I know. But I want you to do it, too." I put my mouth on his. "Ask me, Tourael."

He hooks his hand around the back of my neck, joy toying with the edges of his mouth. "Marry me?" he whispers.

I nod into the kiss, grinning. We both are, smiling so hard my face will get stuck like this, but I let it.

I don't want to look back anymore. I want to, am able to, look forward now.

And the only thing ahead of me is him.

Turn the page for a sneak peek
at the second book in the
Magic and Romance series!

Sports romance gets a *Dungeons & Dragons* makeover when Orok, now a pro rawball star, is forced into a fake PR relationship with a feisty, fan-favorite cheerleader in an effort to bring some much-needed good press to him and his patron god.

Coming 2026

"Let's get this party started! It's karaoke night, bitches, and you know what that means. No heckling. No booing. Everyone's welcome. If you have siren lineage, please warn us *before* your song so the audience can cast disenchantment wards. Now, first up, we have . . . Alexo the Magnificent! Let's give it up for Alexo!"

The crowd applauds. But Seb keeps his grip on my arm.

"Orok," he says over the din. "We can—"

"I'm gonna go closer to the stage." I pause though, analytical eyes sweeping over him, and my emotions take a one-eighty. "Unless *you* want to leave?"

One corner of Seb's mouth lifts. He leans back again, where Thio, in conversation with Marlow and Darian, automatically threads an arm around his waist.

That's one of the main reasons I was able to get some much-needed healthy distance from Seb over the past few years: I knew he had Thio. I knew he was taken care of.

"I'm good, O," Seb says with a helplessly content smile. "I'm engaged. We *won*. You're back in Philly. Everything's great." His smile dims. "Right?"

Right.

Say it.

Right, Seb. Everything's great.

Except I didn't get traded due to my stats—which are the reason Seb thinks I'm back home. I got traded because my old team's managers made my life hell for trying to bring down the camp that almost killed me.

And my new team seems to have the same opinion on the matter.

Yes. We won the lawsuit. That era of our lives can finally be put to rest.

It's this new era that terrifies the shit out of me.

I lean forward to peck Seb on the cheek. "I'll be back. Cheer for me."

Seb still looks like he wants to push me until I crack, and I love him for it. But he relents and gives me a thumbs-up as Alexo the Magnificent's song kicks on: Journey. A pretty standard karaoke pick.

I shove off the stool, a long breath escaping the farther I peel away from my group.

A large portion of the crowd has pressed around the small stage at the back of the room, but I lumber my way through and score a spot on the wall, right up against the edge. Alexo the Magnificent croons the first lines of "Don't Stop Believin'" and a cheer goes up, but I'm pathetically scanning faces in the dim bar lighting for any-one else from the team.

If they're going to believe the fuckers saying that our claims about Camp Merethyl's cruelty were lies, I don't want them here.

I'd hoped this team would be different. That I could be back home in every sense of the word. No one on the Hellhounds has spoken to me about the trial yet, and everyone's been welcoming and kind, if overly formal. I knew once the verdict landed that it'd all come to a head, and I'd hoped I could get in front of it, invite everyone out, play it off as something positive before they had a chance to believe the worst of me.

We're a team. Spells, explosions, obstacles—all that and more gets thrown at us every time we step onto a rawball field. Trust is what keeps us alive.

The Hellhounds don't trust me, do they? It's gonna be the Chi-meras all over again.

I roll my left shoulder instinctively, phantom pain radiating from the sprain I got a few months back, as Alexo the Magnificent takes the midnight train going anywhere. His voice is smooth and pretty damn good, flowing over me in a crooning wash.

My eyes drift to the stage—

And my jaw drops.

Holy.

Shit.

I take back all my previous smartass thoughts about his karaoke name. *Magnificent* is completely accurate.

He's about Seb's height and size, but thinner, slighter, wearing a scarlet satin shirt unbuttoned to his stomach so it billows away from his bare chest, with tight black pants tucked into clunky gold boots. His pale skin is covered in a dusting of gold glitter, and with his overall demeanor, I can't figure out if it's makeup or if he's part pixie.

Alexo sways in the musical interlude between verses, eyes shut, a sweep of gold paint shimmering across each eyelid, his messy tangle of strawberry blond curls gleaming pink in the stage lighting.

Wow, my brain supplies. And then keeps repeating that word in a dumbstruck rollover when Alexo the Magnificent dives into the next verse.

His eyes fly open, a deep onyx-brown highlighted in thick black liner, and as the music builds, rage sparks there. A small pool of it at first, and then it grows, and grows, spreading across his whole face until he's snarling with the swell of the words and music, *livin' just to find emotion*—

Gods, this guy is throwing his whole body into the performance, dancing across the stage, and the crowd starts clapping along. But Alexo seems unaware of them, each word of each verse coming from the very pit of his soul. I almost wonder if I missed him telling the audience he's a siren and he's inadvertently casting an enchantment on us with this routine, but he doesn't have the look of someone casting spells. This is for him. Just for him.

I take a little of it for me, too.

Because I *feel* that yearning he exudes. Where the crowd is fully enjoying the song, dancing and laughing, a partying Thursday night, I go more and more slack as the music carries on.

There's this god who fell out of favor centuries ago—Cendis, the god of small fires. Candlelight, sparks, embers, tiny touches of heat. He dropped away as people were more drawn to raging elemental fire gods, but I always found what he represented to be far more potent. He was the god of *beginnings*. Of having the ability to start a fire in the first place.

That's what I see as Alexo bares his soul with this song. Someone trying with every wisp of their existence to *begin*.

To be free.

My throat swells and I sniff through the tightening of emotion.

The lyrics drop in the last interlude, and Alexo's previous dance moves were a warm-up.

He pirouettes around the stage, back arching, legs kicking up to his face, arms pinwheeling in a mesmerizing braid of limbs and fluidity. All the while keeping the mic cord from tangling, and playing around the karaoke machine with the lyric screen he's not once looked at—and avoiding a few reaching hands from the audience.

I jolt forward at that, shoulders bunching high. I'm close enough to the edge that all I have to do is move to get the attention of the front row. When I glare, they sink back a few good inches.

Because it's unsafe. I don't want him to trip. Obviously.

Alexo doesn't notice. He whirls back into the last swell of lyrics, clinging to the mic with both hands, and singing, *singing* his fucking heart out. Each long note becomes its own mini performance piece, his spine folding so far backward he's defying gravity, and that part of my brain still going *wow, wow, wow* now adds *he's flexible* along with pathetic little whimpers.

The song fades out, Alexo holding in the position of the final note, hands still death-gripping the microphone, eyes pinched shut.

The music barely ends when the crowd explodes, hooting and cheering and clapping.

Alexo's eyes blink open like he's coming out of a trance. His gaze casts over the crowd, a slow smile lifting one side of his mouth—

His eyes land on me.

Acknowledgments

Four years ago, I started watching *Critical Role*. If you don't know what that is, *oh baby*, are you in for a treat! And I'm also about to throw a lot of lingo around that you probably won't understand, but don't you worry, darlin'—I promise, I bring it all back eventually.

Anyway, *Critical Role*, Campaign Two. In the months leading up to watching it, I had fallen more and more out of love with fantasy. I didn't have it in me anymore to *care* about the core root of escapism that had made fantasy such a necessary part of my existence before. (This was right after 2020, in case that wasn't obvious.)

But then, *Critical Role*. And this series epic (there's no other term for it; it's an epic) that was just . . . *fun*. It was all the best parts of fantasy that I loved as a kid, and it held my reservations at knifepoint so I could fall back in love with fantasy again, and *wow*, did I. It reminded me that at the root of fantasy is escapism, yes; but beyond that, deeper still, is the need for joy.

(Joy is a recurring theme in my books, you'll find. Hashtag sorry not sorry.)

I could wax poetic for weeks about *Critical Role*, and the Mighty Nein and Exandria and Nott and Jester and *ohmygodthatcupcakescene??* But I will restrain myself. Until, ya know, maybe a social media post or something, you can't stop me there.

But here? Here, I lay out all this backstory so you know where this book came from. What pieces of myself I carved out to serve up for you. This book is not quite as silly-goofy-irreverent as *The Nightmare Before Kissmas*, but I still hope, on some level, that it brought you joy.

Because it sure as hell brought me joy.

I mean, I got to write a book that's basically self-indulgent Caleb/ Essek fanfiction. Just saying that has me giggling, and I can't help but think how damn lucky I am.

The truth is, it isn't luck at all. It's having a whole lot of incredibly fantastic people on my team. Which, in its own way, is luck, isn't it?

So here are all the people I get to count as part of Team Wizard Book (as it was known in its earliest iterations):

Firstly, Monique Patterson—thank you for this idea, which came entirely from you saying "Why aren't there more fantasy STEM books?" To which my reaction was "Because STEM is mostly technology not magic and—wait. *Could* it be magic? WHAT IF—" And the rest is, as they say, history.

Amy Stapp, who patiently listens to me overreact and is even more patient when I come crawling back a few weeks later and admit I might have overreacted.

Erika Tsang, for helping me flesh out this book beyond the onslaught of DND jokes. Not that DND jokes aren't important, but it turns out character arcs are too. Who knew? (Erika. Erika knew.)

Tessa Villanueva, for your excitement, organization, and for being an all-around delightful person.

Jordan Hanley, Caro Perny (a DND BOOK!!), Lauren Abesames, Emily Mlynek, Sarah Reidy, Ariana Carpentieri, and all the marketing and publicity magic-makers. That you use said magic for my book is beyond dreaming.

Lilith Saur, for giving me yet another *stunning* cover. There is nothing you can't do and I'm so honored I get to watch you create!

All the behind-the-scenes darlings who are wizards in their own right: Lesley Worrell, Rafal Gibek, Megan Kiddoo, Jen Edwards, Jacqueline Huber-Rodriguez, Sara Thwaite, Drew Kilman, Maria Snelling, Katy Robitzski, and Kira Tregoning.

And, as always, to you, my dear, loveliest of readers.

I hope you found some magic in these pages.

I hope you smiled.

About the Author

SARA RAASCH grew up among the cornfields of Ohio and currently lives in the historical corridor of southeastern Virginia. She is the *New York Times* and *USA Today* bestselling author of almost a dozen books for young adults. *The Nightmare Before Kissmas* was her debut adult novel, offering all the joy, irreverent wit, and crackling sexiness of your favorite sweet-as-a-candy-cane holiday romp.